"This multilayered story focuses on t[...] [relationships] and community on personal and spiritual healing and growth. Throughout the story, conflict is laced with whimsy, humour, and stunningly vivid descriptions of fish behaviour beneath the water's surface. A great read that's hard to put down, Holloway's story presents a vision of the future where barriers are overcome through an emphasis on creativity, trust, and group effort. I'm already hoping for the chance to spend more time in the company of these characters. Sequel, please!"

Nancy Oster, freelance journalist, California

"Members of the Pelagic Territory – a realistic yet futuristic network of communities who farm and ranch marine species in the South Pacific Ocean – give sanctuary to former special forces officer Ben. He and the Pelagic settlers are swept up in a clash of world views and must bring the crisis to a resolution. A riveting novel."

Norm Reichenbach, professor of biology, Liberty University, Virginia

"Pelagia beautifully blends fast-paced thrills, complex characters, and compelling near-future science to deliver a terrific read. As a marine biologist and fisheries scientist, Holloway is able to paint a portrait of life on the oceans that is both realistic and hopeful. Present-day themes of radical Islamic terrorism are developed and extended to draw the reader into a dangerous world, where a revitalized Islamic caliphate threatens global catastrophe. Holloway's many years living in the Islamic world enable him to give rich detail to the characters, offering intriguing glimpses into the world view and thought processes of those we in the West so often misunderstand and fear. I know of no other book that so well combines the themes of science fiction, politics, and faith in a realistic, heart-pumping thriller. I'm looking forward to the sequel."

Roger Martin, PhD, environmental and natural resource economist, California

"An exciting adventure set in a near future, where technological and scientific advancements have enabled whole communities to make the oceans their home. In among the action and moments that had me on the edge of my seat, this story explores important and sensitive concepts: the impact of loss and trauma; the many stages of healing; the power of community; the influence of faith; and the way our hearts and our innermost motivations can shape our world. The characters we meet along the way are refreshingly genuine, natural, and believable. I found myself fully immersed in their world and thoroughly enjoyed this read. I would love to have stayed there for longer!"

Stephanie Bryant, science-faith communicator, UK

"A stunning mix of thriller, science fiction, and exploration of religious belief. Marvel at nature, technology, and the activity of God in this tale of people interacting with one another, pursuing their dreams, and seeking to create new communities."

Jonathan Andrews, researcher and writer on the Christian communities of the Middle East and North Africa

"Pelagia is a such an enjoyable read. You're plunged into the story from the first paragraph, and it's a thrill ride from that point onward... Descriptions of the harmonious interaction between the sea and characters are so poetic at times it leaves you aching for that kind of peace and stillness. A great book on so many levels."

Nancy Gabriel, electrical engineer (MIT), California

"As a science-fiction enthusiast and oceanographer, it was a pleasure to read a book that combines both interests. The story moves along at a good pace, and at each stage left me wanting to know what would happen next. The story is set in the near future and the scientific advances it relies on are reasonable projections of current research directions, making the plot believable... Pelagia is an interesting and enjoyable book to read."

Meric Srokosz, professor of physical oceanography, National Oceanography Centre, UK

"Pelagia is an intriguing story with page-turning excitement. I was amazed by the science within the story; wonders of the ocean depths and its other-worldly creatures. I was mesmerized by the science fiction within the story; fantastic futuristic machines and the things they can do. Pelagia even has love and romance. The characters are also well developed. You feel you know them in a short amount of time; both the good guys and the bad. A great read!"

Jacqueline Wallace, author, California

"If you like Clive Cussler, Dan Brown, Robert Ludlum – with a little Jacques Cousteau thrown in – you'll enjoy reading Pelagia. It is a unique, original, fresh, and interesting vision of the not-too-distant future of mariculture, human culture, and the constant battle between good and evil. It is the story of a protagonist you are always pulling for – who has experienced a series of catastrophic personal setbacks that rocked him to his core – salvation, second chances, and those who helped lead him to redemption and healing. Each chapter leads into a new series of unanticipated events that culminate in a satisfying and realistic conclusion."

Rob Fitch, professor of biology, Wenatchee Valley College, Washington

PELAGIA

BETWEEN THE STARS AND THE ABYSS

STEVE HOLLOWAY

LION FICTION

Lion Hudson Limited
Wilkinson House, Jordan Hill Business Park
Banbury Road, Oxford OX2 8DR, England
www.lionhudson.com

ISBN 978 1 78264 339 5
e-ISBN 978 1 78264 358 6

First edition 2021
Acknowledgments
A catalogue record for this book is available from the British Library
Printed and bound in Great Britain by Clays Ltd, Elcograf S.p.A.

*To the steady star of my life, Kitty, whose encouragement,
support, patience – and occasional prod – helped distil this
book from a dream.*

Acknowledgments

Fictional narratives are often conceived in scribbling solitude as the writer captures imagination within a net of words. However, it was connecting with a community of friends and other willing readers that breathed life into the story of *Pelagia* – helped shape it, refine the texture, colour, and character, and finally give it a sheen. These several dozen courageous individuals offered their time to engage deeply with the story, giving me the gift of objectivity which allowed me to view the narrative through their eyes. They sustained my motivation through the many drafts with their honest, encouraging, and insightful feedback.

I would therefore like to thank: Peter and Jan Aijian, Darcy Albers, Celeste Allen, Cheryl Anderson, William Barker, Paul Beam, David Bok, Maureen Chapman, John and Melanie Dodd, Courtney Duncan, Christine Eitzen, Barbara Essex, Rob Fitch, Ruth Forney, Nancy Gabriel, Margaret Graham, Rebekka Greenlee, James Hazleton, Kim Hesse, Eric Holloway, Gina Holloway, Laura Holloway, Martin Horton, Ken Howard, Jason Jones, Alicia Kronick, Jason Lawton, Jim Leftwich, Phil MacInnes, Steve Mack, Kristine Magee, Roger and Tammy Martin, Chris Maynard, Dominic Meering, Karen Miller, David and Nancy Oster, Norm Reichenbach, Mike Shelton, Meric Srokosz, Danial Sutami, Don Thomason, Liza West, Ron Williams, Karyn Wloczewski, The Writers Bloc of Chesham, and Robyn Yates.

I am also deeply indebted to the constructive and ruthless work of professional editors who guided me in polishing the manuscript. They include Fay Sampson, Jaqueline Wallace, Carol Holloway, Joy Tibbs, Mary Davis, and especially Fiona Veitch-Smith, who believed in *Pelagia* enough to recommend it to her publisher.

Of course, I am grateful for many, many others who have shaped my story simply because they have shared in my life journey.

CHAPTER ONE

2 July 2066, Forty-five miles south-west of New Caledonia, South Pacific

A lone gull swept through the last gleams of the day, high above the open sea. The gull dipped and turned on gusts of wind, wings white before the rising darkness of a storm. Below, a yacht's engines strained to stay ahead of the advancing blackness. A man at the helm pressed the throttle further forward, scanning the dials and repeatedly glancing behind.

The bird circled the boat in lazy arcs. Then it wheeled down and away, skimming the waves. Diving suddenly into an approaching swell, the gull left a ring of ripples in its wake.

The gale-driven swells increased. Blackness arched above, dwarfing the lone craft. Clouds of spray and foam swirled through the air, whipped from the waves. On deck, several figures scrambled, slipping about the cockpit as they secured the gear. The crew slammed hatches closed as rain swallowed the yacht in a deluge.

*

Ben felt lightness. His body was almost weightless, then rudely pulled down with a slam. Nausea assaulted him as his mind groped towards a twilit awareness.

A rhythmic roar drew his attention, thrumming through the floor and walls. *An engine?* The plunging and shuddering crashes. *Waves.* His mind began to recognize his environment. *A boat.*

His chest tensed: *Somalia? No, no, that was long ago.* The grip of that terror relaxed and withdrew into a dark memory.

He opened his eyes to darkness. The air was stuffy, musty, and reeking of diesel. *Who uses diesel these days?* He lingered over the smells. *Metal, rust, a whiff of rotten… what was it? Ah yes, seaweed.*

The force of the boat ploughing through the waves again lifted his body,

7

then threw him against a solid wall. He attempted to steady himself. *My arms, legs. They're bound.* He strained against the bonds until he couldn't bear the pain.

Looking around, he perceived only blackness. He could not feel a blindfold, this must be a dark compartment of some kind. *Or am I blind?* He pushed that thought away.

His head throbbed. His tongue felt thick. Bitter. Dry. He must have been unconscious for hours. All his muscles ached from being in one position for so long.

He tensed and rolled onto his back, bracing himself for the next wave. A calm internal voice moved through him. *Be still.* He willed his six-foot frame to relax, allowing years of military training to take over. *First, assess your situation.* But his thoughts were slow to gather. He waited, letting his senses steep in his surroundings.

As he turned his head stiffly, a tiny light swung before him. Gratitude flooded through him. *I can still see.* He squeezed his eyes shut, blinked, and looked again. *A porthole.* A field of stars in a deep twilight sky flashed one way, then the other, across the small opening. *Evening, then.*

The sloping walls hindered him. Squirming to a sitting position, he brushed the walls with his bound hands. Rough texture, prickly. *Fibreglass.* Must be an old boat. Following the wall forward with his fingers, he felt the sharp angle of another wall. A chain rose before him, he could feel bits of dry seaweed clinging to it. An anchor chain, this is the bow.

Rising with effort to a hunched squat, he felt coils of rope under him. Faint whiffs of resin, rust, metal, and mildew. *It must be the chain locker of a – motor yacht? Maybe fifteen, eighteen metres.*

Now that he was moving around, his circulation began to return. The stabs of pain in his limbs felt almost welcome, helping his thoughts clear.

OK, so I'm in the forward locker of a yacht. Waves are rough, maybe there's a storm brewing. What's the last thing I remember? Images of rosewood and brass filled his mind. A restaurant. High windows, chandeliers, linen tablecloths. Of course, the symposium. I was preparing my lecture in Singapore.

A vivid memory taunted him: a half-empty glass of ice water left on the table. He licked his parched lips. *Had someone spiked that?* Possibly... That would make sense – it was the last thing he could remember, and it would explain the unconsciousness. The unwelcome realization slowly formed in his mind: *I've been kidnapped...* Dark memories began to crowd in, he pushed them down. *No time. Focus.*

He twisted around on the piles of rope, exploring the space. Using his legs, he lifted the coils and explored under them. In one corner, his foot struck something metal. He kicked it and heard a rattle. Manoeuvring, he managed to pull it out from under the ropes with his feet and onto another coil next to him He contorted himself to run his hands over it. *A toolbox.* He could only imagine how it got there, maybe a careless workman who dropped it in a locker too deep to retrieve. He blessed the man's laziness.

Straining, panting, he fumbled and opened the latch. The hinges squealed softly; but the noise was masked by the rising storm. Ben exhaled slowly and deliberately and continued the awkward task. Just as he felt he was making progress, his sweaty fingers slipped and the lid clicked shut. He stifled an oath and set to work again. Focusing patiently, he eventually managed to tip the box over, spilling out its contents. Stretching his bound arms as far as he could, he eagerly felt among the pile and identified the jumble of angles and edges: a *wrench, screwdriver, hammer, screws, wire. Pliers.* He gripped them tightly.

Just then the boat plunged wildly, throwing him against the wall, scattering his treasures. He recovered, tensing his legs against the opposite wall amid the continued lurching. Rain rattled in a rising crescendo across the deck above.

Concentrating on the pliers, he turned them awkwardly. Their rusty surface scraped his wrists. *Patience. Concentrate.* With some twisting, Ben manoeuvred the pliers, so the wire-cutting edges closed on the plastic straps binding his arms. He pressed his weight onto the handles, the straps gave slightly. *Reposition, squeeze, reposition, squeeze.* The straps loosened and stretched, then broke. Within seconds, he had freed his legs as well.

Fire shot through his stiff limbs as he stretched them in the cramped space. Taking deep, slow breaths, he rolled to a crouch, and found his balance. With a new presence of mind, he ran his fingertips along the flat wall behind him, and then up. *A door.* It must lead into the next compartment. He pushed gently. It clicked but didn't open. He ran his hand along the frame and found rivets attaching the latch.

Reaching back, feeling in the darkness among the scattered tools, he retrieved a screwdriver and hammer. Quietly, he stacked coils of rope to kneel on. Climbing on them, crouching before the door, he paused to listen. The rhythmic thunder of rain and waves served him now, masking his efforts. Using the screwdriver as a chisel, he sheared the heads of the rivets, timing hammer blows with the crash of the breakers against the bow.

Anger and fear, in equal measures, gripped his chest. Thoughts raced through his mind, in rhythm with his hammering. *Who's on this vessel? Why have they taken me? Where are they taking me?*

One, two, three rivets done. Halfway through shearing the fourth rivet, the boat shuddered and lost headway, pitching him towards the bow. Muffled shouts and the rumble of boots sounded from the stern. *Four or five heavy men at least*, he guessed. Rain slashed on the deck above with a steady roar. Ben breathed deeply, recovering from his fall. He moved quickly to restack the coils next to the door and sheared the last rivet.

With a gentle shove, he cracked open the door and peered into the swaying room. Windows in the cabin revealed only darkness outside, but hazy light filtered under a door at the far end. Stale cigarette smoke, unwashed laundry, a faint smell of teak oil. He took a moment to look around, letting his eyes adjust. A single bunk on each side with unmade sheets and blankets, probably water and fuel tanks under them. A lot of fine wood panelling. A kind of desk with drawers built into the back wall, heavy brass clock above and folding chairs secured to the starboard wall. A cabinet on the port side and a door – probably to a small head. He focused on the door with the light – where did it lead?

The boat swung broadside to the waves. Pitch and roll increased. The craft had lost steerage. Dishes and pans crashed to the floor beyond the door. *The galley.*

He slipped the screwdriver and hammer under his belt and moved stealthily through the small door and into the dim cabin, bracing himself against the rolling. *Breathe. Steady. Weigh your options.*

Glancing up, he spied a hatch leading to the deck. He quietly unhooked a chair, unfolded it beneath the hatch, and carefully climbed, legs instinctively flexing with the boat's movements. The hatch was hinged. Releasing the catch, he lifted it just enough to peer out. Gusts of warm rain and wind whipped at his face.

A rising moon laid a glittering path on the water, the air fresh and clear. At that moment, the boat tipped with the waves and he glimpsed a dark silhouette of land through a break in the curtains of rainfall. *About a kilometre away. Swimmable.*

He stepped down off the chair, to search the room. Studying the starboard bunk, he tugged the ragged mattress off, then the plywood panel beneath. A plastic tank. He shook it. *Water.*

He turned to the port bunk and stripped it to reveal another tank. Reaching into the dark opening, he felt a cold metal surface. Stooping, he sniffed and smiled.

Shouts sounded as an argument erupted in the stern.

A shadow flickered across the sliver of light under the far door. Ben froze. Footsteps sounded just beyond. Someone rummaged through the clutter of fallen galley equipment.

"Where's my knife," he heard distinctly in Arabic. A man's voice, angry. It sounded like a Yemeni or Somali dialect. Dark memories crept again to the edges of consciousness. Ben pushed them away.

"Maybe in the forward stateroom." The noise stopped. Ben waited, aware of the faint sound of his breath, in and out.

The door handle rattled and slowly began to turn. Ben quietly lifted the brass wall-clock from its nail and balanced it in his hand. He flattened himself silently beside the door, holding his breath.

"Found it!" came from the other side. The handle was released with a click. Another rattle, then the footsteps receded to the stern. Ben found he was still holding his breath, the brass clock raised above his head. He exhaled noiselessly, waited ten more heartbeats, then set the clock down.

He continued his systematic search, sliding open one of the drawers in the desk. *Several packs of cigarettes. Matches.* He felt his way back to the starboard bed and, stabbing at the mattress with the screwdriver, managed to tear a piece of fabric off the smelly old mattress cover. Then, reaching down and placing the screwdriver against the side of the tank near the bottom, he struck it sharply with the hammer, matching the boom of the bow ploughing into a wave. The smell of diesel rewarded his efforts. He grabbed at the stuffing of the mattress and held it near the tank, letting it soak up the spreading diesel. He picked up one diesel-drenched rag from the pile and striking three matches at once, he brought them under the cloth to slowly catch fire, then placed it back carefully with the stuffing. *Like the wick of a kerosene lantern.* Small red flames smoked and glimmered in the dark void.

Climbing back onto the chair, he opened the hatch again. Slowly. Quietly. He peered out. *No one.* He lifted the hatch and rotated it carefully on its hinges to lie flat on the deck. Pulling himself up through the opening, he lay prone near the bow. The coolness of the storm awakened his senses;

a teak deck was beneath him, not well cared for. Darkness off the starboard side, a curtain of rain approaching. The deck was clear around him. No one on the bridge above the deck. That was puzzling.

Rolling onto his back, he paused under the deluge and allowed the sweet liquid to stream into his mouth. Thirst barely slaked, he turned again to his stomach and slithered across the deck to the starboard edge of the bow. The wind now lashed his wet body. He shivered, staring into the night, allowing his eyes to adjust again. The squall passed and he again spotted a treeline of palms silhouetted against the moonlit sky, a dark fleeting promise.

A noise, more shouting. Looking back, he saw a figure climb out onto the side of the boat. The man was perched on the narrow catwalk that gave access to the bow from the stern cockpit; he was maybe eight or ten metres away, clinging to the rail mounted on the main cabin as the boat rolled under him. His attention was still fully towards the stern. Adrenaline shot through Ben as he inched closer to the starboard edge of the bow, willing himself to be a shadow.

On both sides of the bow, stainless steel posts were linked with a safety line. Grabbing the cable, Ben swung himself over the side with the roll of the boat. He hung for a moment, suspended above the sea. He glanced at the silhouette of the man against lights from the stern; a searchlight pointed in the water behind the boat. The man's back was still turned to Ben.

Ben looked down at the black waters below. *Large, deep breaths.* Each time the boat tipped, his feet dipped beneath the waves. On the third tip, he released his grip, slipping below the surface noiselessly.

As he surfaced in the warm water, he heard the man on deck shouting in Arabic at someone in the water at the stern, "Cut the rope!" There was an answering shout from the water that was lost in the roar of rain.

Ben kept to the shadow of the bow rocking above him. *Point of no return.* He was committed, he couldn't climb back onto the boat from here. After an eternal minute, the man scrambled back into the stern cockpit. Ben slipped below the water.

The comforting warmth of the sea closed over him. He relaxed, momentarily revived. *This is my element.* He felt the vastness of the ocean all around.

He kicked off his trainers. Sharp barnacles scored his feet as he pushed away from the hull. Moving beneath the surface, with regular, strong strokes, he distanced himself from the threat of his captors. After thirty metres, his lungs began to strain, craving air. But his resolve was stronger. Pressing down the panic, he persisted, stroke by stroke.

Finally, he broke the surface, gasping for air. He turned, face low in the water, treading in place so he could assess what lay behind. Through the rain he spotted a flickering glow in the forward cabin. He made out four men at the stern. *They haven't noticed the fire yet.* The men were shouting at a fifth person in the water near the propeller shaft.

Ben turned again towards the distant and now barely visible silhouette of land. He pressed on through the encircling darkness. The ocean depths below and the black heavens above allowed him to relax and focus his will on essentials: reach forward, pull the water past, kick. He fell into the rhythm of a strength-conserving breaststroke. Stroke, breath, glide. He rose with the wave crests and dipped into the troughs. The rain had eased.

As he swam, disturbing memories arose of previous abductions. Questions obsessed him: *Who are they? Why? What do they want?* He could not afford the rush of panic that accompanied these unanswerable thoughts. He forced them aside and focused on survival. Later there would be time enough to puzzle this through.

The swim seemed endless.

A change in the rhythm of the surrounding swells roused him from his stupor. The waves were now larger, choppier. He paused, treading water for a few moments, trying to make sense of it. *Ah, waves are reflecting off a barrier reef. The land is near.* He swam forward with heightened caution.

His left leg grazed against something jagged. He felt stabbing pains on his calf and thigh, but resisted the urge to recoil. Relaxing, he spread his arms and legs out, flattening himself to float on the surface. He sensed the reef now only a few inches below him. The water rose and fell more erratically as the current swept him over the shallows.

The waves pushed him on. He maintained a thin profile on the surface to avoid being dashed by the relentless swells onto razor-sharp coral. Even so, shallow coral raked his stomach and legs. The saltwater stung the skin now torn and raw beneath his clothing. He pushed from his mind the threat of sharks attracted by the blood in the water.

A final swell lifted and deposited him beyond the barrier reef into the calm, deeper waters of the island's lagoon.

The storm was moving on; the rain lessened until it was pattering lightly around him. The moon broke faintly through the clouds, shimmering on the calmer water. He slowed, turning onto his back to take in this moment of beauty, even in the midst of danger. The quiet splendour gave him heart.

The silhouette of the island became sharply visible, several hundred metres away. Intent on each stroke, he continued towards it until he heard soft splashes ahead. *Waves on sand.*

In the dim light, he saw a band of gleaming white coral sand, separating the sea from the dark island vegetation. A sense of relief rose within his chest, but only for a moment. Then his military training snapped on; steely caution took control.

Turning to his left, he swam parallel to shore, searching.

He spied a rock projecting into the water, like a dark stain across the white sands. He headed for this landing and scrambled over sharp ridges onto tufts of grass. *Leave no footprints to follow.*

He ducked into the palm jungle, weaving his way through tangled brush, moving eastward, hunting for a spot that allowed a clear view across the bay. He almost tripped on a snag of a plastic tarp sticking out from the sand. He pulled it out and took it with him.

The rain had stopped. Starlight shone through ragged rips in the clouds, filtered by the palm fronds waving above. In a fleeting flash of insight under the stars, he realized that, for anyone nearby, this was a normal, peaceful evening. Families sitting down for dinner. Somehow, this gave him solace.

He spotted a blaze, far out on the ocean. *The boat.* He felt a primal joy, knowing he was the cause. There was a flash, then a few seconds later, a deafening explosion. *The galley's butane bottle.*

They may be gone for now, but maybe there were co-conspirators? He knew he must conceal himself – and quickly.

He found a small clearing in the jungle, in sight of the beach, and dropped to his knees. The soil was firmer, sandy more loamy and held together better than the loose sand on the beach. With determination, he began to scoop a hole in the sand using the wide, flat base of a palm frond as a shovel. *Three feet deep, six and a half feet long.* He spread the tattered tarp and carefully piled the dirt on it. Periodically, he would carry the full tarp to another outcrop of rock near him and dump it in the swirling water.

After twenty minutes, the hole was done. Grabbing other fallen palm fronds, he wove the leaves together roughly into panels as he'd learned in tropical survival training. He would need about eight to cover the hole, leaving a gap for an entrance. He carefully laid the finished panels, spread the tarp over them, then used the last batch of sand to cover the tarp. Then he scattered leaves, rotted coconut husks and other debris over his hide, mimicking the surrounding jungle floor.

He wiggled down into his hole, pulling a large palm leaf over the opening as he settled. He carried a stone from the outcrop and wedged it under a corner of the frond, allowing him a clear view of the beach. Deep breath. *Now, the patient wait.* A familiar routine, one he'd experienced many times during his military tours.

Lying still made him acutely aware of cuts, bruises, encrusted blood, pain, and sand gritted between his teeth. Hunger gnawed at him insistently. A line of large black ants appeared and began a parade into his sanctuary. One bit him, then another. He ignored it.

Still he waited. Adrenaline and desperation battled against his exhaustion. He struggled to keep his vigil. The night was now clear, he could make out the burning boat still bobbing, flickering on the sea.

As he waited, Ben's mind entered a kind of trance, unaware of time passing. Pain and danger receded. His mind drifted to memories of happier times, then snapped back suddenly to full alert as a light appeared out on the water: *a searchlight near the boat.*

Shadowy activity around the boat increased; the fire was quenched. The searchlight then swung in systematic arcs over the surrounding waters as another craft advanced towards his beach. Exhaustion pulled at him as he strained to stay alert. Blackness took him.

2 July 2066, Seastead vessel *Ossë*, 500 miles north-north-west of Cape Reinga, New Zealand
(the same day)

"Watanabe-san, you honour us in coming personally to test this new *iki jime* technique and give us the assistance of your engineers." Suliman Battuta raised the steaming green tea as a toast.

His guest raised his own cup in acknowledgment, "It is a privilege, Captain. We've had a good business relationship for years, you provide high quality tuna, this technique will make it even better, increasing profit for both of us. Besides, I have been curious for years about your life here, herding tuna."

"Tuna herding is not as strange as it sounds, Watanabe-san." Sul glanced over at his guest, reluctantly turning from watching the patch of sea busy with divers at work. "My Bedouin ancestors were herders as well, nomadic shepherds. Their clans travelled across the desert with herds of camels and goats. My family merely traded livestock for schools of fish – and they traded the vast Arabian sands for the expansive seas of the Southern Pacific Gyre."

The Japanese businessman chuckled, "When you say it like that, Captain Battuta, it almost makes sense."

Suliman smiled, "Bedouins have a saying: 'When you sleep in a house, your thoughts are as high as the ceiling. When you sleep outside, they are as high as the stars.'"

Ogata Watanabe admired the horizon on all sides. "The open sea is certainly vast and empty like a desert. Some would feel anxious and vulnerable living in such desolation, so far from civilization."

"That may be, but I would have it no other way. There is a deep joy sleeping beneath the stars and above the abyss. We Pelagics find peace, held in our suspension between two vast and measureless realms. A poet from our community wrote, 'We make our lives at the edge of creation, we walk in wonder.'"

"Those are intriguing thoughts, indeed. They almost attract me to your life."

The two men were seated at the table, under a sunshade, on the deck of *Ossë* as it glided just a few metres above a ruffled sea. The deck was the only part of *Ossë* above water. The submerged family quarters and work areas were connected to the upper deck by sleek metal stanchions. Waves moved freely between these supports, passing under the deck and over the living area, allowing a level ride unaffected by sea conditions.

Suliman studied his guest, admiring the aristocratic profile. "Here we are on station, Watanabe-san. Just in time for today's demonstration of the new harvesting technique."

*

Ossë slowed and stopped, with other similar vessels, in a semi-circle around the area of activity. Several small *Dragonfly* utility craft also hovered nearby.

This is good, Sul thought. *Most of the Pod has arrived. Mr Watanabe will get a taste of our community life.* A light but steady breeze streamed through Suliman's dark hair; greying at the temples marked his years. Clear golden eyes below dark brows scanned the sea before them. A salt and pepper beard completed the frame of his face. He was the image of a sea captain from another age; his leathery skin weathered by years of sun, wind, and salt.

There was a buzz of activity as people crowded to find good vantage points on the other vessels, watching with keen interest in this latest innovation for their community. *Dragonfly* workmen used headsets to interact with divers in the water, coordinating the experiment.

One diver waved to Sul, who waved in return. Nemo, *Ossë*'s augmented intelligence agent, conveyed the diver's message. "Captain, Gideon says the *iki jime* gate is in place. The tuna guide for Cohort 32 will now lead the school through the device. Shall we proceed with the trial?"

Sul moved swiftly to the low railing of the deck to observe the activity more closely. The dozen divers had swum away from the *iki jime* gate, a structure suspended twenty metres below the ocean's surface. "Yes, Nemo, proceed."

"This procedure will give your product a much higher price in the Tokyo market. The meat is sweeter when fish are killed in this humane way," Ogata Watanabe remarked, joining him at the railing.

"That's our hope. Thank you, my friend, for sharing this *iki jime* technique with us."

The divers were now all clustered near the *Dragonfly* craft to avoid spooking the approaching tuna. Ogata spoke again, "Your son Gideon has great talent. By the way, how are his studies coming along?"

"Kind of you to ask. He's finishing his final project for a graduate degree at the Marine Institute of Science and Technology in Auckland, an amphibious aircraft. We hope…"

"Sorry to interrupt, Captain," a disembodied voice broke in.

"Yes, Nemo?"

"The tuna guide-bot is approaching the gate."

"This'll happen quickly. Let's move to the bridge. We'll be able to see better on the holo-display." Sul indicated the semi-enclosed area at the forward end of the deck. "Please come with me, Watanabe-san."

"Of course, Captain." They moved from the railing and began walking across the deck to the bridge of *Ossë*.

Ogata spoke to the air, "Nemo, is it? Your name sounds like the Latin word for 'no one'!"

"Yes, very good, Mr Watanabe, sir. It is Captain Battuta's little joke, since I am indeed not human, only an algorithm. I believe it also is an allusion to the name Ulysses gave himself when facing the cyclops in Homer's *Odyssey*. Similarly, it's the name of the captain in Jules Verne's submarine novel, and the name of a Pixar cartoon fish."

"Ah, I see. All marine settings. Appropriate," Watanabe observed.

"Nemo likes to show off at times," Suliman said wryly.

"I do only what I'm programmed to do – that is, what *you* have programmed me to do, Captain."

"Touché, Nemo."

Ogata laughed, "A psychologist would have a field day with this."

*

The two men had arrived on *Ossë*'s bridge, the control room for the vessel, with windows allowing a view out over the bow and both sides. They stood in the centre of the bridge as a blue pool of light took shape before them. Within seconds the holo-display came into focus.

The display resolved into the scene being acted out in the water below them. A school of tuna, numbering thirty-five, emerged from the depths, following their lead fish, which was actually an autonomous underwater robot. With the bot in the lead, the school surged through the *iki jime* gate.

The trellis-like structure was a u-shaped lattice, forty feet across, the top opening to the surface of the sea. As the school entered, passing between the arms of the lattice, sensors tracked each fish, pinpointing a spot just above and behind the tuna's eye. When all the fish had been targeted, a single hail of darts was released, each dart passing through the brain of a fish.

"We're using your idea of sea ice darts, Watanabe-san, so they melt in the flesh."

"Excellent," Ogata murmured, intently watching the scene unfold.

The guide bot stopped next to the forward edge of the gate as the stricken school sank lifelessly behind it, the bodies still carried forward by momentum. Several long-legged, crab-like bots scurried along the matrix of the gate to grasp the drifting tuna with soft pincers, carrying them one by one to a storage container which had been positioned near the entrance. The fish were loaded into the case and immediately submerged inside within a slurry of sea ice.

"Well done, Captain!" Ogata exclaimed, as the holo-display showed the last tuna being stowed in the container.

The men moved outside again, to watch the ocean from the railing.

Divers now swam into position, waiting for the fully loaded container to ascend. As the container surfaced, a sudden cloud of spray alerted them all to the arrival of a *Flying Fish* courier drone. The drone lowered hoists, retrieved the precious cargo with the help of the divers, then pivoted and flew north.

All eyes tracked the drone's path. Within minutes, it had vanished over the horizon. The iced fish would arrive by evening at the Tsukiji fish market in Tokyo.

"This calls for a celebration, Watanabe-san!" Sul announced. "One tuna has been set aside. We'll lunch on fresh sashimi today. Nemo, please invite Gideon and the other engineers to join us, to enjoy the fruits of their hard work!"

"Invitation given," Nemo said. "I've taken the liberty of ordering a plate of sushi for Sophia as well, Captain. She's with Fatima in the work area."

"Sophia?" interrupted Ogata.

"Forgive me," Sul hesitated, "Sophia's my daughter. I apologize that you've not met her yet. She's very shy."

"Ah yes. Now I remember, you told me, she's autistic. Is that right?"

A look of affection passed over Sul's face, "Yes. With Sophia, being autistic is not so much an affliction, but rather a kind of genius. She has a unique way of looking at the world."

"I've heard rumours of her impressive robotic creations."

"Yes, Sophia's designs are in demand throughout the Pelagic Territories and beyond."

"It seems both of your offspring have brilliant minds."

"They do indeed, they take after their mother." Sul smiled and stood up.

Ogata nodded uncomfortably, remembering Sul's recent bereavement, and wishing he hadn't allowed the conversation to stray towards that topic. "I'm so sorry for your loss."

"Thank you, Watanabe-san. Sarah would have loved this demonstration today. She'd have been proud of Gideon." Sul looked into the distance and sighed, then turned to his guest, "Shall we go down for lunch, Watanabe-san?"

Ogata and Sul walked to the lift that would take them to the dining area below.

*

Half an hour later, Sul, Ogata, Gideon and the men and women from Watanabe Enterprises were preparing to eat the fruits of their labour. The table had been set by the engineers in traditional Japanese style, with plates of fresh tuna sliced in sashimi style and sushi in the centre. The two older men sat at one end conversing quietly. The rest looked expectantly at them.

Ogata stood, "*Itadakimasu!*" Turning to Sul as he sat back down, he interpreted, "We are so grateful for this food." The engineers cheered, toasting Sul with small cups of *saké*.

The seven young Japanese engineers, several of whom had changed into elegant kimonos for the meal, began chattering excitedly as they chose plates of food from the serving line. They settled at one of the long tables with their colleagues from the Pelagic colonies, and started to eat.

Ogata watched from his seat as Sul's son put his chopsticks down to draw on a napkin, explaining a concept to the others. Gideon had his father's dark hair, but his eyes were hazel and his features more refined. The other engineers watched him, first silent, and then buzzing with exclamations and comments when he'd finished.

Through the window beyond the tables, a silver stream of anchovies swirled into a ball as a school of bluefin tuna swam into view. The predators flashed through undulating sunbeams as they devoured the scattering baitfish. Scales fell like shimmering rain as the bluefin tuna finished their meal and swam out of view in their search for another.

"Was that another one of your schools of tuna, Captain?" Ogata asked.

"Nemo, which school is that?" Sul directed Ogata's question to the AI.

"Those are part of Cohort 73," came Nemo's voice, from the air.

"Our farming community, the *Arraa'i* Pod, manages eighty-six schools or cohorts of tuna…" Sul's comment was cut short by an alarm.

"Please report, Nemo." Sul stood sharply, and the diners grew silent.

"Captain, the tuna guide for Cohort 67 has gone offline abruptly. We've lost telemetry of the school. Backup systems are not kicking in. I'm checking now."

Everyone around the table looked at Sul, then Gideon, holding a collective breath.

"Captain, it seems that Cohort 67 has been poached. The tuna guide was delinked from my systems, and we've lost control of the school. I've contacted the New Zealand Coastguard, requesting assistance to catch the pirates. However, their nearest ship's over fifty nautical miles away."

"They won't arrive in time," Gideon's voice broke the silence, weighted with frustration as he pushed his chair back. "That's five million US dollars' worth of tuna they've stolen."

"Nemo, are any Pelagic Ranger units nearby?" Sul asked calmly.

"No, Captain. They've all been called out of our sector, responding to an incident at the Marcelli Township."

"What was the last location of the cohort, Nemo?" Gideon asked, now standing.

"Five kilometres, bearing 243 degrees, Gideon."

"Show us on the holo-display." Sul's tone was terse.

A blue pool of light appeared before them on the head table. Several of the engineers cleared plates out of the way.

The blue sphere of light displayed an image of an empty sea. Off to one side, were icons representing another tuna school. A "34" glowed brightly on the flank of the fish guide.

"Nemo, instruct the guide of Cohort 34 to probe for signals from tuna of Cohort 67." The tuna guide detached itself from the school in the display and moved quickly to the centre of the pool of light. More small fish icons appeared, but as soon as they appeared, they disappeared off the screen one by one.

"Nemo, range?"

"They're just beyond the reach of our weapons systems, Captain."

"To be expected," Sul said quietly. "Nemo, extend the sensitivity of the tuna guide's electronics."

"Yes, Captain."

The image sharpened, and a vague shadow appeared near the dwindling members of the tuna cohort. "That's a submarine!" Gideon pointed.

Smaller shadows moved among the remaining tuna. More tuna icons winked out as they watched.

"*Baba*, they're poaching our schools as we watch! We've caught them red-handed," Gideon cried.

Sul was staring at the display. "The resolution of the image is not sharp enough to use as evidence in court, son. We won't be able to identify who the perpetrators are."

Gideon turned to his father, "I could get there in eight minutes on a *Dragonfly!*"

His father looked at him with empathy and spoke in calm, deliberate tones, "Son, you can't get there fast enough. In eight minutes, the pirates will be long gone." The last of the stray tuna icons disappeared from the display as he spoke.

"Baba, let me try!" He walked towards the door.

"Sit down, son. You mean well, but it's too late." Gideon returned to his chair, dejected. The other engineers looked at one another, outraged along with Gideon.

"The poachers are probably using a high-speed *Tigershark.* They love those," Gideon mumbled.

Sul noticed a movement by the door. Sophia had come in without a noise and stood listening near the door.

"Captain, one of Sophia's drones has arrived on site, reporting that the surface of the sea is clear, there's no longer any sign of a vessel in the area."

"Any clues as to the identity of the pirates, Nemo?" Sul asked.

There was a pause, then Nemo resumed his report. "Analyzing the last telemetric records, my guess is that a submarine came near the tuna school and was able to hack into programming of tuna guide 67. Within the last three hours, there have been reports of both *Yakuza* merchant ships and a Caliphate trawler in that area. Either of those could have launched a craft like the *Tigershark* Gideon suggested, from outside our detection range."

"Nemo, please alert the rest of the *Arraa'i* Pod. Move all tuna guides to security level three, bring them close to our Pod. Ask Hafez to develop countermeasures. And send a copy of your analysis to Sophia. She might be able to use it to make the next version of tuna guides more secure."

Sophia peeked around the door, a smile flashing across her small face.

"Yes, Captain." Both Nemo's voice and the display faded away.

Staff entered the dining room to clear the tables. The engineers remained alert, their taut faces revealing their anxiety about the event and their desire to help.

Ogata spoke for them, "I'm so sorry, Captain. This is terrible. We're ashamed that the Japanese criminal *Yakuza* gangs can still act with impunity and our government has failed to control them. Ashamed we still allow pirates in this day and age. We should have eradicated them long ago."

Sul sighed, "Piracy is all too common out here in the open ocean, I'm afraid. By *Yakuza,* by the Caliphate, even by other Pelagic communities. Be at peace, Watanabe-san, we have faced much worse. We will get through this."

"Yes, the dark side of human nature is one thing all communities seem to have in common," Ogata commented.

Sul nodded. "So true. And the outlaws always have the offensive advantage as they probe for our weaknesses. No matter how well designed our systems are, the vulnerabilities only become evident when someone discovers and exploits them."

"What measures have you been taking to combat piracy?"

"The Pelagic Territories deploy some defensive forces, but we don't yet have enough political leverage to fully protect ourselves. Since we inhabit international waters, not our own, there is no law giving us authority to prosecute criminal behaviour. We can submit a complaint to the Pacific Rim Council, but they also have limited jurisdiction."

"Pelagic Territories need to be granted nation status so we can stop these criminals with our own laws!" Gideon said, this time jumping up and stalking out the door.

"Forgive my son. He's impetuous." Sul bowed his head slightly towards Ogata.

"No need to apologize, Battuta-san," Ogata said, waving his hand. "I actually agree with him. My corporation has spoken up repeatedly on behalf of the Pelagic Territories during negotiations with the Japanese government. You recently petitioned the Pacific Rim Council again regarding nationhood, isn't that right?"

Sul looked out the window thoughtfully, "Yes, we petitioned, and they turned us down for the third time. The international implications of recognizing the Pelagic Territories as nations, they said, are… complicated."

Sul straightened up and spoke to the diners, "I'm sorry this has ruined our meal, and after such a triumph." He turned towards the engineers with a smile, "You all did very well." He applauded them.

Ogata rose and bowed towards Sul, and the Japanese engineers rose and did the same. "We appreciate doing business with your Pod, Battuta-san. Thank you for an excellent feast. We'll leave you now, to sort this out."

Sul rose and bowed in return. "You're kind, Watanabe-san. Thank you." He watched as Ogata and his colleagues filed into the hallway. One of their company craft would be standing by at the surface to take them back to Japan.

*

Sul walked, deep in thought, towards the left edge of the great sea window. A door slid open, revealing his office, built beneath the bow of *Ossë*.

The far wall, which was curved, was filled with display screens. The upper screens, at eye-level, provided views of activity on the bridge and surrounding the vessel. The lower ones displayed sensor readings of the ocean conditions surrounding *Ossë* and cycled through telemetry of the tuna cohorts managed by the *Arraa'i* Pod. A desk below the screens was piled with papers and several computer pads. As Sul slid into his chair at the centre of the desk, before him an active holo-model appeared showing the position and movement of vessels and tuna schools belonging to the *Arraa'i* Pod. A window above and down both sides of the screens opened to the sea around the bow of *Ossë*. A giant sunfish was passing by. It looked ungainly but swam nimbly as it fed on a swarm of jellyfish.

Sul gazed out the window. *How powerless we are to stop this thievery.*

A soft tone sounded. "Yes, Nemo," Sul said without looking around.

"I trust I'm not interrupting, Captain. Paul Whitestone has an urgent request."

"Thanks, Nemo." Sul swivelled his chair towards the centre of the room where another holo-projector displayed. In a moment, his friend appeared before him, seated in a barn, with horses in the background.

"From your face, Sul, I see you're having a bad day."

Sul's smile turned wry. "You know me too well." He sighed. "We've just lost another tuna cohort to pirates."

"Sorry to hear that. A whole cohort? That has to hurt. What are your options?"

"Not many at this point. I think the pirates will get away with it."

"That's terrible, Sul. I'm sorry." Paul paused, giving his friend a moment, then said, "Are you free to chat?"

Sul smiled, "A chat with you, Paul, will improve my day. What can I do for you?"

Paul shifted uncomfortably on his stool, "Well, I'm concerned about a young man I mentored a few years back. Name's Ben Holden. He came to mind earlier today."

"One of your premonitions, Paul?"

"Possibly. I can't shake the feeling that he's in trouble. Ben's been in Singapore lecturing at a symposium. I've been trying to contact him but can't get through. The organizers said he didn't show up for his scheduled presentation yesterday and no one has seen him since just before dinner last night. His things are still in his hotel room, but the bed wasn't slept in. I'm concerned."

"How can I help?"

"Sul, I see you and the *Arraa'i* Pod are north-west of New Zealand. I'm sending you some coordinates. Would you be able to scan the sea between you and New Caledonia around these coordinates? I'm uploading them to Nemo. Could you let me know if you find anything?"

The area of ocean appeared on one of Sul's screens. He studied it. "That's within reach of our observation drones. I'll get back to you in the next hour or two. Remembering how many times your premonitions have proven true, Paul, I suspect we'll find something interesting."

"Thank you, Sul. That'll ease my mind."

"No problem, my friend. Talk to you soon." The image faded.

"I've released three drones towards the coordinates, Captain." Nemo's voice pulled Sul back to the moment. "They should send us information in about forty minutes."

"Thank you, Nemo. Keep me posted."

3 July 2066, Îlot Brosse, South Pacific
(the next day)

The drone of a small outboard motor humming roused Ben. The sound, stark and lonely in the vast quiet darkness of the small hours, drew Ben back towards consciousness. He woke, groggy and achy, but immediately focused.

Through the opening in his hide, dripping from a recent squall, Ben spotted points of light a quarter mile away, moving parallel to the reef. *An inflatable.* Dread gripped his stomach. The points turned into beams, sweeping the water's surface, as the craft sought a channel into the lagoon. Someone in the bow shouted directions. The dinghy slowed as it breached a break in the reef barrier, and then muttered across the shallow lagoon, moving back and forth to avoid the treacherous coral heads just below the surface.

As it neared the island, the dinghy turned to cruise parallel to shore, finally beaching several hundred metres from Ben's hide. Four men got out and spread to search the area. Systematically, silent, intent, thorough, their spotlights swept the sand, rocks, brush, and palms.

Several times they passed near Ben's refuge, their beams piercing through his palm leaf cover. Ben held himself motionless, gripping the hammer he'd kept in his belt during the long swim.

At one point, a man stood a few feet away. Ben could have stretched out and touched his boots. Ben slowed his breathing, willed his body to relax and remain motionless. He stared at a trailing shoelace.

A rustle nearby, the searcher stopped and swept the light over the area and came to rest on a land crab creeping across the dried palm leaves. It had a taken a bleach bottle as its shell. The man cursed and moved on.

Several tense hours passed as the search continued. The men gathered back at the dinghy to confer in subdued voices. In the pre-dawn stillness, words drifted over the water to Ben's ears. He strained to hear their Arabic. "… the Emir… not happy … Yunus … furious … almost dawn … must leave."

A faint line of light broadened in the east. The men packed their equipment and climbed back into the dinghy, motored across the lagoon, crossed the coral reef and then out to sea. Ben sighed. Relief flooded his weak, tired body.

The pre-dawn light increased. Still lying prone and peering through the small opening, Ben's eyes followed the retreating craft. It approached a dark object a quarter mile out on the ocean. He recognized the silhouette of a conning tower. *A submarine.* The men clambered aboard, pulled the dinghy up, and disappeared into the tower. The sub slipped silently beneath the waves.

*

Ben remained in his hole long after the submarine had left. Watching. Expecting the threat to return. He no longer had the strength to climb out, to escape. An empty hopelessness pooled in his spirit.

The sun climbed higher in the sky, its rays burning through his shelter. He woke again and again, prodded by the insistent heat, thirst captivating his every thought. As he opened his eyes, the sun sparkled off the sea, tantalizing.

What is that? A shadow crossed the opening as a lone gull landed on the ground next to the entrance to the hide.

Through bleary eyes, he saw the gull step towards him, then pause, pulling a leg up to rest on one foot.

His head felt light. *Hallucinations will come soon. Maybe this gull is one of those.* He tried again to lift himself from the hole, to scare the gull away, but was only able to bump the woven panels above. Loosened sand sifted down, irritating his eyes; he blinked away the grains and looked out.

The gull turned its head, beady eyes seeming to focus on him. Behind the bird, Ben imagined he saw people emerging from the sea.

Impossible. Hallucinations, he thought. But then arms were pulling him from his shelter. Memories rose in his mind as darkness overwhelmed him.

CHAPTER TWO

14 November 2053, Seattle, Washington
(thirteen years earlier)

God, I hate public speaking, Lisa Holden thought nervously as butterflies battled in her stomach. Her professor, Professor Hakim, had negotiated a speaking slot for her at the North American Geophysics Conference. She had to deliver her presentation in less than half an hour's time. *Deep breaths, it's only a talk.* The breaths didn't help.

"You have to tell others about your research," Professor Hakim had insisted. "Your findings are revolutionary. Being heard from the podium will help your career."

Picking up her mobile, she called her husband. "Hi, Ben? I need to talk to you. I'm a mess. I'll be on in twenty minutes."

She heard Ben chuckle. *That doesn't help!*

"Relax, Lise, honey. You always get nervous at these things, and you always do fine. You got rave reviews for that talk at the university last month."

"But this crowd's five times larger, Ben."

She heard muffled whispers, then a small boy's voice. "Mom, Dad says you'll do fine." More low voices, then, "You'll do great! We're rooting for you. Dad said to tell you to break a leg!"

Tears came to her eyes. "Thanks, Sammy," she said, "You've made mommy a whole lot braver."

"It worked, Dad! Mom said, thanks. Why do we want her to break a leg?" She heard Sammy moving away from the phone. Ben came back on. "With both of us on your side, how can you possibly go wrong? The fact that your work is excellent might help as well."

Lisa took a deep breath, "OK, you goofs," she said. "Thank you. That's what I needed, a lift from my boys."

"Break a leg," Ben repeated, punctuating his blessing with a kiss into the phone.

"But why, Dad?" she heard Sammy's insistent voice again.

"Thanks, Ben. Love you." She hung up and began sorting her notes for the hundredth time.

*

"So, as you can see," Lisa swept her arms to direct the audience's gaze towards the colourful holographic display, "this map shows a sampling of data for seismic activity collected over the last five years. When we've finished our analysis, we'll have a much better understanding of seismic dynamics at the edges of the North American craton – that portion of the North American continent which has been stable for billions of years. Working with the US Geological Society and the Federal Emergency Response Agency, we hope to refine protocols based on likely critical events. The algorithms I have developed will exponentially increase our ability to predict catastrophic quakes and thus save human lives."

Applause surged from the audience as the holographic map faded. "Thank you," Lisa nodded, smiling faintly and blushing as she walked away from the podium.

Later, at her booth in the display area, underneath holographic maps, she met swarming crowds. Professor Rashida Hakim joined her to field their questions. Rashida's support encouraged Lisa as much as the crowd's interest. After a half hour of intense interaction, the wave of people flowed towards the dining area. Lunch was being served.

Lisa sighed. *I'm glad that's over.* The attention had almost overwhelmed her.

"Well done, Dr Holden!" Rashida said. "The praise is well deserved."

"Thank you, Rashida. I couldn't have done it without you," Lisa said as they together began to close down the display.

One last delegate lingered at the display, gazing at the map overhead. The small, wiry man was dressed in a dark suit, a bit formal for Seattle. Olive skin, black hair, a distinctively trimmed beard beneath a prominent nose. He now approached her, eyes flashing. Professor Hakim glanced at him, then gave the man a look Lisa could not interpret.

The man turned from the professor to address Lisa. "Thank you, Dr Holden," he said. "An excellent presentation. Your research into the dynamics of seismic stress zones moves predictive science to a new level."

He extended his hand, with a smile. "Let me introduce myself, Doctor. I am Dr Abdul Qawwi, Senior Researcher of Geophysics and Tectonics at the Caliph University in Mecca. I am engaged in similar research focused on faults around the Indian Ocean. May my research assistants consult with you on the algorithms you've created? I believe that, through collaboration, both our efforts would move forward more efficiently."

Smiling awkwardly, Lisa shook his hand lightly, then released it.

The professor stepped between them; there was an edge to her voice, "Thank you for your interest, Dr Qawwi, but Dr Holden hasn't finished processing the data. It may take another six months. She's working under a federal grant, so the data is governed by the Security Protection Act. I suggest you submit your request to the State Department."

Was that anger flashing across Dr Qawwi's face? "Yes," he said, smiling again. "Of course. The Caliphate will make a request. Thank you again, Dr Holden." He bowed slightly to Lisa, ignoring Professor Hakim.

Rashida tugged on Lisa's arm as they turned and walked towards the cafeteria area, away from the man still examining the holographic display. Lisa was glad to leave. "That was awkward, Rashida," she said turning to her professor, "May I ask why you reacted to him that way?"

"That man is Salafi, probably part of the New Caliphate." Rashida almost spat the words. Seeing Lisa's questioning look, she said more softly, "They have killed members of my family."

3 March 2054 Mecca, Saudi Arabia
(three and a half months later)

Abdul Qawwi sat tapping his knee with his fingers. The lavishly decorated lobby seemed more appropriate for the leader of a Caliphate in the thirteenth century than the twenty-first. Abdul Qawwi did not approve of this outdated style; it reflected the glories of the past, not the future. However, he also knew his disapproval did not matter, it was still an honour to have an opportunity to talk with the Caliph.

A vizier, one of several political advisors to the Caliph, entered the room. "Dr Qawwi?"

Abdul Qawwi stood. "Yes," he said, as he bowed slightly.

"The Caliph is ready for you." The vizier tilted his head towards the door to his right.

Abdul Qawwi smiled, anticipating this encounter. *The Caliph will be thrilled with this idea, inshallah, if God wills.* He'd taken care over the last few weeks to route his proposal through personal contacts, to avoid prying eyes.

Abdul Qawwi followed the vizier to another well-appointed hall, but much smaller. Through the doorway he could see the Caliph seated regally. Abdul Qawwi discretely studied the man he'd heard so much about, but not yet met. The popular press had compared him to the great warrior Caliph, Saladin.

Power emanated from this man, the power of life and death. Abdul Qawwi suppressed the fear that now gripped his chest. *This man is revered as God's Shadow on Earth. His power and influence increases year by year.* Abdul Qawwi entered the room, bowing deeply, willing his breaths to be deep and slow.

"Dr Abdul Qawwi? Please take a seat," the forty-something Caliph gestured towards the chair to his left.

Abdul Qawwi sat as the Caliph regarded him quietly. Moments passed. Abdul Qawwi felt unnerved.

Finally, the Caliph spoke. "Doctor," he began, his voice measured and clear, "I found your proposal intriguing. However, I wonder if the plan you propose is plausible. Can one really start cascading seismic cataclysms on the North American continent?"

Abdul Qawwi found his voice. *"Inshallah,* we believe so, your Eminence. Let me show you."

Abdul Qawwi nodded towards the waiting vizier, "Sir, have my files been uploaded?"

"Yes, Dr Qawwi. Use this." As Abdul Qawwi rose to his feet, the vizier handed him a remote control.

Abdul Qawwi projected holographic maps, casting vivid colours within the walls of white marble.

"Here is the North American craton. A craton, your Eminence, is the stable portion of the continent. This craton extends from the centre of the USA up through Canada. Notice the seismically active areas around the edges.

"In the north-west, we can see the Cascadia subduction zone. This is where, over millions of years, tectonic plates have collided, forcing one edge to bend under another." The subduction zone glowed blue. "In the south-west are the Hayward, San Andreas and Imperial Valley faults, deep cracks revealing more evidence of boundaries between tectonic plates." As Abdul Qawwi named them, these fault lines shone as golden, jagged splits down the state of California.

"And that red area east of the Cascadia zone?" the Caliph interrupted.

The fiery red area pulsed. "That is the Yellowstone Caldera, a huge subterranean space full of molten magma. We'll leave that caldera alone. Scientists predict that an eruption in this area would release so much debris into the atmosphere that it would lower the temperature of the whole world, bringing about a prolonged winter and a new ice age."

"Yes, we should avoid that," the Caliph commented dryly.

The Caliph's remark interrupted the rhythm of Abdul Qawwi's planned presentation. He fought down a rising anxiety. Breathing deeply again, he continued. "Moving further eastward, over in the Midwestern US is the New Madrid seismic zone. This region is prone to frequent earthquakes due to tectonic plates grinding against one another. On the easternmost coast, there's also the Ramapo fault, an area weakened by multiple earthquakes thousands of years ago." A colourful mosaic of fault lines and seismic activity areas now filled the hologram.

"I have done preliminary modelling of the information accessible from public data. We have also collected private data, at a cost."

Even as the Caliph murmured his approval, Abdul Qawwi could sense his impatience. He spoke at a faster pace. "Of course, faithful geologists, brothers and sisters in the Islamic community, have shared their data freely."

The Caliph stopped him by waving his hand. "Dr Qawwi, all this is interesting, but come to the point. I have other engagements."

Abdul Qawwi took a breath, then told him his idea.

"Impressive." The Caliph rose and paced around the holograph. "Can this indeed be done?" The Caliph studied the map for several minutes. A bead of sweat formed on Abdul Qawwi's brow.

"Your Eminence, I require one last set of data. The most important. It is vital for the plan's success."

"So?" The Caliph looked directly at Abdul Qawwi, and despite the calmness of his voice, Abdul Qawwi felt a visceral threat, a sudden sinking in his stomach.

"There's a slight complication, Eminence. A scientist by the name of Dr Lisa Holden. She has designed an algorithm to process the seismic data. We need the results of this algorithm to carry out this plan. However, the American State Department has firmly refused to grant us access."

"Then, persuade the doctor to give us this data."

"That is not an easy task, Eminence." Abdul Qawwi averted his gaze.

Finally, the Caliph said, "What do you need?"

Abdul Qawwi told him.

He turned to the vizier, "Abdul Ghafoor, please have Dr Abdul Qawwi's theory checked by our scientists."

The vizier was busy taking notes on his pad, then looked up, "Yes, your Eminence."

"Before sunset, Abdul Ghafoor."

The Caliph swept out of the room without a backward glance. "Yes, your Eminence," the vizier said to his retreating form. Abdul Ghafoor turned to Abdul Qawwi. "Return at five p.m. and I'll give you the Caliph's answer."

As Abdul Qawwi bowed low, drops of sweat fell from his brow onto the floor. When he looked up again, the vizier had gone.

3 March 2054 Mecca, Saudi Arabia
(the same day)

Abdul Qawwi strode purposefully out of the palace of the Caliph and towards the Grand Mosque of Mecca which contained the *Ka'ba*. It was almost time for midday prayers.

Abdul Qawwi joined the crowd of men filing into the vast courtyard of the Grand Mosque. Bending next to a streaming fountain, he began the ritual cleansing, wadhu, in preparation for prayer. He thoroughly washed his right arm from the fingertips up to the elbow, then his left. Next, he rinsed his mouth three times, cleaned his teeth with a finger, then he splashed water and wiped his face with his right hand. Both wet hands were swept over his head. Next, he completely washed each foot to the ankle. All the while, he murmured prayers of dedication. With his wet hands, he wiped across his hair to the back of his head and then down the sides of his beard. He paused to silently acknowledge that his intention to pray was pure.

As he rose, several men came to greet him. These were *jihadis* he'd worked alongside in several European cities. *Fellow foot-soldiers of the Caliph.*

He joined the mass of worshippers demonstrating the unity of believers by walking anti-clockwise around the huge draped structure, the *Ka'ba*, performing the pilgrimage rite of *tawaaf*. Through loudspeakers, a *muezzin* sang out the call for the worshippers to join in prayer.

Abdul Qawwi stood to pray on the white marble surrounding the

Ka'ba. On either side of him stretched a circle of men, one of many circles of pilgrims around this black cube, which every Muslim in the world faced during prayers, as the focus of devotion. He began the familiar rituals and postures of the daily prayer, *Salaat*, with the others. In unison, the worshippers raised their hands, chanting, *"Allahu Akbar*, God is Great." The words resonated around the courtyard and through his soul.

He folded his arms along with the rest, continuing the ritual. *"Bismillāh ir-raḥmān ir-raḥīm*. In the name of Allah, the Merciful and Compassionate, Praise to Allah, Lord of the worlds," they chanted.

These are my brothers. Together we're spreading God's truth throughout the earth. He was deeply moved, as he worshipped as part of the crowd.

Abdul Qawwi bowed, placing his hands on his knees. *"Subḥāna rabbī al-aẓīm*, Glory to my God, the Exalted," echoed around him and through him. *We're building the New Caliphate, the Homeland of the Faithful. Together we'll win many more to the one true faith.* Together we will end six hundred years of world domination by infidels!

Abdul Qawwi straightened then prostrated himself. His forehead and nose touched the cool marble floor beneath them. *"Subḥāna*, our Lord on high be praised," he recited, a deep peace surrounding his heart. His spirit soared.

He immersed himself in eternity, in the holiness of Allah. He continued the *Salaat* prayer. As he finished the final *rak'ah*, he recited to the angels on his right and left who watched over his life, *"Assalāmu 'alaykum wa raḥmatullāh wa barakātuhu*, Peace be upon you and God's mercy and blessing." He stood and then filed out with the worshippers, leaving others to finish their *tawaaf*.

Abdul Qawwi stepped out of the Grand Mosque area, refreshed, and turned towards the shops across the main boulevard. At the sound of running footsteps behind him, Abdul Qawwi turned, "Ah, brother Mustafa. And these are your friends?"

"Sheikh Abdul Qawwi," Mustafa responded. "Do you have a few moments to join us for tea? We have with us a new brother, Robert, from Perth, who has come for his first *'umrah*."

An eager young man with blue eyes and a red fuzz of hair, his head freshly shaven to join in the worship at the Grand Mosque, looked at Abdul Qawwi with reverence. Abdul Qawwi held out his hand for the young man to shake. "Welcome, brother!" He shifted the conversation easily from Arabic to English. "I hope you have been blessed on your pilgrimage. Join me at one of the tea shops. I have some time to chat before my appointment at the Palace this afternoon."

"You honour us, Sheikh," the young Australian said.

Abdul Qawwi smiled, "Mustafa is a good brother. He and I have worked together in Europe." Mustafa led them to one of the opulent hotels that looked across to the sacred site of *Al-Masjid al-Haram*. Crowds were lighter than normal since this was not the primary pilgrimage season, the *Haj*.

The restaurant was crowded, but Mustafa had reserved a table near a window, where they could look out on the milling pilgrims. Mustafa signalled to the waiter, who promptly filled their table with tea, small bowls of pistachios, almonds and dates, as well as plates of falafel, *yugmish* and sweet *luqaimat*.

Flanked by bodyguards, a young central Asian man draped in the traditional two white cloths of pilgrimage walked in, looking around for a seat. Their table had one extra chair and Abdul Qawwi graciously gestured to the pilgrim to join them. The young man sat down, thanking him. Abdul Qawwi nodded in return.

Mustafa addressed Abdul Qawwi, "Sheikh, I was just giving Robert lessons on the recent history of our faith."

"It's exciting to be living in a time when Islam is regaining its rightful place in the world," Robert gushed. "But Sheikh," he spoke directly to Abdul Qawwi, "in your opinion, how did our brothers lose their way, during those many centuries when Islam ceased spreading, when good Muslim lands came under the yoke of colonial infidel powers, those who brought an end to the original Caliphate?"

"That is an excellent question, brother," Abdul Qawwi nodded. "Muslims did lose their way during those centuries. They no longer followed the teaching and traditions of the first believers. They were seduced by their colonial masters and wandered off the true path. They ignored the example of *al-ṣalaf al-saaliḥ*, the first generations of followers of Muhammad, peace be upon him. They failed Allah's test and were found unworthy."

"More than three hundred years ago, in the 1700s, Mohammed ibn 'Abd al-Wahhab showed us the way back to the true path. He taught us to imitate those who lived at the time of Prophet Muhammad, peace be upon him. 'Abd al-Wahhab's teachings have been revived, and once again Islam is spreading through the earth as it should."

Abdul Qawwi noticed and approved that this Australian man had trimmed his beard and moustache to the proscribed lengths. "I see you've been taught this true path as well."

"Yes, Sheikh. While a teenager, I wasted my life in drugs and whoring. I was drowning in my own filth and arrested for crimes I had committed. Then, in prison, brothers came alongside and taught me the clean life, the true way."

"Robert, you are among the flood streaming into the House of Islam today. Heed the lessons you are learning. Early this century, groups like Taliban, Al Qaeda and ISIS thought they could spread Islam quickly, primarily through Jihad, confronting the world powers as warriors for the faith with the intent to bring all people into the right path. They underestimated the resolve and power of the infidel West. We, the next generation, have learned from what they did wrong. We've learned to be patient, to pursue the long game. Today, we extend the influence of the New Caliphate subtly and with wisdom. Now it is spreading as Allah intends." Abdul Qawwi paused, feeling a deep sense of privilege for his own vital role in this drama.

The central Asian man had been sipping his tea and nibbling at the dates and nuts on the table, listening. He glanced at Robert, then directed his gaze at Abdul Qawwi. "Bullshit," he said quietly.

Startled out of his lecture, Abdul Qawwi narrowed his eyes and held the gaze of this interloper. "Excuse me, brother?"

The young Asian did not blink, and boldly returned the stare. "You *Salafists* are a stain on the community of faith. You believe the Lord of the Universe wants to keep all believers trapped in a primitive way of thinking from fifteen hundred years ago. The world has moved on. Good Muslims engage the modern world on its terms while still submitting to Allah with their whole beings."

The young man ate a date, almost delicately, then looked at Robert. "Brother, they use their man-made rules and regulations as the only measure of a true Muslim, but in reality, they are intent on building a political power base. They do not care about the state of your soul, only that you adhere to their interpretation of how the first community of Muslims at Medina lived so they can control you."

Robert's eyes flashed between this young man and Abdul Qawwi; confusion flooded his features.

Mustafa sprang to his feet, along with several others at the table, moving with aggression towards the speaker, who lifted his right hand above his head.

In response to this gesture, the six burly bodyguards came over from nearby tables. Mustafa and his associates slowly sank back down into their seats.

The young man stood, brushed pistachio shells from his white clothes and looked coolly at those around the table, then stopped and focused on Robert. "Do not be led astray by these *Salafists*, earnest pilgrim. Keep to the true path, the *dīn* of the Qur'an. You have been warned."

He dropped a large bill on the table to pay for the tea and refreshments for everyone, then turned and walked away with his bodyguards.

Abdul Qawwi strove to contain the fury of impotence he felt. These false teachers are bold, he thought, but they will take their proper place among the unbelievers.

He looked back at Robert, "That man is an agent of Satan, brother. He only tests your faith by twisting the truth. He pretends to live the true faith, but in reality is far from Allah."

Confusion faded from Robert's face, and he nodded.

"Sheikh, it is your vision, what you described, which fires my heart. But what of those, like this man, who call themselves Muslims but have become complacent and do not strive, those who no longer practise the Jihad of spreading the faith?"

Abdul Qawwi studied this young man, he liked him. He made a mental note to talk to Mustafa about ways to pull Robert into their campaigns. "Yes, Robert, you are right to be concerned. A man cannot keep one foot in the House of Islam while the other is in the House of War, where the infidels reside. A soul cannot be divided like that; those who are not wholly in Islam commit the blasphemy of worshiping something other than Allah – maybe money, power, or status. They are lost unless they come to their senses. That man was obviously rich, and a slave to his riches; that is his god. It is as Allah wills."

Robert nodded thoughtfully. "Yes, Sheikh. Thank you."

Abdul Qawwi glanced at the clock. He stood, "I'm sorry, I must leave now for my appointment."

Everyone at the table stood and bowed as they embraced briefly, grasping each other above the elbows and brushing cheeks in farewell, comrades in the effort to spread the Caliphate. Abdul Qawwi walked out the door. His mind still simmered with anger at the words of the young critic, robbing him of the peace from his *Salaat* prayers and the pleasure of his impending meeting.

Chapter Three

10 June 2054, Redondo Beach, California
(three months later)

"Dad, Dad!" Sammy called from the water. He emerged, waves rolling gently around him, then sat on the sand to struggle with his obstinate fins. The diving mask still gripped his face.

"Sammy! What did you find, son?"

The boy jumped up and ran across the sand to his father, fins flapping in his hands, snorkel jiggling against his cheek.

"Dad, I found a colony of sand dollars!"

"Just out there, in about twenty feet of water?" Ben asked, pointing beyond the waves.

The boy was dumbfounded. "Yeah, how'd you know?"

Ben laughed, "Because that's where I found them, about eighteen years ago, when I was about your age."

"They're so cool, Dad. They have short purple spines and they're standing, lined up like someone stuck them on their edges in the sand," Sammy enthused.

Ben smiled.

Lisa walked over to join them, three ice cream bars in hand. "Provisions for the explorers?"

"Yay, Mom!" Sammy snatched one from her hand.

Ben smiled at his wife. "One of the many reasons I love you is because you know just the moment to bring us food!"

She smiled back, "That's easy. Any moment is a good time to bring food for you two."

Ben laughed again. "True, that."

"Did you choose this spot because of the colony, so Sammy would find the sand dollars?" Lisa asked, amused.

"Maybe," Ben hedged. "I can neither confirm nor deny." She rewarded him with a poke in the ribs.

Warm sand. Hot sun. The young American family huddled together, licking their ice cream bars before they could melt. Ben looked around. *How I'd love to rest in this moment, and not leave tomorrow.* Ben was only twenty-seven but experience from former tours had taught him that memories of these moments, of this sense of belonging, of family, were his places of rest and hope, helping him persevere through gruelling military tours.

Lisa was wistful, "I always dread it when you leave, Ben. I never know where you're going. I never know what dangers you'll face."

Ben glanced at his wife, his expression softening. "I'm sorry, Lisa. I know it's hard. But you understand *why* I can't disclose more details."

She sighed, turning her gaze to the fluffy clouds sailing across the blue, blue sky. "Yes, my father warned me what it would be like to marry a Special Forces man."

"This could be my last tour," Ben offered, snuggling closer, enjoying the softness of her skin.

"No, these fears will pass, Ben." She looked at him, "I know how important your work is. You're protecting us all. I value that." She finished off her ice cream and turned her gaze again into his eyes. "Let me just savour this moment with my two boys."

He gave her a quick hug and shifted the topic. "So, is all the data in now, from your probes around the craton?"

She nudged him with her elbow. "You're changing the subject," she accused playfully.

"You bet I am."

"OK." Her eyes danced. "Yes, the data's all in now. When it's been fully processed, we'll have a comprehensive picture of seismic vulnerabilities of the North American continent. It's thrilling. The algorithm is already running through the numbers at home, as we speak. Homeland Security asked me to add another layer of security to my system last night, to ward off hackers. Could you help me set up the additional biometric encryption before you leave? Seems like someone with a master's in engineering should be able to figure that out."

"I'll have to charge you," he said laughing. "Sure, show me what I need to do when we get back."

Lisa stood, gathering the ice cream sticks from Ben and Sammy and tossing them in a nearby bin. Sitting back down, she said, "I saw on the news this morning that the LA riots are spreading towards the beach cities."

"Yes. I heard that too. The rise in house prices is pushing people into the inner-city areas. Crime has been increasing and tempers are flaring, especially during summer."

"It sounds like the shooting last week of that man in Carson sparked this wave of unrest. I heard there were fires and looting in Lawndale."

"Do you want to move in with your sister in Glendale while I'm away?" A flicker of concern flashed across Ben's face.

"No, no, we'll be OK. If we get lonely, we'll move over there after I'm done running the algorithm. I'll just keep everything locked up and stay in touch with the neighbours."

"Dad!" Sammy said, jumping to his feet. "Grab your mask and fins! Let's go look at the sand dollars some more."

"Sure, buddy, race you into the water!" He gave Lisa a peck on the cheek, gathered his gear and ran with Sammy into the sea.

Lisa watched them rolling in the surf as they pulled their flippers on. Sammy was giggling. Ben picked him up and threw him into a wave. "My boys," she sighed.

12 June 2054, Redondo Beach, California
(two days later)

It was almost midnight. Abdul Qawwi and Yunus Saleh sat with two other men in the dark car, tinted windows rolled down a few inches, so they could watch for movement in the houses on this tree-lined street of typical beach homes.

Dawood Naji's pudgy shadow fidgeted in the back seat. Abdul Qawwi turned in a hushed whisper, "What is eating you, Dawood?"

Dawood Naji quieted. "Sorry, Sheikh," he said. "I've just had bad news today about my sister, Aisha."

"The one who is a student at UCLA, with the scholarship arranged by the Emir?"

"Yes, that's the one. She won a scholarship through the Emirates orphan programme; our parents died when we were children." Dawood Naji hesitated. "She's been attending classes, wearing her hijab. Several of the students taunt her because of her clothing. She ignored them, as was proper."

"The infidels have no sense of decency. This is the price we pay for holding to the righteous path."

"Yes, Sheikh, of course. But…" he hesitated again. "This is so shameful."

"You can tell me, brother. What is troubling you?"

"Aisha had been promised to her cousin, Rajih, but she confessed to me this morning that she'd been raped on campus a few months ago. One of the boys from class caught her alone and robbed her of her virginity. She hasn't told anyone else. Her shame will be discovered if she marries Rajih."

There was profound silence in the car.

"If we were back home, under the Caliphate, the rapist would be forced to marry her. But this was an infidel," Dawood Naji spat.

Abdul Qawwi looked at Dawood Naji with pity, "I'm sorry, my brother. Your sister has lost her chance at a happier life because of that infidel. She cannot marry Rajih. The household of the Emir, who has taken care of you as orphans, could not be shamed like that. It is as God wills. I am genuinely sorry, she is beautiful. This is our struggle, to overturn the depraved culture of countries like this one. To put people on the right path."

In the half-light, the gleam of a tear rolled down Dawood Naji's face. "You're right, Sheikh. This is why we struggle in our Jihad on the righteous path."

"It will soon be time, brothers," Yunus Saleh interrupted with quiet urgency, his eyes darting around the street constantly. His thin frame barely contained its intense restless energy.

The street outside the car was dim and shadowy. Above the trees, the red glow from the riots half a mile away flickered, reflecting on the low clouds above.

*

Lisa paced from room to room. It had been less than twenty-four hours, but already she missed Ben terribly. Her loneliness was most acute during the night. She checked and rechecked that the doors and windows were locked, as was her habit. *Can't be too careful, with the riots nearby.*

According to the ten o'clock news, angry demonstrations were moving towards their area.

Lisa peeked into her office to see the reassuring blinking between the computer and data device.

All that data I've gathered, now becoming something that can save lives.

41

The algorithm was due to finish in about five hours. With a pang, she realized she hadn't yet backed up the latest version she had programmed earlier today. That can wait until tomorrow. *Tomorrow. Only a few hours away now.* She glanced out the window at the dark sky.

I'm so thankful Ben helped me finish encrypting the system before he left. One less thing to worry about. She continued watching the flashes for a moment, then gave audio commands to the machine: "Time lock until 9 a.m. tomorrow."

"Time lock for 9 a.m. 13 June 2054 requested. Please confirm," a voice requested from the device.

She held her right hand up as she faced the camera. A beam from the device played across her hand and her face. "Confirm," she commanded.

"Lisa Holden. Biometrics confirmed. Time lock set."

I'll be at the university office by nine. Now I can sleep more easily.

Her slippers whispered on the carpet as she made her way to the room at the end of the darkened hall. The door was slightly ajar. She pushed it open. There was Sammy, curled up, asleep, around his new computer tablet. He'd been reading up on sand dollars and had delivered a short lecture to her at dinner time. She smiled as she recalled his enthusiasm.

Sammy stirred, then opened his eyes and looked at her. "Mom, I have to pee!"

Lisa laughed, "Well then get to it, sport! You know where the bathroom is!"

Leaping out of bed, he scampered down the hall. A moment later she heard the flush. The bathroom light went out. Sammy returned to the comfort of his bed. Lisa bent over him and kissed his forehead. "Sweet dreams."

He was already asleep.

She strolled through the house a few minutes longer, praying for Ben. *Lord, keep him safe.* Lisa took a deep breath and relaxed. *It's late. So much work to finish tomorrow.*

After changing into her nightgown, she crawled into bed. *Too large and empty.*

She switched off the light. A few moments later, she drifted off to sleep.

*

The last light in the Holden house went out. Most of the houses on the street were now dark.

"That's her bedroom, Sheikh," Yunus Saleh said softly. "The boy's gone back to bed, and now the woman has too."

Abdul Qawwi nodded. "We'll wait a few more minutes to make sure she's asleep. Then we'll move."

They watched fifteen minutes more. The Holden house remained silent and dark.

The four men climbed out of their car without a sound. Abdul Qawwi whispered terse reminders, "Dawood, go to the other end of the street and watch. Stay near our other car. You have your cocktails?"

The man nodded, holding up bottles with rags. There was a slight whiff of petrol. He stole down the street, in the shadow of trees and the cover of bushes.

"Yunus, stay here. You know what to do after we leave the house. You have your bottles?" The man nodded, pointing at a row of four bottles on the curb. He crouched by the rear fender.

"Shakeel, you stay with me." The two men crept silently to the yard of the darkened home – stopped, watched and listened. No evidence of movement from inside.

"You're sure there are no alarms?" Abdul Qawwi hissed to the shadow next to him.

"Yes, Sheikh. This house only has locks."

Approaching the back door, Abdul Qawwi applied a thin sheet of plastic to a pane above the knob. He touched a small device to the plastic and was rewarded with a barely audible crackle. He peeled back the sheet, now with the shattered window stuck to it, and slipped the film with glass behind a bush. Reaching inside, he unlatched the deadbolt.

The men paused again, listening. No sound came from within. Shakeel sprayed the door hinges. Abdul Qawwi turned the knob.

The door swung open silently. Slinking inside, Shakeel closed the door behind him.

*

Twenty minutes later, two figures walked quickly from the rear door of the darkened house, through the back garden and over the fence. Abdul Qawwi picked up a bottle from under a bush, where he'd placed it earlier in the day. Shakeel grabbed another. Pulling off the tops, they stuffed rags inside the bottle necks. Shakeel moved along the fence until he was outside the neighbouring house with its white clapboard siding.

Abdul Qawwi lit the rag and threw his bottle through the kitchen window that they'd left open at the Holden house. Shakeel threw his at next door's wooden walls. Flames leapt up quickly. Shakeel moved another two houses down and launched yet another petrol bomb. Their work done, the two men turned and sprinted between the dark houses, back to the car.

Dawood Naji returned from his destructive spree leaving yellow fires flickering behind shattered windows. Yunus Saleh ran towards his comrades, his set of Molotov cocktails successfully shattered under parked cars. The four men hurried each other into their car. The neighbourhood was quickly waking up, lights came on. People were running into their yards and the street in bedclothes, yelling. Security alarms filled the air. Neighbours rushed to the flaming homes and pounded on doors, others trained hoses on burning vehicles.

As they drove away, Abdul Qawwi registered the fires set by operatives on other nearby blocks. *Blazing up nicely. The operation is going well.* He smiled – but Abdul Qawwi was not content. Persuasion had required more than he expected.

13 June 2054, Redondo Beach, California
(the next day)

The hotel room overlooked the runways of Los Angeles International Airport. In the midnight hours, two men gathered around a glowing screen. The small, thin, screen operator, Omar, was typing rapidly on the keyboard. Sweat poured from his brow. Nearby, a small oval device flickered as it processed his requests. A red light blinked on at the end of each sequence.

Omar paused, looking up, "Sheikh, I'm not familiar with this encryption software. The information on the device is coded with the biometric data of a... Lisa Holden."

Abdul Qawwi cursed briefly, his voice breaking in anger. "She's dead, Omar!"

"I can do no more." Omar leaned back from the keyboard. "*Inshallah*, our technicians in Mecca can go further, but I have my doubts."

A thought came to him and Omar used his screen to query the device once more. "Ah! Maybe all is not lost. There seems to be another biometric profile that will open this data. Let me see if I can identify it from the intelligence files. A few minutes, Sheikh."

Abdul Qawwi drummed his fingers on the table near the keyboard. Omar's left eyebrow twitched. Finally, a face and a name appeared in the screen. "Here it is, Sheikh. A Ben Holden. Her husband?" Omar asked, turning around.

"Yes." Abdul Qawwi looked out of the window at planes landing and departing. "Get me a flight to the Caliphate tonight."

Omar quickly switched tasks on his computer, to secure a reservation for the Sheikh.

*

As the new day dawned, fire crews swarmed around the burnt properties. Morning fog billowed above from the nearby beach, drifting silently through the trees that lined the street. The lights of the squad cars cast an eerie glow in the mist.

Torched houses, collapsed and steaming, contrasted with the untouched homes next to them. Here and there were burnt hulks cradled in melted asphalt, which only the night before had been family cars.

Fire fighters recovered the bodies of Lisa and Sammy in the early hours. No other fatalities. News of the deaths spread rapidly in this close neighbourhood. Everyone had loved the Holden family. Emergency crews stretched yellow tape between the singed trees in front of the desolate scene.

As the sun rose higher, the curls of fog lightened to a silvery sheen. One by one, neighbours came over and stood at the edge of the lawn. Police interviewed families, bundled in blankets, tears streaming as they huddled in the early morning chill.

By the time the sun peeked over the roofs, a large crowd was gathered outside the smouldering shell of the Holden house. Children, on their way to school with parents, stopped to find out what had happened. A little girl collected flowers from the gardens edging the road. She ducked under the tape; the police did not stop her. She laid the flowers on what had once been the Holden's welcome mat.

16 June 2054, Bosaso, Somali Emirates
(three days later)

Cockroaches are social insects. This clan had been dwelling deep in the cupboards of the bazaar's shops and tea houses for generations. Milling and multiplying in the damp darkness, they thrived on an ample food supply. Mingling among this current generation were several creatures that the other cockroaches ignored, treating them as part of the cupboard debris. This was because they were not of the clan. Humans might mistake them for cockroaches, but the clan knew better. These counterfeits hid in the darkest corners, motionless and inert.

Now it was 6 a.m. The bazaar already bustled with morning shoppers and breakfast gatherings. Most of the cockroach clan had already returned to the cupboards to sleep off their nocturnal adventures.

However, the counterfeits began to stir. They jostled past the resting clan. One of the cockroach bots crept towards the crack in the cupboard door. Its antennae pressed through the opening to the outside. It sat there, waving, as if testing the air, then ventured into the open space, scurrying under the baseboard, and then along the circumference of the musty shop. Several others followed suit, maintaining a discrete distance between each one.

In shops all along the street, similar imitation cockroaches also emerged, acting in ways that only another cockroach would notice as unnatural. A few approached a café where three men sat sipping tea. Climbing up a table leg, one cockroach clung to the underside of the tabletop. Others manoeuvred themselves into position, scattering under nearby chairs and tables, maintaining line-of-sight with each other. The bots began to beam pinpointed flashes of invisible infrared light back and forth, relaying the conversation above them to a hidden transmitting station at the edge of the bazaar and beyond the range of surveillance scans.

The men talked in low voices, oblivious of the small listening robots.

"No phones? Nothing electronic on you, right?"

Abdul Qawwi's companions glanced at each other then looked back at their leader. "Sheikh, of course not. We know the protocols. We also did an electronic sweep of the tea shop. There are no transmitters or bugs here."

"I need to ask, brothers. Some forget. Our enemies are vigilant."

"We understand. We didn't forget." A taller, older man chose a samosa from the plate on the table, popping it into his mouth.

"Good. What do you have to report, Yunus Saleh?"

"Sheikh, tomorrow Team A on the *Eastern Star*, will travel south, and Team B on the *Palermo*, will head north – *inshallah*, if God wills."

It has taken us almost a year – but finally we've infiltrated the crews, Abdul Qawwi thought to himself. Aloud he said, "Excellent. The Emir will reward you." Abdul Qawwi sipped his tea and then unfolded a well-worn map, laying it on the table. "The *Star* must be sunk here. And the *Palermo*, here."

"Yes, Sheikh, all has been arranged. The men are willing to be martyrs in service of the Caliph. They know their families will be well rewarded, *inshallah.*

16 June 2054, Desert outside Bosaso, Somalia
(the same day)

"Are you getting this?" a young man with headphones asked, turning towards Ben. Three men crouched in a small cave, a well-hidden listening post carved into a hillside above the coastal city of Bosaso.

"Yes, Malik. Optical laser links are good. I'll move another bug in to give us eyes." Ben adjusted controls on his pad's display. "There! They've got a map of the Suez Canal, as we suspected. I think they're discussing a dirty bomb placed on the second ship, the *Palermo.*"

Hameed, the third member of the team spoke up: "I'm sending a message to the Commander." Hameed listened a moment, a hand pressing his headset, then relayed the news, "Command will send a team to intercept both ships ASAP."

Malik spoke quietly, but with deep conviction, "These men are acting out a travesty of true Islam."

Ben glanced at his colleague.

Hameed clicked his tongue in agreement as he kept watch on an array of screens providing a 360-degree view around their cave hideout from sensors tracking visual, thermal, and electronic activity. His eyes shifted systematically between the screens. "All's quiet," Hameed observed. "No activity nearby."

Malik closed his laptop, "OK guys, this is a wrap. Let's pack up. Need to reach the extraction point in three hours."

The men were tense, but quiet and efficient as they shut down their operation, dismantling and stowing the equipment. They had done this many times before. The journey from their observation post to their pick-up point was always the most dangerous part of each mission.

Without warning, the ground erupted under them.

Hameed's quick reflexes saved them. With one fluid motion he armed and dropped a taser grenade into the hole which had opened beneath their feet. In the resulting confusion, Ben and Malik kept their footing and escaped from the cave. Shots ricocheted around them, one struck Hameed in the head and he died instantly. Ben and Malik scrambled outside.

The two men stumbled out into the night, rolled down the hill, sprang up, and sprinted to cover at the other edge of the ravine. Their suits changed colour, blending in with the terrain, sand, and shrubs around them, while also masking their body heat.

The landscape stood stark and desolate, but the expanse arching above sparkled with stars. A soft night breeze sighed from the east, where the coast beckoned them. The moon rose, an immense half disk, on the eastern horizon. *Under other conditions this could have been beautiful,* Ben thought as he crouched, looked around, and then sprinted.

Malik's tight breaths and rapid footfalls were barely audible over the pounding of Ben's own heart. The two scrambled to the next, higher hill, offering a wider view of the area. As they threw themselves down at the crest, Ben pulled night vision binoculars from his pocket to scan the far side of the ravine. *No movement near the cave entrance.*

Malik was scanning the other approaches to their hill with his binoculars. He caught Ben's eye and shook his head.

With Hameed dead, Malik was in command. Ben could see his lips moving. Malik's helmet, translating his facial movements into words, transmitted a soft electronic whisper within Ben's helmet. "Five clicks to the extraction point."

They both looked cautiously along the route to their destination to the north-west, sweeping their binoculars back and forth.

A movement caught Ben's eye. His blood chilled. In front of the rising moon, the silhouette of a vehicle, no larger than a small dog, glided on treads across the sand. *A sentinel drone. Can't let it find us.*

"Malik!" He mouthed silently. His mouth was dry.

"I see it. Let's circle out of its range. You go to the west, I'll turn north and then both of us beeline to the beach."

Malik and Ben each tossed a dust-coloured ball – a countermeasure designed for just this kind of situation. The balls spun across the sand, away from them, but just outside the drone's sensor range. The balls emitted sounds and a thermal profile typical of humans on the run.

One ball rolled to the east. The other to the south-east. After a few seconds, the sentinel drone detected the presence of the eastward rolling sphere and raced to intercept it. Spurts of dust erupted along the trail of the orb. The men waited motionless for a few long moments as the sentinel sped off.

Once the drone had crossed the next ridge, the men split up. Zigzagging rapidly but silently through the scrub of the desert, they headed north-west.

17 June 2054, West Coast of Bosaso, Somalia
(the next day)

Having rendezvoused on a low ridge above the beach, Malik and Ben lay next to each other, a few hundred metres above the predetermined extraction point. They watched and waited, wary.

The beach was serene. Waves in regular procession crashed along the shore under the moonlit sky. It was still a few hours before dawn.

"Ben, wait here. I'll go and make sure the beach is secure." The voice came softly into Ben's helmet as Malik slipped into the darkness of the gully.

Ben acknowledged with a soft click of his tongue. He watched his partner's shadow melt between the shrubs and disappear into the shadows of the canyon.

He waited. The silent moments ticked by.

Static exploded abruptly in his ear. Ben's muscles tensed.

"Malik?" No answer.

Ben backed deeper into the cover of shrubs. His gaze swept the beach below.

No. Malik. Two dark figures dragged a limp body out from the mouth of the ravine and onto the sands below. A third figure stepped out from a cluster of boulders.

Malik's mike was open, Ben heard one of the figures say in Arabic, "This one is a traitor to the Caliph."

The other prodded Malik's form with a foot. "Wake up *khaa'in*, traitor."

Ben heard Malik groan. The speaker squatted down and looked directly at Malik. "Why do you serve the infidels, instead of your brothers?"

Malik rose on an elbow and returned the gaze, reciting the *shahaada* quietly, "There is no god but Allah, and Mohammed is his prophet." Then he added, "You, my brother, practice *shirk*, replacing worship of Allah with worship of your ideology and Caliph."

With increasing dread, Ben watched the crouching Islamist pull a pistol from a holster. "I send you to *aljahim*, hell, *khaa'in*," the crouching man said quietly. He pulled the trigger.

Malik! Even as he thought it, he knew it was too late. The report of the gun echoed in his soul, shocking him into action.

"Search the area. The one the Sheikh seeks is out there. Two escaped our ambush."

Ben began moving. He darted from shadow to shadow. There might be others lying in wait. He pushed away the image of his friend's assassination. He pushed away grief. *Survival requires my senses to stay alert.*

Making his way into open countryside, he trusted his suit to conceal him. The reverberating shock of the assassination played with his emotions, making him feel vulnerable under the bright moon. He steeled himself and glanced back. *Still no sign of pursuit.*

He dashed into the shadow of hills, looking warily around him. He stopped and listened, then moved deeper among the dunes. After twenty minutes of this, he waited in a shadow. *The secondary extraction point is three kilometres further. I must get some bearings.* Slowly, cautiously, he crept to the top of the nearest dune.

As he topped a gentle rise, he felt the sting of a taser dart on his thigh. He stiffened and fell. Darkness closed around him.

*

As he woke, Ben held himself still, his senses alert, silently absorbing his situation.

Smells like vomit. He licked his lips and tasted that it was his own.

He tuned into a rhythm of movement beneath him. *On the sea.* He groaned quietly. His arms and legs were bound, his torso bouncing roughly against the bottom and rubber sides as the small dinghy skipped over the waves. Cracking open an eye, he saw glittering stars against the paling sky. *Nearly dawn.*

Nearby, someone spoke quietly into a radio in Arabic, "We've got the infidel pig you're seeking, Sheikh. We're on our way to rendezvous with the submarine *Qarash*. Just ten minutes out. Then we'll bring him to you for questioning, *inshallah*. We took care of the other two, the apostates."

A moment of silence. The man listened to an inaudible response, then barked orders to another man at the tiller. "It's arranged. The sub is a hundred metres ahead, ten degrees to starboard. Slow down. Wait here for them to surface."

The dinghy slowed to a stop. A foot prodded Ben, but he did not respond. Then a knife scraped his cheek. Ben opened his eyes. His captor holding the knife sneered, "The infidel's awake." With the words, a smell of decay wafted over Ben.

Ben looked beyond the rim of the dinghy. Nearby, the sea boiled, as a conning tower rose from the depths, silhouetted against the first light of dawn. Indistinct words came from the radio. "Yes, Captain, we're ready," grunted his captor. "Open the hatch."

A shadow flashed across the sky, followed by a thundering boom.

The emerging forward deck of the submarine erupted in flame. The explosion almost flipped the dinghy. Ben's captors crouched low and yelled into the radio. No reply. Seven small velocicopter aircraft swooped in, encircling the submarine and dinghy.

Soldiers rappelled down lines from the aircraft, dropping onto the submarine deck and into the water around the submarine and dinghy, guns pointed at those in the boat.

The dinghy crew froze, eyes glued to the gun muzzles.

Confident hands reached into the boat to sever Ben's bonds while the copter dropped a self-inflating raft into the nearby water. The copter lowered other men with a stretcher into the raft.

Frogmen swam with Ben to the raft, and carefully lifted him in. The men in the raft checked him with efficiency, while strapping him to the stretcher. A corpsman above winched the stretcher up to the copter. Other medics pulled the stretcher in and did a thorough check of Ben's vitals. One gave a thumbs-up signal to the pilot. The rescue copter with Ben veered away, racing back to the command ship over the horizon.

Below, more soldiers swarmed aboard the damaged submarine, watching closely as the crew came out and knelt onto the deck.

It was a flawless operation.

CHAPTER FOUR

18 June 2054, Diego Garcia Island, Indian Ocean
(the next day)

Fed, rested, showered, and fresh out of a two-hour mission debrief, Ben sat waiting, fidgeting uncomfortably with the standard-issue utility cap in his lap. He was outside an office of 1st Marine Raider Battalion Command. A sergeant opened the door to usher him in. "The colonel will see you now," she said.

Ben rose, entered, and stood to attention, looking at the back of his commanding officer. The sergeant slipped back out, closing the door with a soft snick.

Colonel Jimenez stood at the window, observing the staging area below. "The teams out there are heading to the Suez to avert an attack." He turned to face Ben. "Thanks to your team we got the necessary intelligence in time to intervene."

The colonel moved from behind his desk and came over to Ben. "At ease, lieutenant," he sighed. "Lieutenant Holden," his eyes flicked to a file open on his screen, "Ben…" he said, almost tenderly, as he held the young man's gaze. "I must tell you terrible news. There's no easy way to do this, so I'll come right to the point. Your wife and son, Lisa and Sammy, died during the riots in Los Angeles, five days ago."

Ben's face fell in disbelief, the world crumbling under him. "Sir… that can't be. I just left them. We had a day at the beach. They were fine. Sammy was about to start first grade…"

Jimenez held Ben's gaze. "I'm sorry, son."

"No," Ben pleaded weakly.

The colonel struggled to continue. "I'm afraid there's worse news, son." He paused, not really wanting to continue, but unable to avoid it. "The police found evidence that their deaths were not accidental. An investigation is in progress, to find their murderers." Compassion softened his hard features.

The sergeant opened the door again and looked in. The colonel waved the young woman over. Ben swayed on his feet. Colonel Jimenez rushed around the desk to support Ben; the sergeant took the other arm.

"Murdered?" Ben's eyes blinked. It was too difficult to comprehend.

"I'm very sorry, son. This must be a terrible blow, especially after your recent ordeal." They held Ben for a moment, until he was able to stand on his own again. Ben glanced at them, grateful.

"How could... how did this happen... sir?" Ben looked full into the colonel's eyes. The man averted his gaze.

"Evidence was destroyed by a fire in your home, son. Apparently, arson."

Ben was silent, searching the colonel's face for something that would lift the terrible weight of this news. There was nothing.

"Yes, sir," Ben said slowly, then was silent, staring at the carpet.

"Sergeant Kim, please escort Lieutenant Holden to his quarters. Pick up his papers on the way out. He is released for bereavement leave." Ben began to walk with the sergeant, unsteadily, towards the door.

"Yes, sir." The sergeant quietly led Ben out.

The colonel turned back to the window. His gaze focused on the young men and women on the tarmac, loading the copters. A profound sadness shadowed his face. His lips moved in a silent prayer.

2 July 2054, Camp Pendleton, San Diego
(two weeks later)

Ben sat in the consultation room, glaring at the psychologist, a captain. "I've done my tour, put in my time and am eligible for a discharge. Why have I not received it?"

"Soldier, change that attitude immediately or this meeting stops," the psychologist said in a tone that belied his sympathy for the young man.

Ben settled into his seat, visibly calming himself. "Yes, sir."

"Lieutenant Holden," he glanced at the file on his screen, "Ben. You've been through immense trauma this past month. Your counsellor recommends treatment for another four months at least."

Ben looked the man straight in the eye, "Sir, am I eligible for a discharge?"

The psychologist shifted uncomfortably. "Yes," he replied. "You have an exemplary record, young man. Two purple hearts. A bronze and silver star. Excellent recommendations."

He paused a moment, referring again to the file. "Excellent. But, unfortunately, there is a problem, and we see it here in this meeting. You haven't yet come to terms with your recent tremendous trauma and loss. The murder of both your field officers in Somalia, resulting in the loss of your team. Capture. Then hearing of the murder of your wife and child. This series of events would have destroyed most men."

Ben continued to stare calmly into the captain's eyes, "Yes, sir. I understand. However, I respectfully request a discharge. You cannot force me to stay."

"No, son, we cannot," the man said wearily. "But I believe it would be in your best interest to remain in service until your treatment has been completed. However, if a discharge is what you want, you may be discharged."

"Yes, sir. Thank you, sir. When will the papers be ready?"

"The day after tomorrow."

Ben stood and saluted. As he walked to the door, the psychologist called out, "Ben?"

Ben glanced back. The captain, standing at his desk, said quietly, "Good luck, son."

Ben walked out the door.

The psychologist sighed and closed the file on his computer. He stared at the wall opposite his desk for a long while.

2 July 2054, The Grand Mosque, Mecca, Saudi Arabia
(the same day)

Vizier Abdul Ghafoor entered the small dark room where a single spotlight was focused on Abdul Qawwi, who sat at an empty table. The vizier stood by the door, thumbing through his computer notepad, pointedly failing to acknowledge the nervous guest.

As the silence stretched, Abdul Qawwi fidgeted then blurted, fear tinging his voice, "I thought I was meeting with the Caliph, Excellency."

Timing is everything. Let him sweat a bit longer. The vizier ignored Abdul Qawwi's comment, continued looking at his pad, swiping through pages for a few more minutes.

Finally, he fixed Abdul Qawwi with steely eyes. "The Caliph doesn't meet with those who fail, Sheikh. The New Caliphate is built by those who succeed."

A stricken look spread across Abdul Qawwi's face.

He is right to fear me, the vizier thought, as he examined his pad again.

"Apparently, you had the infidel woman, Dr Lisa Holden. Yet you failed to obtain the necessary data for the plan you proposed to the Caliph."

Abdul Qawwi looked at the table. "Your Excellency, we learned too late that she'd put a time lock on her data device."

The vizier continued to read from his pad, "The data encryption was apparently keyed to her biometrics." He waited a moment, then looked directly at Abdul Qawwi. "The data device became useless once she was killed."

"Yes, Excellency. But we've discovered that it is also keyed to her husband's biometrics."

"We'll come back to that." He let the silence hang. "And you killed her child."

"Excellency, we did not want to leave a witness. The torture of the mother was … messy. The child was struggling wildly, even in bonds." Abdul Qawwi whispered now, trying to hide his trembling voice. The memory of the child's death came vividly to mind, as it had so many times before. Especially at night. He wished he could forget that...

The vizier waited again, smiling within himself, knowing that he was effectively tearing down the arrogance of this minor Sheikh.

"So, again. We gave you valuable resources. To capture this man." He glanced at the pad, "Ben Holden. We gave you resources to set an ambush in Somalia. And once more you failed. You had him, and then you lost him. Even worse, those who rescued him have captured one of our submarines, and its crew. And now… it seems Ben Holden is secure within the American military base."

Abdul Qawwi was silent now, staring at the table. Sweat trickled down his brow.

The vizier waited, allowing several minutes to pass in silence. He savoured Abdul Qawwi's agony, knowing the corrosive effect this had on Abdul's soul and will.

The vizier's voice shifted subtly to a more honeyed quality. "I have intervened. I did not want to see talent wasted, Sheikh Abdul Qawwi. Prior to these failures, I see that you had an excellent track record, *alhamdulillah.*

You served the Caliph, rallying the faithful across Europe. This did not go unnoticed."

Abdul Qawwi looked up, a flicker of hope crossing his features. "Thank you, Excellency."

"The state of Somalia has petitioned to become a satellite of the New Caliphate. The Caliph has graciously accepted their request. I am developing a plan and organizing a team to bring the peoples of Somalia into the New Caliphate, *inshallah.* Your talents could be of use."

"Excellency…" Abdul Qawwi began.

The vizier held up his hand, speaking with measured words. "This is a *conditional* mercy, Sheikh. You will become part of my team, but the loyalty I'll require from you is *absolute.* The task will not be easy."

"Thank you, Excellency!" Tears streamed down Abdul Qawwi's cheeks.

The vizier smiled, *it was so easy to recruit and ensure loyalty among followers.* "I'll be watching you, Sheikh Abdul Qawwi. Any further failure will result in a consequence far worse than prison." A guard had entered the chamber noiselessly. "Go with this man to your quarters. Tomorrow, *inshallah,* I'll tell you your duties."

Abdul Qawwi stood and bowed low to the vizier. "I am your servant."

As Abdul Qawwi left the room, the vizier made a mental note to keep the file open on Ben Holden. *Once I've tamed this upstart, Dr Qawwi's plan could still work. We will work on it in Somalia. What a great triumph this will be, to make infidel America vulnerable to the Caliphate.*

9 July 2054, Redondo Beach, California
(a week later)

"Ashes to ashes, dust to dust." The familiar refrain played over and over in Ben's mind.

Ben had never really thought about the words before. He sat in the bobbing rental boat. The GPS map showed that he was a few hundred metres from the beach, probably above the sand dollar colony, but he could only see mist. A thick morning fog surrounded him, with a pearly sheen from the first light before dawn. There was a touch of rose on the eastern edge.

Ben stared at the two ornate canisters on the deck before him. Lisa's sister had taken care of everything; cremating the bodies of Lisa and Sammy, organizing the memorial service that Ben had found it excruciating to attend. Afterwards, she had told him where the urns with the ashes were stored.

Yesterday he'd finally been able to collect them, to face their cold reality.

He picked each one up, with a caress. His hand trembled. *Ashes. Is this all that there is to a life?* The question felt threatening. In a sudden rage, he threw the containers far out into the sea. He heard them land. Distant splashes muffled in the fog. He shook his fist. "Those ashes are not my Lisa and my Sammy!" he yelled.

The world did not change; he stood still in the calmly rocking boat. Tendrils of fog swirled uncaringly around him. Something inside him went cold, steely. He sat down, gunned the engine, and spun the boat back to the harbour.

12 July 2054, Redondo Beach, California
(three days later)

Stewart met his friend for coffee a few mornings later. "Howya holding up?" It was a polite question, but he knew the answer just by looking at Ben.

"OK," Ben said over his steaming cup. "Not a lot of sleep."

That sounds like an understatement, Stewart thought, studying his friend. "Yeah, I get that…" He wasn't quite sure what else to say. What do you say to a friend who just had a wife and son murdered? I guess you just be there, be a friend.

He and Ben had known each other for years. They had played beach volleyball since high school and had won a number of tournaments. His wife had been good friends with Lisa – in fact, she'd introduced Lisa to Ben. Their little girl had looked up to Sammy like a big brother. The two families had been tight throughout the years, kept in touch while at graduate school, moved near each other when they started their careers – Ben into the military, Stew into the police. The murders had devastated Stewart and his family, but that was nothing compared with what Ben must be feeling.

"Stew, were you able to look at the file on the case?" Ben's eyes were bright.

Too bright, thought Stew.

"Yeah, buddy, I did. Not too much there. Resources were stretched thin during the rioting. Because some of the riots were within five blocks of your house, they wrote off the arsons on your street as part of that mess. It was only after they were able to get around to autopsies…"

Ben's coffee jiggled, burning his hand.

"Sorry, buddy. It isn't a pleasant thought. The *investigation* did reveal indications of… sorry again, torture. By the time they returned to the scene, the fire crews had compromised any evidence that might have been there."

"Why would anyone torture them?" Ben was incredulous.

"I have no idea. They did conclude the fire in your house and the ones along the street had been started to cover the murders." Stewart handed Ben a small memory cube. "Here's everything they have on it. The case is closed for now, there are no leads. My supervisor gave me grudging permission to give this to you."

Ben took the stick and stared at it as he took a sip of coffee. He looked at his friend, "I can't thank you enough Stew. The situation eats away at me. I need to find some kind of closure."

"It's the least I can do, buddy. Want to come for dinner tomorrow night? We'll be having my famous sea bass chowder."

Ben hesitated, "Thanks, Stew, but I'm not ready to be with people yet."

"Yeah, I understand. Let me know if I can help." Stewart looked at the clock, "Gotta run, buddy. I go on patrol in fifteen minutes."

Ben stood and shook his hand. "Thanks, Stew, this gives me a start."

12 July 2054, Redondo Beach, California
(the same day)

Later that day, Ben stood before his home. The yellow crime tape had been taken down, but fire crews had sealed the house as condemned. Dried flower petals were still strewn on the welcome mat. He blinked at the scene, uncomprehending.

His eyes were red from many sleepless nights; every time he drifted off, he heard the screams of Lisa and Sammy calling for him.

As he looked at the blackened house, memories flooded his mind. Vividly, he remembered Sammy waving from the front window. Lisa at the front door, reaching out to embrace him, happy to have him home. *Home. This was my sanctuary, my life.*

He shook himself and took in the bigger picture. The street was lined with other burnt out husks of homes. The road was scarred with black marks where torched cars had lain. Across the road was the Singh home. In a flash, Ben remembered that his neighbour, Ajeet, had surveillance cameras which covered the front garden and street. He strode over and knocked on the door.

Ajeet answered, "Ben! I heard you were away on tour… I am so sorry, Ben… about Lisa and Sammy." His words dwindled to an awkward silence, then Ajeet continued softly, "I've had trouble explaining to my little boy why Sammy is no longer around as a playmate."

Ajeet glanced across the street, and said to the air, "It is beyond terrible. I can't imagine…"

Ben let the discomfort settle around them, and in the following silence he extended a hand said, "Thanks Ajeet for your kind words. Yes, it has been a terrible, terrible thing."

Ajeet took in Ben's haggard face, "I can see it's been rough on you. If there's anything I can do…"

"Well since you mention it, there is, Ajeet. You have a security system here. Do you still have surveillance images from that night?"

Ajeet brightened. "Sure I do. The system stores up to a month's worth of images. I can't think why I didn't think of that. And, come to think of it, the police haven't asked… Would you like to take a look at them? The camera angles would cover part of your garden…"

"Yes, please." Ben followed Ajeet into the house.

19 July 2054, Redondo Beach, California
(a week later)

Ben was doing a quick clean of the condominium he'd rented down the street from his burnt-out home. Dirty clothes were thrown in the closet, a week's dirty dishes stowed in the dishwasher. He collected food wrappers, coffee cups, and papers from the tables and stuffed them in the trash. He'd ordered in Chinese and had some cold beers in the fridge. The doorbell rang.

Ben opened the door, "Hey, Stew, thanks for coming over!"

"Well, I couldn't very well pass up the offer of a free meal, buddy. There's some brews to go with that, right?"

Ben laughed, "Of course."

As they shook hands, Stewart held Ben's and looked at him. "Ben, buddy, you look terrible. Like something the cat dragged in. Still not sleeping?"

"Not much, Stew. Nights are rough."

"Yes, they would be. I can't imagine."

Ben pulled him in. "Mu Shu pork – your favourite, I think?"

"Good memory, Ben. And I think I smell Kung Pao chicken, another winner. What's the occasion?"

Ben pulled some bottles from the refrigerator and waved to a chair. "Sit down, I'll explain."

They served steaming food from the cartons onto plates. Stewart flicked the caps off the bottles. As they started eating, Stewart said, "I'm all ears."

"OK, I've been doing some investigations of my own into what happened that night. The file you gave me was an excellent starting point."

The chopsticks stopped halfway to Stewart's mouth. He met his friend's gaze, "Ben, is that a good idea? Detectives have closed the case down at the precinct, there were no new leads."

"Hear me out, Stew." Ben pleaded.

Stewart studied him for another moment, doubt on his face. "I'm listening, Ben."

"Follow me," they picked up their plates and beers and went into the second bedroom of the condo. Two tables and a few chairs were the only furnishings. The walls were covered with maps of the area around Redondo, printouts of news reports, charts and photos. Coloured strings extended between the pinned-up documents.

"Whoa, buddy, what have you got here?" Stewart set his plate and bottle on a table and inspected the cluttered wall.

"Stew, I am convinced that the murder of Lisa and Sammy had nothing to do with the riots. Someone planned this and used the riots as a cover."

"Yes, there was a suspicion about that Ben, but the case turned cold. But walk me through it, let's see what you got."

The food was forgotten as Ben explained his research. Stewart asked sharp, insightful questions, and repeatedly made Ben support the logical steps to his conclusion.

After about an hour, Stewart sat down. He picked at the now cold Kung Pao with the chopsticks. "You build a good case, Ben. I think you are right about the riots being used as a cover."

He sighed, "But I don't see how this gets us any closer to identifying the perpetrators.".

Silence hung between them for a few moments.

Ben opened a folder on top of one of the tables. "There's this." He pulled out two grainy photos. "I got these from my neighbour's surveillance footage."

Stewart looked at the pictures. One was of a man running across the lawn, the next was a close-up of the face. He studied this last carefully. "Features could be Asian, Hispanic, Arab even, but the quality is not good. Won't be useable with facial recognition software. And you think this is one of the attackers?"

"I think I have a way we can find out." Ben explained the plan to his friend.

"OK, you might be able to pull that off, Ben. Not many others could. Let me talk with my supervisor tomorrow and see if I can get permission for you."

"Thanks, Stew, that's all I can ask."

Ben saw his friend to the door and shook hands with him once more. "I'll try, buddy," Stewart said as the door closed.

Ben nodded, grateful. He stood there staring at the shut door for a few moments. The silence crowded in on him and he was alone again with his ghosts. He walked over to the fridge, pulled out another beer and popped the cap.

23 July 2054, Redondo Beach, California
(four days later)

A few days later, Ben dressed like a local Muslim and discretely followed Stewart, now in uniform, from mosque to mosque on a Friday during the five different prayer times. Stewart would introduce himself and pull the pictures out and ask if anyone had seen the man in the grainy photo. Ben was always among the men crowding around to look. He inconspicuously watched the reactions of the others and listened to them talk in Arabic or Urdu afterwards. So far everyone had complained that the photo was so poor that they couldn't recognize who it was.

Stewart kindly thanked them and moved to the next mosque.

This was the sixth mosque they had tried. Stewart made his introduction and pulled out the photo. Men crowded around and looked. Ben noticed several of the men stiffen, but then compose themselves. Like everyone else, they said they did not recognize who was in the picture. Stewart thanked them and left.

Ben stayed and went through the preparations for prayer with the other men in that mosque. One of the men who had reacted was whispering quietly to another in Arabic. Ben silently blessed his Arabic teacher at Fort Bragg, then did his ablutions near enough to overhear. "That looked like the Sheikh, brother!"

The other nodded, "We must tell them that the police are asking around; I'll go now." The first placed his hand on the other's shoulder, "Good, he will reward you."

Ben quietly slipped away from the men filing into prayer and waited outside. *The second speaker was a young Arab probably from Yemen, judging by the dialect,* Ben guessed. The man came out shortly after prayers finished. He looked both ways on the street, then started a quick walk deeper into the neighbourhood.

Ben shadowed him at a distance. After about half a mile, the man turned into a narrow alleyway. Other men loitering at the entrance to the alley stopped him to exchange a few words, then let him pass.

Ben slipped into a diner across the street, ordered a sandwich and beer, and watched the alley. Fifteen minutes later, the man came out again, exchanged greetings with the lounging men, then headed back towards the mosque.

Ben ate slowly, watching the entrance of the alleyway. Every time someone approached, they were quietly challenged by the men he now recognized as guards of some sort. Most were allowed in – but a few were refused and moved on their way.

That evening, Ben rang Stewart to give his report. "Let me look into what I can find out about that area," Stewart said. "It seems familiar, somehow. Let's meet at Leo's on the pier tomorrow."

24 July 2054, Redondo Beach, California
(the following evening)

The next night Stewart walked into the busy restaurant at the end of the pier. Outside, the sun was just setting. He slid into a seat opposite Ben as a waitress came over to their booth.

Stewart gave her a smile, "I'll have a large bowl of clam chowder and a beer." She tapped the order into the pad in her hand.

"Make that two bowls, and I'll have a scotch," Ben chimed in.

"Stepping up your game a bit – scotch." Stewart noticed the empty glass in front of his friend, "Is that your second?" He studied Ben more carefully, "Or your third?"

Ben waved it off. "It's been a tough day; I'm just relaxing a bit. I was doing some investigation of that neighbourhood. Seems there are a number of alleyways guarded by rough characters."

Stewart noted that Ben looked even more exhausted than yesterday. "You're not getting much sleep, buddy. Those bags under your eyes could hide bowling balls."

"I'm OK, Stew." There was an edge to Ben's voice.

"Chill, buddy. Just concerned."

"Noted. What did you find out?"

"Well, asking about that place touched a raw nerve down at the department. Apparently, you're not the only one watching it." Stewart paused, studying his friend,

"You won't like this next part, Ben. I was told today in no uncertain terms that you are to stay away; a very sensitive operation is in progress. When I told them what you were doing, my boss almost went ballistic. If they find you nosing around, they will arrest you."

"Stew! I'm following the only clue I have to Lisa and Sammy's murder. The murderer may even be there in that neighbourhood now!" Ben was unconsciously clutching the table, knuckles white.

Stewart's voice softened, "Yes, I fully understand, and if the dirt-bag is there, the police will find him through their operation. That's what we do."

Ben forced himself to be calm before his friend, then leaned across the table towards him. "OK, Stew, I understand. But... can you throw me a bone? This is about Lisa and Sammy. Can you give me some hint at who shattered my life?"

"Yeah, Lisa and Sammy..." Stewart looked out the window for a few minutes, at the ceaseless progression of waves in the twilight. He relented, turned back to his friend and said, "OK, it seems that that area is a hotbed of activity for a group of Islamists who are part of the New Caliphate."

"The New Caliphate." Ben seemed to age ten years before Stewart's eyes, sagging into the booth. "I know these guys, I encountered them on my last tour. They were the ones who killed the other members of my unit and tried to kidnap me."

Stewart sighed, and looked at Ben with compassion. "It doesn't get better buddy. Apparently, this is a centre for radicalization and recruitment. They've tried to make it a no-go area for the police, but undercover work is going on. That's why we need you to stay away. Sniffing around will endanger their operation and their operatives."

The food arrived at that moment, interrupting him. Ben stared at the bowls of chowder, then looked up at his friend.

Stewart's voice became very focused and intent, "I had no idea they were the ones that nabbed you off Somalia. I should not have told you that information about the New Caliphate." Stewart held his gaze, "Ben, do not go all vigilante on me. I'm already very concerned about you. Promise me you'll stay away from that area, or I will report this conversation."

Ben's hand shot out and grabbed the glass of scotch. He downed it in a gulp and glared at Stewart. "Really? You would report me?"

Silence hung between them.

"Forget it! Some friend you've turned out to be." Ben slammed the cup down, then rose unsteadily out of the booth.

Stewart jumped to his feet and stood in front of Ben, a hand on his chest. "Buddy," he said softly, "You need help."

In one fluid motion, Ben grabbed the hand, twisted around and pulled Stewart over him, flipping him onto the table. Chowder went everywhere.

The restaurant was shocked into silence, all eyes on them.

Ben glanced around then strode out.

The manager ran over and helped Stewart to his feet. "I'm fine, thanks," Stewart said, staring after Ben. "Sorry for this mess," he said without looking over, "I'll pay for the damages." Beyond the door, there was only a dark night.

31 July 2054, Lawndale, California
(a week later)

Ben sat huddled in his dingy coat on a piece of old cardboard, leaning against the cold bricks. A rusted shopping cart with a sleeping bag and a couple of carrier bags was next to him. He clutched a bottle of cheap malt liquor close to his chest, taking sips from time to time, keeping in character.

He feigned sleep, but carefully watched the entrance of the alleyway down the street. He was getting to know the players. This is the third time Baldy has stopped by today. The Guards let him through without a challenge. Ah, and Longbeard just showed up. Same time as yesterday.

A squad car pulled up in front of him. Two policemen got out and walked over, "Get up. We're taking you in for loitering."

No, I'm so close! Ben bit his lip, mind scrambling for what he could do next. After a few seconds, the officers grabbed Ben under the arms and hauled him up. One opened the rear door as they pushed him into the car. The loungers across the street watched for a moment, then returned to their activities.

At the precinct, the officers put him in an interrogation room where he waited, alone, for an hour and a half. Finally, a detective came in and sat across from him. He looked at a file on his computer pad, then at Ben. "Ben Holden. Your friend Stewart told us about his conversation with you. He gave us your description, told us to watch for you. It took a few days, your disguise was effective."

"Is there a charge?" Ben said with steely quiet.

The detective looked at him for a few minutes, then said, "That depends."

"On what?"

"On whether we find you anywhere around that neighbourhood again. If we do, I have a court order to arrest you. Stewart is an exemplary cop, you could easily ruin his career."

Ben stared at the table.

"What's it going to be? You gonna help your friend Stewart or go to jail?"

"I'll stay away," Ben whispered.

"Good. Remember that. I like Stewart, and you are apparently a decorated Marine, so I'm giving you a pass this time. If I find you at this table again, you are going up for a felony. Obstruction. I'll make it stick." He paused, glaring at Ben, then said, "Now get outta here." The detective got up and walked out the door.

Ben left the police station and walked down the street in a daze. A neon sign on the liquor store across the street beckoned. Ben paused, then walked over and went through the door.

CHAPTER FIVE

14 January 2055, Sonoran Desert, Arizona
(six months later)

Heat radiated from the asphalt. As he drove down the highway, Paul Whitestone patiently scanned the barren landscape that rippled in the heatwaves. *There.* A car splayed on the gravel, on the opposite shoulder next to a cactus shimmering through rising air. Paul tapped his brake as he surveyed the situation. Skid marks suggested that the vehicle had crossed the centre line, spinning off the pavement. The driver's door gaped open, swinging in the wind.

A young man sprawled on the front seat with legs out the door, dusty jeans and scruffy shoes etched in the bright sunlight.

Passing the scene, Paul made a U-turn and pulled up behind the car. He rolled to a stop; a billow of dust drifted over the truck. A lizard sunning on a nearby rock scuttled into the brush.

The young man's car appeared off-balance, right front tyre askew. *Most likely, bearings have gnawed through their housing. Must've been a constant squealing the last fifty miles or so.*

From his truck, Paul turned his attention to the man slumped in the car staring into the desert; he brushed a fly from his face. Paul sat in his truck for a few moments, observing him through windscreen. *Sandy-haired. Good looking but hasn't shaved in a while. Probably near roasting in that car.*

Vehicle after vehicle flashed by in air-conditioned indifference.

Paul lingered in his truck another moment, then opened his door. His boots scrunched on the gravel as he approached. He kicked the broken right front wheel and then crossed over to the driver's side. *He might be thirty years old, maybe more.* An empty liquor bottle lay in the gravel nearby. The young man gazed vacantly at the horizon.

"Looks like a serious problem," Paul offered. The young man glanced at him; his bloodshot eyes looked as desolate as the desert. They slid away, staring into the distance again.

The sun burned harshly in the still air. Blinding light reflected off the desert sand. More cars flashed past.

"It wasn't your fault," Paul said softly. "Your family is at peace now."

The young man reacted as if he'd been stung. In one fluid motion, he leapt from the car, grabbed Paul and pinned him onto the scorching car hood. He glared into the older man's calm eyes.

"What're you saying?" he spat, teeth clenched.

Paul spoke quietly, as he repeated, "It wasn't your fault, your wife and son. The murder. You're not to blame."

"What do you know about my wife and son?" The young man's voice was a mix of fury and astonishment.

"Only what I just said, son."

"How can you know that? Who are you?" Pain and fear flickered across the young man's features as he released his grip and took a step back. Paul slid off the hood and stood watching.

He then brushed the dust off and continued, "My name is Paul. Paul Whitestone. I saw you on the side of the road here. I recognized that you were having some trouble and stopped. I have a sense for these things, and as I walked over, I had a flash of understanding that you've experienced some terrible losses." The young man stood in stunned silence.

"Are you a psychic or something?" he finally asked.

"No," Paul said simply, then changed the subject. "Look, I guess you might be needing food and shelter at this moment. I can help you, son. I can offer you some assistance, help you get back on your feet."

The young man took a few steps forward, viewing Paul with suspicion. "And why would you do that? Why would I come with you?" His eyes narrowed. "What're you after?" He instinctively shifted his weight into a fighting stance and took a deep breath.

Paul unconsciously took a defensive step back in response. "Look, no offence intended, son. I can walk away, and you can continue sitting in that car. However, it looks like you don't have a lot of options, way out here. I can drive you to town, give you a meal. We run a shelter. Then you can decide your next steps on a full stomach."

Paul held the young man's gaze, his own grey eyes radiating honesty. *I'm glad to see there's some fight left in you,* Paul thought. *Where there's fight, there's hope.*

"I guess I could use a ride outta here," the young man mumbled, dropping his gaze and relenting. "Name's Ben."

Paul reached forward and shook Ben's hand. The two of them moved towards Paul's truck. Glancing in Ben's car, Paul noticed a grungy duffle bag and rucksack in the rear seat. He retrieved them, handing them to Ben.

Silently, they clambered into the truck cab, and Paul started the engine. Ben sat hunched over, the bags in his lap.

As they pulled away, loose grit sprayed from the truck tyres and settled on the wreck left baking in the sun.

15 January 2055, Grit, Arizona
(the next day)

Crisp, flowered curtains framed the window, glowing in the morning sun. Bright gingham cloths adorned the tables. The floor shone from last night's polishing. A dozen men and a few women shuffled along the serving line for breakfast at the homeless shelter.

At just thirty-two, Ben Holden felt like a shadow of the man he'd been two years ago. Back then, he'd been part of an elite military unit, living with his wife and son in California. Those days were distant, merely a dream.

He sat alone near a window, desert dust shifting from his clothing onto the chair and floor. He gazed out at the abandoned buildings along the road. The clapboard structures looked like empty husks crowding what must have been a lively main street some time ago. *Wonder what happened to this town.* Glancing down, Ben picked at his plate of scrambled eggs, now cold.

Someone slid into the chair across from him. Ben continued eating without looking up. The silence stretched. The wall clock marked the seconds in ticks.

Finally, Ben glanced up. He was startled as familiar grey eyes met his gaze. *The man with the truck.*

Ben stiffened. "What do you want?"

"Thought you might like some company. I can leave if you'd rather be alone," the older man said. Ben studied him. Dark hair greying at the temples. Clear grey eyes. High cheekbones, maybe some Indian background. *Looks fit, radiates vitality.*

Ben hardened his face and repeated, "What do you want?"

Paul broke into a warm smile. "Well now, that's the question I'd ask you."

Confusion flashed across Ben's face. "What do *I* want?"

"Yes."

Paul let the silence hang between them. To Ben, the silence felt insidious, dangerous. It chipped away at the wall which was protecting him from the pain, the endless grief.

"Nothing. I want nothing. Leave me alone," he snapped.

"All you're finding in solitude is pain, son," said the older man gently.

Anger stirred in Ben, an anger carefully fashioned to protect him from darkness and despair. "You don't know me, Mr Whitestone. What can you know of my pain?" The words tumbled out more harshly than he intended. A silence hung between them.

"Ben, I know pain," Paul said quietly, looking out the window, "Three years ago, my twin sons died in a bus crash on their way home from summer camp. I wish I had died with them. My life fell apart; my wife left, then divorced me. I lost my job with Homeland Security in DC. I retreated from the world into alcohol." Paul's words were blunt, but his voice broke slightly.

Paul turned to look at Ben as he continued. "I fell into a dark spiral. I found that the bottle could muffle my thoughts and deaden my pain. It helped at first. But quickly the bottle became my master and cast me out on the streets."

He sighed, "I reached a point where I was ready to die. But this niggling thought told me I still had a choice. I could die or I could fight. I decided to fight. But I couldn't fight it on my own; I couldn't have won that battle without my friends, this shelter, and then the rehabilitation programme. They have helped me take every step forward that I was willing to take."

Ben's gaze was on his plate.

"I don't know your personal pain, son, but you have no corner on the market."

Ben looked up from his plate and saw grief darkening those grey eyes. He had to look away; he saw his own anguish reflected there.

Something in Ben gave way. He said quietly, "You're right, though I don't know how you know. My wife and son were murdered some months ago, while I was away, on tour in the Gulf." His voice trailed off. Then, he whispered, as though to himself, "My life stopped."

"And yet, here you are, Ben," Paul offered. "Alive."

"Yeah, I'm alive. What's that to you?!" Ben reacted, slamming his hand on the tabletop, eyes glaring. People in the dining area looked around at them.

Paul ignored them, the grey eyes probing Ben's. Steady, calm. "Self-pity is as terrible a taskmaster as alcohol, Ben. They'll both smother any last bit of life in you."

Ben slouched back into his chair, then murmured, "I love my wife. I love Sammy. They were the core of my life."

"Yes, and now they stand before God. They're at peace."

"You can't know that! All I know is they are no longer with me." He stared at the remains of his eggs. He lifted his head and scowled at Paul. "What do you want?" The scowl wavered, and he turned back to his plate.

"I want to see you released from grief and pain, Ben. There's a way out. I found it, and so have others. But to get there you must *want* to live, to fight for life again."

He paused. "Ben. What do you want?"

"I want you to leave me alone!" The cauldron of rage simmering in Ben's heart exploded into flame at this statement. "I don't believe in fairy tales, in some God that takes care of us! Peddle your sanctimonious crap to someone who cares. I can handle myself!" With this, Ben lurched to his feet and strode through the door at the back, towards the sleeping quarters.

Paul followed him and leaned against one of the shelter's bunks, watching Ben stuff his meagre things into the duffle bag.

"The choice is yours, Ben. You can leave. You can reject the help I'm offering. Or you can stay and allow someone to walk through this pain with you."

The young man ignored him.

"Sometimes people have to hit rock bottom before they'll ask for help. I guess you aren't at the bottom yet."

"Leave me alone," Ben mumbled.

"Here's my card. Call me anytime." Paul laid his business card on the bed next to Ben's bag, then turned and left the room.

*

Just before lunch, Paul passed the now empty bed. The card was gone.

30 January 2055, Sonoran Desert, Arizona
(two weeks later)

"Dad!" The cry jolted Ben into consciousness, and he blurted out, "Sammy?"

The mid-morning sun had already seared his face as he cracked open bleary eyes. *Sand. Rocks. Scrub bushes. A barrel cactus. A large black bird with an ugly red head sitting on the cactus. A buzzard. Not a good sign.*

A movement caught his attention. He sat up, painfully shook his head, and looked again. *Is that Sammy, behind the cactus?* Grief gripped Ben's heart like a vice. "Don't go, Sammy," his voice rasped.

He squeezed his eyes shut, then opened them again, squinting and scanning, taking in a wider view. *I'm in a small canyon. No, a dry riverbed. An arroyo.* The sun was shining much too brightly over the far cliff face, causing needles of pain. He rolled over and slowly sat up, groaning, sore and bruised.

Why am I here? Sand caked the side of his face and his arms. He brushed it off, wincing as the grit rubbed against raw scrapes. His faded military fatigues were stiff with grime.

Just cactus and scrub. No one else around. The buzzard slowly turned away then lazily flapped into the sky. *Sorry, buddy, there's still life in me.* Standing up, he rotated his head and neck slowly left then right, wincing at the pain.

Rocks and debris lay around him in a pile. Less than five feet away was a crumbling rock wall, stretching up ten feet from the arroyo floor. *Did I fall from that cliff? What happened last night?*

Glancing down again, he saw two sets of coyote prints circling the spot where he'd lain. His heart beat more quickly as he realized how vulnerable he'd been.

He turned away from the glare of the sunlight. Surveying the cliff before him, he sought a way up. *Maybe there'll be a clue up there as to how I ended up down here.*

Further down, part of the cliff face had crumbled into an easier slope. He shuffled in that direction.

Bit by bit, he clambered to the top, and scrambled along the edge until he was above the spot where he'd regained consciousness. He scanned the arroyo. *No sign of the buzzard. Gone to find an easier meal.* No Sammy either.

Ben glanced around and saw a sagebrush that was crushed, and next to it signs of his stumble and fall into the ravine. Behind it stretched a line of footprints leading back through a valley between two low hills. He began following the erratic trail.

As he plodded along, memories surfaced in his muddled mind. A smoky, dark room. *It was a bar. A serviceman gave me a lift there. And forty dollars. He must've felt sorry for me.*

I just used that money to get wasted.

Ben sat down heavily on a boulder, shaking his head, trying to pull his thoughts together.

In a dim recess of his mind, alarm bells were ringing. *Is this what I've come to? Blackouts. Waking up at the bottom of a cliff. Just a piece of meat for buzzards and coyotes?*

And was that Sammy calling to me? Was that real? He put his head in his hands. Of course not.

The relentless heat forced him to rise and look for some kind of shelter. He continued following the tracks. The desolate landscape stretched out on all sides. After a few moments, he climbed a small rise and spotted a highway ahead.

In the time it took him to shamble the few hundred metres down the hill, only one car sped by. He neared the road. *My green rucksack!* Clothing lay scattered next to a saguaro cactus. *Wonder where my duffle bag went.*

He walked over and took inventory. It was hard to concentrate. His head throbbed. *Wallet's gone. Someone left me to die out here.*

I should be angry. He felt a strange aloofness from this tragedy.

I should be dead.

Half-heartedly, he collected his things, as his last bits of motivation blew off in the gusts of desert wind.

Standing, uncaring, next to the road, he gazed down the weathered strip of highway. Again, he sensed Sammy, this time sitting a few metres away. "It's OK, Dad." Blinking, heart racing, he looked. The feeling of his son squatting nearby was strong, yet the patch of ground was empty. The sense of presence persisted. "Choose life, Dad."

He heard a distant hum, and down the road he noticed a glint in the heat waves. A car was hurtling towards him. On an impulse, he stepped closer to the highway and put out his thumb. *Do people still pick up hitchhikers?* Miraculously, the car slowed and pulled over. The door was pushed open.

Ben climbed in with a glance over his shoulder. The impression, presence of Sammy was gone.

31 January 2055, Grit, Arizona
(the next day)

Ben talked with the driver enough to be sociable, a plausible story of hiking in the desert. The man looked Ben over and Ben could tell he didn't believe him. But he didn't kick him out either. For most of the four-hour trip, Ben feigned sleep, thinking about his experience. Eventually, the driver dropped him off in Grit, Arizona, before pulling back on the highway west.

Dawn was breaking, the sun's rays just beginning to cast a golden hue on the fronts of the buildings. Ben willed one foot to step in front of the other down the familiar, shabby main street. He had learned the oil fracking boom that built this town had ended decades ago.

He leaned into the steady desert wind, his six-foot frame hunched, a bedraggled rucksack on his back. Litter and dust whirled around him in the gusts. A tumbleweed spun down the street, only to be caught, straining in the wind, on a fire hydrant in front of an abandoned store. Shop windows all down the street looked permanently shuttered. *A dying street. A deserted town.*

Ben's mind wandered to the voice and image of Sammy entreating him in the arroyo and on the highway.

A dream? It felt real. A vision?

Whatever it was, it had nudged him to a decision.

In the lonely morning, a light beckoned from a window ahead, a light Ben had been hoping would still be there. He opened the door to the homeless shelter. An old-fashioned bell mounted on the door frame jingled an inappropriately cheerful welcome. Ben stepped inside. Behind a worn reception desk, a young bearded man slept in a chair leaning against the wall, eyes closed, faint smile on his lips.

Ben cleared his throat.

The man startled awake, the sudden movement causing his leaning chair to slip to the floor.

"Excuse me," Ben apologized.

"Sorry, you surprised me!" The receptionist scrambled to his feet. "You're here early." Regaining his composure, he continued, "How can I help you?" He peered more closely at his visitor. "You look like you could use some coffee. Help yourself. Over there."

Ben glanced down the counter, where a red light glowed on a steaming pot of coffee. Ben found his voice, "Thanks. Coffee would be good. It'll warm me up."

Looking around the open space, Ben noticed the familiar crisp curtains framing the windows, the same bright cloths on the tables. He shrugged his rucksack off onto a chair and filled a mug. A box of pastries sat next to the coffee maker. His mouth began to water, and his stomach reminded him that he hadn't eaten in a couple days. He filled a mug and took two pastries. Both hands full, he shuffled back to his table.

The young man from the reception counter came over with his own mug of coffee. "Do you mind if I join you?"

Ben paused and then gestured towards the nearest table. "Suit yourself." They both sat down.

"Anything I can help you with?" the staff member offered. Ben noticed that the man was a few years younger than he was.

Ben gulped down some of the warming brew, and took a bite of a pastry, stale but wonderfully sweet, before setting his mug down. The man waited patiently, while Ben rummaged through his coat pockets, retrieving a crumpled business card.

"I'm looking for someone. Maybe you can help me?" Ben pushed the card over to the young man's side of the table. "He offered to help me a few weeks ago."

The card was crumpled, with evidence of water and weather damage; the writing faded. Scrutinizing it, the shelter worker could just make out the name. "Oh! You're looking for Paul Whitestone. He'll be in later this morning. Why don't you wait here? The kitchen will be serving breakfast in about an hour. You're welcome to join us."

"Thanks. I could use some breakfast." Ben then slid his eyes away and resumed drinking his coffee. He wasn't interested in talking more just now. He turned his attention to the movements outside the window. A few early morning delivery trucks rumbled by.

The staff member understood Ben's need for quiet. "You've been here before, so I assume you know where the bunk area is. Through that door there. Feel free to stash your things on one of the empty beds. Go ahead and settle in after you've had enough coffee."

Ben acknowledged this with a simple nod.

The bell jangled again. "Excuse me. Back to work." The receptionist hurried away to assist a couple who had entered.

Ben resumed his concentration on the world outside the window. As he gazed into the desert, an image of his wife formed in his mind. *Hey, Lise, I miss you so much. What are you smiling at, my love?*

"Ben, this is a good choice," his heart heard her say.

The coffee cup trembled in his hand.

*

Hours later, Paul arrived at the homeless shelter as usual. His consulting work for Homeland Security paid the bills, but this was where his heart was.

At the reception desk, he heard of Ben's return. Surprised, he sought out Ben and invited him to share lunch. A few minutes later, holding their food trays, they backed through the screen door to the outdoor dining tables.

"Let's sit in the shade," Paul suggested, as they moved across the small, walled courtyard. Smooth white pebbles covered the pathways, river stone from a nearby arroyo. Several branching saguaro cactuses dotted the area. A prickly pear plant with flat fleshy leaves and ripe red fruit stood in one corner. *The staff have done a great job; they've turned this into such a beautiful garden.* Paul realized how long it was since he had been out here.

Four old wooden picnic tables were already filled with residents of the shelter, who happily ate in the noontime heat, sheltered by faded umbrellas. The two men moved past them, heading for the far corner where an empty gazebo beckoned, a small table with benches under the shade of a roof crafted from ancient mine timbers. As they approached, a spotted gecko crept up under the eaves with a chirp.

The coolness of the gazebo drew them in and they sat down with their trays.

Paul looked across the table at Ben, who hunched over his food, his grief like a cloak, pulled close for protection. His face looked haunted.

"I don't know much about you yet, Ben," Paul began. "You were pretty quiet during that first truck ride here, and our last conversation didn't go well."

Ben looked up, meeting his gaze. "Yeah, sorry." He flashed a sheepish half-grin.

That's encouraging. Paul held the warm burrito in his hand for a moment before biting into the stuffed tortilla. After chewing for a moment, he pressed on. "So, where're you from?"

"I'm from Redondo, one of the beach cities of Los Angeles."

"I know the place. The way you hold yourself and move, you look like you have a military background. Camp Pendleton?"

"Yes, sir," Ben said, reverting out of habit to military respect. "United States Marine Corps Special Operations Command, 1st Marine Raider Battalion."

"I'm a fan. I was an Army Ranger, myself. You've seen action?"

"Yes, sir. A few missions on the African Horn. Two tours."

"I heard that those tours were brutal. Your country is indebted to you. Thank you, son." He met the young man's eyes with his gaze. "Don't call me sir, Ben. Paul is fine. We're no longer in the service."

"Right, si-," Ben stopped himself, "OK, Paul." They turned their attention to their burritos.

After a few moments of silence, Ben looked up. Paul was encouraged, *I see a spark in those eyes.*

Ben ventured, "It's been eating at me, Paul. How did you find me, that first time out in the desert? It was as if you knew exactly where I was. It was strange, you seemed to know something about me and..." he hesitated, "and my family."

Paul felt warmth towards him. "That's a hard question to answer. Let's just say that it's a gift I seem to have been given. That morning I felt a compulsion to drive out into the desert, looking."

"Looking for what?"

"You. But I didn't know that until I saw your car. As I got out and walked towards you, I had that sudden insight about your family."

"Well, however you did it, it was impressive." Ben said with a faint smile. "Does this kind of thing happen often to you?"

Paul laughed, "Yes, often enough. Can have uncomfortable consequences at times. Like you throwing me on the hood of the car. That was also impressive... and painful. Nice move by the way."

"Thanks, part of my military training." Ben thoughtfully dipped tortilla chips into salsa, then looked at Paul. "Do you believe in God?"

"That's out of the blue, why do you ask?"

"I've thought a lot about our last talk, that stuff about the bottle and self-pity becoming my master. It's like I was caught in a death spiral. You finding me in the desert like that, well it felt almost like a divine intervention." Ben was looking into the sky, watching the drifting clouds.

"Yesterday I woke up," Ben continued quietly, "battered and bruised in a dry riverbed. I have no idea how I got there. Last thing I could remember was being in a bar drinking until I couldn't think any more. Someone robbed me, then left me to die by the side of a road. I must have come to in the night, then wandered off and fallen over a cliff. The next thing I know I'm waking up covered in sand. It's late morning, the sun is blazing over the canyon wall and then I saw… and heard my dead son, Sammy." Ben's voice faltered.

Paul took a bite, waiting for the story to come out. He watched Ben carefully.

Ben pulled himself together. "Sammy called to me, he woke me up. Without him, I think I would have just laid there and become food for the coyotes." He looked at his plate. "That moment when I heard him felt like another intervention, like someone is looking out for me. Part of me wants to believe all this was God. But…"

"But how could a good and all-powerful God allow your family to be treated so cruelly, and be taken from you?" Paul said bluntly.

Ben froze in his eating and looked at Paul, "Yes."

After a moment, Paul pushed his plate to the side, and spoke directly to the young man. "You've come back to the shelter, Ben. Why?"

"When I woke up yesterday, Sammy's words brought back something alive in me. A desire to fight, to get my life back. You said you were able to do it. Your own story gave me a little hope, I suppose. I kept your card." Ben pulled out the tattered paper.

"I'm glad you are listening to the part of you that chooses life," Paul smiled.

"I want to stop the pain, but I don't know how. My dreams torment me. Grief and rage are eating away at me."

"You can rid yourself of these, but it will be the greatest battle of your life, *for* your life. It will take a different kind of courage from the kind you needed on your military tours."

Ben's attention was fully on Paul now.

"The kind of courage you need now, Ben, is the courage to change direction. Changing direction takes mental, even spiritual courage. Courage to say 'no' to your addictions. Courage to face inner darkness instead of running from it. Courage to keep choosing life… and hope. Do you have that kind of courage?"

"Choose life. That's what Sammy said." Ben watched the gecko.

He met Paul's gaze, "What do I do next?" Ben voice had grown in strength and a hint of resolve. "I have so much pain, anger… so much grief inside me."

"Well, son, I'll walk with you as far as you will allow me to. We both want your healing, let's see what we can do together. This shelter is connected to a rehabilitation programme; if you choose, you can join that programme and become a resident here. They have tough rules, you will have to… keep choosing life to stay."

"Sounds daunting, but I would like to try. Thanks," Ben said.

They got up together and carried their dishes through to the dining area and put them in the trays. A young man was cleaning the serving line.

"Oscar, those were terrific burritos," Paul said, then explaining to Ben, "Oscar here is our cook."

"They were great!" Ben agreed.

The dark haired youth looked up with a smile. "Thanks. Come back for dinner, we're having seared tuna tacos with avocado and mango salsa."

Ben gave a genuine smile, "Can't wait."

Paul was thoughtful, "Tuna, quite a high-end item. Oscar, do you know where the tuna came from?"

Oscar paused, thinking. "I believe the tuna was a donation from the Southern Pacific Pelagic Territory co-op. Why?"

Paul nodded, "Just curious. One of my oldest and closest friends from college days is developing tuna ranching in the Southern Pacific. It would be like him and his clan to donate part of their harvest to organizations like ours."

Chapter Six

9 April 2055, Grit, Arizona
(two months later)

John Robinson, director of the rehabilitation centre, approached Ben as he was cleaning up after breakfast, scrubbing down the breakfast line. John was black and 220 pounds of pure muscle. He'd been a bounty hunter earlier in life, then went on the skids with drugs. He came to the homeless centre to clean up his life, and there he met Alice. They married after John had been clean for a year. That was five years ago.

John watched Ben for a bit, then approached him.

Ben looked up, "Hey John."

"Hey, Ben." John walked over.

Ben straightened, "What's up?"

John seemed to come to a decision, "I have a proposition for you; you've done well in the programme, stuck with your twelve-step group and carried your share."

Ben gave a wry grin, "This place is tougher than bootcamp."

"That's the point." John smiled in return. "The proposition is this: We've planted six acres of jojoba bushes outside of Grit. We're hoping the jojoba oil will provide a new source of income for the shelter and programme here. I need someone to manage the equipment. Agri-bots mainly. Word is that you have an engineering degree. Interested?"

Ben nodded, it wasn't a hard choice, "Sure, I like mechanical things."

John smiled, "Good."

Two days later, Ben began work on the jojoba plot. He studied the agri-bot systems online at night in the bunk house, and managed the bots tending the fields during the days. The crops thrived under his administration.

*

21 May 2055, Grit, Arizona
(six weeks later)

Six weeks later, John brought a young man to Ben while he was working out in the field. "Ben, this is Tim." Ben looked at the thin youth and extended a hand. "Glad to meet you, Tim." Tim lowered his gaze.

"Interested in an assistant?" John queried.

Ben looked Tim over. He was a gaunt, dark haired Latino young man whose body showed the ravages of a life with drugs. Tim's eyes rose to meet Ben's. "Pretty good with your hands?"

Tim nodded.

"Willing to work hard, keep the rules, and follow instructions?"

"Yeah," the young man said quietly.

Ben watched him for a minute, then said, "OK, I'll give you a chance."

Tim started out well. As a first project, Ben had him install a new drip irrigation system for the field. It took Tim a bit longer than expected but he did a thorough installation. More projects and responsibilities were delegated to him in the following days, weeks, and months. Tim rose to the challenge each time.

Ben was pleased with his work and cultivated a friendship with Tim. They'd often meet up for dinner after a long day in the fields.

19 July 2055, Grit, Arizona
(two months later)

Ben sat alone in the diner. He'd been waiting patiently for two hours, hoping Tim would show up for their usual dinner together. Ben ate slowly, wondering. *The accident spooked him.*

The director, John, had joined them in the field earlier in the day as they set up a high efficiency windmill to draw water up into the holding tank. Tim had been running the backhoe, preparing an area for new jojoba plants. There was a large boulder next to the water tank and at John's request, Tim had driven the excavator over to dig it out. Ben didn't see how the accident happened, he just heard the creaking timbers and the snap. He whirled around just in time to see part of the tower collapse on John.

Ben had rushed over and lifted the wooden beam off his friend's leg, then ran to the shed for the first aid kit to stabilize John until the medics arrived. The break looked nasty. Once Ben had makeshift splints on it, he looked around for Tim who was nowhere to be seen. The backhoe engine was still humming, but the driver's seat was empty.

That was hours ago. Ben waited at the diner a few more minutes after finishing his meal, still hoping. Then he paid his bill and out onto the streets of Grit.

He walked into the dark and smoky bar and looked around. *I once loved coming into this atmosphere. The smells, the dim lights, the muddle of noise. It used to be my sanctuary, my solace. But now it repulses me.* This was the third bar he'd visited that evening.

There, that furtive figure in the dark corner booth. Is that Tim? Ben took a seat at the bar and watched for a bit. A waitress came over and set a drink in front of the man in the booth. *Yes, it's him.*

Tim sat staring at the cocktail.

Ben walked over and quietly slid into the booth opposite his charge.

Tim looked up, "Leave me alone."

Ben just sat quietly and considered his friend. "You afraid of heights, Tim?"

The younger man looked up, startled. "A bit, why?"

"Imagine you are at the top of a two-hundred-foot drop onto rocks. Toes at the edge. What do you do?"

"Step back, of course. What's your point?"

"That drink there is the edge of the cliff. There's no safety railing between you and the drop. It's your decision."

Tim's hand edged back from the glass. Ben could see the memories of addiction rise in Tim's face.

Ben's voice softened a bit. "You didn't show up at the diner like usual, Tim. Why?"

Tim looked at him like a beaten dog. "I didn't mean to knock over the water tower. When it fell on John, well, I panicked." He looked at the drink again.

"Yes, you made a mistake today Tim. I've been there, I can understand what you're going through. The tower is a write-off. John's leg was broken. He's OK, his leg's in a cast. We can build a new tower."

He let a few seconds tick by, holding Tim's gaze. "But here's the hard choice: you take that drink and you drop two hundred feet. Probably, it'll be fatal. Not today maybe, but you know what it'll lead to. You've seen it happen to friends."

Ben's words were brutally loving. "In the end, you'll fall into the abyss. You'll drink yourself to death."

He paused for the words to sink in. "The other choice is to leave that drink on the table, come back with me and eat humble pie: face the consequences of your actions."

Tim's hand trembled. "I'm not sure if I can," he whispered.

Ben put his hand on top of the trembling one. Tim looked up. "Today I'll be your safety railing," Ben said. "You can still hop over me and take the drop, or you can get up and walk out with me. We can go back and face the consequences together. I'll be your sponsor back into the community."

Ben watched the struggle play out across the young man's features. He could see the point when the battle was won. Tim looked at Ben and stood, grabbing his hat and coat from the seat. They walked out together. The drink remained on the table, untouched.

Ben drove Tim to the hospital to visit John, whose leg was in a cast, suspended above the bed with pulleys and wires. John smiled at them as they entered.

"Hey, Tim. You might need some more lessons in driving a tractor." Tim didn't meet John's gaze.

"Look, man, it ended OK. I'm alive. What's more, I forgive you." John held out his hand.

Tim looked at John with a bit of awe. "Thanks," he stammered as he shook the hand.

Then Tim told John about the incident in the bar.

"Good choice, Tim. My broken leg was worth that."

Tim was incredulous. "Really?"

"Kid, I've broken many bones in my life. Bones heal more quickly than a broken life."

The three chatted for a while; Tim mentioned that Ben had offered to be his sponsor. John gave Ben a look. "That's quite a commitment." Ben just nodded.

Visiting time was up; a nurse came in to shoo Ben and Tim out. As they were leaving, John motioned Ben back in.

"Well done," he said simply. "Today you showed real progress, caring for Tim. You proved something to us, and more importantly, yourself. Oh, and how would you like to live in a real home instead of in the transient bunks? Come, stay with us. Alice brought the idea up yesterday."

CHAPTER SEVEN

19 November 2056, Grit, Arizona
(a year later)

The young woman blinked blearily at Paul from the reception desk, "Ben?" she searched the screen in front of her. "I see that he logged into the power plant last night. No sign of him logging out, Dr Whitestone."

"Thank you. Sorry to wake you. I know I'm here before opening time."

She smiled at him sheepishly and murmured, "No problem."

Paul's feet knew the familiar path. He'd been at home here for many years, serving as an advisor and sponsor to members of the community.

The security door clicked open, responding to his badge and biometrics. Paul pushed through, past the café and the dorm for transients, then out of the back door to the community's main compound. The residences along the wall were dark; people were still sleeping.

The eastern horizon lightened. Subtle bands of red, orange, and green streaked the deep blue of the early desert sky. High, wispy clouds caught the golden glow of the coming dawn sunlight. The air was cool and dry. The fragrance of nocturnal cactus flowers, still open from the rain a few days before, drifted in the air. The simplicity and beauty of a desert morning always refreshed Paul's heart.

At the base of the hill stood a power station, a small building which backed up against the circumference wall of the compound. Paul descended the white gravel path to the station door. The security system again responded to his badge, unlocking the door with a quick, quiet beep. He entered a dark, silent control room. A blue glow in the far corner highlighted an intent expression on the face bent over a screen.

Paul allowed the door to close behind him with an audible click, to announce his entrance. "Good morning, Ben. Have you been here all night?"

The younger man looked up, startled. "Ah, hi, Paul. Is it morning already?" He rose and glanced at the window through which the first rays of the sun poured in, spilling over the horizon. "That was a short night," he sighed and stretched.

"What are you working on?" Paul asked, marvelling at the gifts emerging from the man he'd found wasting away in the desert just a year and a half ago.

"Oh, I'm installing an array of super-conducting batteries. They'll buffer the power output from the fusion reactor here. It's an Alchemist III model. We installed it last year, but already it's been straining during peak energy times. So, I proposed a few weeks ago that we install this array instead of purchasing a larger reactor. Much cheaper. The Council approved my proposal."

"Right, I remember that," Paul said. "So, this is it?"

"Yep. Metallic hydrogen models. Perfect for the environment here."

"Spoken like a true enthusiast," Paul laughed, "You seem to have a knack for this kind of thing, Ben. I appreciate your good work managing the jojoba fields and now developing the power systems at the shelter. Are you enjoying yourself?"

Ben considered and said slowly, "Yes. I do enjoy this. I've always been fascinated by power generation, especially at the atomic level. And reactors like this one are interesting to work with. What brings you down so early?"

"I was looking for you. Care to join me for breakfast?"

"Sure, let me put this last battery online, then I'll call it quits for the night." His hands danced over the screen, "Done and done! Breakfast sounds good." Ben stood up and stretched. "I can't believe a whole night has gone. I'll have to catch up on sleep later."

Paul led the way as they left the power station, past the residential homes, some with light now peeking through cracks in the curtains.

Up the gravel path. Through the dimly lit transient dorm, where bedraggled men, towels in hand, were shuffling to the showers. Into the bright and fragrant dining room, where a breakfast buffet was being set.

"Waffles this morning. Bacon and eggs," Paul announced, glancing at the serving trays being put in place.

Ben's eyes brightened. "And coffee." The green light on the coffee machine gleamed with promise.

Collecting trays, they made their way down the line with other early diners and carried their meals to a window table.

"As I crossed the compound, I realized that it's been nearly two years since I found you sitting in that wreck of a car." Paul's face had a bemused expression.

Ben caught his grey eyes. "Has it been that long? Still feels like yesterday."

"You've come such a long way in such a short time, Ben. I would not have predicted that the despairing man who threw me onto that scorching car hood back then would become the man dreaming about fusion reactors today."

"Yeah," Ben smiled ruefully, "I was in bad shape, wasn't I? Sorry for roughing you up a bit that day. I realize now you could have put up quite a fight if you wanted."

"No worries, son."

"I remember now, it was touch and go in those first months. I wanted to change, but I often despaired of breaking free from my addictions. Thanks so much for introducing me to John and Alice Robinson. Even now I'm amazed that they took the risk of sponsoring me."

"They saw your potential." Paul studied Ben. "John also came to this community as an addict. He understood where you were coming from. He identified with you."

"Yes, he did understand, though at first I resented his strictness. I fought against the rules and structure the Robinsons imposed on me."

Paul nodded. "Yes, the fight is part of the process. You've experienced first-hand how hard it is to break from your old masters. They won't let go without a struggle."

Paul smiled, cutting into his syrup-drenched waffle.

Ben looked out the window, to the desert beyond. "I needed what the Robinsons were giving me, even though I repaid them with a lot of grief."

Paul nodded, pleased with the self-awareness Ben was showing.

Ben's face grew grim at the memory. "That 'tough love' people talk about."

"You know it's as tough for those doling it out as for those on the receiving end."

Ben looked Paul in the eye, "Yes, I realize that now. It must be very tough. John stuck to his guns. He made me prove that I could be trusted. He gave me something to fight for."

"They were a good fit for you," Paul picked up a slice of bacon and nibbled it.

Ben looked up at his mentor, dripping waffle suspended halfway to his mouth. "John reminds me of a coach I had in high school who pushed me beyond my limits, but ultimately helped me become a better athlete. John made me finally admit that willpower alone couldn't keep me from the lure of alcohol."

Paul put his fork down, looking squarely in Ben's eyes. "I'm proud of you, Ben. You've allowed suffering to do its job, strip away your self-deceptions. You've been able, finally, to fully face your grief without denial, or excuses. To accept it; that takes courage of spirit and heart."

Ben slowly chewed some more bacon. "Looking back, I feel like I've been throwing off a kind of childish self-centredness. My own heart deceives me, I so easily rationalize my destructive habits."

"What else have you learned?" Paul asked, encouraging Ben to stay in this reflective mood just a bit longer.

Ben stopped yet again with fork poised in the air. "Well, now I see that, while I cannot change the past, I can change how I feel about the past and how much it affects me now. Like losing Lisa and Sammy. I still deeply feel the grief and loss. Yet now those emotions are – what's the right word? Tamed? That's the best way I can put it."

Ben looked at Paul, "I almost feel I can move on with life, the overwhelming weight of those emotions are reduced to manageable levels."

Paul sighed, recognizing the words of a journeying soul. He remembered his own battle with grief after the death of his sons. "Almost is good enough for now, Ben. You have been given a gift, Ben, a start towards a new life."

"Yes, a new life. Thank you," he said simply.

"It's your life to spend, use it well. I am grateful to see you sitting across the table from me in your right mind, Ben, taking an interest in the physics of fusion reactors, of all things."

Paul smiled as he watched Ben return to his breakfast with gusto.

"And, I received my one-year sobriety chip yesterday. A whole year!" Ben enthused, between mouthfuls.

"Congratulations! That's a great achievement." Paul was thoughtful, looking at Ben. "You'll never be fully cured, of course. Keep your guard up. You will be tested again."

"I'm ready. I've learned so much about myself. I think I've kicked alcohol forever."

A shadow of concern crossed Paul's features. "May it be, Ben," he said quietly. It was his turn to look out the window and watch the heat shimmer on the landscape. "Take care. Overconfidence can lead you into a trap."

Ben glanced up. Paul could see the remark hit a nerve.

"Point taken," Ben admitted. "I'm probably not out of the battle completely yet."

Ben looked at the rising sun, "I think I'll go for my run while the day is still cool."

Changing the subject, Paul brought up his reason for this meeting, "Before you go. Your work with the agri-bots and reactors show you have aptitude and a bright mind, Ben. Have you ever considered going back to university for your PhD?"

Ben put his utensils down and looked at his mentor. "A year ago, I would not have considered it." He paused, turning to look at the busy street outside for a moment, then back at Paul. "But now could be a good time. I'd enjoy the research; I've been intrigued by my readings in particle theory, especially muons. They might be a key to the next generation of fusion reactors."

Paul's expression turned thoughtful. "Ben, if you're serious about this, I know the Chancellor at Caltech in California. An old friend from Homeland Security. I could put in a good word for you. You must, of course, pass all their entry requirements, but I think you could do that. And I suspect there might be scholarships or grants available. Interested?"

Paul was gratified to see the light brighten in Ben's eyes. "Yes. Why not?" Ben said quietly.

"I'll call him later today." Paul said, smiling.

5 January 2057, Grit, Arizona
(a month and a half later)

The lights were already on in the gym as Ben stepped from the locker room. Paul stood in the ring, relaxed, waiting for him. Ben ducked between the ropes. He bounced out onto the canvas with little jumps, testing the spring of the floor.

Paul smiled, "Are you sure you're up for this? Have you trained lately, Ben?"

Ben grinned, dancing around, "I should be asking you that, old man. Shall I go easy on you?"

"Brave words. Can you back them up?" Paul said with a smile, standing alert and with a quiet stillness.

Ben slowed to a walk, circling Paul. Without warning, he sprang towards Paul. But Paul wasn't there. The lunge took him through empty air.

"Lucky," Ben said.

"Maybe," Paul replied, with another faint smile.

Warier this time, Ben stepped around his friend looking for a weakness. Paul followed his circling walk, turning in place to face him.

Paul's arm twitched. Ben moved in with lightning reflexes to take what he thought was an opening. Next thing he knew, he was on the ground looking up at a smile. "Pride comes before a fall," Paul teased, helping him up.

"Impressive." Ben massaged his bruised ego.

"It's a variation of an aikido move, called the Heaven and Earth throw," Paul said. "I learned it years ago from a fellow Army Ranger. His father was a master in several martial arts. We whiled away many hours of down-time practising moves."

"Can you teach me some of them?" Ben asked, keen to hone his skills.

"Ah, a little humility creeps in. That's good. Remember, in sparring, your mental state is even more important than physical training and techniques. Wisdom and experience can often defeat brute strength."

"You've a compelling way of demonstrating that!"

"Addiction eroded the edge of your discipline, Ben. Try again."

Ben tried a move and was on the ground again. Ben got up and rubbed his shoulder. "More humility."

Paul laughed. "Ah, humility. One of my favourite definitions of humility is the ability to simply see things as they really are."

"Things as they really are?" Ben rose and stretched, watching Paul.

"For example, we all tend to think more of ourselves than we should. Pride is a weakness, easy to exploit."

Ben lunged, saw and anticipated Paul's feint, but ended up on the mat nonetheless. He laughed. "Yes. Guilty as charged."

Paul danced and shook himself a bit. He held Ben's gaze, "Things as they really are. I must, with ruthless honesty, understand my own strengths and weaknesses. Accept them."

"So, for example, me assuming being younger and quicker, I could take you down. Bad assumption." Ben grinned.

Paul smiled, walking around Ben. "Yep, one lesson. Another part of humility is to see others as they really are. If I like a person, I tend to see only his good parts. I ignore his darker side. If I hate a person, I tend to see only his bad side. I refuse to acknowledge the good in him as well. A normal human habit."

"Are you going to lecture or are you gonna spar?" Ben danced around Paul, springing on his toes.

Paul fluidly moved his weight onto his hands and swung his legs under Ben, toppling the younger man onto the mat once again.

Ben sobered a bit with the wind knocked out of him.

"How well do you know yourself, Ben? Tell me something you have learned recently." Paul sprang to his feet and offered Ben a hand.

"OK, OK. What have I learned?" Ben walked around, getting his breath back.

"Well, addiction and self-pity feel good, like they're my friends, but really, they're my enemies. Blaming others for my problems and soothing myself with alcohol has corroded who I am. I haven't been taking responsibility for things I could change." Ben and Paul circled one another carefully.

"Good, but it sounds like you're just parroting what you hear in your support group." Ben moved, and Paul knocked him on the mat again.

Ben jumped up, consciously controlling his emotions, watching Paul carefully. "Well, I was angry about losing my wife, son, and life." He saw a vulnerability and deftly put his mentor on the mat. He felt good about that.

Paul smiled. "Well done. What did you do about that?" He got up and circled with Ben again.

"This last year has been about learning to channel my anger into the fight to regain my life." Ben lunged, and Paul blocked. They danced.

"And…?" Paul moved in under Ben's guard like lightning, but Ben pivoted away.

"I reckon I faced down the pain and grief, I embraced them." Ben gasped as Paul landed a blow.

"Then I walked through them." Ben feinted, Paul moved in, and Ben grabbed his arm, pulled Paul into a roll over his body and slapped him on the mat again.

"I'd say they're no longer my masters." He gave a hand to Paul and pulled him up.

"So, it was all due to your will and effort?" Paul said wiping sweat from his brow.

Ben stopped, held up his hand while he breathed and thought. "No, I might have believed that a few months ago. But honestly, looking back over the last two years, I now know I couldn't have done it without you, the Robinsons, and the rest of the shelter and rehabilitation staff."

Ben reflected more, "You've been mirrors to my soul, helping me see myself more as I really am." Ben smiled. "Lesson learned."

"Maybe lesson one has begun to be learned," Paul said, clapping him on the back. "Lessons have to get from here," Paul tapped him on the forehead, "to here." Paul pointed to Ben's chest over his heart.

Ben reflected, "True. I understand that now. I had to face down my loss and grief to rip away the dark filter those emotions put on my heart. The filter distorted how I saw the world."

"Losing Lisa and Sammy, losing your team, being captured. These all severely dented your faith in humanity, maybe your faith in the goodness of life itself." Paul took a step back, watching Ben.

"Yes," Ben said quietly.

"What's the truth, though?" Paul was now jogging in place.

"The truth is that there are evil people. But there are also good people: you, the Robinsons, this rehabilitation programme. You've all demonstrated that to me."

Paul stretched again. "You were a bit of a terror when you came. Many would have left you to your own devices. The Robinsons saw a good heart underneath the anger, bitterness, and self-pity. They took a chance on you and took you into their home."

They took defensive poses and walked around each other again, looking for an entry.

Paul went on, "When you look at people with cynical eyes, you will only see bad people with bad motives. This is only a half truth. When you see others with rose-coloured glasses, you will only see good people with good attitudes. Also, half true. Look with mature humility, then you'll see people and yourself as we really are."

Paul moved in, thinking Ben's guard had dropped. In a flash, Ben took the older man's momentum, rolled, and threw him on the mat again.

"I've found your weakness; just let you start a lecture." Ben grinned. Paul laughed from the mat, then jumped up.

"Not bad." He said rubbing a shoulder. Let me show you that 'Heaven and Earth' move."

"I'd like that, thanks."

Paul began walking through the technique slowly, allowing Ben to follow and mimic.

*

After an hour more of workout, then showers, Ben stood outside with Paul. The Primal Gym's retro neon sign flickered above them. The downtown area of Grit was empty, shops closed. In this dark alley, there were only streetlights for company. At the end of the alley, beyond main street, in the residential areas, people were tucked into their homes behind softly lit curtains. "I'm heading back to the centre," Paul said.

"I think I'll take a walk. It's a beautiful night." Ben's eyes were drawn to the starry expanse. Moonshine glowed as an aura above the hills outside of town. *The moon will be up soon.*

"OK, see you later." Paul waved and walked down the alley towards the brightly lit main street. Ben turned the other way down an alley, which emptied onto a boundary road. As Ben turned and began walking, he heard a soft scrape behind him. Adrenaline whispered through his system. He did not turn his head but kept walking across the boundary road and towards the open desert. There was more cover there. He neared a telephone pole.

A pebble quietly crunched under a tread. An almost inaudible click. Ben dropped and rolled to land behind the pole. A double tap on the wood above him; he looked up, shocked to see two taser darts embedded there. *I hate tasers,* he thought, remembering Somalia.

A ditch was behind him, paralleling the road. He silently melted into its shadows, moving along the bottom, keeping the pole between him and his assailant. Senses in high alert, he now heard the soft purr of a motor car maybe thirty metres down the road. *There's more than one.*

Two metres away there was a creosote bush growing from the side of the ditch. Using it as cover, he peered through the scraggly branches. *I'm glad there are no streetlights here.* In the starlight, he saw a faint figure moving towards him. He wished for his camouflage suit and glanced down the road where the car was, headlights were off. *Yes, another figure there too.*

"Did you see where he went?" one asked quietly in Arabic.

"Shh, he's near. In that ditch, I think. Be wary, the Emir says not to underestimate him. Cover your side of the ditch." Looking back, he saw the first man had a gun. The second stepped away from the car and Ben could clearly see him silhouetted against the milky way. There was a taser in his hand. *I must stay out of range of the taser.*

Ben scuttled quietly along the bottom of the ditch towards where he had spotted the first man. He was no longer there. *He must have taken cover in the ditch, like me.* Ben froze, keeping absolute stillness, listening.

"I hear your breathing, *kaafir*."

Ben slowed his breath.

"Ah, you understand me. Then listen, I can shoot along the ditch. I would certainly wound you, perhaps kill you. There's nowhere for you to go. Climb up into the light, and I won't have to shoot."

Ben chose to obey; he still had some options if he could get close to the man. The other was now walking towards them. *Better to deal with them one at a time; I've gotta stay away from that taser..*

Ben rose slowly. "Here I am. Don't shoot," he said in fluent Arabic.

His assailant rose as well. He had dark features and clear eyes. A long beard hung to the middle of his chest. *A Salafist, probably New Caliphate;* Ben recognized the look.

The man scrambled onto the tarmac, pistol pointed at Ben's torso. "Come up on the road, slowly."

Ben did as he was told, stealthily closing the distance between them.

"Move back!" the man said, recognizing Ben's tactic.

Ben stepped up on the road and stood there.

"My reflexes are quick, *kaafir*. I can shoot your knee out before you can get in reach. Turn around." Ben did so.

"Move towards the car." Ben could sense the muzzle pointed at him. He walked forward, slowly, looking at the other man advancing. It was only thirty seconds before the second man was in taser range. *I'm running out of options.*

A yelp came from the man behind him. Ben ducked and rolled to his right. He landed again on his feet, ready to fight. He saw the silhouette of Paul Whitestone, bent over the gunman. Paul had wrested a gun from the man and was stashing it in his belt behind his back.

Whirling around, Ben saw the second man sprinting towards the car. In a second, the engine revved and the car lights came on. "Over the embankment, Ben!" Paul grabbed the assailant, hurling him back into the ditch at the side of the road. He and Ben followed, diving then rolling to a crouched stance in the ditch. The car roared past.

Paul had the assailant in a lock, immobilizing him. He stood up, whipped out the gun and fired at the car. It was too far away, and disappeared quickly into the night.

"You OK?" he asked, looking Ben over in the faint starlight.

"Yes, shaken, but OK." Adrenaline still pumped through Ben's veins.

"Who is this guy?" Paul asked, dragging the struggling man to his feet.

"I have no idea." Ben looked him over. The man glared at them. "He speaks Arabic and called me a *kaafir*. I would guess he is an extremist, probably New Caliphate."

Ben turned to the man, and in Arabic said, "Who are you!?"

The man just stared at Ben impassively.

"Is he someone you met during the Dependency Wars?" Paul studied the man.

Ben shook his head. "Don't recognize him."

Paul made a quick call to the local police station, "Sergeant, we've had an assault out on Mesquite Drive, by Saguaro Alley. Yes. Yes. We have the assailant, but a possible accomplice has fled in a black Nissan sedan. Licence plate BNG8224. Yes. Thank you, we'll wait for your car here."

5 January 2057, Grit, Arizona
(later that evening)

Must be close to midnight. Ben sat on a bench in the tiny police station, waiting to find out about the man who'd assaulted him. **So far the police had told him nothing.** The prisoner inside the holding cell eyed him, a sly grin playing around his mouth. Ben had pestered him with questions in Arabic, but he remained silent.

He just stared at Ben.

Paul was behind the next door, in the interrogation room, giving a statement to the sergeant. It would be Ben's turn next.

A guttural whisper startled him. "Ben Holden?" the prisoner sneered. "I've been looking for you for many years. I remember your wife Dr Lisa, right? I enjoyed her immensely. She begged for more. No, wait," he cackled, "she cried for mercy. She was gibbering when we were finished. I slit her throat."

Ben launched from the bench and grasped at the man through the bars. "Who are you?!"

"Oh, and your little boy, Sammy? He was crying, begging for his father. I ran the knife across his jugular vein." The prisoner talked nonchalantly while methodically ripping open a seam of his shirt.

With a dawning premonition, Ben called quickly towards the station desk in the next room "Sergeant!" The answering sound of running footsteps came down the hall as he turned back to the prisoner, who sneered while popping a pill into his mouth. "I'm off to *aljanna*, paradise, *kaafir*. Give my regards to the Emir. Oh, and Abdul, Yunus and Dawood. You'll soon be meeting all of them."

Within seconds the prisoner was convulsing on the cell floor. The policeman fumbled for his security fob to unlock the cell. By the time they reached the prisoner, the man lay still. The officer put his hand up to stop Ben from entering, then checked the pulse of the prisoner. He was dead. When the officer turned back, Ben was gone.

A moment later, Paul Whitestone came running into the holding area. "Ben!" he called, looking around.

The officer was checking the prisoner's vital signs. "Your man has gone. Out that door. Looked like he was in shock. Or rage. I couldn't tell."

Paul slammed open the door, looking up and down the street. Both directions were dark and empty.

20 February 2057

(a month and a half later)

Ben stood in the redwood forest, allowing the majesty of the surrounding giants fill his senses. Brilliant sunlight filtered through the soft green of the branches above, illuminating intricate patterns of ferns and giant clover on the forest floor. A holy stillness burned around and through him.

A line from an Elizabeth Browning poem came to mind, "Earth's crammed with heaven, And every common bush afire with God."

He began to walk through the glade. Moses might have felt like this, he thought.

"Ben."

The familiar voice electrified him with an exquisite thrill. He peered around. He saw no one. He walked slowly between the redwoods.

"Lisa?" he called. Then he ran, searching through the trees. The forest opened onto a bright, broad meadow.

Someone stood in the centre. Ben stopped short, unable to take his eyes off her.

It was his wife, but not his wife. She was vividly real, and far more beautiful than in life. It was as if the bright beauty within her had burned away the shell of her body, revealing her essential nature.

"Forgive me, Ben," she said, gazing into his eyes, directly into his soul, triggering a flood of pent-up longing and grief. Tears streamed unbidden down his cheeks.

"Forgive you?" He didn't understand. Seeing her was almost more than he could bear.

"Forgive me for having to leave you, Ben. I love you still." Her face was alight and there was a softness in her voice that pierced him.

"It wasn't you, Lise, it was them. They murdered you... and Sammy." He shook with involuntary sobs.

Sammy ran into the meadow, clung to his mother, and turned a smiling face towards Ben.

Lisa's tender eyes held him. "You must forgive them, Ben. Stop clinging to anger and bitterness. Withholding forgiveness only hurts you, my love. It doesn't affect them."

"Forgive them?"

"Yes," she said simply, "for me and Sammy."

"For you," Ben whispered.

With an act of will, he released the cloud of anger and bitterness. As he did so, the conflict that had raged for so long in his heart receded, like a tide from the shore.

"Ben, I want you to be whole again. You must forgive yourself as well." The words hung in the holy quiet. Ben was now beyond grief and anger. And as her words sank into his heart, he became that stillness. Accepting. Forgiving.

"It is time, my love. You must let us go." Ben started towards them, but then stopped. An invisible Presence was between him and them. "We must go," Lisa said simply, gazing at him. The Presence whisked them away as though by a wind. "Bye, Dad," Sammy's small earnest voice echoed in the air as Ben stood in the now empty meadow, alone under a warm sun.

*

Ben woke and found himself lying in a pool of his own vomit next to a dumpster. He groaned, opened his eyes. *That dream felt much more real than this alleyway.* He felt achy and groggy, yet something was different.

He probed his soul where there had been anger and found only stillness. *Only peace.* What's happened?

A moment later a police car turned the corner at the end of the alley. A spotlight shone on Ben. One of the officers got out and walked over to him, disgust flashing across his face.

"C'mon, buddy. Let's take you down to the station and get you cleaned up."

Ben staggered to his feet. "Thank you," he whispered.

The officer was surprised. "You are the first one who ever thanked me."

He helped Ben into the back of the squad car. As they exited the alley, Ben looked back. *That was a holy place.*

21 February 2057, Ajo, Arizona
(the next day)

John Robinson was waiting outside when Ben was released from the station. Seeing the disappointment in John's face reminded Ben that he would now have to climb a hill of consequences for his choice to cower in the bottle.

John drove Ben to a motel a few blocks away to clean up. After Ben showered, they threw his old clothes in the dumpster out back, and then drove on to a diner on the highway into town. They slid into a booth by the window and ordered breakfast. Ben was starving hungry and cleaned his plate in a few minutes.

John took his time with his food, watching Ben. Finally, he said, "Tell me what happened."

Ben laid his cutlery down and looked into his friend's eyes. Then dropped his gaze to his empty plate.

"I didn't know the man who held me at gunpoint."

John took a bite of his bacon, "Yeah, Paul told me about that. But what happened in the cell?"

Ben looked out the window. "That man taunted me. He said he raped… my wife. And cut Sammy's throat."

The words hung in the air between them.

"It all came rushing back, the grief and pain. It was overwhelming, John." Ben looked at his friend, watching for reassurance.

"So, you went back to your old friend, the bottle, to numb those feelings." John's words were matter of fact, not giving him an inch. "Not much of a friend."

"No." Ben dropped his eyes again. His mind drifted to a scene of sparring with Paul; he heard Paul's voice challenging his overconfidence.

John sighed. "I can't imagine the anger you must've felt. I'm not sure how I would've handled it."

Silence hung between them. Ben knew what was coming.

"You know the rules, Ben. You agreed that any violation of the 'no drink' rule would mean you'd have to leave our house."

"Yes." Ben said again, simply.

"I think you broke Alice's heart. And she's a pretty tough cookie."

"Last thing I wanted to do," Ben agreed. "For what it's worth, tell her I'm sorry."

"Listen, Ben. I've come as a friend..." John's voice trailed off.

"I know. Thank you, John. You helped me clean up this morning, brought me clothes and given me breakfast. You didn't have to do that. You've probably broken several community rules yourself."

John took another bite of bacon. "So, what are your next steps?"

The peace from the vivid dream steadied Ben. It gave him new hope, even an unexpected resolve.

"I want to reapply to the rehabilitation programme in the community."

"You'll be back to square one, in their eyes, because of your relapse." John looked at his friend intently. "You'll be back to sleeping in the transient bunk room. You'll have to re-earn the trust of the community." He hesitated, "And of me and Alice."

"I know. I'm willing." Ben paused, then added quietly, "It's like Paul said; I've just had a clear view of who I really am. This... situation showed me how much grief and anger were still simmering just below surface. How raw and vulnerable I actually am, behind my mask of bravado. I needed to see that."

Ben stared at his fork. "But this time, something else happened. I can't explain it. Maybe I saw a vision, a dream, or... whatever. But it has lifted a cloud that was hanging over me, John."

John studied Ben for a few moments silently. "So maybe there was a good thing hidden in something terrible."

Ben smiled. "You sound like Paul."

Ben followed him to the car. As they drove to Grit, neither of them spoke. John paused in front of the shelter to drop him off.

Ben stepped onto the curb. John reached across to the passenger door, grabbed the handle, and looked up at Ben. "I... *we* want you to succeed, Ben."

Ben nodded and John pulled the door closed. He walked into the shelter. The bell jangled above him.

27 February 2057, Bosaso, Somali Emirates
(a week later)

The room was dark and oppressive.

The angel of death is here. Abdul Qawwi tried to fix his mind on life as he turned towards his mother, who lay still, propped up by pillows. Rugs embroidered with Qur'anic verses draped the walls. One covered a niche by the bed, behind which he could hear medical monitors beeping quietly, counting down her final hours.

A man sat cross-legged in the corner, chanting the reassuring *shahaada*, "*Laa illah 'illa Allah wa Muhammadun rasuul Allah.* There is no God but God, and Muhammed is his prophet." Abdul Qawwi breathed deeply. *These are good words to hear when taking one's final breath.*

Next to the door, Abdul Qawwi's wife, Hazima, sat with their son, Rafi. They drew closer to each other as Abdul Qawwi entered the room. Abdul Qawwi nodded to his wife on his way to his dying mother's side.

"*Ya 'Ummi ilghaaliya,* dear mother," Abdul Qawwi said, sitting by the bedside. Her body had shrunk from her suffering, her breaths were laboured. The eyes that opened to him were bright, but rimmed with red.

"*Ya ibni ilghaali,* my beloved son, you have come," she whispered.

"Yes, of course. As soon as I heard. Are they taking good care of you? The Emir has sent his best doctors." Abdul Qawwi glanced at the men quietly talking together by the machines.

Abdul Qawwi fought back tears. "Do you remember the answers you must give when the angels question you?"

"Yes, Abdul Qawwi, long ago. I'm as ready as I can be. I've kept the pillars." A flicker of fear crossed her face.

Abdul Qawwi took her hand, it felt so fragile. "Dear *'Ummi,* I owe you so much. I've worked hard so that you'll be proud of me."

"Yes, Abdul Qawwi. You are a good son." She stroked his cheek, "Yet, as I stand at the door of death and eternity, these things don't seem important any more. I cannot carry them to the next life. It is only Allah that matters in the end.

"I feel my life draining away. Soon I'll go to be questioned by *Munkar* and *Nakir,* the angels who will judge my faith. The deeds of my life will be weighed in the *miizaan,* to see if the good outweighs the evil."

"Of course." Abdul Qawwi looked into her eyes and saw they were growing distant. Looking beyond him. Suddenly they grew wide with wonder.

"I see your father, my mother. Many are gathering, Abdul Qawwi."

Abdul Qawwi turned to look behind, but there was no one. His skin crept.

Her hand suddenly gripped him with an unbelievable strength. "Abdul Qawwi, oh! It's beautiful, he's beautiful." She turned to him with a look of amazement, "Abdul Qawwi, we misunderstood." Then alarm slowly spread across her features, "He knows my life; I... I must stand before him and give account. But there is so much love..."

The sentence was not finished. Her breath rattled, and she sank back into the pillows, lifeless. Her features which had showed dread now relaxed into death with a shadow of joy. The man in the corner came quickly to the bedside and whispered the creed again, into the ear of the dead woman: *"Laa illah 'illa Allah wa Muhammadun rasuul Allah."*

Abdul Qawwi heard someone sobbing, then realized it was his own voice.

14 March 2057, Bosaso, Somali Emirates
(two weeks later)

After the requisite time for mourning, Abdul Qawwi returned to the palace of the Emir, near the town of Bosaso on the north coast of Somalia. He'd been invited to tea with Abdul Ghafoor, Emir of the Somali Emirates. Before being appointed Emir, Abdul Ghafoor had been one of the Caliph's chief advisors. He had recruited Abdul Qawwi to help him bring Somalia into the New Caliphate. They worked well together and had successfully rebuilt the failed Somali nation.

The two sat on the balcony overlooking the gardens. The sea sparkled beyond the grove of date palms; a fountain splashed softly in the courtyard below. Servants stood just inside the doors, out of hearing. Abdul Qawwi glanced across the table at the man he now counted as an ally. *Yes, an ally but like a snake charmer allies with his cobra.*

"I'm sorry to hear about your mother, Abdul Qawwi. She was a good woman."

"Thank you, Emir. I'm grateful for the care you provided during her last days." His grief still felt fresh. The last few words from his mother still echoed in his mind.

"Of course. You are my vizier, I will care for your mother as though she is my mother." Abdul Qawwi nodded at the acknowledgment.

"Your wife and your son, they are well?"

"Yes, Emir. Thank you." Abdul Qawwi waited patiently. *He has invited me here for a reason.*

"Do you remember the proposal you presented to the Caliph three years ago? The plan to trigger earthquakes that would devastate North America?"

"Of course, Emir." Abdul Qawwi brightened. *This was interesting.*

"As I recall," the Emir interrupted, "the project was halted due to a lack of key information."

"Do you still have the data device we obtained... from that mission, Emir?" A haunted look clouded Abdul Qawwi's features as he recalled that night, the boy silently staring at him across the room as his young throat was cut. He shuddered. *That had been unplanned, terrible; the boy's eyes still glared at him.* The Emir didn't notice Abdul Qawwi's reaction.

"Of course, I still have the device, and the data are still locked within it." The Emir tapped his finger lightly on the table, looking out onto the garden.

"It can only be opened with Ben Holden's biometrics. We lost track of him, Emir." Abdul Qawwi watched his mentor closely.

"Yes, quite. Well, I've continued investigating. A few months ago, I found him in Arizona. Apparently, he's in a rehabilitation facility, for alcoholics."

"You did not mention this to me, Emir."

The Emir waved his hand, oblivious to the edge in Abdul Qawwi's voice. "No, I did not want to trouble you while your mother was on her deathbed."

Abdul Qawwi was thoughtful. More likely, you waited until I was not available, so you would not have to share the credit for this success.

Recent sanctions against the Caliphate, led by European and Asian leaders, had greatly angered the Caliph. The North Americans had inspired these sanctions. And, the frequent disruption of Caliphate plans by covert foreign units was eroding their influence across Europe, North America, Australia, and South-East Asia. New recruits for the Caliphate were drying up as their credibility dropped. An attack on the North American continent could significantly weaken these efforts against the New Caliphate.

Whoever undermines Western powers will gain the Caliph's favour, Abdul Qawwi mused. The Caliph is getting old. A triumph like this might even put someone in position to become the new Caliph.

"Of course, Emir. Very kind." Abdul Qawwi waited a moment, then asked "Were you able to capture this man Holden?"

"No, our attempts have been thwarted so far. We'll watch for another chance. The device you retrieved still sits secure in my office, waiting to be decrypted. Since the infidels are now alert to our efforts to capture the man, it may be a while before another opportunity presents itself." An opportunity squandered by incompetence.

"We can wait, Emir. The next time we will succeed, *inshallah*." Abdul Qawwi said smoothly, while sipping his tea and looking at the Emir over the rim.

CHAPTER EIGHT

9 July 2066, Seastead vessel *Ossë*
(nine years later)

Undulating light wavered and flickered across his closed eyelids as Ben began to wake. He felt a subtle vibration and a sense of movement around him. Otherwise all was quiet.

An unnatural silence, almost absolute.

A small hand lightly touched his chest. Then there was a whisper, "A deep soul, Nemo."

Ben stirred, startled. The hand pulled away. He heard the soft footfalls, like a child running from the room.

The strange silence left with that small presence. Now sounds filled the void, the soft gurgling of water. Ticks, creaks. A whoosh of air cascading through a ventilation system.

He opened his eyes with an effort, to deep blueness rippling with sinuous bands of light. *Where am I?* He blinked. It took a few moments to realize that the blueness was the surface of the sea, gliding several metres above an enormous sloped window. The room was full of sea light.

He pulled his arm out from under the covers, to run it along the top of the bed. The blanket was smooth wool.

A quick movement of the head brought nausea. Glancing around more slowly, he noticed the few furnishings in a small room. *A wooden table and chair, beautifully crafted. A large carpet with rich reds and blues. Where am I?* The floor beyond the carpet was the colour and texture of smooth seashell. It curved up to merge seamlessly with the window and form the other walls and ceiling of the chamber. An elevated, carved wooden door, perhaps a closet, was on the wall nearest him. There were two other doors; one was ajar, opening onto a corridor.

He heard a distant chime, then a voice announced from the hall, "Captain, the professor is awake."

Footsteps approached. A large man, with a smile nestled in his beard, entered the room. His eyes were friendly, calming Ben's initial flash of alarm.

"Professor Holden, I'm so glad to see you awake. I am Suliman Battuta, captain of *Ossë*, the vessel you are on. It is an honour to meet you, though I would have preferred better circumstances."

Sul stood by the bedside while Ben struggled to sit up. Sul helped him with a practised skill. He moved pillows to support Ben.

"You've been asleep for five days. We were worried about you. You had lost a lot of blood and were severely dehydrated when we found you on the beach. Close to death, Professor. We found it necessary to sedate you the last few days to allow your body to recover."

"What?" Ben asked, still not quite able to process the conversation. "Who are you?" His tongue felt like sandpaper. "Where am I?"

"I'm Captain Sul, Professor. You're on my ship." Sul repeated gently, then added, "You are safe."

Ben sat up and stared for a moment at his host. Sul continued, "I'm sure you have many questions – not least, how you came to be with us. Take some time to wake more fully and bathe. If you feel up to it, dinner will be served soon. Please join us. Solid food will be good for you. I'll be happy to answer your questions at that time. Or later after a rest, if you prefer."

Ben noticed that someone had clothed him in lightweight sleepwear. As he rubbed his eyes, a piece of gauze taped to his wrist grazed his cheek.

"You've been on a liquid diet these last few days, Professor." Sul touched the intravenous drip standing next to the bed, no longer connected.

"Uhm." Ben massaged his neck gingerly, struggling to take in all this information. He winced at the pain radiating down his back. "Please call me Ben. But...." His thoughts were chaotic, he wasn't sure what to ask.

"Relax, Ben. We're here to help you. You're in good hands. You'll have to trust me on that for now – until we can get to know each other better." Stepping towards a door on the opposite side of the room, Sul continued. "You'll find a shower through that door there. Please refresh yourself."

Sul opened the small wooden door. "You'll find clothes in this closet when you're ready. May I help you get out of the bed?"

Ben nodded, swinging his feet to the floor. Sul helped him to stand.

"Food does sound good, I feel famished." Ben took a step, then another.

"Nemo," Sul said as he helped Ben steady, "Please have Cook prepare red snapper for tonight."

"Yes, Captain."

"I trust that red snapper will be acceptable, Professor... Ben." Sul turned his attention again to Ben, who was still standing by the bed and taking in the surroundings. "Take your time. No hurry."

"Thank you," Ben mumbled, struggling to adjust. His thoughts were slowly organizing themselves. "Yes. Fish sounds good."

"Nemo will guide you to the upper deck, when dinner is ready."

"Who's Nemo?"

"Oh, I'm sorry. Nemo is our family's augmented intelligence agent – and my first mate on the ship as well." Sul's eyes smiled, "I'll leave you to get ready. Will you be OK on your own?"

Ben shuffled a few more steps, balancing himself with a hand on the wall. "Yes, thank you."

"Good, about an hour until dinner, then. See you on the main deck." Sul turned, stepped into the corridor, and the door clicked shut behind him.

Ben willed strength into his limbs and took some more steps, still touching the wall. Each step more confident than the last. He paced around the room a few times, practising. He walked near the door, it slid open. *Not locked. I'm not trapped in here.*

He then shuffled across the soft wool carpet into the bathroom.

Another ceiling-to-floor window opening onto the sea lit one side of the room. A moon jellyfish, with four rings in its pulsating translucent body, drifted by the window, giving an indication of *Ossë*'s speed. *What is this place?*

"Sorry to intrude, Professor." Ben stopped, startled, and looked around. "I didn't mean to surprise you. I'm Nemo, the family Augmented Intelligence Agent that Captain Sul referred to," continued the pleasantly modulated voice, evoking the image of an English butler. "Just wanting you to know that these are one-way windows. Your modesty is preserved."

"Nemo, where are you?"

"I'm in the circuits of *Ossë*, Professor. I am an algorithm."

"Oh, right, of course. Well, thanks for the information."

"My pleasure, Professor. The captain has assigned me to answer your queries."

Satisfied that he was alone in the room, Ben stripped and stepped into the shower. The deluge of warm water refreshed him. As he bathed, sharp pains prompted him to inspect his body. Someone had stitched wounds closed in several places. On his temple. On his right side. One near the femoral artery in his leg.

"Nemo, who treated my wounds?"

"Dr Sul, the captain of this ship, has treated you, Professor. He was trained at Cambridge."

Ben examined the neat stitches. "Nice work. So, the captain is a doctor too?"

"Yes. Dr Battuta has extensive experience in emergency health care. Four years in the emergency unit at Gleneagles Hospital, Singapore, and six years as a medical officer during the Dependency Wars on the Horn of Africa."

"Impressive credentials. And his name is Sul Battuta, is it?"

"Yes, Professor. His full name is Captain Suliman bin Hassan bin Ibrahim Battuta."

"Suliman bin Hassan? Sounds like he's from the Middle East somewhere."

"Yes, Professor, Captain Sul is of Yemeni Bedouin descent. His grandfather took on a new name when he decided to build his life, and those of the generations to come, on the ocean. He adopted the name Battuta, after a well-known explorer of the fourteenth century."

"Yemen, now part of the New Caliphate, right?" A part of Ben tensed.

"Yes, Professor. Captain Sul's ancestors left the area before Yemen joined the New Caliphate. Would you like to hear more about the Caliphate, then?"

"No thanks, Nemo, I know enough about them." There was a moment of silence as Ben revelled in the cascade of fresh water. A thought struck him, "Is Captain Sul part of the New Caliphate?"

"No, Professor." Ben relaxed at this and considered what information he most needed to learn in this strange situation.

"Nemo, what can you tell me about this ship?"

"You are on the seastead vessel, *Ossë*. This is an Immersed Mono-hull design, displacing 3,450 tons, with a flying deck bridge. It was manufactured from seacrete grown over a graphene composite matrix."

"Hmm," Ben said, turning off the spray. "That's a bit over my head. Can you put that in simple terms?"

"Sorry, Professor." A slight pause. "I gather from your background you might have no experience with the Pelagic Territories or its residents."

"You see from my background? Do you have intelligence files about me?"

"No, Professor. Just public domain records."

"Where did the captain find me, Nemo?"

"You were rescued from Îlot Brosse, an island near New Caledonia."

"Îlot Brosse?" He stopped, staring at the blue vastness beyond the window as he readied himself for the next, more important question.

"Why did they rescue me, Nemo?"

"I'm sorry Professor, I must defer to Captain Sul. He'll answer that question when you dine with him."

"OK." Ben pondered this response. *Is it a complicated answer?* He changed tack, "Nemo, where are we now?"

"*Ossë* is at about 35 degrees south latitude and 172 degrees west longitude. About 900 miles south-south-west of Tonga and 780 miles north-west of Auckland, New Zealand. We're currently on a heading of 111 degrees true, travelling at 8.5 knots."

"So, it seems we're in the middle of nowhere, then?"

"Not literally nowhere, Professor, but I understand the idiom. On our current course, the nearest static habitation is a sea farming community built around a seamount: the Marcelli Township complex, 180 nautical miles south-south-west."

"I've heard of the Pelagic Territories, but you're right, I don't know much. Please fill me in. Actually, give me a basic overview of the Pelagic Territories." Ben lathered his hair.

"The Pelagic Territories is the name given to settlements in international seas, outside the territorial waters of continental nations. Over this last generation, local self-governing townships and nomadic communities have formed. Now they are making alliances, building territory-wide civil governments, resulting in the current Pelagic Territories. There is a loose confederacy between these territories. This confederacy has begun negotiating with terrestrial powers for recognition as nations in their own right. Currently, we're in the South Pacific Pelagic Territory."

"Ah yes. I read about those talks between terrestrial and Pelagic communities over the past fifteen or so years, whether these territories should become nations."

"Yes, those negotiations are ongoing. However, as you are probably aware, people have been establishing homesteads in the open ocean seasteading for at least forty years."

"For that long? Wow," came Ben's voice, distorted under the shower spray again. "And back to my earlier question, tell me again about this ship?"

"You are currently in the submerged living quarters of *Ossë.*"

"*Ossë* sounds Norwegian."

"Very good, Professor. It is at least Scandinavian. It's a name borrowed from a Tolkien tale, a favourite of the Captain's. According to Tolkien, in his book, *Silmarillion, Ossë* rules over storms on the sea."

"A fan of Tolkien? Interesting. So why do I not feel like I am on a boat, Nemo?"

"Because you are presently under the ocean. The bridge and deck are suspended above us via connecting columns. Waves pass between the underwater and above-water sections, which can be raised and lowered with buoyancy tanks to allow for varying sea conditions. No part of this vessel rests on the surface of the sea. This allows the whole vessel to remain stable."

"Interesting. Who else is on this boat?"

"This boat contains the Battuta family and a few staff."

"The Battuta family?"

"That would be Captain Sul and his two children, Gideon and Sophia."

"No Mrs Battuta?"

"Tragically, Suliman's wife died three years ago."

"I'm sorry to hear that. Must have been a great loss."

"Yes, it has affected the captain and his children very much. However, they are journeying through the grief process and adjusting."

"I can understand that. Are they on their own out here in the open sea?"

"The Battuta family travel as part of a nomadic community, which they call a Pod. They are seasteaders constantly travelling the South Pacific Gyre. This Pod is one of many in the emerging South Pacific Pelagic Territory."

"Wait. A Pod?"

"Yes, Professor. A wry allusion to dolphin and whale pods. Marine mammals travelling as extended family units. The Battutas travel with other families related to them. They are a nomadic clan."

"Fascinating. So, how do they earn their living? What do they do in this Pod?" Ben asked, lathering his body.

"*Ossë* is one of twelve vessels in this Pod, ranching tuna fish, species *Thunnus maccoyii*, while also engaging in other marine-based enterprises."

"They herd tuna?"

"Yes, they manage schools of tuna while following the currents in the Southern Pacific Gyre. This herding community is known as the *Arraa'i* Pod."

"*Arraa'i*. I know a bit of Arabic, that sounds like the word for goat or camel-herder."

"Yes, Professor, correct."

"Nomadic tuna herders, ranching southern bluefin tuna?" Ben reflected on this novel concept. "Supplying tuna for which markets?" Ben turned off the water, grabbed a towel and began drying his hair vigorously.

"They market to all the terrestrial nations of the South Pacific."

Stepping from the shower, Ben towelled himself off. He patted gingerly around the stitches, cuts, and scrapes.

Ben stepped back into the bedroom and took clothes from the closet. "Nemo, these clothes fit well," he observed, dressing.

"The captain asked me to take your measurements as you slept, Professor, via sensors in the bedroom. Clothes were made to your size."

"You were thorough, thank you." Ben looked at himself in the mirror. A gaunt face looked back with bloodshot eyes. Fine stitches ran down one cheek, a few scrapes were in the healing process. *You've seen better days*, he mused.

Moving towards the door, he said, "Please direct me to the dining room."

"Certainly, Professor. Turn right as you exit. Follow the passageway about thirty feet to a lift. That will take you to the bridge, which in turn opens to the deck. The table has been set this evening on the main deck behind the bridge. Captain Sul is waiting for you."

Ben stepped into the passageway. A child's face peered at him from the corner of a doorway across the hall, then quickly pulled back into the room.

He paused, puzzled, then continued following Nemo's instructions. "Who was that, Nemo?" he asked, seeing if Nemo was still tracking with him.

"Sophia, the captain's daughter. She's very shy."

"And curious," Ben said remembering the small hand that woke him. Ahead stood a small lift, door ajar. He stepped inside and was whisked upwards.

*

The lift door opened and Ben stepped into a small room he recognized as the bridge. The walls were lined with shifting images, a wide semicircle of holographs, and a set of panels displaying a complex array of images and figures. Windows above the panels looked out over the sea. He could hear the soft, rhythmic murmur of the vessel cutting through the waves below, but he felt airborne. This part of *Ossë* seemed to be suspended several metres off the ocean.

Stepping around the lift pillar, he entered an open deck. The fresh sea breeze and salty tang were invigorating.

He spotted Captain Sul seated at a small table in the centre of the deck. Sul rose and approached to shake his hand. "Welcome again, Professor… Ben. Please join me for dinner."

"Thank you, Captain. A beautiful evening." Ben admired the vista around them; placid seas under drifting clouds, which were shifting from grey to a flaming red. It was late afternoon, just before sunset.

He turned his gaze towards the captain, who was also taking in the view. *Could be in his late forties?* Sul's hair was receding, greying at the temples. He had a strong brow above sparkling dark eyes. A full salt and pepper beard framed his face.

Sul seemed to notice Ben's scrutiny. With a smile he recited verses in what sounded like Farsi.

Ben tilted his head, unable to make sense of the words.

"Those are words of the Persian poet, Rumi," Sul explained. "He was an early Islamic mystic who was enthralled with God's love for him. In English, you might say:

"On a day when the wind is perfect, the sail just needs to open and the world is full of beauty."

"Hmm. Appropriate." The sun now rested on the edge of the horizon.

"Yes. In these latitudes, the weather can be very pleasant. Perfect tonight for dinner on the main deck." They sat down at the table, already set with salad, freshly baked bread, and cheese.

A bell sounded and Sul walked over to open a nearby dumb waiter. He set plates of roasted fish on the table. "Ben, this red snapper was harvested today from the farms at Marcelli Rise and prepared, Yemeni style, in a clay oven. I thought something light would be a good first meal for you."

"Thank you, you're very kind."

"I hope you don't mind, I'd like to offer a word of thanks before we eat." Sul lifted his hands, palms upward, thanking God for the beauty of the day and the gifts of family and friends.

Ben observed quietly, I do indeed feel grateful to be alive.

Sul moved to fill their glasses with wine, but Ben put his hand over his glass.

"Sorry, I am a recovering alcoholic. I'll have to pass."

Sul withdrew the wine glasses and bottle, stowing them in the dumb waiter. "Apologies, Professor. I didn't know."

"No apologies necessary," Ben smiled, and he warmed to this man, so he disclosed a little more. "I've had to live with the consequences of my poor choices. So now I live with the fact that I'll always be at risk of returning to alcoholism. Best not to tempt resolve."

"Of course, Ben. Forgive me."

Sul shook out his napkin and took the first bite, to encourage his guest to begin eating.

They savoured the food for a few minutes in silence. Then Sul directed his voice away from the table, "Nemo, update on the children, please."

"Yes, Captain. At five, Sophia dined on sashimi, sea salad, and rice. She's currently in the holo-suite studying today's telemetry from sensors shadowing moon jellyfish. Gideon hasn't dined yet. He's out testing his latest model of *Kestrel*."

"Thank you, Nemo."

Ben stopped eating for a moment, curious about his host, "You have two children, Captain?"

Sul smiled, "Yes, Ben. Normally my two children dine with me. However, I arranged to dine just with you tonight, to make sure all is well with you. I thought you might have some questions about your rescue."

"Indeed, I do, Captain. Please tell me about your children first."

"I'd be delighted. My Sophia is nine. Her passion is for all things that live in the sea. Plus, she has a genius for marine robotics."

"I met her already, and saw her below on my way here. She ducked behind a door."

"Yes, she is shy; she's autistic. She's also curious about visitors. I hope she didn't bother you."

"No, no bother."

"And then, Gideon is my twenty-two-year-old son. One of his passions is designing amphibious craft; ones able to operate in both sea and air. Another passion at present is his girlfriend, Sally Marcelli."

Sul paused. "In fact, tonight Gideon will be dining with her at the Marcelli family home in Marcelli Deep. We're just 175 nautical miles away from the Marcelli Township."

"Ah yes, Nemo mentioned the Marcelli Township to me, though I am a bit confused. What's Marcelli Deep? I've heard in the past about something called the Marcelli Ring. Are they all related?"

Yes, they are." Sul looked at Ben, "I can see why you are confused, since they all bear the name 'Marcelli'. They are located along a submarine ridge. The Marcelli Township is made up of three different areas: the Ring, the Rise, and the Deep. Marcelli Ring is the main town, built in a ring around a seamount. About forty nautical miles south-east from the Ring is Marcelli Rise. The Rise is the mariculture section of the Township where seafood for local consumption and export is grown. Our snapper came from there. The third area is in the waters between the Ring and the Rise, Marcelli Deep, the industrial park of the Township, where light industry and services are based. Placing these activities in the Deep keeps them from affecting the relatively sensitive ecosystems of the marine park in the centre of the Ring and the mariculture farms of the Rise."

"Thanks. I can almost visualize it." This description reminded Ben of something he'd heard before. "In fact, I might've met someone from Marcelli a few years back."

They both ate in silence for a while before Ben ventured the next topic. "Sounds like you have fine children, Captain. Nemo mentioned that you recently lost your wife. I'm so sorry."

A shadow of sadness passed across Sul's face. "Yes, three years ago. An abiding grief. And yet, somehow, life moves on."

Ben was silent for a few moments, gazing out at the sea. "I lost my wife and son, twelve years ago. I understand a bit about grief. If you don't mind me asking, how did your wife die, Captain?"

Their eyes met. "Well, Ben," Sul began, "my wife died in a freak accident during a storm. Sarah had gone onto deck to secure our equipment. There was a lull in the storm, so she thought it was safe enough to venture out without a harness and line, but a rogue wave swept her overboard. It took us hours to find her body."

Sul's eyes softened as he passed the question back, "Tell me about what happened to your wife and son, Ben. We who grieve find solace in talking with others who have walked similar paths."

Ben's lips stiffened as the familiar wave of grief welled inside him. *The surge of pain is less, but still there.* He turned his eyes back to the horizon. "You're right. It's good to talk about it." He took a deep breath and continued in sombre tones. "While I was on a military tour in Africa, our house was burgled. My wife and son were both brutally murdered."

A stricken look flashed across Sul's face. "That's horrible, Ben. My heart goes out to you."

Ben continued quietly, "During my tour, everyone in my unit was killed, and I was kidnapped by agents from the New Caliphate. Apparently, the New Caliphate was also involved with my wife and son's murders. And, the New Caliphate may have been behind this incident you saved me from."

Sul carefully put his fork down and looked at Ben. "That is very disturbing news, Ben. Our Pod also has a history of conflict with the New Caliphate. If they were behind your abduction, then this is a very serious development. Let me think on this a bit. But, please tell me more about yourself. Losing your unit, then your family in rapid succession, a catastrophic blow. And yet you survived."

"It almost destroyed me," Ben admitted soberly, "I tried to track down their murderers, but failed. Losing that hope, and closure, I began to numb my grief with alcohol. My life was spinning out of control. I thought the numbness would provide a refuge, but that was a terrible strategy, with lingering consequences."

Ben focused on a star emerging in the darkening blue of the evening as he finished up his meal. Wiping his mouth with the napkin, he finally continued, "It's taken me years to work through my grief. Many people have helped me. I sit before you, alive and healing, because of them."

Silence framed his words.

Sul broke the spell, "Remarkable. Wise words, Ben. May I ask, are you a man of faith?"

Ben glanced at his host, "I would call myself a man of little but growing faith. Until recently, I have had little reason to trust in powers outside myself. Some people with stronger faith in higher powers have helped me step out of my private darkness and see the world of light again."

"Faith can be contagious. My community here helped me in a similar way after my wife's tragic passing."

"I'm grateful that now I am learning to draw strength and faith from the memories of my wife and son."

"Wisdom is sometimes drawn from deep and dark wells," Sul said quietly.

"Rumi also said," Sul's voice rose as he began to chant.

> **"Don't run away from grief, O soul.**
> **Look for the remedy inside the pain.**
> **Because the rose came from the thorn**
> **and the ruby came from a stone."**

"Beautiful words. May they come true for both of us." Ben watched clouds drifting in ephemeral grace through the azure vault of the sky. The moment was etched in his mind as he reflected on the common ground he had with this man who was otherwise a stranger to him.

Sul pushed his finished plate to the side and offered the bowl of fruit to his guest. "Nemo tells me you have been asking him questions," he suggested.

Ben chose a tangerine and began to peel it. "Yes, Nemo has been helping me understand about you, your boat, your nomadic community. However, he told me to ask you personally about my rescue."

Sul smiled. "Yes. I wanted to explain that to you, Ben, face to face."

"I see."

"It seems we have a mutual friend, Ben. Do you know Paul Whitestone?"

Ben started at this name and his anxiety retreated. "Yes, Paul has been like a mentor to me."

"Well, Paul is an old friend of mine. He contacted me about a week ago, convinced that you were in trouble. Apparently, you had gone missing from an event in Singapore."

"Yes, I was speaking at a scientific symposium."

"Since our Pod was near the area he suspected you to be in, he asked if we could join in the search. Thankfully, we did find you."

"Wow." Ben's mind raced, searching for words. "How did Paul know I was in trouble? That man seems to have access to things beyond himself."

"Yes, we've experienced his unique prophetic gifts many times." Sul studied Ben. "It sounds like you might have heard one of his words of insight before."

"Yes, I did, in fact. He intervened in my life in a dramatic way when I first met him."

"His words of insight are almost always dramatic. So, Ben, who do you suspect kidnapped you? And why?"

That word kidnap suddenly evoked a tumult of memories. In a flash, Ben relived the trauma of the capture and escape. His heart beat thunderously in his chest, and his fists involuntarily clenched. He took a deep breath, willing his mind to return to the present, safe now. He ate another tangerine one section at a time, allowing his emotions to settle.

"I've been asking myself that, who and why? It might connect with the answers I've been searching for over the past twelve years. Perhaps something to do with my wife's research on seismic modelling. You see, my wife had a device which could only be decrypted with our biometrics, either hers or mine. Right now, the best motive I can figure out is that someone, maybe from the New Caliphate, wants to access that data. I have no idea what they want with it, although I did talk to my wife's professor who told me some chilling ideas of how the data could be weaponized."

Sul sat back, pondering, as Ben continued.

"The last thing I remember was preparing for my seminar at the Fusion Symposium in Singapore. I was at the Raffles Hotel restaurant, enjoying Thai food and a lemonade. I suspect that someone drugged my food or drink, because I awoke trussed up in a dark locker in a boat, en route to who knows where."

"Well, the good thing is, your captors failed. You escaped. We found you. Now you're safe within the Pod."

"Yes, I'm very grateful to you, Captain." Ben collected his thoughts, breathed deeply and changed the subject. "You called me 'Professor' and seem to know a lot about me. How do you know who I am, Captain?"

"As I said, Ben, our paths are only crossing due to our mutual friend, Paul. He filled me in a bit. However, I've heard about your work independently, Professor. I too follow the development of fusion science. I believe your research into harnessing the sun's energy via cold fusion, by deflecting muons into deuterium and tritium Cheng matrices may benefit the whole world. Especially if we're able to utilize natural background radiation sources of muons."

"I'm impressed. Not many people follow such arcane science."

"I'm an enthusiast of energy research. *Ossë* is powered by an Alchemist IV reactor, a carbon-nitrogen transmuter, which is much more efficient than the old nickel-copper models. What led you to study particle physics and fusion?"

Ben warmed to this man; he seemed genuinely interested. "I was living in the rehabilitation community Paul works with, recovering from alcoholism. The people in the community noticed my qualifications in engineering and began giving me responsibilities over things like agri-bots, then the community power plant. These activities fanned into flame interests which had lain dormant for years. At one point, Paul suggested I pursue a PhD in physics, and recommended me to Caltech. I jumped at the chance. Eventually, my study of muons led me to some novel avenues for research, which my professors invited me to pursue."

"Impressive, Ben. Well done! And now you've become a leader in that field."

"Well, many things had to fall in place. It feels like a series of coincidences, really."

"I don't believe in coincidences," Sul said simply.

Ben laughed, "You sound like Paul."

Coffee arrived, steaming, via the dumb waiter. Sul moved it to the table, and they continued their conversation as they enjoyed bittersweet sips. Ben shifted the subject.

"So, please tell me more, Captain. What do you know about my captors?"

"My best guess was also that they are agents of the New Caliphate. My Bedouin ancestors came from what was once Yemen, now part of the New Caliphate. I still have many family connections there. However, the Caliphate consider my clan who form this Pod to be traitors and apostates. They have been harassing us for several generations. But that's a tale for another day. I've kept you from your rest too long already. You're still weak."

Ben laughed, "Yes, Doctor. You're right. Even this little bit of activity has tired me. I think I'll go grab a good night's rest."

"Good." The two men stood and shook hands. "Can you find you way back?"

Ben nodded, "Yes, I think so. If I get lost, Nemo can straighten me out." He walked back to the bridge and the lift to his quarters below. The conversation with Sul had stirred up old memories and emotions.

CHAPTER NINE

11 March 2057, Redondo Beach, California
(nine years earlier)

Ben's eyes drifted across the bluffs to a patch of beach two hundred metres south of the pier. The air was still cool, the clouds muted the scene in shades of grey. Last night's rainstorm had disrupted the normal crowd of joggers' and surfers' morning routines. The beach was empty.

There. Ben focused on the shore below the cliffs. *That's where we last were together as a family. Only three years ago.* His gaze drifted out beyond the surf line. How strange: the sand dollar colony is still there. As if nothing has happened. His heart wrenched remembering Sammy's excitement that day.

Turning away, Ben wandered up through a small park next to the pier. That vision, or whatever it was, next to the dumpster in Ajo had changed him. The loss of Lisa and Sammy no longer overwhelmed him; the black despairing grief was giving way to acceptance. Even a kind of peace. Paul had been right. Ben walked for hours, weaving through familiar streets in the neighbourhood. Every corner and vista held a memory. He found Catalina Drive.

Walking down his street, he stood in front of their house. It was boarded up, fire damage still evident three years after the attack.

He paused before inserting the key into the front door. *The last time I stepped out this door, my life ended.*

He shrugged off the thought and opened the door, stepping into the entryway. *Still smells like smoke.*

Flyers and letters from real estate agents had piled up below the mail slot. He kicked the mail out of the way.

He wandered. Memories, like ghosts, inhabited every charred room. The kitchen broom closet: Sammy and I hid there to surprise Lisa for her birthday. The living room: I held Lisa on that sofa as we wept over the miscarriage of our first child. The hallway: Darting in and out of rooms during Nerf gun battles, Sammy's clever water balloon prank that drenched Lisa.

He opened the door at the end of the hall. Sammy's room, still cluttered with all the accumulated treasures of a six-year old. This room had not been damaged much by the fire. *Sammy could just be at school, except for the dust. And smell of smoke.*

One last door to open. He hesitated, reluctant. The master bedroom. He turned the handle and entered. He was overwhelmed by the bloodstains on the carpet. His legs crumpled and he fell onto the bed. Once again, he wept for his family.

*

He collected a few electronic memory cubes containing pictures and movies of their years together, along with the few undamaged wall photos. *Lisa. Sammy.*

As he glanced at one of the devices in his hand, words of a conversation floated to the surface of his mind. He remembered the day at the beach... and afterward. Lisa was securing her data with a biometric encryption package ordered by Homeland Security. *We'll encrypt it with both my biometrics and yours, Ben,* she'd insisted, *as a safeguard.*

The device's sensors had scanned my face, irises, vein patterns of my hands, and fingerprints. At the time, it had all seemed so unnecessary. "But honey, the data is just geological. Why do we need such intense security measures?" He remembered the conversation.

He searched the drawers, floor, and every inch of the room, even though he knew the university staff and government agents had done the same after the fire. Following Lisa's death, the university had eventually asked him about the missing device, but at the time he assumed it had been destroyed in the fire.

The face of the man who had taunted him in the jail flashed before him again. His mind connected the dots. *With Lisa gone, only my biometric profile can open the encrypted data. Is this why they hunt me?*

He spent another hour searching the house, any place Lisa might think to hide something. Nothing, not even a glob of melted plastic to show it had been burnt in the fire. Nothing. He stood for a moment in the living room. Shadows lengthened outside.

He lingered in the moment, and a spontaneous prayer of gratitude rose in him: *Thank you for those years with Lisa and Sammy.* Ben wasn't sure if anyone was listening – although he knew Paul was convinced someone was. Still, it was heartfelt and gave him some sort of closure.

Finally, he said goodbye to what was once their home but now was just an empty shell of a house. On the way out, he reached down, retrieved a real estate flyer from the doormat, and slipped it into his pocket. It was time to sell the house, it no longer held ghosts.

11 March 2057, University of California Los Angeles
(the same day)

Ben passed through the quad and between several campus buildings until he found the entrance to the Geology department. He'd been here only once before, more than a dozen years ago when Lisa had been accepted into the degree programme. He studied the list of names inside the door. *There it was. Professor R. Hakim, Room 318.*

That morning, he'd had breakfast with Stew, in that restaurant out on the pier. They had laughed and bantered, easy with each other again. Ben was grateful to have his friend back. Stew had listened to Ben's suspicions about Lisa's data device and had suggested he visit his wife's professor. Stew was being considered for promotion to detective. Ben understood why.

Ben rode the elevator to the third floor and approached Room 318. The green sign on the door indicated that Professor Hakim was available. Ben opened the door.

Dark flowing hair with a few streaks of grey, in her early forties and the kind of woman who seemed to age well. She looked up from her desk, "Yes?"

"Professor Hakim, my name is Ben Holden."

"Ben Holden, Dr Lisa Holden's husband?" Ben nodded. The woman got up, walked around the desk and shook Ben's hand.

"What a long time it has been, Mr Holden. I am so very sorry for your loss; and ours as well. Your wife was one of the brightest students I've had. Her work with the data from the seismic monitors was promising, even revolutionary."

"Take a seat." She waved to a chair and sat in another one facing Ben. Ben pulled out a pad of paper and pen.

"Such a puzzling tragedy. Were her murderers ever brought to justice"

"No, Professor. That case has been closed and unsolved for years. That is why I've come to see you."

The professor brightened, "How can I help?"

"Do you know what happened to that data device containing Lisa's algorithm?"

Professor Hakim leaned forward, "No, I assumed it was destroyed in the fire. Do you think it still exists? We would love to get our hands on that. Lisa had a breakthrough in her algorithm that day, I remember. Indications were that this new version could give a whole new level of resolution and insight to plate dynamics."

"I'm investigating whether the device was destroyed in the fire or not. Lisa told me that the government required her to increase the encryption on the device. Do you have any idea why that was needed?"

Professor Hakim leaned back. "The data, and especially Dr Holden's algorithm, would provide the most detailed mapping of active faults in the North American continent. I actually requested that the project be classified until we understood the implications better."

"Was there a reason for that?"

Professor Hakim looked at Ben for a moment, as if deciding what to say. "At the last geological conference Dr Holden and I attended, special interest was shown in her project by a scientist from the New Caliphate. Call it a hunch, but he seemed too interested. As a precaution, I requested the classification."

"Do you remember his name?"

"No, sorry…" A thought crossed her mind, "You don't think…"

"I don't know, but it is a helpful bit of information." Ben wrote a few things on his pad and said under his breath, "New Caliphate. That might explain some things."

Ben looked back up at the professor. "You mentioned the implications of Lisa's research, would you mind telling me your concern?"

The professor looked out the window. "Such a detailed model of North American faults, extending down deeper into the earth than we've ever seen before…"

"If someone strategically placed an explosive charge…" Ben offered.

"No, a common scenario in the movies, but in reality, even a nuclear weapon would unlikely set off more than a local quake."

She thought in silence for a moment. "During the years of fracking for oil, the technique was correlated with multiple small quakes in the vicinity of fracking activity. I believe the theory was in pumping in large quantities of water as required in the process, it acted as a lubricant, and released the tension along fault lines. Theoretically, if a super-lubricant were pumped into areas of high stress along major faults, one could trigger a major earthquake, maybe even a cascade of quakes. Your wife's data would, again theoretically, give the clearest picture yet of where these high stress areas were and how to access them."

Ben was taking notes furiously while his thoughts put the facts together.

CHAPTER TEN

29 April 2066, Seastead vessel *Ossë*, off the coast of Chile
(nine years later)

In the southern hemisphere, the cold Humboldt current slid quietly up the coast of Chile and Peru. The winds blowing up the coast, along with the earth's rotation, contrived to drive the surface waters away from shore and out into the Pacific Ocean.

As the surface waters moved offshore into the open seas, they were replaced by cold, nutrient-rich waters upwelling from the dark depths. Phytoplankton bloomed abundantly in this swell of nourishment. This, in turn, attracted swarms of anchovies with gaping mouths to gorge themselves on the bounty.

Schools of tuna waited, biding their time in the depths. These cheetahs of the sea had crossed an ocean seeking opportunities like this. Now the predators darted in, slashing through the school of fattening baitfish. Terror sent the anchovy shoal to draw tightly together, then flash and wheel as one in their instinctive but futile defence.

As the anchovy fought for survival, from a distance, a pod of dolphins sensed their struggle and changed course to join in the feast. Circling the shoal of anchovy, the dolphins blew fences of air bubbles to cause the bait ball to tighten.

Above the waves, sea gannets screamed and dropped from the sky, diving several metres into the sea to snatch their share of the meal. An ever-increasing crowd of predators charged the swirling shoal of fish.

One tuna swerved away from the pandemonium to pursue a tantalizing anchovy. However, despite the tuna's speed, the small prey easily stayed ahead, luring its predator away from the bait ball.

Several other small fish now flashed alongside the tuna, forming an unusual pattern: above, below, to each side and behind. They changed direction suddenly and nimbly, shadowing the tuna movements and staying in perfect formation. Intimidated, the tuna broke off the chase, flicking back towards the feast.

The small robotic anchovy then moved closer together and returned to the seastead ship, *Ossë*.

*

On *Ossë*, nine-year-old Sophia Battuta climbed down the short staircase into a darkened room. Clothed in a loose-fitting, flowery, one-piece suit, her long dark curls bounced around her olive-skinned face. The studio was filled with the hum of machinery and subtle gurgle of water flowing across the ship's outer shell.

"Silence, Nemo," she requested.

"Ask politely, Sophia."

"Silence, *please*, Nemo," she repeated in a gentler tone. All external sound was quenched; the silence cloaked her, and she sighed with relief.

"Holo-interface."

Noticing no response, she added, "*Please?*"

"Well done, Sophia. Even augmented intelligence agents function better with a bit of politeness."

As she lowered herself to sit cross-legged on the floor, a pool of light congealed in front of her. "Load bait fish number four… *please.*" The image appeared within the light: a southern tuna swimming strongly, jinking right and left, but staying in the centre of the light pool. She leaned towards the image, transfixed.

"Slower, please, Nemo." The image moved more slowly. The same swim segment, recently recorded by Sophia's robotic anchovies, now repeated in an endless loop. "Show muscles, please," she whispered.

The tuna image was stripped of skin. Waves of electrical impulses visibly rippled from the brain of the tuna to the muscle groups and synchronized with the swimming movements.

"Now, bones, Nemo." Muscles faded, then the organs, and the skeleton of the tuna now swam before her, looping repeatedly in the light pool.

"Slower?" a pause. "*Please.*"

The image slowed; movement was barely perceptible. Sophia gazed intently as the sequence replayed, over and over. Then she stood to walk around the holo-display, examining it from different angles. After fifteen minutes she sat again and whispered, "Layers."

Now, with each sequence of the loop, a layer of muscle and associated firing of neurons was added, until the complete tuna again swam before her in exaggerated slowness.

"Layers, again, please."

An hour passed, the relayering was repeated over and over. Sophia blinked, lifting her gaze. "Stop, please, Nemo."

The ghostly tuna froze before her, whole again in its skin.

"Interface, Nemo." She waited in silence, then said, "Please."

"What kind of interface would you prefer, *Ameera*?"

"Palette." Another pool of light appeared next to her on the floor.

"Match bones." The first tuna appeared as a skeleton in the new holosphere. A range of labelled icons, various substances, appeared below the new skeleton. Sophia chose "aluminium ceramic composite" by dragging the icon over to the skeleton. The colours and texture of the holographic bones morphed to emulate the composite.

By wiggling her fingers at the original image of the live tuna, she initiated the looping action sequence again. Scooping the ghostly copy with her hand, she set it alongside the original tuna image and wiggled the fingers of both hands in unison. The two fish now swam a spectral, synchronous dance together. They looked similar, however Sophia discerned that they did not yet move exactly alike.

"Magnify, *please*."

"Very good, Sophia."

Concentrating, Sophia adjusted the bones in the composite copy until its movements aligned with the original.

Meticulously, through each cycle and layer, she chose and placed materials from the palette. She created muscles and their electrical connections. Sensors for eyes and lateral lines. Skin, gills, scales, and fins, all matching the form and movement of the original. She then configured a small computer interface to run the new model. Two hours had passed.

"Sophia, your father says it's time for dinner. Tomorrow you have an early appointment with *Eima* Fatima."

Sophia seemed to ignore the comment, still engrossed in her creation. "It's time to stop," Nemo coaxed softly.

Both tuna images stopped moving. Sophia sighed and rose, waving her hand over the two light pools. They faded into darkness.

"Ready for food, *please*."

"Yes, *Ameera*, it's in the dining room," Nemo reminded her.

Sophia padded down the corridor to a room with a large window that looked out at an underwater vista. A small plate of sashimi, rice, and pickled seaweed salad was softly spotlighted on a table. Pulling over a chair, she ate, one thoughtful mouthful at a time, while gazing out of the artificial sapphire window to the deep indigo beyond; she watched the patterned ripples of the surface gliding a few metres above her.

Her brother, Gideon, peeked in. "You OK, Soph?"

She nodded, without turning towards him.

"Love you, *'ukhti*! Meet you for breakfast tomorrow!" he called as he left.

Sophia smiled.

Ossë shifted course, and the moon came into view, shining full in a cloudless sky, a rippling image through the seawater. Shafts of silver moonbeams danced through the infinite blue before her. Phosphorescent plankton flashed as they struck the windowpane, like sparks of creation passing through the primal void.

Sophia finished her meal, rose, and padded down the corridor to her quarters. Lights faded behind her as she moved down the hallway towards her bedroom, until only a ghostly blue, shimmering sea light was left in the abandoned passage.

"Tomorrow, you'll be at *Eima* Fatima's, *Ameera*. She'll review your projects and hear about your goals, what you'd like to do next week."

Sophia stopped and looked upwards. "Tell her thank you, Nemo. I love Aunty Fatima."

"I'll tell her in the morning when she awakes."

Sophia crawled into bed and pulled up the blankets. A few moments later, her father, Suliman, came to tuck her in. She hugged his neck, then snuggled back under the blankets. Suliman smoothed her hair and kissed her on the forehead. He said a quiet Arabic prayer over her. "Love you, *Baba*!" she whispered afterwards.

"You are my most precious fish in the sea, *Ameera*." Sophia giggled. "Sleep well."

The lights flickered out as Suliman left. Sophia heard Nemo speak to her father as he left, "Captain, Paul Whitehouse wanted to inform you he has taken on a role as consultant of the Pacific Rim Council and would like to set up a meeting with you tomorrow…"

Their voices faded down the corridor.

The silvery surface of the sea glided silently outside the window.

"Now," Sophia whispered, "Nemo, tell me a true story. *Please*."

"*Ameera*, we're cruising in an area where the Pacific, Nazca and Antarctic tectonic plates join as one, deep under the sea. Remember the sensors you placed last year around the active black smoker about 2,600 metres deep?"

Sophia nodded.

"Telemetry data from those sensors shows me that hundreds of life forms are swarming around the vents of that subterranean volcano."

The child sighed and smiled, snuggling deeply under her bedcovers. Faint starlight filtered through the sea and glimmered across Sophia's peaceful features from the window above.

"I can see a forest of bearded worms around the hot vent, weaving in the rising current as they feed on the minerals and methane. There's a white Vulcan octopus stalking across a bed of mussels, which are teeming with ragworms. The octopus is creeping up on a white vent crab, which in turn is looking to snip a snack from the hoods of one of the red bearded tube worms. An eelpout cruises nearby, its tapered body hovers over the mussels. The octopus edges fluidly towards the worms. I see one arm slowly stretching towards the crab…"

Nemo's voice faded as slow rhythmic breathing from the bed announced a child in blissful unconsciousness.

CHAPTER ELEVEN

6 June 2066, Bosaso, Somali Emirates
(six weeks later)

Abdul Qawwi stood next to the flower-strewn coffin of Emir Abdul Ghafoor. Though only in his fifties and in good health, the leader of the Somali Emirates had died of a heart attack during Friday prayers. After the death had been confirmed, Abdul Qawwi had stepped in quickly, overseeing the bathing of the body and wrapping in the *kafan*, the funeral shroud.

The Caliph himself had requested that Abdul Qawwi lead the crowds of the faithful who came to pay their respects in the *janaazah* prayer, the funeral prayer for the dead. Abdul Qawwi stood at the head of the crowds in the courtyard around the Greater Bosaso Mosque and raised his voice to begin the ritual. He felt elated. *Allah, you have raised me up. Now I lead thousands to honour your servant. Allahu Akbar, you are greater.*

When he'd finished reciting the prayer, he escorted the casket to the burial site to be lowered into the ground facing the direction of the *qibla*, towards the sacred stone at Mecca, the *Ka'ba*. Abdul Qawwi sprinkled three handfuls of earth into the grave while reciting words of the Qur'an, "We created you from it, and return you into it, and from it we'll raise you a second time."

The gravediggers completed the burial as Abdul Qawwi led the last collective prayer for the dead. Afterwards, he stood attentive while the crowds dispersed, comforting and offering condolences. Then he escorted the Emir's family to waiting limousines, to show them honour.

As he helped the last family members into the cars, his hand furtively brushed against the device barely detectable, wrapped in a handkerchief, in the pocket under his robes. The data device of Lisa Holden. He smiled to himself. *The poison was undetected. Now at last I am rid of that weakling, who would never have carried out my plan.*

Secretly, at his bidding, agents had continued shadowing Ben ever since the last kidnapping attempt. *Now I'm free to make my move.* He would not repeat Abdul Ghafoor's mistakes. Abdul Qawwi suppressed a chuckle.

5 July 2066, Bosaso, Somali Emirates
(one month later)

A pearl-white airship, with sleek lines, pushed away from the terminal. Its tether lines pulled it along grooves in the tarmac. Arriving at the launching point, the ship slipped its moorings to sail into the bright desert sky. It climbed eastward over Bosaso, above the dramatically widening vista of the northern Somali coastline.

"Ladies and gentlemen, enjoy the verdant expanse below. Thirty years ago, this was just shifting sand, an empty desert." Emir Abdul Qawwi beamed at the impeccably dressed gathering of international dignitaries, who had been specially invited for the cruise. Abdul Qawwi's black hair was beginning to grey. He glanced around at his audience, seated comfortably in the dirigible's plush gondola. *Influencers of the nations.* Pride swelled within him as he looked beyond this gathering to the beautiful Somali landscape through the wide windows.

Abdul Qawwi gloried in this moment, casting his mind back a few years. He reflected on Emir Abdul Ghafoor; they had met when he was a mere vizier to the Caliph. Together they had partnered, all those years ago, to establish the Somali Emirate, rebuilding a destitute nation.

Abdul Ghafoor had been appointed Emir of Somalia by the Caliph, and in turn had appointed Abdul to be his chief vizier. For nine years, Abdul Qawwi had observed, and patiently manoeuvred, using his role to provide favours for powerful friends, cultivating their obligations towards him. He sponsored key projects, widening his access to the network of Emirati leaders. With the death of the Emir Abdul Ghafoor, Abdul Qawwi was able to finally realize his ambitions. The web of supporters he'd patiently groomed enabled him to defeat his opponents.

Just this month, the Caliph appointed him to be Emir of Somalia.

But for Abdul Qawwi, it was not enough to have this honoured status. *We must break the defiance of the infidel powers. We, the New Caliphate, must secure our destined place in the world.* The Allied West Europe, North and South America, Australia, Israel, and even traitors in the Gulf states still formed a ring of resistance, restricting the efforts of the Caliphate. To ensure that the truth of Islam finally spread to all nations, this resistance must be eroded, then crushed. *Abdul Ghafoor wasted too much time. We need to act now to release the power encrypted in the data device. I'll finally accomplish what I have been destined to do.*

Abdul Qawwi would use his new position to move his long-delayed plans forward quickly.

The moment of reverie past, Abdul Qawwi remembered his audience in the dirigible. He smoothly resumed the presentation. "That multi-layered band of forest and grassland along the coast is the result of years of patient geo-engineered transformation. Plant species suitable for this coastal habitat have been systematically introduced. Natural, ecological succession strategies have been put into play."

The French ambassador turned to him. "Excuse me, Emir. Please explain these ecological succession strategies."

"Thank you, a good question, Ambassador Jeume." Abdul Qawwi welcomed this opening to showcase the miraculous changes accomplished by the scientists of the Caliphate. "As you well know, the limiting factor in desert environments is water."

"Yes, of course," the ambassador nodded.

"With the development of modern fusion technology, the energy needed to desalinate seawater has become inexpensive and plentiful. Underground desalination plants have been installed all along the coast, supplying enough water to support progressive reforestation."

"And this progressive reforestation?"

"Yes, it begins with quick-growing species, local grasses. These grasses hold and condition the soil. Over time, we progressively introduce plants, shrubs, and then young trees. The desert is transformed into woodland, eventually becoming a mature forest. The spreading forestland in turn attracts many varieties of bird and animals, some formerly native to Somalia, some new. Out of this, a dynamic ecosystem evolves between plants and animals. The changing ecosystem attracts increased rainfall, so that after a few years there is less need for desalination. We then channel more of this fresh water to nearby cities and farms. The combination of a healthy environment and increased agriculture has allowed us to make significant steps towards self-sufficiency."

"Amazing, indeed." The French ambassador's words were echoed by many others onboard.

"Through these efforts the coastal ecology has become sustainable. The forestland will now continue to expand on its own, reversing desertification."

"Incredible!" There were murmurs through the gondola.

"Yes, Ambassador, distinguished guests, engineered ecological succession is only one skill of the New Caliphate."

"Now, if you'll all notice the lighter green band on the inland edge of the forest below us. This is new farmland. It has been expanding inland at a rate of a half a kilometre, or a quarter mile, each year."

The gondola filled with an appreciative buzz.

"*Alhamdulillah,* praise be to God for this miraculous transformation!" Abdul Qawwi continued, "We've come a long way as a nation. Can you believe that just forty years ago, northern Somalia was a failed state, caught in a downward spiral, the people were starving, corruption was rife, our economy and civil structures were in disarray."

Heads nodded. Many in the room remembered.

Abdul Qawwi waved to the window on the opposite side of the gondola. "Across the Gulf is the Homeland of the Faithful, known as *Watan al-Mu'miniin.* You have heard it referred to as the Heart of the New Caliphate, hub of more than a dozen satellite Emirate states.

"Somalia has received much financial and technical assistance from the Caliphate. Ten years ago, the Caliph formally invited Somalia to become a satellite Emirate, providing even more support. Brothers and sisters from the Caliphate migrated to the Somali Emirate and took key positions in government, finance, science, and education. With this intervention, the downward spiral was rapidly reversed. Corruption was rooted out, the Rule of Law was established, infrastructures were rebuilt. This increased stability attracted international business, which strengthened the economy. Many of you here have been part of these changes; international support has been a crucial factor in the rejuvenation of Somalia."

The dignitaries smiled as they looked around at each other.

"Where there had been despair, now there is a stable society. Somalis now have hope for a bright future and believe that this same hope should spread through the earth, the blessing of Islam."

Abdul Qawwi's thoughts drifted to recent news. Just last week, Indonesian security forces shut down one of the Caliphate's more promising cells in Jakarta. A month ago, the Kenyan defence ministry shut Caliphate-sponsored schools, based on information sent to them by infidel intelligence.

Nonetheless, my plan has finally been put in motion. Even while he was speaking to this crowd, it was being executed. Yunus Saleh has captured Ben Holden in Singapore;

even now the infidel is on his way here and I will soon have my hands on that crucial data.

His thoughts were interrupted by a young man approaching, whispering an urgent message in his ear.

Abdul Qawwi looked at his guests, "Excuse me, my friends, I must attend to an important matter. The Minister of the Interior will continue guiding your tour." Abdul Qawwi swept his eyes around the gondola, making eye contact with important dignitaries. Bowing deferentially, he directed their attention to his minister, who had come to stand behind him, also dressed in the flowing robes of his office.

"Thank you, Emir," said the young official, quickly adjusting his head covering and moving up to the podium. "The changes in Somalia over the past twenty years have been nothing short of extraordinary. I lived here in the city of Bosaso during the days of poverty…"

Abdul Qawwi made a quiet exit through doors at the rear of the gondola and followed the messenger through a short corridor.

His minister's words had evoked memories of his own. *I've come a long way from the slums of Mukalla.* Life had been chaotic in the coastal towns of Yemen when he was a child. His father had died during the al Qaeda insurgency. His mother had raised him and his brother. Then his dear brother, had died fighting in the conflicts. *He is now in paradise.*

Finally, after many countries in the Arab Peninsula, including Yemen, had become consolidated into the New Caliphate, stability and civil order returned.

With this advent of peace, Abdul Qawwi's mother found a permanent home for the family, allowing him to resume studies. He excelled at school. Village elders recognized his leadership potential, which was confirmed as he rose quickly through the ranks in Caliphate youth programmes.

He won a scholarship to the Sorbonne University in France and graduated with honours in geophysics. More importantly, during his university days he took a lead in local Muslim clubs, organizing Caliphate activities.

As a result, he was given a full scholarship to pursue a doctorate in geophysics at the Caliph University in Mecca. During his graduate studies, he met experts at a variety of international conferences. He used these trips to spread the influence of the Caliphate across Europe.

One of those conferences had been in Seattle, where he'd seen the work of Dr Lisa Holden and recognized its potential.

Abdul Qawwi entered the carpeted reception room and snapped at the messenger, "Yes? What's so important to take me away from the VIPs, Mahir?"

"Many apologies, Emir." Mahir grovelled and bowed before his superior. "But you did say that if we heard from the operatives, we were to let you know immediately."

There was a pause, Mahir was clearly uncomfortable. "I must warn you, Emir," his voice rose with anxiety, "things haven't gone as we hoped."

Abdul Qawwi moved despondently into the adjoining control room. A pool of light glowed in the centre of the dark space, illuminating a technician at a desk near the door who was adjusting the display.

The mist in the blue globe of light quickly resolved into an image of three uniformed men, Abdul Qawwi barked, "Leave!" The technician fled through the door, which hissed shut behind him.

"Yunus Saleh, you oversaw the operation. Report!" Abdul Qawwi commanded, glaring at the men in the hologram. They squirmed uncomfortably. He was disgusted by their timidity.

"Sir," Yunus Saleh pulled himself to attention. "The prisoner Ben Holden has escaped, Emir."

"Escaped?" the Emir growled quietly. "I was told he'd been captured and bound."

Yunus dissolved into fidgeting distress. "Yes, Emir, he was. We had him in the boat, but somehow he escaped during a storm. We searched the sea around us, the nearby island. But... but, he seems to have vanished!"

"Nonsense, no one vanishes. This Ben Holden isn't a *jinn*."

"You're right, of course, Emir," Yunus Saleh agreed, though his face betrayed his words. "Somehow the prisoner escaped. Our boat was destroyed by fire. The Caliphate submarine that was to take this prisoner had to rescue us."

Fury rose in the Emir, "There's no excuse for such incompetence. We need access to his wife's data to complete the plan sanctioned by your Caliph!" The Emir gained control over his rage, though his gaze on Yunus Saleh remained an icy threat. "You and your operatives failed to get that information the first time, Yunus. You had the wife in your grasp and yet you killed her before obtaining the data."

All three men lowered their heads as he railed at them. Abdul Qawwi studiously avoided mentioning that he was also involved in, even led, that first failed attempt.

"Then under Abdul Ghafoor's orders, you had this Ben Holden in the American desert. He escaped; we lost Shakeel to martyrdom. We must adjust our plans once again." Abdul Qawwi glared at the men for a bit, as he mulled over options. *Such ineptitude!*

The Emir fingered the gold thread on the edging of his robe, "I'll give you one more chance, Yunus Saleh. Find Ben Holden. Get his biometrics to unlock the data."

"We won't fail, Emir."

One of the other men in the hologram, Dawood Naji, spoke up, "Emir, when we had the prisoner, surveillance reported that the *Arraa'i* Pod was also in the area. The tuna-herding community with the apostate captain, Battuta."

"Yes?" Abdul Qawwi lifted his head with interest. "Yunus, investigate whether the *Arraa'i* Pod has interfered with our work. I wouldn't put it past that apostate, Suliman." He spat the name.

"Yes, Emir, Excellency," Yunus Saleh bowed. The two other men bowed with him.

The pool of light dissolved into darkness. Abdul Qawwi stared into the room now filled with shadows, his mind vexed. *How does this Holden fellow keep eluding us? It shouldn't be this difficult.*

Chapter Twelve

9 July 2066, Caliphate vessel *Shaheen*
(four days later)

The *Uthman ibn Affan* class submarine was small and lithe, designed to operate undetected in the depths. It hung motionless twenty feet off the ocean floor. Tucked under a rocky overhang, it was a shadow within a shadow, barely discernible in the 280-metre deep waters.

Nearby swarmed a shoal of bioluminescent firefly squid. The light emanating from this swarm failed to reflect off the specialized skin of the sub. The squid scattered as a swordfish sliced through the shoal, devouring many as it passed.

A remote sensor drifted quietly out of one of the submarine's torpedo tubes. The cigar-shaped device whirred just beyond the rocky overhang. It hovered, motionless, listening with electronic ears.

Inside the sub, bearded faces huddled over the consoles and instruments, lit by a dim red light. Yunus Saleh paced the small space of the operations room. "Report!"

"Nothing yet, *Qaa'id*, Commander." The acoustic technician pressed the headphone against his ear, watching the screen intently before him for any sign of nearby vessels.

"Keep watch another few hours, just to be sure." Yunus Saleh paced the control room, glancing at instruments. The crew worked to keep the *Shaheen* stationary, intent on avoiding detection. This was critical to their mission.

The executive officer stepped into the control room, motioning Yunus Saleh over to the chart table. "*Qaa'id*, we've detected the *Arraa'i* Pod moving south-west of Durand Reef, 78 degrees and 65 nautical miles away. A satellite photo from yesterday showed that one vessel is absent from the nomadic group. We believe that vessel is *Ossë*."

"Wah! The craft of Suliman Battuta, that apostate! Tell those manning the reconnaissance drones to broaden the search area. Let's see if we can find *Ossë*."

The radio operator spoke in subdued tones into his headphones. Then he turned to Yunus Saleh. "*Qaa'id*, they've extended the search area."

Yunus Saleh tapped his finger on the chart table. "Have them search the whole path again. From the sea where we lost the prisoner near that island to the present position of the *Arraa'i* Pod, Ahmed."

"Yes, *Qaa'id*." The radioman spoke again into the headset. Yunus Saleh began pacing brisk circles in the cramped room.

After five minutes, Yunus Saleh slowed his pace and stopped to glare at the radioman. Ahmed avoided his gaze, eyes fixed on the console. He trembled slightly under the scrutiny. Yunus resumed his pacing.

Fifteen more minutes passed. The radio operator pressed his hand to the headphone. He turned to catch Yunus Saleh's attention, anxiety on his face. "*Qaa'id*, our reconnaissance drones haven't yet found *Ossë* along the course. They also can't confirm the current location of the *Arraa'i* Pod yet."

"Keep looking, Dawood Naji. I wouldn't be surprised if Suliman is somehow involved in this. He may even have the prisoner on board his ship. What are our options?"

Ahmed brightened, "*Qaa'id*, I believe we should test out the Emir's new device, the Sea Snake *ḥanash ilbaḥr*. Why don't we place a sea snake device near that seamount the Pod always passes?"

Yunus Saleh's face relaxed. "Excellent idea, Ahmed. Yes. Send for *ḥanash ilbaḥr*. Set a trap on the Danseur seamount."

"Very good, *Qaa'id*."

A few hours later, the submarine left the sheltering overhang, descending into the darkness below.

10 July 2066, Seastead vessel *Ossë*

(the next day)

The approaching dawn turned the ocean golden, as light clouds reflected the rising sun.

The morning star still glimmered in the east. The sea was calm. Rolling swells passed beneath the deck of *Ossë*. Ben felt as though he was gliding on a magic carpet above the sea. He and Sul were eating an early breakfast on deck.

Sul had been explaining more about how they rescued him. "So, with the help of Paul, we were able to guess your location. We detached ourselves from the Pod and headed towards New Caledonia. Gideon launched several of Sophia's gull reconnaissance drones to see if any vessels were in the area. The gull sent back reports of a yacht and a submarine registered to the Caliphate. The gull also detected an infra-red signature in the forward locker of the yacht – not somewhere you'd expect to find a warm body."

"That was me." Ben moved uncomfortably in his chair at the memory.

"Sophia's devices are versatile. Several of her anchovy-bots were released and sent to tangle and disable the yacht's propeller."

"Ah, that's what happened with the propeller. I'm grateful for those bots! That problem you created with the propeller distracted the crew and allowed me to escape." Ben remembered all the activity beyond the galley door. Then a question came to mind. "The kidnappers must've had surface radar. How did they not detect your ship?"

Sul smiled. "Not only did we have to evade surface radar, we also had to hide from the sub in the vicinity which was scanning the area with sonar. Through some tactical cloaking, again mainly thanks to Sophia's designs, we were able to move into the area without detection."

"So, you'd been watching these vessels for some time, then?"

"We watched for hours. When we saw the boat burst into flames, we suspected that was your doing. However, we couldn't detect you in the boat or in the water. We then monitored the enemy search parties. So, in fact, they were the ones who led us to your island hiding place."

"I hid myself well."

"You did indeed. You almost hid yourself too well. The gull drone finally detected a faint heat profile and stood guard near your hide. Gideon and his crew took a risk to retrieve you. And none too soon. I believe another half hour and you'd have died from blood loss and shock. Even when we had you safely onboard, I wasn't sure whether you would recover or not."

They were silent for a few moments as relief and gratitude washed through Ben. "Thank you, Captain Sul, I am indebted to you and the community here."

"So pleased we could help, Ben."

The sky brightened. Lights from other seastead vessels in the Pod began to wink out. Their shadowy silhouettes arced out across the sea towards the horizon.

"My captors spoke Arabic, they talked about a sheikh." Ben channelled the rising anger into clarity, remembering every detail.

"We were able to confirm both were Caliphate vessels. The hostile sub waited and watched. They may be there still. They didn't want to lose you, that is certain. Your wife's data must be very important to them."

"Yes," Ben sighed, feeling a pang of the old grief. "And this is the third time someone has tried to kidnap me."

"The third time?!"

"Yes, the first one was while I was deployed in Somalia, twelve years ago. I thought it was just chance that I was the only survivor from my unit. Now I'm not so sure; I believe we were ambushed. The second time was nine years ago when I was living as part of Paul's community. Not a pleasant memory."

Ben told Sul the story of the attempted kidnap on the road outside Grit.

When he finished, Sul thought for a while. "I must bring all this information before our *majlis*, the governing council for our community, Ben."

"Yes, I would not want to endanger your community." Ben stared at the distant horizon.

Sul looked at Ben with compassion. "Hospitality and even sanctuary are deeply held values in Bedouin culture; we extend these to you freely. And I believe that since God has brought you here to this point, he will show us the way forward. We do not balk at danger, nor do we appease bullies."

Ben studied Sul, and another seed of hope was planted in his heart.

"Ben, tell me the last things you remember before waking up in the boat, that might help us understand your situation better."

Ben leaned back as he began to recall.

Chapter Thirteen

28 June 2066, Raffles Hotel, Singapore
(eleven days earlier)

Ben stopped just inside the door of the Tiffin room; it had a world-class reputation for Asian fusion food. Instinctively, he surveyed the room, ignoring hunger pangs. *Later.*

I wonder what this journalist's angle will be. Is she pro-fusion or one of those concerned about the impact on the environment? And I still need time to run through my presentation for tomorrow's seminar. Better keep it short.

The room was buzzing with animated conversations in many languages. He recognized some familiar faces he'd met at previous Fusion Conferences and acknowledged each of them with a simple nod.

She said to meet near the buffet. He spotted a young woman seated by the window, picking at the tablecloth and watching the door. She glanced towards him. Their eyes met. Her face brightened. As he walked towards her, she stood up.

She waved her hand. "Professor Holden?" she called lightly across the few tables between them. He waved back and approached. "I'm Cathy Freeman with the Science Today show," she smiled.

"Professor, thank you for agreeing to this interview. I find your work with muons fascinating." She paused, smiled. "But I'm getting ahead of myself."

Ben chuckled politely and shook her hand. "I'm glad that the British public are interested in muons. Most people find particle physics to be a dry topic."

"Well, the implications of your research are what people find intriguing. Do you mind if I record this? We might edit some of it into a podcast to accompany the article."

"No problem."

"I've taken the liberty to order tea and snacks while we chat."

"Excellent." Ben sat down.

She rose and poured tea and milk. "Sugar?" Ben shook his head. Cathy moved the cakes and tiny sandwiches to within easy reach of Ben, and sat back down.

"OK, then. Let's start." She pressed the on button of the recording device and assumed a more conversational tone.

"Thank you, Professor Ben Holden, for joining us on Science Today. Professor Holden is a researcher at Caltech, exploring the properties of an elementary particle called the muon. Professor, what is a muon?"

Ben nodded, "A muon is a negatively charged electric particle, smaller than an atom. Muons are produced when cosmic rays collide with matter in the upper atmosphere of the earth. They're like electrons, and have a negative charge, but muons are about two hundred times heavier than the electron. They constantly bombard us, at the rate of around 10,000 per square metre of the earth's surface."

"Bombard us? Are they harmful?"

"No, muons safely pass right through us."

"So what makes them so useful, Professor?" Cathy reached across and chose a small watercress sandwich.

He paused thoughtfully. *My favourite type of question.* "Well, let's see if I can express this clearly. Let's go back twenty years, to a man named Stuart Cheng who discovered the Cheng matrix. The Cheng matrix is an environment in which hydrogen ions, essentially free protons, can become inserted into the nuclei of other atoms. The breakthrough of the Cheng matrix enabled scientists to develop viable Low Energy Nuclear Reactors."

"Low Energy Nuclear Reactors. Which do what, exactly?"

"In Low Energy Nuclear Reactors, hydrogen ions are added to the nucleus of another element, causing it to be transformed. In the case of nickel, when the hydrogen proton is added to the nucleus of the atom, it is transformed into a copper atom, copper being the next higher element on the periodic table. Are you following me so far?"

Cathy pulled up a periodic chart on her computer pad and studied it, then wrote something in her notes. "So, during this reaction process, the nickel is actually changed into copper. The alchemist's dream, one metal being transmuted into another. However, I suspect those alchemists would not have been impressed by nickel becoming copper."

Ben laughed and sipped some water. "No, I expect not. Their goal was to transform lead into gold. They'd probably leave in disgust and go search for the Philosopher's Stone instead. Where was I? Now, when the hydrogen proton is added to the nickel atom, an immense amount of energy is released. Seventy-six per cent of the energy we use today comes from the energy released by the transmutation process."

"Seventy-six per cent, I hadn't heard that. Impressive." More notes.

"Yes, this is a huge amount of power, produced by a relatively simple process. Low Energy Nuclear Reactors have made energy essentially free, transforming the world we live in. We're no longer dependent on fossil fuels, which were a non-renewable resource. Economies of nations are no longer revolving around the availability of oil, and no longer under the sway of the nations with the largest oil fields. Now all societies have equal access to inexpensive, renewable energy. This has revolutionized how we produce food, do industry, travel, work, and play. Back in the early 2000s, our grandparents wouldn't even recognize what our children now take for granted."

"And, of course, the benefits to our environment have been nothing short of miraculous," Cathy added. "Try those smoked salmon and cheese. Exquisite."

Ben hesitated, then bit into one and smiled. "Yes, they are. Where was I?"

"Changes in how we obtain and use power," Cathy prompted.

"Yes. While there have been some significant advances, there's still a lot to do. Unfortunately, even an essentially free, renewable energy supply is not enough to usher in a utopia. Even with centuries of progress in technology, human nature has not changed – sadly. Technology can always be used both for good and evil, to build and to destroy. But that's another topic."

"Yes, let's stay with muons," Cathy smiled wryly. "Perhaps we can schedule a later interview on human nature."

"Yes, back to muons. Now scientists are exploring the next breakthrough in energy production. My research team is seeking to replace those electrons orbiting the hydrogen atom with muons. Muons are heavier than electrons. So, as they orbit, they'll be drawn in closer to the hydrogen nucleus. Theoretically, this allows more hydrogen atoms to be packed closer into a Cheng matrix. This, in turn, increases the chances that two hydrogen atoms will fuse to produce a helium atom. Such fusion will release immense amounts of energy. This is called muon-catalysed fusion."

"Muon-catalysed fusion. Amazing." The interviewer glanced at her notes. "Now if I understand rightly, Professor, your current research is focused on developing configurations of energy fields to guide muons to where we want them. Tap into all those muons that pass through the earth and focus them into a hydrogen-rich environment." She looked at her notes again, "Into this Cheng matrix, for example."

"That's right, Cathy. If the process we're researching can facilitate the fusion of hydrogen into helium, we may release incredible energy, the same energy as that which powers our sun. At least that's our working hypothesis. Still, we have a lot of research before we reach that point. However, initial findings have been encouraging," Ben smiled.

"Fascinating. At the Fusion Symposium, the keynote speaker, Dr Haverson, mentioned that he'll be keeping a close watch on your research over the next few years. He pushed your research into the limelight."

"Kind of him to say that," Ben demurred.

Cathy shifted topics. "Many of our listeners would like to know more about you, your background, to glimpse the person behind the science. Have you always been interested in science? In physics?"

Ben laughed. "Science, yes. Physics was during my early university years."

"Science then. What influenced you as a child?"

"I've always been fascinated by how things work. I was that child who liked to take things apart. When I was seven, my mom gave me a corner of our garage and a small workbench. Any of the appliances that broke she would put on the workbench for me to play with. I discovered circuit boards and motors. As I grew older, my interest gravitated to the software and hardware that ran such devices." In his memory, he saw the family's augmented intelligent agent in pieces on his workbench. *It took me a month to bring that AIA back to life.*

"So, you were mainly interested in electronics and programming?"

"Well, in the early years. On my tenth birthday, my parents gave me a chemistry set. One of those sets with safe chemicals and experiments. Boring, really."

Cathy laughed, "Yes, I know the type."

"However, that set sparked my curiosity; my tendency is to always colour outside the lines. I started looking for and experimenting with chemicals not in my set. A friend and I got a hold of potassium nitrate, sulphur, and charcoal. We made our own gunpowder. Then we created fireworks, experimenting with which metals made which colours. I'm surprised I survived that part of childhood, actually." He chuckled involuntarily.

"Did your parents know about this?"

"No, we did these experiments at my friend's house. His parents were very busy, so we had plenty of time to experiment." Ben felt wistful. *Carefree days.*

"Hmm… I might cut out that part about the gunpowder and fireworks. We have young listeners. Don't want to give them ideas."

"Of course."

"Professor, from these childhood stories it sounds like you were a bit of a nerd, busy with experiments. But," Cathy consulted her notes, "I see that later you were quite athletic. You joined the military, a special forces unit?"

Conversation is moving into sensitive areas. "That's right, Cathy. I made California all state basketball in high school. I joined the marines after graduation and was stationed at Camp Pendleton in California. I did two tours in the Dependency Wars. Though I'm not free to talk about those missions… sorry." Ben felt cautious now.

"Yes, I understand." Cathy noted something on her pad, then looked up at him again. "It was a few years after you left the military that you decided to apply for PhD studies. What was your motivation to pursue that?"

Ben paused. *The hardest period of my life.* Now, though, his heart was at peace, he could talk about it more easily. "That was a hard time in my life, Cathy." He assessed her, then continued. "My wife and son had been brutally murdered while I was on a mission, and during that mission my entire unit was killed."

Cathy's hand froze, she looked up with a stricken face, "That's terrible! I'm sorry. I didn't mean to touch such a nerve."

Ben smiled sadly, "No, it's OK. I've come to terms with it. When I was released from the Marines, I went into an alcoholic tailspin. A community that works with the homeless helped me step back from the edge of self-destruction and walked with me until I had control over my life again."

"Wow," Cathy looked at him for a minute, then wrote some notes.

"That experience gave me a deep appreciation for life and living it well. I was inspired to focus on using my aptitudes in physics to help and serve. My professors at Caltech encouraged me, maybe saw something in me. Anyway, I owe these recent breakthroughs in muon and energy research to that community and my teachers."

"That's inspiring. What a story." Cathy gazed at him, then wrote more notes. "Athletics, special forces. Were you a big risk taker as a child?"

"Well, no more than any active boy. But if we're talking about courage," this was an easier topic for him, "it was my father who inspired me, really. He was one of the bravest men I ever knew."

"Tell me a story of your father's bravery."

"Every year, my father and I would go camping on the Kings River, in Kings Canyon National Park in the California Sierras. We'd hike a different fork of the Kings River each year, camping and fishing together for a week. It was the high point of every summer.

"One year, we were on our own in the upper reaches of the South Fork of the river. We were eating lunch at our camp by the river's edge, watching our fishing lines in the water. The river was running high from snow melt." Ben was transported back to the time. Fond memories with his dad rose again as he retold the story.

"Suddenly two kayakers came down the rapids, hit the rocks, and were thrown out of their boats. Dad jumped to his feet. He pulled a coil of rope from the tent and quickly tied a bowline knot loop under his armpits and gave me the coil. 'Tie this around that pine there, Benny,' he told me. Then he jumped right into the raging river. He pulled them both out of the freezing rapids. He saved their lives."

"That's amazing. How old were you?" Cathy was scribbling notes.

"Just twelve. Holding that line with my dad on the other end is still etched in my memory."

Cathy looked up. "Wow." She glanced at her watch. "I'd like to hear more but unfortunately our time is up. Is there anything else you'd like say, maybe to kids listening?"

"Something I read years ago sums it up for me: 'The exploration of science is systematic wonder.'"

"'Systematic wonder.' That's quotable. Well, thank you Dr Holden. It's been a pleasure." Cathy pressed the recorder and the light faded.

As she packed her gear, Cathy glanced at Ben then across the room. "Ben, do you know those two men near the far wall? They kept glancing over during the interview."

Ben looked over at the two men, now leaning forward, in earnest conversation with each other. "No, I don't recognize them." Ben's instincts went on alert.

"Yes, of course. Probably nothing." Cathy paused, "They just seemed... a little too interested, if you know what I mean. And their expressions didn't look friendly to me."

The men got up and were walking to the exit, their backs towards him. Ben shook off a sense of apprehension. No time to follow up now, maybe later. After the presentation.

He stood and shook hands with Cathy, and she left. The afternoon was late and there was so much left to do. Time to look over my notes, maybe over some Thai food...

CHAPTER FOURTEEN

11 July 2066, Danseur Seamount, South Pacific
(two weeks later)

On the eastern side of Danseur Seamount, robotic miners chewed away at the vast ferro-manganese crust covering the undersea slopes. They excavated, night and day, filling an endless stream of bucket loaders which were conveyed down from the surface, and then sent back up again full of ore. This mineral harvest was processed by Williams Marine Ores at Marcelli Deep. Most of the mineral products would be sold among the Pelagic Territories, with surplus exported to the terrestrial nations. The underwater Pelagic Array – the combined security, management, and communication network of the Pelagic Territories – tirelessly supervised the work of these robotic miners as one of its many tasks.

On the western side of this seamount, out of view of the electronic eyes and ears of the Pelagic Array, a small craft shaped like a hump-backed torpedo whirred in the darkness a kilometre below the ocean's surface. Tractor-like treads hung just below the stabilizing fins on either side of the body. The craft cruised to where the Danseur undersea mountain rose from the depths and lowered its treads. Buoyancy tanks filled with water, pulling the craft down until its treads gripped the silt of the slope. Then, like a grotesque caterpillar, the vessel inched upward, crushing coral fans and brittle stars in its path.

Still hundreds of metres under the surface of the ocean, the craft reached a ledge. Detecting the change in slope, it slowed to a stop. The craft used ground-penetrating sonar to pinpoint a suitable spot. A drill bit emerged from its underside and began to bore a hole into the mud. As the hole deepened, a cylinder on the back of the craft slid forward and slotted into the silt of the new pit. The craft fixed its load in position on the mount. A cap fashioned to look like a stone was placed over the sea snake to camouflage it, then the machine backed away.

The tools retracted; propellers lifted the delivery craft off the mount. Retracing its path away from the weaponized site, the device stirred up the mud to erase its tracks, then whirred away, disappearing into the depths.

Under the rocky lid and inside its chamber, *ḥanash ilbaḥr,* the sea snake with acute electronic senses and the patience of a machine, lay listening, waiting for the opportune time to strike.

11 July 2066, Caliphate vessel *Shaheen*
(the same day)

Yunus Saleh was grateful that the holographic transmission was low resolution. *The Emir won't notice the beads of sweat on his face.* He waited tensely as the blue pool of light formed before him again. The Emir's image emerged and came into focus.

"How is the plan progressing?" the image barked. Outside the view of the camera, Yunus Saleh clenched his fists. *Thank Allah this man is three thousand miles away.*

Taking a deep breath, he began, "Emir, sir. *Alhamdulillah,* praise be to God, we found an area on the Danseur Seamount far from the monitoring of the Pelagic Array. We successfully planted the *ḥanash ilbaḥr.* All went smoothly, without detection, *inshallah.*"

"How can you be so sure they didn't detect you?"

"We watched, Emir, sir. No signs of electronic or acoustic monitoring. No activity indicating suspicion. *Ossë* is not expected to arrive for another thirty-six hours. The sea snake is still well outside the range of *Ossë* sensors. It'll become our eyes and ears when the vessel passes by."

"Well done, Yunus."

Yunus Saleh's fists relaxed slightly. "Thank you, Emir."

"Is the boarding party ready?"

"Yes, Emir. They're shadowing the path of *Ossë,* remaining just beyond their sensor range. They'll be ready, *inshallah.*"

For a moment, the Emir appeared to be lost in thought. "Very well, Yunus Saleh. Keep me posted." The image faded.

Yunus Saleh turned and snapped at the lieutenant standing behind him, "Get me an update on the boarding party!" The man ran from the room to find the information.

11 July 2066, Seastead vessel *Ossë*, South Pacific
(the same day)

On the bridge of *Ossë*, a display flashed, and a soft tone sounded to attract the captain's attention.

"Yes, Nemo," Sul said, while monitoring and assigning positions for vessels in the *Arraa'i* Pod.

"Captain, the Pelagic Array near the Danseur Seamount has detected an anomalous echo. Neither biologic nor one of the known Pelagic or terrestrial craft."

"Thank you, Nemo. Monitor the area as we approach it. Let me know if the echo reoccurs."

"Yes, Captain."

*

Rising from deep sleep, Ben found himself staring into the vast blueness beyond his window. He could feel the azure sea extending around him as *Ossë* slipped silently through the waters. As this immensity seeped into his waking senses, it awoke wonder in him. For some reason, the memory of his dream with Lisa and Sammy, so long ago in that Ajo alley, came to him. *Lisa would love this; Sammy would go bananas.*

He revelled in the sense of peace.

What is that shining out there?

Slipping from the bed he walked over to investigate. In the pre-dawn darkness, luminescent creatures pulsated; small, shimmering necklaces in the deep blue waters. The creatures moved through galaxies of phosphorescent plankton.

Fascinated, he pressed closer to the window. The exquisite ballet extended through the water as far as he could see. As *Ossë* progressed at a languid speed, the delicate creatures slid along the window.

"Nemo, what are these, a kind of jellyfish?"

"No, Professor, they are salps, part of the tunicate family. They are feeding on the plankton bloom we're passing through, caused by the upwelling along the Louisville Seamount Chain beneath us. The bloom has attracted the salps."

A shadow lanced across his field of vision. Then another and another. Within seconds there were thirty or more frenzied fish, feeding on the salps.

"Are these the tuna being ranched by *Ossë's* Pod?"

"Yes, Professor. This is Cohort 34."

"How many tuna fish does the Pod manage?"

"According to today's telemetry, 27,946."

"How is the ranching done?" Ben watched the flurry of activity, mesmerized.

"Each of the eighty-six cohorts under management of the Pod follows a tuna guide, a robotic fish designed by Sophia. I'll call one to the window if you are interested."

"Please."

The room brightened behind him. One tuna detached itself from the school and swam just outside the window, slowing to keep pace with the speed of *Ossë*.

"That's a robot? It looks just like the other tuna!" Ben's eyes darted back and forth, comparing the fish pausing before him with the shapes flashing in and out of view in the window.

"Yes, Sophia's an excellent craftswoman. Her designs are in demand throughout the Pelagic Territories."

"How does a tuna guide control the school of fish?" Ben appreciated the fine details of the tuna robot before him.

"It begins when the schools of fish are still young, just after spawning. Tuna juveniles are conditioned at the hatchery in cohorts, with a guide assigned to each cohort. Each tuna guide emits a unique and repeating pattern of pressure pulses. The juveniles sense this through special cells along their lateral lines."

"Lateral lines?"

"That's an organ along the side of fish that gives them the unique ability to detect pressure waves in the water around them. The young fish become conditioned to follow their guide's pattern of pulses. Once they've been imprinted with the unique pattern of their cohort guide at the hatchery, they'll follow it throughout their lives."

The sea before Ben was clearing now, returning to an empty, endless blueness.

"The guides contain sensors which monitor the health of the tuna. This data is forwarded to Pod computers like me for analysis. This data is used to manage the health of the schools."

"Fascinating." Ben turned away from the window, walking to the bathroom to shower and shave.

Nemo's voice followed him. "As the nomadic Pod moves through the

Southern Pacific Gyre, they identify feeding grounds for the schools. They can also protect the schools."

Ben lathered his face. "So, these tuna guide bots are bellwethers, watch dogs, and security blankets all in one. Fascinating."

Nemo paused, "I'm not familiar with that phrase, 'security blanket'. Did you mean it in the sense that the fish feel more secure around their guide?"

"Yes, that's correct."

"Thank you. I'm building a context in my lexicon for that idiom. Yes, Professor, now I see. Those allusions do parallel the tuna guide functions."

As Ben shaved, a stray salp appeared in the mirror and drifted across his field of vision. A tuna shadow flashed through the reflection and the salp was gone.

"Very impressive. So, these tuna guides are managed by the Pod?"

"Yes, they are networked into an information management system. The guides transmit data to each other and the Pod's computers. We then share this information with other Pods distributed widely throughout the Pelagic Territory. In this way we can also monitor factors like the population of sharks and other predators. The guides are alerted, for example, when sharks are detected near their feeding grounds. They defend the tuna."

"That's amazing." Ben wiped his face on the plush towel.

"Excuse me, Professor, the captain informs me that breakfast will be ready in twenty minutes. Would you like to join him?"

Ben was pulling on his shirt. "Yes, thank you. I'm almost ready."

After dressing, Ben headed down the corridor to the lift. Part of his mind mulled over the genius of these tuna guides. Another part continued to ponder his situation. *Was it chance that brought me here among these people? Of course, Paul would say that it was not chance that brought me here, but the God he believes in.* He was startled to find that when he considered Paul's point of view, a sense of hope warmed his heart.

A breeze met him as he opened the lift's door onto the ship's bridge. The ruffled sea glowed rosy in the early morning light. A thin mist scudded before the wind, not quite a fog. The combined effect gave the view a subtle, almost surreal beauty.

Stepping around the lift, he was surprised to see Suliman kneeling on a prayer rug, hands uplifted, the rising sun full on his face. Ben stopped, embarrassed that he had disturbed such a private moment.

Hearing his footfall, Sul lowered his arms and turned to him. "Good morning, Professor. Ben. A beautiful morning!" He rose, came over, and extended his hand. Ben took it.

"Please, come join me. Breakfast will be ready in a moment."

"I'm sorry to disturb your prayers."

"No matter. Please, I am finished." Sul folded his rug as he stood.

Ben paused for a moment, then, "If you don't mind me asking, are you Muslim?"

Sul glanced at him. "Your question's simple but requires a more complex answer than you might have patience for."

"No really, I'm very interested,"

"As I mentioned to you yesterday, I'm a descendant of a Bedouin tribe, from Yemen. While Bedouin are Muslim by birth and by culture, I have chosen to follow *Isa al-Masih*." He saw a confused look pass over Ben's face, then resolve.

"Jesus the Messiah," Ben translated the Arabic, smiling. "So, you're a Christian?"

"I prefer calling myself a follower of Jesus. The name 'Christian' tends to be entangled in various cultural interpretations, religious traditions, and institutions. I'm not strictly Catholic, Protestant, Orthodox, or Evangelical, for example. I respect those traditions and centre my faith, as they do, on the person of Jesus. I'm from a line of Bedouins, extending over several generations, who have all chosen to give heart allegiance to *Isa al-Masih*, and who integrate our faith with our Yemeni culture.

"We simply try to follow the teaching and person of Jesus motivated by what he has done to bring us reconciliation and peace with God."

Sul beckoned Ben to join him as he moved towards the tables and chairs.

"Come, sit here and enjoy the morning with me."

"Tell me how you chose this unusual life you lead," Ben invited.

"Well, I must tell you first about my grandfather, Jadan al Hada, who was of the Abyan tribe of Yemen. This tribe has been Muslim for as long as can be remembered. My grandfather grew up by the sea near Aden, in a town called Shuqra. Early in this century, he was given an opportunity to leave for a degree at the University of Plymouth, England. His studies were in marine biology."

"This was during the civil war in Yemen. Is that right?"

"Yes, he felt lucky to leave that danger and chaos. At the university he was exposed to many new ideas. During his first few years at Plymouth, grandfather Jadan joined a group who were studying the Bible. I believe he took part because he was so disillusioned with the Islamist narrative of groups like Daesh, Taliban, and Al Qaeda, actively preaching in Yemen at that time. He despised the Salafist emphasis of these groups because he felt they wanted to pull Yemen back into medieval thinking, to the time Salafists consider to be the Islamic Golden Age, the early Muslim community in Medina. At least this is what my father has told me."

"Sounds like your grandfather was searching for freedom from rigid thinking?"

"Yes, that's right. The story handed down from my grandfather to my father, to me, is that he continued to read through the Bible, especially the teaching of *Isa al-Masih*. He was particularly intrigued by a passage in the Gospels, where Jesus was teaching about the type of people that receive God's favour or blessing. He was deeply attracted to the person of Jesus and the things he taught."

"That's fascinating. I haven't heard much about Muslims reading the Bible and seeking Jesus."

"Well, it's common, even though you might not hear about it in the news." Sul chuckled. "This was the beginning of his journey to a new faith. He read the Holy Books over and over, observed the lives of Christians, had heated discussions with friends, and spent hours pouring his heart out to God. After a few months, he became convinced that Jesus was the one for him to follow. He was baptized quietly in the Catholic Cathedral at Plymouth in 2019. He thought he'd avoided public notice, but his family quickly learned of it and they ordered him expelled from the clan. They labelled him as an apostate from Islam, publicly proclaiming that he was dead to them."

"Wow, what a high price to pay," Ben observed.

"Yes." Sul looked out over the sea, thoughtful. "My grandfather was disappointed by the reaction of his family, but he never regretted his choice. This life my family and I now lead is a direct result of that choice, and we have no regrets either."

Out of the corner of his eye, Ben noticed a light flashing on the dumb waiter. Sul saw it as well.

"That's our breakfast." Sul went over to collect the plates. "Some fresh kippers have arrived by drone. The cook has whipped up Kippers Florentine, with poached egg and sea salad on the side."

"It looks delicious, thank you!" Ben drew in the delightful aroma. "Please tell me more of your family's history."

"I don't want to bore you."

Ben waved it off. "Not bored."

Sul brought glasses of orange juice and cups of tea, then sat again.

Ben sampled his kippers. "This is great. I've heard rumours of experiences like your grandfather's. I've never heard a story first-hand."

"Kind of you to listen. Stories like this must be told, new generations need to understand how different life was then." Sul lingered over a few bites and then resumed. "Well, in 2021, my grandfather finished his degree. He did not want to return home to Yemen in the middle of a civil war still raging between the Houthis in the north and Mansur Hadi-led forces in the south. However, his student visa had expired, so he had to leave Britain. Other European nations were closing their borders. The Covid-19 pandemic added to the significant reduction of immigration quotas. There weren't a lot of options for my grandfather."

"Yes, that was a tough time. What did he do?" Ben sipped his tea.

"Well, he and a friend, Carlo Marcelli – whom he met in his Bible study group – were working for one of their professors for a few months after they graduated."

"Carlo Marcelli?" interrupted Ben, "Is he the one Marcelli Township is named after?" A short pause, "and would Gideon's Sally be a descendant of Carlo?"

"Very observant, Professor." Sul cast an assessing look at Ben. "Yes, the teacher made arrangements for my grandfather and Carlo to join an ocean farming project in Indonesia, raising sea cucumbers to sell to the lucrative Chinese market. They jumped at the chance. After a few years' work, they managed to accumulate significant capital."

"That turned out well. But there's a big difference between working in ocean farming and moving your whole way of life onto the open sea."

"Well, Carlo was a brilliant marine engineer. As family legend has it, he wanted to use his capital from the sea cucumbers to invest in a pioneering design: a seasteading vessel, an early precursor to our *Ossë*. It was a wild idea for that time. He wanted to farm commercial marine species beyond the range of the national economic exclusion zones."

"To work in the region of ocean outside the international boundaries which extend off the coast of terrestrial nations?" Ben asked.

"Yes, his dream was to live on the open sea and Jadan wanted to join him. There were few laws or regulations governing the open oceans. Carlo and my grandfather saw it as an opportunity. A new frontier."

Ben let Sul eat for a moment, then asked, "How did they make a living on the open sea in those days?"

"Well," Sul continued, "here was their first idea: Carlo designed a mobile fish-aggregating device."

"Fish-aggregating device?" Ben queried between bites.

"Fishermen all know that baitfish shelter under floating objects. The baitfish attract larger predators. Fishermen through the ages have designed and anchored raft-like devices to attract bait fish and their predators. Then the predators, commercially valuable species like tuna, mahi-mahi and even swordfish, could then be found in predictable spots, where the aggregators were anchored. Far easier than hunting fish in the open ocean."

"So Carlo improved a known technology." Ben drank his juice.

"Yes, traditional aggregators were anchored. Carlo's innovation was designing mobile devices that could be controlled remotely. Carlo and grandfather Jadan deployed the first portable aggregators in the Indian Ocean, to attract yellowtail and skipjack tuna. Essentially, this was the start of sea ranching, as they herded schools of tuna along their natural migration routes using the aggregators to manage them."

"A simple and clever idea." The sun was bright in the sky now; the morning haze had burnt off. Ben relaxed in the warmth.

"Yes, mobile aggregators fit well with a nomadic lifestyle. Grandfather revelled in being a Bedouin on the sea. However, it was more difficult for Carlo and his Italian wife to live always on the move."

"I think I hear a parting of the ways coming."

"Yes. Their success had already attracted many to join them. Grandfather was a sheikh, from a leading tribe. Many like him, seeking freedom to practise their faith as followers of *Isa al-Masih*, were drawn to his example."

Ben was impressed. "It reminds me of the American colonies several centuries ago. Some of the settlers of those unexplored territory were also seeking religious freedom in America," he mused.

"The narratives are similar," Sul agreed. "Many of the early seasteaders had challenges like your ancestors, as they pioneered and learned how to live on the open sea. People were also drawn to a land, or sea, of opportunity."

"Many people from Carlo's extended family in Italy also had joined the seasteaders at that point. They hit on the idea of settling seamounts located in international waters. They chose a site in the southern Pacific

Ocean and founded what is now Marcelli Township. Both grandfather and Carlo found different paths forward that worked for their clans. They parted as friends and the families remain close to this day."

"That reflects well on their character, and their bond of friendship. So, the families in your Pod still are all part of the same clan?"

"Yes, as my grandfather's early nomadic community grew, it divided into multiple interdependent communities, and spread across the Indian Ocean. Our Pod is among about thirty others that are part of our extended clan."

Breakfast finished, empty plates now lay between them.

They lingered, enjoying each other's company as the beauty of the morning washed over them.

Ben saw a solitary squall in the distance, spreading a shadow of rain on the surface of a glimmering sea. To their right, off the starboard quarter, the waters boiled with tiny silvery fish leaping out to escape a predator.

"I'm thinking about your comment that we seasteaders are similar to those who opened up the American West," Sul reflected. "Communities forming beyond the laws of nation states attract many types of people. Not just ones seeking religious freedom."

"You're right. In the Wild West, there were some motivated by adventure, wanting to explore and conquer new frontiers." Ben searched his memory for character types.

"And, of course," Sul added ruefully, "some of them were predators living by robbing others: outlaws, pirates, and conmen, whose goal was to relieve settlers of their hard-earned profits. We have those."

"In the Wild West, because of those predators and outlaws, settlers had to band together and develop ways to protect themselves. This eventually evolved into a safe civil society in which people could raise their families in peace." Ben reflected as he watched a shearwater high in the sky flex its sleek charcoal-edged wings, then dive and snatch a fish for breakfast.

Sul nodded, "And today, the outlaws on the open seas also are forcing the Pelagic Territories to find ways to ensure peace, safety, and justice. In the early years, we quickly recognized the importance of forming networks to work together and help each other."

"So, those were the early days of the Pelagic Confederacy?"

"No, there was no confederacy yet. Communities were networking in various ways. Some moved around, nomadic, like ours. Some were static communities, like Marcelli Township. Small communities were scattered across many of the oceans, pursuing a wide range of ocean-based enterprises. We were all exploring how to survive and thrive in this barren setting."

A thought struck Ben. "Your grandfather began this new way of life in the Indian Ocean, but now your Pod makes its home in the South Pacific, as do those in the Marcelli clan. Why did you all move so far from where he began?"

Sul smiled. "You are inquisitive. The curiosity of a scientist?"

"I'm enjoying your history. Please continue if you don't mind."

"As you wish. Yes, we lived in the Indian Ocean until I was around seven years old. At that time, a band of Yemeni raiders attacked our community and seriously damaged our vessels."

"Yemeni raiders?"

"Yes, pirates regularly plunder merchant ships in that region. Some were recruited by leaders in Yemen and sent to punish us as a clan. Even to this day, many clans in Yemen consider our Pod, and similar Arab descent Pelagic communities, as apostates from Islam."

"What a long time to hold a grudge."

"Indeed. Tragically, a third of our community was killed that day, before we could fight off the attackers. I remember my mother comforting me as we watched our home sink."

"What a terrible situation!"

"Yes, we felt very vulnerable. This incident was a turning point for our clan. Our ruling council, or *majlis*, convened an emergency meeting, at which the decision was made to relocate, far from the continuing threat. They decided to move to the South Pacific."

"Put more distance between you and the New Caliphate."

"Yes, just distance wasn't enough. We worked with Marcelli Township and other willing members of the pelagic community to established alliances with each other and terrestrial nations including Australia, New Zealand, Chile, and Peru. Eighteen other nomadic Pods moved with us to the new territory. Life was better for us in the South Pacific Gyre. There was ample room for all of us to establish new livelihoods. Soon after that we organized the first Pelagic Territory. That was almost twenty years ago."

Light clouds drifted across the blue expanse. The day was bright and sparkling.

"You were the pioneers, others followed you. You are like the tuna guides Nemo was telling me about earlier."

Sul laughed.

"Nemo showed me one of the tuna guides," Ben continued, "and explained how they work. What a brilliant idea!"

"My father first came up with the idea. It was his specialty when he studied at the Marine Institute of Science and Technology in Auckland."

"Ah, so he inspired Sophia, then?"

"Yes, my father's designs were primitive compared to Sophia's. My father spent the year after his PhD working with Huang Hatcheries, which was just a start-up at that time. Building on my father's research, Huang Hatcheries, which became Huang Marine Research, developed the first prototypes of fish guides."

"What a brilliant innovation." The engineer in Ben rose to the topic.

"Before this invention, we collected wild stocks using the mobile aggregating devices. However, with the addition of these guides, we could control the whole lifecycle of the southern tuna, from juvenile stage through to harvest and shipment to market."

"Amazing."

Sul stood and beckoned to Ben to join him walking around the deck. "Look at that, Ben. The ocean stretching as far as you can see from horizon to horizon. Limitless room to innovate and flourish. Our most precious asset, a gift."

"I can see that you love your way of life, Captain."

"I am a second-generation Pelagic. My whole life has been spent living on the sea. I view it as an immense privilege."

"It sounds like an incredible life: pioneering, matching your wits against nature, learning how to live in a new environment."

Sul's voice sobered. "Don't over-romanticize it. Over the past twenty years, terrestrial nation-states have become uncomfortable with the growing wealth and power of the seasteaders. Some view us as a threat because we inhabit formerly ungoverned and open seas. This has further forced settlers to organize our loose territories into stronger political bodies, able to negotiate new international laws, economic agreements, and diplomatic alliances."

A sudden roar from behind interrupted the conversation. Ben instinctively spun around. Sul chuckled. Off the port side of *Ossë*, a manta-shaped craft rose on three rotors.

"Don't be alarmed, Professor," Sul shouted above the noise, "it's just my son, Gideon, showing off his new machine."

As he spoke, the canopy on the forward end of the aircraft sprang open. A dark-haired, athletic young man with bright eyes under thick brows emerged and sprinted across the wing. He leapt onto the deck of *Ossë* near them.

"Nemo, please put *Kestrel* away," he called over his shoulder.

"Yes, Gideon," Nemo responded.

The canopy closed. The winged craft dropped back into the sea, slipping from sight.

The quiet of the morning returned, almost.

"*Baba!* Any breakfast left? Oh, you must be Professor Ben," Gideon paused to shake Ben's hand. "Great to see you up and about."

"Breakfast is in the dumb waiter, Gideon. I anticipated you would be hungry," Nemo informed him.

"Neem, you're the man!" The young man dived for the plate and brought it to the table with breathless energy. "I'm famished."

"*Baba*," he said between mouthfuls, "I hear the Pod is gathering tomorrow. Will we be forming a Star?"

Chapter Fifteen

12 July 2066, Seastead vessel *Ossë*
(early the next morning)

Sophia slipped quietly from under her covers and stood peering into the dark waters beyond her bedroom window. Translucent comb jellies slid along the outside of the glass, winking in blue flashes. There was no need to ask Nemo to create silence in these quiet hours of the morning. Everyone on *Ossë* was deep in sleep. She'd had enough sleep, so she wandered out the door in her pyjamas.

"Nemo, my *Egg*, please," she requested in a hushed voice.

"Yes, *Ameera*, your craft is being prepared."

Sophia glided down the corridor like a shadow. She paused at the door to the guest room. "Nemo, please open the door."

"The professor is sleeping, *Ameera*."

"Just to look."

The door slid open. Ben slept peacefully under the sea-filtered starlight. Sophia stood in the doorway.

"Has he suffered, Nemo?"

"Yes, *Ameera*. Great suffering. News reports tell about his wife and child who were killed. He was taken by cruel men. He has had to fight and lose friends in battle as well."

"I feel his sadness."

"You have a sensitive heart, *Ameera*."

Sophia stepped away from the door and continued down the corridor. She heard Ben's door sigh shut behind her.

The lift opened silently as she approached. "Down to the *Egg*," she whispered.

The walls of the small cylinder glowed a subtle blue around her. She felt the lightness of descent.

Reaching the lowest floor, the lift opened to a spartan corridor, a place of work in contrast to the comforts of home on the level above. The second door on the left opened into a small humid chamber. Slings dangled from the ceiling, equipment was hung around the walls and organized in shelves in the corners. In the centre of the room was a pool of seawater that opened to the depths below and in the pool floated an ovoid vessel that looked like half an egg. The family affectionately referred to it as Sophia's *Egg*. Spotlights glimmered above and under the platform, illuminating the sea underneath the slowly moving *Ossë*.

She stepped across a short bridge onto the craft. The bridge retracted as she moved to the centre of the vessel. A small brass sign on the floor was engraved: "To Sophia on her 9th birthday. With all our love, Gideon and *Baba*." A clear dome now rose from one side of the vessel and encircled her small figure, sealing as it closed on the other side. The *Egg* began to glow softly.

"Go," she said quietly. Mooring cables released. The *Egg* dropped below and behind *Ossë* into the heart of the sea.

A wave of phosphorescence sparkled against the windows. Two guardian drones resembling amberjack fish also dropped from *Ossë*. Swimming on each side of the *Egg*, they took stations as sentinels. The *Egg* drifted astern of *Ossë* into the silent solitude of the night sea, suspended among shifting pillars of moonlight.

"Lights off." The glow around the small sphere winked out. Sophia stood silently in her *Egg* as it slowed to a stop. Her eyes widened in the dark, as she turned to take in the full wonder of the infinite blue expanse. *My sea.*

After twenty minutes of silent communion, she said quietly, "Squid, Nemo."

"Yes, *Ameera*, a shoal of giant squid is feeding eighty metres below us."

The *Egg* now descended, deeper into the blackness. The glittering phosphorescent became less frequent. It was now almost absolute darkness outside, but at the edge of vision Sophia could discern darting shadows.

"Red light," Sophia said. The orb's faint glow clicked on again, giving shape to the giant shadows. Giant squid, *Architeuthis sp*. Sophia watched, entranced at the rushing activity around the vessel.

Putting her hands on the sapphire glass, Sophia peered closely at a passing four-metre long squid. It slowed, caught by her gaze, then stopped, suspended in darkness on the other side of the dome and, for a few seconds, returned her gaze.

In an instant, the squid turned to reach for her. Its tentacles struck against the dome.

Sophia didn't flinch. The large squid, a modern-day kraken that weighed much more than the child, hovered for a moment. It sent exploratory tentacles to touch the shield gently, then withdrew. The squid floated next to the glass contemplating this mystery. Sophia and the creature stared eye to eye, one alien to another. Amberjack-like guardian bots emerged from the darkness. The squid flicked a tentacle at one of the robots, hoping for dinner, and was rewarded by an electric jolt. It flashed away, leaving a cloud of ink in its wake.

In the glow of the craft's lights, the squid flashed in red arcs as they fed on a school of anchovy wheeling around the *Egg*. Sophia was spellbound by these dogfights of survival in the heart of darkness.

Other shadows now flashed through the melée. One of *Arraa'i* Pod's tuna cohort had dived to join in the feeding frenzy, but veered back to the surface on encountering the squid; losing some of their company to the monsters. The waters cleared and the giant cephalopods faded from their feeding crimson to the colour of the sea. They winked out of view, one by one. Scales from the school of anchovy drifted into darkness beyond the lights.

The sea around Sophia's *Egg* was once again primal blackness.

"Light. Surface." Lights underneath the craft shifted to a soft white as they rose through the expanse. Fairy lights gleamed again around her shell as the *Egg* rose through the dancing moonbeams. These star flashes of the sea gave way to their astral sisters spread across the heavenly expanse as the vessel broke the surface. The dome slid silently back into the body of the craft. Sophia stood in the open air, afloat on a mirrored sea, an innocent Venus upon her magical shell with sentinel escorts swimming at each side.

"All off."

"Yes, *Ameera*." The light around the ovoid vessel faded to darkness. The subtle vibration of the craft ceased.

The night extended around her. A rich, vast canopy with a shimmering host that looked down upon their reflections in the calm sea. Within the soft breeze of this tableau of peace Sophia knelt on her *Egg*, letting her spirit commune with the Other.

"Thank you, Lord," she whispered. Nemo was silent.

After almost an hour of prayerful stillness, Sophia rose to her feet, stretching her limbs. "Home."

"Yes, *Ameera*," Nemo said again. The sapphire dome curled around the tiny figure. The craft moved silently towards home, sinking beneath the surface of the eternal sea. As it neared *Ossë*, it rose towards the docking bay to return its charge to her bed.

*

Gideon paced across the deck of *Ossë*. The stars shimmered brightly over the sea, a furtive breeze touched the surface here and there with cats' paws. The chill that lingered from the early hours invigorated him. A faint red glow was growing on the eastern horizon. Dawn was not far off.

"Neem, bring *Kestrel* to the port side of *Ossë*. Stay in silent mode, please. I don't want to wake the family," Gideon said, without taking his eyes off the far skyline.

"*Kestrel* is on its way, Gideon."

"Thank you."

Small footsteps approached from behind. He turned to see Sophia. Her sphere of silence was on, and as she drew near, the world grew quiet. He smiled down on her.

"Good morning, *Ameera*. You're up early." She smiled and continued to gaze downward. Gideon was touched again with the love he felt for his mysterious sister. She lived in her own world, yet he felt she saw deeper into what was around them than anyone he knew.

She glanced for a moment into his eyes. "Come?" she said quietly.

Gideon looked at the diminutive figure, wishing he knew her thoughts more fully. "You want to come with me on *Kestrel*?"

A quick nod and another smile.

"Of course, *Ameera*. You'll have to narrow your bubble of silence, so I can hear during the journey, though."

"Yes," she said.

"Gideon, Sophia would like to bring some observation drones on your trip today." Nemo filled in for his less communicative charge. "She's ready to monitor the flocks of sooty shearwater birds which are migrating through this area."

What a welcome treat. She wants me to help with her project. Gideon discarded his plans to test new offence protocols for *Kestrel*.

"Of course." He looked down at her. "You must wear an exposure suit. And bring your observation drones as quick as you can." Sophia immediately ran off. *I guess that means "yes",* Gideon thought wryly.

"I'll ensure she brings everything necessary," Nemo said.

"Thanks, Neem. Where does she want to go, exactly?"

"A flock is feeding about four and a half miles south-east. You'll need to allow her about an hour to observe their social behaviour."

"OK, plot a course for us."

"In process."

Kestrel rose like a hushed shadow on the port side, ready to be boarded. Gideon jumped lightly from *Ossë*'s deck onto the hovering craft. He pulled a small ramp out from a slot, creating a bridge to the deck. Opening the canopy, he climbed into his seat to prepare for the flight.

A few minutes later, Sophia emerged in an exposure suit and ran across the deck, hugging a box to her chest. Gideon jumped out of his seat, stepping lightly across the ramp. "Here, Soph. Let me help you with that."

He set the box in one of the rear seats, then helped Sophia into the co-pilot's seat and stowed the ramp.

"Box," Sophia said. Gideon handed her the box and clipped her harness on.

"Thank you," Sophia said clearly, still looking at the box.

"Wow, sis! A thank you! You really are growing up!" Her eyes flickered at him for a second. She smiled shyly and averted her eyes once more.

Buckling into the pilot seat, Gideon leaned forward to set the controls. A display rose before him as the overhead canopy whispered closed. Then *Kestrel* rose into the air and swung onto a course south-west.

"OK. Today we're on a shearwater expedition!" Gideon sang out. He loved exploring with his latest design. *Kestrel* levelled out at twenty metres above the sea, cruising towards a brightening ring of light on the horizon.

Soon a gigantic flock of dark grey seabirds came into view, wheeling silhouettes against the glowing horizon. "What's the best position, Nemo?"

"We'll keep *Kestrel* about two hundred metres from the centre of the flock," Nemo said.

"Make it so."

The sleek craft rose silently to take the position just beyond the feeding flock.

"Now what?" Gideon asked, looking at Sophia.

"Open," she said, staring straight ahead.

"OK. Opening canopy." The covering silently unlocked and slid open. A fresh breeze swirled in and around *Kestrel*'s cabin, bringing with it the deafening cries of the shearwaters. Gideon breathed in the fresh air, then watched his sister.

"Silence," Sophia said. The world muted around them.

Sophia opened her box, revealing six dusky grey, delicate objects set in foam. The slender, narrow-winged birds with forked tails reminded Gideon of miniature terns. As Sophia touched them, one by one, they came to life. She tossed each one out of the craft. The small robotic birds flapped into the pandemonium of the wheeling shearwaters. Gideon could see each bot lock onto and shadow an individual bird in the flock. After taking readings of the chosen shearwater, each device moved to another bird.

"Outside," Sophia said.

"Outside?" Gideon repeated, looking at her. *How unpredictable she is!* Sophia unclipped herself. She scurried into the back of *Kestrel*'s cabin to retrieve two safety lines. Without looking at Gideon, she held one out to him.

Gideon took the safety line. She clipped one end of hers to an eyebolt on the craft and the other end to a ring on her exposure suit. Then she crawled along the outer surface of *Kestrel*, perching on its skin.

"Wow, sis, you never cease to surprise me." Gideon followed Sophia's lead. He secured his safety line, crawled out, and sat next to her.

The sun was up now. The day brightened in a clear sky. A strong breeze brought up fine salt spray, almost a mist. The ocean was a vast expanse before them, as far as the eye could see, a ring of sea and a vault of sky. *A beautiful day to be alive,* Gideon thought. He carefully reached over and hugged his sister. She stiffened but allowed him. Gideon smiled at her. "Thanks, sis."

As they admired the view, Sophia burst into a spontaneous laugh of pure joy. Gideon joined her. They revelled in their own flying carpet, seventy metres above the sea's surface and just beyond the gyre of seabirds. After about forty-five minutes, the flock began to disperse, individuals and groups ranging out over the sea, seeking other prey.

"Gideon," Nemo interrupted the moment, "I'm monitoring a reconnaissance drone, ten miles to the west. It seems to be carrying out a search pattern and is moving towards you."

"Whose is it, Neem?"

"Unknown."

Gideon looked westward, his heart beating faster. "We should find out. Neem, can you detect whether it's using sonar in its searches?"

A moment's pause. "No indication of sonar. It's searching with radar and most likely visual pattern recognition algorithms. We will be in its detection range in six minutes."

Sophia leaned towards Gideon and whispered.

"Great idea, sis."

"Three, Nemo. Please." Three of the six white robotic terns returned to Sophia's outstretched hand. She slotted them carefully back into the box. Gideon and Sophia crawled back into the cockpit and snapped on their harnesses as the canopy closed.

*

Twelve minutes later, the sea-coloured search drone flew near what was left of the flock of shearwaters. Three tern-like devices flew different configurations within the lingering confusion of birds, triangulating on the drone, and taking data. The drone's sensors paid no attention to them.

Ten minutes later the drone had moved beyond the horizon. *Kestrel* rose from where it had been hiding beneath the sea and moved near the few shearwater birds still lingering. The canopy opened. Three tern drones emerged from among the shearwaters and entered the vessel, landing on Sophia's hand one by one. She placed them in the box with the others. The canopy closed.

Kestrel pivoted in the air and sped back to *Ossë*.

12 July 2066, Seastead vessel *Ossë*
(the same day)

Captain Sul stood on the bridge of *Ossë*. In front of him was a holo-display showing the current positions of the Pod seasteads within it. Nemo was speaking, "Captain, the *Murex* AI has handed over pilot control to me. That's the last of the Pod vessels to check in."

"Very well. Thank you, Nemo." Sul's senses were on full alert, as he scanned the near horizon from the deck of *Ossë*. "Yes, I see *Zephyr*, as well, coming into view."

Gideon and Ben approached him on the bridge. Sul glanced over, signalling them to wait a moment.

"Direct all the guide fish to herd the tuna schools into a ring around our Pod. Four miles in diameter."

"Yes, Captain. The ring is forming."

"Direct the crafts into the Sea Star configuration now." He walked back under the roof of the bridge, waving Gideon and Ben in to join him. They stood around the pool of light with its miniature vessels. Sul studied the images in the pool. Clouds of tiny silvery dots indicated the schools of tuna. As they watched, the fish curved into a ring surrounding the twelve tiny yellow vessels of the Pod.

Sul turned to his son and Ben. "Thanks for your quick thinking, son. The data you collected on that unknown drone this morning was important."

"Well it was Sophia's idea, actually, *Baba*," Gideon commented, his eyes also watching the display. "We were collecting data on shearwaters, and Nemo alerted us to the drone. She suggested we submerge and leave some of her devices in the flock to collect information on the drone."

"It was well done." Sul glanced at Gideon then concentrated again on the display. "From the data collected, we've confirmed that the search drone was a Caliphate craft."

Sul turned back to the holographic display, "Which school is that one, lingering so far outside the ring?"

"That is the *Murex* vessel's school, Cohort 16. The guide fish is still herding the school into the ring," Nemo answered.

An elegant dance emerged out of the seeming chaos of fish and craft manoeuvring in the display. The virtual silver shadows formed a shining circle of life around the cluster of crafts. The vessels, in turn, aligned into a twelve-pointed star in the centre. Sul felt pleasure as the design sharpened. He looked over at Ben and said, "I suspect the people searching for you are indeed connected with the Caliphate, Ben. That spy drone's behaviour indicates that it was looking for something important. The timing is suspiciously close to your escape."

Ben was thoughtful. "Yes, I would agree."

Sul's face grew sombre. He compared the holographic display with the movement of vessels he could see beyond the deck. "If these are the Caliphate's men, we must take extra precautions. I've sent out six gull observation craft to alert us should other reconnaissance craft come near our Pod."

The holograph view panned out to include the six gull bots, "They have been persistent." Ben looked up from the display to Sul. "I'm sorry my presence endangers your clan, Sul."

"The Caliphate views our Pod, apostates, as a threat. You are just one more excuse to persecute us, Ben."

"That was generations ago."

"They regard those who leave Islam as they interpret it to be worse than unbelievers. Apostates must be punished, even through the generations. Now that they have guessed that we are giving you sanctuary, they have even more reason to attack."

Sul's features softened as he met Ben's gaze. "I understood the risks when we rescued you, Ben. We won't be intimidated by aggressors. However, if their activities are this hostile, we need to bring this matter before the *majlis*."

"*Majlis*? Oh, your council."

"Yes, our decision-making body, made up of representatives from each family in the *Arraa'i* Pod." Sul's mind returned to the details of managing the next events. "Nemo, give me the forecast for sea conditions on our route for the next forty-eight hours."

"The sea state is predicted to be calm to smooth for the next three days, Captain. Wave height no more than a half metre."

"Good, thank you. Lower the Pod vessels to align at 1.2 metres above the sea surface."

"In progress, Captain. The Star will be aligned and the vessels ready to link together in six minutes."

The twelve craft drew closer and closer, manoeuvring into their invisible, assigned slots, their decks all facing inward.

"In position, Captain."

"Very well, Nemo, extend the gangways. Connect the Star." He gave an involuntary sigh of relief.

Outside, beyond *Ossë*'s deck, the Pod now burst into life.

Rattling noises and activity surged around the circle of crafts as crew members swarmed above deck to toss ropes between vessels. Children stood at the railings, watching in anticipation.

Some of the young adults swung into action, pulling the swivelling ramps from under each deck, connecting with and making them secure with neighbouring seastead homes. Other crew members attached flexible poles between the boats. Even the children took part, taking the ropes adults pulled in and wrapping them securely to cleats, helping to adjust the shock-absorbing poles to maintain distance between the crafts. In a few minutes, the floating star was complete.

The captain of each vessel signalled to Sul when their vessel was secure in the Star. Sul watched their icons turn green in the display. "Deploy underwater sentries," he instructed as the last one blinked on. Amberjack-shaped shadows were sent out from *Ossë* and from several other crafts, quickly forming a protective perimeter under and around the vessels.

"Sound the all-clear, Nemo." A long, low tone boomed out from *Ossë*.

Swarms of cheering children rushed from the decks, flinging themselves into the swim area formed in the centre of the Star. Splashes, screams, and joyful shouts echoed around the circle as they called others to join them. Families unrolled ladders from their decks down to the water. The children scrambled up, only to jump back in. Adults crossed the catwalks to converse with neighbours. Others began arranging tables and barbeques for sharing picnics.

"Nemo, is all secure?" Sul asked.

"Yes, Captain."

"Prepare the undersea room for the *majlis* to convene."

"We're readying refreshments now, Captain."

"Good. Thank you, Nemo. Also, we'll have a Pod clinic later today. Schedule appointments, please."

"I have made the announcement, Captain. There are a number of regular check-ups. Aneesa on *Evenstar* has a fever. Aisha has finished her chemotherapy regime; no cancer remains. No other health concerns registered."

"Good to hear. I'll see patients starting at four p.m."

"Noted, Captain."

"Come, Professor." He relaxed and smiled at Ben. "Time to meet with the council. We must decide how best to handle this situation. I've asked Paul Whitestone to join us by holo-view."

*

The window above the undersea meeting room was a curved half-dome which formed the bow of *Ossë* as it glided beneath the surface. As the sun rose to its zenith, it sent shafts of light through the shimmering surface of the sea above, brightening the room. Ben took a seat near the broad window, mesmerized by a cloud of small silvery fish streaming past. The school turned and flashed, dancing to the silent music of the sunbeams like synchronized motes of dust.

From his seat next to the window, Ben watched as men and women from the local Pod entered the meeting room in ones and twos. On entry, each greeted Sul, touching his hand or shoulder with a quietly spoken

"Sheikh," acknowledging his status among them. Then Gideon and a few of his friends welcomed the visitors. Ben noticed that each newcomer would circulate around the gathering before sitting, taking time to greet the others in their group in turn.

When visitors came to greet Ben, he felt their awkwardness. *I'm not just a stranger, I'm a potential threat.* Still, most smiled encouragingly at him and offered a word of welcome.

Finishing his duties as eldest son, Gideon threw himself down next to Ben. "These are the leaders of our Pod, Ben, gathering for this special *majlis. You* are the topic of the day."

Ben gave a wry smile, "I understand the concern. There could be a lot at stake."

"I love sitting in to listen to the *majlis.*" Gideon surveyed the room, "Plus, *Baba* says it's a necessary part of my training as his son and, of course, being part of the community. This one should be interesting."

Some in the small group pulled chairs into a rough semi-circle facing out the window. Others sat on mats on the floor or on cushions. The room hummed with friendly conversation.

A blue ovoid sphere materialized mid-air, in front of the window just left of the centre of the bow. The ghostly visage of Paul Whitestone appeared in it. Many rose and went over to greet Paul as though he was there in person returning after a moment to their seats.

Sul now left his position at the entrance, bringing with him a small, upholstered stool. He sat on this in the centre of the semi-circle, the expanse of window behind him. Sul held his hand up. All conversations hushed.

Sul lifted both hands, palms upwards, and the group joined him in chanting: "*Bismillāh ir-raḥmān ir-raḥīm.*" Sul remembered Paul was with them and shifted to English. The group continued chanting the opening prayer in both languages:

> **"In the name of God, the merciful, the compassionate;**
> **Praise to God, the Lord of the worlds.**
> **We believe that there is no God but God, and that Jesus the**
> **Messiah is his Word."**

A chorus of "*Ameen*" murmured around the room.

"Thank you for coming." Sul's eyes scanned the group as he smiled.

"This *majlis* has been convened to discuss the situation we find ourselves in. The main decision we need to reach today is whether we, united as a Pod, want to continue taking responsibility to provide Ben Holden with sanctuary. Or whether it is time to send him to another sanctuary, to protect us from attack." He paused before turning towards the holo-image.

"I've asked Paul to join us via holo-link, since he was the one who asked us to intervene and rescue Ben in the first place. Paul, perhaps you could say a few words to begin?"

The image Paul seemed to grow more solid within the blue sphere of light. Paul looked around, surveying the assembly. "Thank you, Sul, for the invitation." Looking over at one older man, he inquired, "Hassan, how is your daughter?"

"Aisha is fine now, *Mustabsir*, seer. God has indeed gifted you with insight, in the word you spoke over her a few months ago. The medicines Captain Suliman prescribed are working, she is cancer free. She is now pestering her mother to be allowed to swim with the children in the Sea Star." A quiet hum of laughter circled the room. They all were intimately familiar with Aisha and her close brush with cancer.

"Good, so glad to hear she is doing better." Paul cleared his throat. "Well, for those of you who haven't yet heard, let me fill you in a bit on who Ben is, and why he is with you. Ben had become a good friend of mine when he was in Arizona."

People seated near Ben turned their heads to glance at him with approval. *I see being a friend of Paul's carries weight here,* Ben thought.

"About a week and a half ago," Paul continued, "during a time of quiet reflection I sensed that Ben was in serious trouble, off the eastern end of New Caledonia. I knew Ben was supposed to be at the Fusion Symposium in Singapore, so I tried to contact him there. I checked his hotel. The hotel staff couldn't locate him. He hadn't shown up for his appointed presentation. No one knew where he was."

Murmurs filled the room as the Pod members considered this new information.

"I had a strong sense that this was an emergency. Realizing that your Pod was in the area, I called on Sul. I told him who Ben was and what I knew about him and his situation. Can you take it from there, Sul?"

"Thank you, Paul. That's a good introduction. Nemo has reconstructed the events leading up to the search and rescue of the professor. It will be displayed in the holo-interface. Nemo?"

A new green pool of light appeared amid the assembled group, and a map began to take shape. The main lights dimmed, and the window tinted grey to allow the images in the holo-display to become more distinct. A three-dimensional map displayed the sea off the eastern coast of New Caledonia. The area Paul had described shone a lighter blue.

Sul continued, "Nine days ago, *Ossë* broke away from the Pod and sped to the area of ocean Paul had asked us to search. We didn't know what we were getting into, so we approached cautiously, staying at a distance to ensure that we would not be detected."

A tiny green image representing *Ossë* moved over the curve of the horizon.

"We launched several gull reconnaissance drones to survey the area."

Three small yellow gull shapes emerged from *Ossë*. They flew in systematic patterns covering the highlighted area. Yellow trails traced their flight paths.

Ben drew his chair closer to watch. Several men moved aside to allow him in. His attention was riveted to the display as the story of his rescue played out before them, step by step, the gull drones searching. The drones detecting a thermal signature in the bow of a yacht. One drone diving below the surface and detecting a submarine nearby. Sophia's anchovy robots being sent from *Ossë* to disable the yacht by tangling its propellers. A fire flaring in the forward compartment. *Ossë* submerging to avoid detection. Discerning a heat signature in a hole near the shore on Îlot Brosse. One gull drone landing to keep watch near Ben's hideout. *Kestrel* arriving. Men dragging a limp figure out, transporting him back to *Ossë*.

Ben relived each step: sounds, smells, emotions, and sensations.

The lights brightened again. Sul stood. "The hostile submarine which was attempting to capture Ben bore design distinctives of the Caliphate. We tried to track its escape. But it took evasive action through thermoclines and submarine canyons. We lost it."

The crowd sighed.

"There are a number of these small and stealthy subs in operation. We aren't sure how many. They belong to various countries and factions. We were not able to confirm who was operating this one. However, it's reasonable to suspect that the sub was under Caliphate control, since Ben mentioned to me that he has been the focus of the Caliphate for some time.

"Just yesterday, Gideon and Sophia brought information back about an unfamiliar drone searching the area near our Pod. We confirmed that the drone was also of New Caliphate design."

Murmurs increased through the room, many looked over at Ben. Sul held his hand up to restore silence as he turned towards Ben. "Ben, please tell the *majlis* why the Caliphate might be pursuing you."

Ben stood, silent for a moment as he scanned their expressions. "First, let me thank you for your generous welcome and protection since my rescue. I am deeply grateful. As to the Caliphate, I can only hazard an intelligent guess as to their motives. My wife, Lisa, was a geologist, researching a more detailed seismic model of North America. She and my son…" Ben's voice faltered.

The listeners held their breaths and waited.

Ben composed himself. "Lisa and my son, Sammy, were brutally murdered several years ago, while I was away on military duty. I now believe they were murdered during an attempt by the Caliphate to steal my wife's data."

"Why would this information be so important to the Caliphate?" a short but sturdy man rose and asked Paul with a level gaze.

"Hafez, I believe I can shed some light on that," Paul spoke from his holo-image. "Dr Lisa Holden's research related to seismic vulnerabilities on the North American continent. It seems that the Caliphate plans to use this information to cause earthquakes to destabilize nations on that continent."

Hafez's wife, Fatima – a thin, wiry woman with intense eyes – stood and asked Sul, "Sheikh, this sounds like a problem for North America. Our hearts feel for our North American brothers and sisters. But is this our fight?" Her tone indicated that she thought it was not. "Why doesn't Ben appeal to America or Canada to protect him?" A murmur of agreement hummed around the room.

"A question we must consider, Fatima, in this council. We must decide if this is our fight," Sul said.

Paul spoke again, "The US government currently is in tension with the Caliphate over their recent attempt to undermine the Indonesian government through their radical cells. It is a very sensitive situation. They won't strike out against the Caliphate unless there's strong evidence that this is indeed an attack ordered by the Caliphate; they don't want to make the current fragile diplomatic situation even worse. We don't yet have the compelling evidence they would require."

Sul looked around the room, "As members of the *Arraa'i* Pod, you all know the agenda of the Caliphate. Our fathers and mothers, grandfathers, and grandmothers suffered at their hands."

Hafez rose, all eyes in the room turned to him. He spoke quietly, "The Caliphate works constantly to expand their sphere of influence, but they are overstepping their bounds. There comes a point when we must decide what we stand for… and what we won't stand for." A murmur of agreement swept through the room.

Paul nodded. "There's danger here, of course, brother Hafez, if we decide that this is the moment to draw that line in the sand. However, by handing the current situation to someone else, we only are postponing the deeper threat for another day. We're allowing it to fester and grow in strength. Eventually your children and grandchildren will inherit a problem deferred; possibly stronger and more deadly. If Ben's situation had not happened in your vicinity, they would merely look for another reason to persecute you, whom they despise."

There were murmurs of assent.

Paul continued, "Let me remind you of Edmund Burke's famous quote: 'All that is necessary for Evil to triumph is for good men – good people, people like you and me – to do nothing.'"

Hafez nodded and said, "Thank you for that reminder, brother Paul. Brothers and sisters, we must weigh this in our hearts. Even before Ben joined us, we were already under threat. Remember that, earlier this year, Caliphate pirates stole almost a third of our stock. They want us, the apostates, to fail. Every success of ours is a threat to them."

"That's right." Fatima, stood again. "You are right, *habibi*, my dear. Removing Ben from our community may lessen the current danger, but it won't change the long-term threat. They have been acting with impunity, not respecting our territorial agreements and laws."

The room had grown quiet; a thoughtful, collective hush.

After a moment, Paul cleared his throat to draw their attention again. "I think Sul and I can find assistance from terrestrial nations to develop any defensive measures you choose to take. New Zealand, for one, would not like to have this kind of lawless activity on their doorstep."

Ben felt the community weighing the threat. He was the current inciting incident, but he realized it was not ultimately about him. Eyes glanced at him and flickered away. Many were quietly talking with neighbours and nodding among themselves.

Sul broke the silence. "I have personally granted Professor Holden sanctuary for the moment. He has been my guest, I have offered him bread and salt, shared meals with him, so, I have taken responsibility to protect him as is our Bedouin tradition. However, if he is to continue living here, it must be by agreement of the *majlis*. As Paul has just said, his presence endangers us all. So, we all must be unified in this decision to extend him sanctuary... or not." A hum of earnest discussions picked up, filling the room.

What a closeness they have as a community; they depend on and trust one another, Ben mused.

Sul called for attention again. "As far as we know, no one detected us when we brought Ben back here to the Pod. After Gideon's experience with the drone yesterday, further investigation revealed other, similar drones searching our waters, most likely hunting for Ben. This forces us to decide today what is best for us, for Ben, and for the wider community. We're committed to freedom within our territory. We must decide what will be the best way forward for us and other nomadic pods in our region."

Paul spoke from the holo-viewer. "I have known Ben Holden for almost eight years. He is a man of integrity and I'd vouch for him. I appeal to the *majlis* to allow him to stay with you, at least until we understand his situation more fully."

More murmurs swirled around the room. Sul caught Ben's eye. "Ben, if you don't mind, would you please step into the hall for a few minutes while we discuss this among ourselves."

"Of course. This is an important decision for you." Ben looked around the room, "Please know that I am as concerned for the safety of the *Arraa'i* Pod as you. I am grateful, no matter what the decision is." He rose from his seat and left the room. The door whispered shut behind him.

*

Ben wandered down the hall. As he passed a doorway, he heard the familiar young voice, "Silence, Nemo."

He peeked in the door. Sophia was seated on the ground, softly illuminated by a blue holo-interface in front of her. Several arrowhead-like shapes were active in the light pool within the viewer.

Nemo spoke to him. "Sophia is setting up a study of Humboldt squid, an important food source for our tuna. She is currently observing smaller schools of Humboldt squid, in anticipation of the larger populations we'll encounter in a few weeks, when we'll turn north into the Humboldt current."

"Can Sophia hear me?"

"No, she has activated her sphere of silence, in which all incoming sounds are cancelled. It encompasses a two-metre diameter around her. This absolute quiet helps her work without distractions. Her autistic nature makes her very sensitive to noise."

After a moment, Nemo spoke again, "Excuse me, Professor, the captain has requested that you return to the meeting."

A second holo-interface had appeared next to Sophia. It contained the outline of a squid, but just showed the internal organs.

Ben was fascinated but dragged his attention away from Sophia and the virtual squid. He returned to the observation room in the bow.

Sophia turned to look at the empty doorframe. "Storms," she mouthed silently.

*

The room was quiet as Ben re-entered. All eyes were on him.

"Thank you, Ben, for your patience," Sul began. "We needed time for a candid discussion among ourselves. The Caliphate's current activities are a concern to all of us."

"Of course, Captain. I'd do the same in your position." Ben took a deep breath, waiting for what would follow. Already a part of his mind was working through contingency plans.

"I have good news, Ben. The *Arraa'i majlis* has agreed to grant you sanctuary. We've also contacted other Pelagic leaders through our network in the South Pacific Territory and made them aware of what we've decided. We've had confirmation and support from the Territorial council. This threat may affect them as well. Until we understand more, we agree to keep the knowledge of your presence within a small circle of responsible leaders only, extending beyond that only on a need-to-know basis.

"Paul is now contacting friends in the New Zealand command to negotiate assistance in case we need it."

Many of the men and women in the room now rose, coming over to shake Ben's hand. Some embraced him. Some lingered and chatted. Ben thanked each person in turn, keenly aware of the gravity of their decision. Slowly, they began to filter from the room. Sul was at the door, exchanging news and greetings with many as they left.

Finally, only Ben, Gideon, and Sul remained. Sul and Gideon began clearing up. Ben stepped in to help, moving chairs back to where they'd been before the meeting.

"That was… generous, Sul," Ben began, as he moved closer to the captain. "A remarkable community."

Sul put his hand on Ben's shoulder. "Your plight has put a face to the threat, and the need to stand up to the Caliphate, Ben. The *majlis* understands this. We've discussed the implications at length. We're much better organized and prepared to defend ourselves at this stage. Certainly not as vulnerable as when my family was attacked when I was a child."

Ben relaxed a bit under Sul's reassuring hand. "Ben, I believe this decision will be a milestone for our Pod. Perhaps even for the entire South Pacific Pelagic Territory. We must draw a line, making it clear that we refuse to tolerate intimidation and persecution."

"Thank you," Ben said simply, looking into Sul's eyes.

"Of course." Sul met his gaze. "On another note, the *majlis* members brought up another bit of news. It turns out that a Chilean delegation is due to arrive tomorrow afternoon at the Sea Star. It's time to discuss the size of the anchovy fishery this year, to negotiate the quota for the Southern Pacific Territory. It would be best if you were away while the Chilean delegation is visiting. I've asked Gideon to take you with him tomorrow morning when he visits the Marcelli Township."

Gideon jumped to his feet, "Great idea! This will be fun, Professor. I've been looking forward to talking to you. I hear you served in the Marines Special Operations Command. I leave next week for my required tour of duty in the Pelagic Rangers. We'll be doing exercises in the west all next month." Ben smiled and took a step backwards at the onslaught of enthusiasm.

Sul smiled, "Don't talk his ear off, son." He turned to Ben as he stood up to leave, "Ben, we'll talk more when you return. There's much to think through. Many, many decisions to make."

Then, he cautioned his son, "Leave in stealth mode, Gideon. We don't know who might be monitoring us. And we don't want the Chileans to ask uncomfortable questions. I'm sure their security systems are already surveying the area in preparation for their visit."

"Aye, aye, Captain Dad," Gideon assured him. As Sul stepped out, Gideon resumed describing the upcoming trip to Ben. "*Kestrel's* now secured under *Oyster*. We can enter her through one of the access hatches in the *Oyster* bilge. The Sea Star gives us easy access. We just have to cross a few vessels via the walkways."

12 July 2066, *Arraa'i* Pod Seastead
(the same day)

Ben and Gideon left the sea room for the lift. As they walked down the corridor, Sophia stood at the doorway of her workplace, studying the texture of the floor. *"May* I come, *'akhi?"* she asked the carpet.

Gideon stooped in front of his sister to look up into her downcast eyes. She didn't meet his eyes. "Yes, *Ameera,* we'd love to have you come with us. How about a barbeque with Uncle Hafez and Aunt Fatima?" She glanced briefly at him, flashing a faint smile before looking down again.

Shyly, she grasped Ben's hand. Gideon gave Ben a startled look. "She never does that. You must've made quite an impression!" Ben looked at Gideon, shrugging his shoulders, but holding the small hand firmly. The three went up in the lift together and walked out on the top deck, into the sunlight.

The sun danced before them on a rippling sea, under a clear sky. A soft wind blew from the west.

Ben studied the bridge and deck with interest. "In the re-enactment, they mentioned that this vessel was submerged for a time. I see a covering hidden in the roof of the bridge. Can it seal over the deck? Is that how *Ossë* can fully submerge?"

Sophia giggled at the thought.

Gideon looked at his sister, "Sophia loves being underwater."

Pointing at the top of the bridge structure, he said, "Yes, you are right. That shield curls down from the bridge and fits in this groove on the deck."

Ben walked closer to look, "Yes I see. Neat trick."

Gideon laughed, "Most of *Ossë* is already underwater. About five years ago, seastead vessel plans were upgraded, taking the next natural step. Now we can completely submerge. This allows us to ride out more violent storms in relative calm. And just two years ago, we tweaked the design again, adding some stealth components. Now we can avoid detection when necessary. Came in useful when we were looking for you."

"I'm glad you did. I'm grateful, not only for the rescue, but also the chance to meet your clan and all of you." Sophia squeezed Ben's hand in response to his gratitude.

*

Conversations wafted across the water as people walked between gangways linking adjacent vessels in the Sea Star. Friends caught up with each other's news. Children frolicked and laughed together in the central pool.

Two vessels away, a woman waved, "Gideon, come! Bring your friend. And Sophia! My favourite girl!" she called out. "Hafez is grilling tuna for lunch. With some toe-curling spices."

They crossed the gangways. Gideon stopped to chat as he passed familiar people on the boats. Sophia drew closer to Ben. Her grip tightened.

They arrived at *Oyster*. There, the older woman, Fatima, who had spoken at the *majlis*, was seated next to Hafez, who was carefully overseeing the tuna steaks on the grill.

"*Ameera*, I see you have a new friend," Fatima said, looking at Sophia with gentle and loving eyes.

"Will you come to your auntie today?" She held her hand out, palm upward. Sophia released Ben and walked over to lay her young hand on the wrinkled one. The woman caressed Sophia's head with the other hand, reciting an Arabic blessing. Sophia smiled and then sat close to Fatima on her bench.

Hafez looked up from grilling the fish, "So you're the famous Professor that *Ossë* pulled from a shallow grave!" he said, his eyes alive with humour.

"Yes sir, and it very nearly was my grave." He shook Hafez's hand, "Please call me Ben."

"Ben, then. Please sit. You'll stay for dinner, yes?"

The smell of the tuna reminded Ben how long it'd been since lunch. He glanced at Gideon.

"Of course, *'ammi*. You couldn't eat all that by yourself," Gideon teased.

"I worry it won't be enough for your appetites," the old man responded smiling. He bent over the grill, then looked up with feigned anguish, "and I as a good host will be left with nothing but a wistful glance, as you clean your plates."

Gideon laughed, "I'll control myself, *'ammi.*" His tone shifted to more serious matters, "We must leave on *Kestrel* before dawn. I'm taking Ben to Marcelli Township tomorrow before the delegation arrives."

"I understand *ibn 'akhi*. I'll leave our boat open this evening, so you two can reach your craft berthed underneath *Oyster*. I'll ensure the way is clear and reconfigure security protocols. We are on security alert level three."

"Please try not to wake us. We old ones need our sleep," chided Hafez, a twinkle in his dark eyes.

Fatima pulled chairs out from the shelter of the bridge arranging them around the barbeque grill. She then began distributing plates and utensils. "*Tabbouleh* and pita are on the table. Are the tuna steaks ready, *habibi?*"

A disembodied voice interrupted the conversation, in Arabic.

Hafez spoke to the AI, "Moosa, We've guests. Please speak in English."

"Of course, Captain, sorry. Today's delivery drone is approaching. Shall I ready this morning's tuna harvested from the *iki jime* gate for shipment?"

"Yes, thank you." Turning to Gideon, Hafez added, "Prices are good today in Singapore. We sold an auction lot to Alladhin Fish Importers for a high bid."

Then, he resumed his instructions for Moosa. "There should be an order of groceries for us, as well."

"Yes, Captain, I see it on the manifest. I'll have it stowed after delivery."

"Thank you, Moosa." Hafez said.

Sophia walked over to Gideon, whispering in his ear.

Gideon nodded, "Moosa, please check today's shipment for *Ossë*. Have Sophia's new robotics arrived? The routing would be from Cheng 3D printers at Marcelli Deep."

There was a pause, then, "Yes, there're two new models of tuna guides and a prototype of a moon jellyfish. I see a note. The printing of the new amberjack guardian has been delayed. It won't be in this shipment."

"Thank you, Moosa. Please ask Nemo to prepare our tuna for shipment as well. From the *Ossë* freezer."

"Nemo confirms that it has been done," came Moosa's response.

Ben was intrigued. "So, Gideon, are there daily deliveries?"

"Yes, Professor. Sometimes two or three times a day, depending on volume."

Sophia sat down next to Fatima, who handed her a plate of food. Sophia picked at it politely but didn't eat much.

"Sophia, *habibti*, there's more to the world than sushi and sashimi. Try a bite." Fatima leaned over with a piece of grilled tuna. Sophia obediently took a small nibble.

Hafez looked up at Ben from the grill, "I hear that you're new to the Pelagic Territories, Professor. Sorry, I mean, Ben. We've a delivery drone network in constant motion. The network serves nomadic pods like us, as well as the static pelagic communities like Marcelli Township, where you'll go tomorrow."

"A delivery drone network. Makes sense for this nomadic life," Ben said, waving his hand around the Sea Star.

"Yes, the *Flying Fish* network takes our tuna stocks to market. It also brings our supplies. The coordination centre for our sector of the network is at Kermadec Seamount. From there they sell our goods bound for the South-East and East Asian markets."

"There!" interrupted Gideon, pointing towards the horizon. "The *Flying Fish* is approaching from the north-east."

A faint blur became visible on the blue horizon, a tiny grey cloud on the line separating sea and sky. It grew rapidly as Ben watched. Now he could distinguish a flattened wing shape amid a swirling cloud of rainbow spray, skimming just off the sea's surface.

Gideon shielded his eyes with his hand, "This is one of the new delta wing drones."

"Ah, I'm familiar with that design. It uses ground effect pressure the sea's surface causes the aircraft pressure wave to reflect, lifting the craft. Flying requires less energy. I've been wanting to see it in operation," Ben acknowledged.

Conversations increased among the people gathered outside on the Sea Star. Everyone was aware of the approaching craft. Children and adults scrambled out of the central pool to prepare for the arrival.

Hafez looked up from his grill, "Professor, I read that during the pioneer days of America, people in towns would flock to the Wells Fargo station to meet the day's stagecoach, eager to see if their family had parcels." He offered the guests more tuna hot off the coals. "I think it's the same excitement here every time the delivery drone comes. It's an important link between us and the outside world."

Gideon set his plate down, "Here, come with me Ben, we can watch *Oyster* prepare its container for the drone."

Ben set his half-finished plate down with a wistful look, then followed Gideon. They took a catwalk on the outside of the bridge and moved to where they looked down on the bow of *Oyster*. From underneath the starboard side of the vessel a container was being released and carried to the surface using a special track system slotted into the hull of *Oyster*.

The wing-shaped drone came within two hundred metres of the Sea Star then switched to a hovering mode. A bay opened on the forward part of the aircraft. Conveyer belts carried out containers to a staging platform; the goods to be delivered to *Arraa'i* Pod. And on each vessel around the Star, containers were positioned to be fetched. Out of the ship, smaller utility drones ferried containers back and forth, delivering containers from the *Flying Fish* drone to vessels in the Pod, and Pod containers to the drone.

Ben and Gideon watched one small utility drone approach *Oyster*. It dropped the delivery container on the port side, where it was grappled and secured by a slotted tethering line.

"That's the container for Hafez and Fatima," Gideon commented. Thumps reverberated through the decking at their feet as the container then disappeared under *Oyster* to be stowed.

The small cargo drone then slid to the other side and picked up the container containing *Oyster*'s tuna, ready for market, whisking it back to the mother drone.

Within fifteen minutes, the whole Pod had been serviced. The utility drones were stowed in the larger aircraft, which then turned and sped away towards the north-west.

"Very impressive." Ben marvelled at the efficiency.

"It will be stopping at the Tomlin Pod next, I believe," Gideon observed as he followed the direction of the *Flying Fish* craft. "They are about fifty kilometres north-west of us. They are also tuna herders."

*

Walking back to *Oyster*'s deck, Ben and Gideon sat again with the family around the barbeque and picked up their still-warm meals.

"This is great!" Ben said, making short work of his tuna steak. Hafez gave him another.

"Ben, tell us about yourself. Where did you grow up?"

"I was raised in one of the beach cities of Los Angeles. My father worked for the electric company there as an engineer." Ben dreaded answering questions about his past.

"Never been in that part of the world. Too far north." Hafez smiled. "Brothers or sisters?"

Ben hesitated, "I had one younger sister, who died when I was eighteen."

"I'm so sorry, how did it happen?" Fatima asked.

Ben looked at her kind face, then continued, "It was a skiing accident. She took a run that was beyond her skill level, and lost control."

"That is terrible."

"Yes, it changed the dynamics of our family. My mother, especially, grieved for many years." *So much sadness*, Ben thought.

"Gideon called you Professor, Ben." Hafez changed the subject, seeing the look on the young man's face.

Ben was grateful, "Yes, I did my undergraduate studies in physics, at University of California Santa Barbara. Then got my Masters in electrical engineering while I was in the Marines. I received my PhD in particle physics from Caltech in Pasadena, California, a few years ago. I've been teaching there part-time, but giving a lot of time to continuing research in particle physics…"

A siren interrupted their conversation.

Hafez leapt to his feet. "Excuse me Ben, I must get to my station." He sprinted into *Oyster's* bridge area.

Everyone on the vessels around the star froze for an instant, then there was a flurry of movement. Fatima hurriedly folded the chairs and table to stow inside. Dishes and food were stashed in a dumb waiter, to be transported back to the kitchen.

"What's going on?" Ben exclaimed, puzzled by the commotion. Children scrambled up ladders from the sea and into their homes. Coals from barbeque pits were dumped into the sea.

"We must hurry back to *Ossë*, Ben," Gideon said, grabbing his arm. He questioned the AIA, "Moosa, what triggered the warning alarm?"

"One of the perimeter scouts spotted unidentified aircraft heading this way."

"Probably another Caliphate reconnaissance drone," Gideon muttered. "Planes with no identification always mean trouble."

He squatted before his sister again, "Sophia, I must carry you because we must move quickly. This is an emergency."

Sophia pointed at Ben.

Gideon looked at Ben quizzically, "OK with you?"

"Sure," Ben said. He carefully bent down and picked Sophia up. He could feel her tense, but she didn't struggle.

The three began to race across the ramps towards *Ossë*.

As they pounded onto *Ossë's* deck, Sul was waiting for them. Ben set Sophia down as Sul began to direct them. "Gideon, take your sister below." Sophia followed Gideon to the lift.

"Ben, stay here with me, please. You might be able to help."

Ben stood in the bridge with Sul. He took in the information on the screens and studied the hologram of the Sea Star in the centre. Seasteads around the ring began flashing a green "ready" sign.

"Captain, I've sent three more scouting gulls to eight thousand feet to give us advanced notice of the approaching craft."

"Good. Thank you, Nemo." Sul stepped back, pulling Ben deeper into the bridge area. A clear panel rapidly curved down from the roof and slotted into the deck, sealing the bridge.

"Status of the Pod vessels, Nemo?"

"All are ready, except *Pleiades*. Their shield's just closing now. Done. All vessels are now under my control, Captain." The holographic display of the pod showed all vessels green.

"Begin submersion sequence. Bring the Sea Star down to 30 metres. Ensure all lights are out, Nemo. Defence protocol level 4."

"Submersion in progress. All exterior lights extinguished. Interior lights shifted to red. Electromagnetic fields dampened. Tuna schools being dispersed randomly and diving away from the surface. Defence protocol 4 being executed, Captain."

"Very good, Nemo."

Ben watched out the window as the Sea Star sank as a unit, still connected as a ring. The water crept up to the decks of the vessels and then slowly up over the windows. Sul's eyes moved between the display, to the instruments on the bridge panel, and to the vessels outside.

Sul looked at Ben and explained, "We needed to respond right away. Best not to be detected right now. We're in an area where there's almost no shipping or aircraft activity. There's no reason for anyone else to be out here. Likely this is another Caliphate search drone."

"That's what Gideon said as well."

"Nemo, has the aircraft been identified yet?"

"Yes, Captain, I confirmed the design is indeed a Caliphate craft, though it is still showing no identity beacon," Nemo informed them.

Ben watched Sul's intense concentration. The responsibility for the Pod rested on his shoulders.

The waves swirled above the shield as they continued sinking. Within six minutes of the alarm, the sea had fully covered the Pod vessels.

Gideon walked back onto the bridge, now the control room for the entire Pod.

"How is Sophia?" Sul asked.

"She's OK, *Baba*. All the commotion is scaring her. Fatima came over and is talking to her. She's calming down. She asked for sashimi as I was leaving."

"That's a good sign. Thank you, son."

Outside the shield, lights from the vessels dimmed to red as they continued to submerge. They were only ghostly shapes outside the window now. The surface of the sea glimmered far above them. Darkness steadily increased.

"Depth, Nemo?"

"Twenty-two metres, Captain. Hull integrity of all vessels nominal. No alarms. Protocol 4 fully executed."

"Thank you. What is the status of the unidentified aircraft?"

"We'll be in their surface sensing range in five minutes, Captain. Without identification, we must presume it to be hostile."

"Nemo, deploy countermeasures. Plot solutions for likely scenarios if we need to employ defence protocol 5. Ready *Kestrel*."

"Yes, Captain. Hafez has taken *Kestrel* out of the mooring clamps. He is bringing it under *Ossë* for Gideon. Sonar-absorbing drones have been released." A school of anchovy-like devices emerged from vessels around the Pod. They formed an undulating umbrella over the submerged crafts.

"I'll go down and prepare to take *Kestrel*, *Baba*."

"Thank you, son. Hopefully, you won't have to use it. Its combat capabilities haven't been fully tested yet."

"I think it could easily splash this spy plane, but best to leave it alone and not announce our presence."

Sul looked at his son, "Splash?"

Gideon grinned, "Destroy it and put it in the water, *Baba*", he said as disappeared below again.

"Thirty metres, neutral buoyancy, Captain." There was deep twilight outside the window. A shadowed and silent world. "We're within their sensor range. The enemy drone will pass within a quarter mile of us."

"Take us down another fifteen metres, Nemo."

"Yes, Captain." The darkness increased incrementally outside the window.

Ben and Sul stood in silence. Their eyes flicked back and forth between the holo-display and the dim silhouettes of the Pod vessels across the sunken circle.

A silvery stream of bubbles erupted from a vessel near them.

"Nemo?" Sul whispered.

"Captain, *Nautilus* had a fault with their ballast tank. Air has escaped." Nemo responded, barely audible.

The bubbles ascended to the surface far above them. They waited.

"The hostile has detected the stream of bubbles. It's now circling our area, Captain," Nemo broke the silence. The icon depicting the hostile drone in the display changed course and began circling above them.

"Release more anchovy countermeasures. Surround the Sea Star."

"Yes, Captain." Another silvery cloud surged out, creating a thicker protective shield around the submerged vessels.

They waited in the silence and darkness. The Sea Star was motionless in the deep.

"They've dropped a sensor package. I detect that it is a sonar and pressure-wave array, Captain."

Blue dots floated in a ring on the sea surface in the display, just a few hundred metres west of their position.

"The array has released several active sonar probes."

Steady pings sounded as the probe descended slowly through the water column. Faint at first, then steadily becoming louder. The display showed the probe's trajectory would pass by the Star on the southern edge, within eighteen metres. Robotic anchovies swarmed to that side of the Sea Star, creating a barrier between the probe and the community. The pings faded into the depths below. There was silence again.

"The hostile is still circling, Captain."

A concussive explosion shattered the silence. *Ossë* trembled.

"The enemy drone has dropped a depth charge, one hundred and fifty metres south. It was set to explode at twenty metres."

"Go to fifty metres, Nemo. Slowly. Avoid emitting pressure waves as we go down."

"Yes, Captain."

Another explosion. The deck lurched. Ben found himself gripping the edge of the control panel. *Relax, stay calm.* "That charge went off at eighty metres north by north-west, depth of thirty metres, Captain. *Pleiades* reports a leak from the explosion." A moment passed, "They have sealed it."

"Thank you, Nemo."

Another tense few minutes, then another explosion. Further away.

"Two hundred and fifty metres east. Depth forty metres, Captain."

"They are framing their search area with depth charges. Intervals of ten-metres depth. The charges must be pressure sensitive, rather than timed." Sul assessed the information from the display.

Pinging began again, closer. An object was falling in the holographic display, just above them. Ben pointed. A blue blinking icon was descending from the surface.

Sul estimated the path of the object. "That one's probably set for fifty metres, and it looks to land on *Oyster*'s deck."

Ben's gaze was riveted on the display. He turned to Sul, "Captain, let me go and deflect the charge away from *Oyster*, so it explodes lower. Is there a way for me to get out there?"

Sul looked at him, "It's dangerous, Ben." He thought a moment then nodded towards a door, "There's an airlock on the starboard side of the bridge, with diving gear stashed in the bridge locker. Nemo, open and prepare the airlock."

Sul locked gaze with Ben. "I don't have to tell you to be careful, son."

"I can do this." Ben ran to the indicated door, which slid open before him.

In a matter of seconds, Ben was in the airlock, and grabbed his gear. "Nemo, close the bridge airlock. Bring us back up to thirty-five metres slowly." The inner door shut on Ben.

"Yes, Captain." There was a slight whoosh as the door slid closed. Sul watched through the window. Ben leaned against the airlock wall and donned his fins, pulled the mask over his face and adjusted the rebreather harness. He put the regulator in his mouth and gave a thumb up. Seawater rushed into the chamber, flooding it rapidly. The outer door opened.

Within seconds, Ben was out in the frigid water, swimming quickly towards the deck of *Oyster*. He could see the blinking orb, still metres above the submerged ring. Ben changed course and began swimming up.

From the corner of his eye, Sul noticed a shadow darting among the anchovy countermeasures. "Nemo, what is this animal?" As he watched, the vague shadow ate one of the robotic fish, then immediately spit it out.

"Captain, it appears a small herd of fur seals are hunting in this area."

The animal saw Ben and swam down and glided around him, inspecting. Ben glanced at this interloper, but then kept his eye on the blinking orb. The seal looked up and saw the object Ben was watching, and in a fluid movement went up and bumped the orb with his nose.

Sul flinched, but the orb continued to fall in a slightly deflected course.

The seal swam around the blinking ball several times, then took it in its mouth, carried it several metres higher in the water column, then dropped it again. Sul's mouth went dry.

He could also see Ben visibly trembling now, he hadn't had time to get into an exposure suit. *He's getting too cold, hypothermia will set in soon.*

Ben manoeuvred to stay under the ball as the seal repeatedly snatched it in its mouth, then dropped it around the ring.

Sul's face was grim. The hostiles will notice that the device has not exploded yet.

Several other seals had now joined the first. Ben was tracking the orb as it was passed from seal to seal. One swooped under the ball, caught and carried it up and outside the ring; it must have bit down on the orb because there was a deafening explosion.

Red lights started flashing on the panel, the deck slowly began a slight tilting under Sul. "Nemo?"

"Several vessels have experienced structural damage; repair systems have closed compartments to maintain buoyancy. Compensating now, Captain." The tilting stopped and began to slowly return to level.

"Release more countermeasures, Nemo." Some of the small robots were now falling, put out of commission by the blast.

"Released, Captain."

*

Sul studied the scene outside the window. Two seals were drifting down, not moving. *Stunned by the concussive blast,* Sul thought. Ben was just settling on *Topaz's* deck, also inert. One of the seals twitched, then slowly righted itself. It swam over and nudged the other seal, who then also began to move. They quickly left the area.

Sul noticed Ben had stopped shivering, but lights on the mask indicated he was breathing. *Next stage of hypothermia will be setting in, along with the shock.*

Pinging filled the air again. "Another depth charge has been dropped over our position, Captain." Sul saw it falling, another blue blinking light above them. It would fall on *Murex. What depth is it set for?*

Sul noticed activity across the ring, two divers had emerged from *Murex*, but they were too far away to catch this new orb before it hit the deck. To Sul's immense relief Ben began to stir. He looked towards *Ossë* and waved at Sul awkwardly. Sul pointed up.

Ben slowly turned his head in the direction indicated and saw the new orb falling. He seemed a bit disoriented but forced himself to move in the direction of *Oyster*.

At that speed, Sul was not sure Ben would get to the charge in time. Ben seemed to come to himself and made a dash to reach the orb just several feet above the deck. Ben gently pushed it with both hands to the edge, then released it to continue sinking into the dark waters beneath.

From inside *Ossë*, Sul watched the drama of Ben's heroic swim to save *Oyster*, and the Pod. "Nemo, tell everyone in the Pod to brace."

"Done, Captain." Alarm screens flashed. "Brace."

"Ensure the countermeasures counterbalance the force of the explosion and no echoes of the ring get back to the drone."

"Calibrating, Captain. Done. I also will have some of the anchovies appear stunned from the pressure wave."

"Good, Nemo." Sul watched as Ben pulled himself into a ball and clung to some cleats on the deck of *Oyster*, next to *Ossë*.

"Good, well done, Ben. Hold tight," Sul murmured.

The nearby explosion rocked *Ossë* when it came. Some of the Pod icons in the display flashed red.

"Damage report, Nemo?"

"This explosion was at fifty metres, Captain. It resulted in cracks in several of the Pod hulls, but no additional leakage."

Sul looked out the window and saw Ben's form drifting from the deck of *Topaz*. The two swimmers had recovered quickly from the explosion and caught the limp Ben, carrying him back inside. "Have *Topaz* immediately treat Ben for hypothermia and shock. Please give regular reports on his status."

Time ticked by slowly as Sul intently watched the displays around him. The Caliphate drone continued to circle above for another ten tense minutes. Then it veered off and continued its search mission.

Its operators must have concluded, correctly, that the fur seals had detonated the charge, Sul thought.

"We're now out of sensor range of the hostile, Captain. It has passed over the horizon and broken contact with the sensor package on the surface."

"Please instruct the Pod to remain here for thirty minutes, just to make sure."

"Yes, Captain. Done."

"Ask *Kestrel* to retrieve and disarm the sensor package."

"*Kestrel* has acknowledged and is proceeding."

Ten minutes later, Nemo said, "Ben is responding to treatment, Captain. He is now coming around."

Sul waited, watching the screens and damage reports. It could have been far worse if not for Ben's quick action.

After thirty minutes, Sul relaxed. "Secure from defence protocol 4. Maintain protocol 3, Nemo."

"Defence protocol 3, Captain."

"Begin preparations for surfacing."

"Yes, Captain."

*

All the crafts in the Sea Star were now on the surface. Water streamed off the decks back into the sea, as families emerged outside. Divers dropped into the water and swam around the Star, inspecting damage to the seastead vessels. The mood was sober.

Ben walked across the ramp from *Topaz*, with unsure steps. He grasped Sul's outstretched arm. "Thank you, Ben!" Sul hugged him, "That was well done. Your actions saved the Pod from certain discovery." He glanced at Ben with concern. "How are you?" he asked.

Ben was quiet. He felt sore, and light-headed. "Still in a bit of shock, I think, but I'll be OK." He was aware of the activity around him, as a blur.

He was surprised at the memories that surfaced as he lay on the deck of *Oyster*.

CHAPTER SIXTEEN

12 April 2063, Grit, Arizona
(three years earlier)

An object glinted in the clear early morning sky, drawing Ben's attention. He gazed up, pausing his repairs of the small agri-bot. Sweat dripped from his brow.

A sleek, miniature dirigible floated over the south end of the jojoba field.

Ben stood, scanning the area. *Who's controlling that thing?*

A hundred metres away, a young woman sat on a rock, intent on her computer pad. Another pesky hiker? On our land, the signs are posted and obvious. Why the dirigible?

Crouching again, he finished installing the replacement circuit modules and closed the access panel. "Test sequence," he said. The small machine whirred to life cycling through its routine: forward, back, right side, left side. Then the hoeing arms and sensor probes cycled through their sequences. "Good to go," he murmured to himself, satisfied. Then a bit louder, "Begin standard work sequence."

"Normal work sequence," the machine acknowledged. The agri-bot scooted off under the jojoba bushes to carry out its tasks. The bot would weed, monitor, water, and fertilize the nut-laden bushes being raised to produce the valuable jojoba oil.

Ben stood. Brushing dust off his jeans, he walked towards the young woman. He called out, "Excuse me, can I help you?"

"Stop right there," her voice was blunt and loud. She didn't even look up.

Ben scowled. "You're on private land," he said, continuing towards her.

"Stop!" she commanded, still intent on her screen. "Don't come any closer."

"I don't know who you are, but this is our land," Ben warned, his voice edged with menace.

"My drone detects a diamondback rattler, four feet in front of you. Behind that bush on your right. Your call." She looked over at him with a sweet smile. The sparkle of her blue eyes startled him.

As if on cue, Ben heard the distinctive rattle, just behind the creosote bush in front and a little to the right. He froze.

"If you want to talk to me, I suggest you walk to the left," she said pleasantly.

He took the circuitous route she indicated. She stood as he approached.

"You're trespassing. What're you doing here?" a brusqueness covered Ben's embarrassment.

"Hi, my name is Maria. What's yours?" She offered her hand.

"Uh, Ben. Ben Holden." He paused, taking her hand warily.

"Good to meet you, Ben. Is this your jojoba field here?" Her hand waved towards the crop.

"It belongs to the rehabilitation programme. I, uh, was fixing an agribot."

"And you want to know why I'm invading your territory?"

"Um, yes," he said, a bit too quickly; she was distracting.

"I'm helping you and your programme out, Ben. I'm surveying the invasive grasses in this valley. If there was a wildfire, those grasses there would pose a threat to your crops." She pointed to a scruffy clump of plants.

"Um," Ben mumbled again, not sure how to respond.

"You see this red grass between the creosote bushes?" She gestured, taking a step towards the jojoba field. "It's red brome and highly flammable. A fire would spread rapidly, engulfing that grass like tinder between the bushes. You need to clear the grass from this field to keep it safe. I suggest that you program your bots to clear a ten-metre fire break, rather than the four you currently have."

He followed her gestures, and then glanced back at her. She waited.

"Ben, should I be using sign language?" she said, smiling again.

"Oh… Sorry. Thanks."

"Thanks… For saving your life? For the advice? Both?"

"Yes, both, of course." He pulled himself together. "And your employer is…?"

"You're welcome, Ben," she said, eyes dancing. "I'm with the National

Park service. Your land borders a national park over there. These invasive plants respect neither boundary nor border. So, we survey beyond our borders. Whatever jeopardizes your plantation also jeopardizes our park, and vice versa."

"Can we begin again?" Ben asked, realizing he hadn't made the best first impression.

"Glad to. I'm Maria. Maria Romero," she said, extending her hand once more.

"Uh, Ben. Ben Holden," he took the hand lightly.

She looked at him quietly for a moment. "Let me guess," she said, "you're the one that owns the weird device in the mine down in the valley."

He nodded, surprised she would know about that.

"So, what is it?" she asked.

"It's a muon collector," he said, now concerned; it was a sensitive device. "How did you find that?"

"A *muon* collector? I came across it the other day while checking on bats that roost in the mine. I also monitor bats." Another long pause.

"So, you collect muons and fix bots. Funny, you don't look like a nerd," she said, studying him.

He looked at her quizzically.

"You're too good-looking," she answered his unspoken question. "But, if you're into fixing bots, it wasn't too big a jump to assume that the muon thingy might be yours as well."

Ben didn't know how to respond. He wasn't keeping up. Her blue eyes were diverting.

"Muons? Are they edible?"

"Muons are sub-atomic decay particles from cosmic rays entering the atmosphere. No, not edible; they're invisible and right pass through you. I study them." He'd found a safe subject.

Maria looked him over for a moment. "I'm thinking you don't get out much, Ben." She smiled. "Want to have dinner with me in town tonight?"

His thoughts whirled. This was moving too fast. "Uh, I guess."

"Good. Coyote Café. Seven tonight. You buy me dinner in return for saving your life." She stashed her computer into a leather satchel at her side.

The drone swooped in, humming overhead. "See you tonight." She walked away, down the hill into the valley. The drone followed above. She turned to wave at him, smiling.

Ben watched her until she disappeared around a canyon wall, then shook his head.

*

That evening, Ben studied the reflection on the window, superimposed on the garish desert sunset outside. She was beautiful.

"You can look at me directly," she suggested. "I won't bite. I love this place," she said, covering his embarrassment. "Did y'know it's over a hundred and twenty years old? My mom told me my great-grandfather met my great-grandmother here. And they have a real human cook back there in the kitchen, sweating over a grill." Ben saw the chef's head bobbing behind the pick-up counter.

"Maria," he said, composing himself, "I'm sorry. I haven't been around people socially for a while."

"I guessed as much. Shall I give you a better introduction of myself?"

He smiled gratefully. "Please."

"Well, I grew up in a very different place from here. My family are seasteaders, living on the Marcelli Ring out in the Southern Pacific."

He was intrigued. "That *is* far away. You're certainly a fish out of water."

She laughed. "I knew I'd like you. I came here to finish my master's degree in ecology. I wanted to go somewhere new, completely different from where I grew up. What better place than a desert? My family once was from around here before they emigrated to the Pelagic Territories. So, I returned to find some of my roots."

Burgers and fries arrived in baskets, along with milkshakes.

"Will you go back to the sea when you've finished your degree?" He pushed a basket towards her.

"Yes," she said simply. "I do want to travel and experience new places while I'm young, before life ties me down. But my first love is the ocean and living at the seamount."

"Seamount? Is that an island?"

She smiled, "No, not quite an island. It's an underwater mountain rising almost to the surface of the ocean. In the centre of Marcelli Ring, the undersea mountain rises to within four metres of the surface at low tide. Near enough to touch it without using a rebreather."

"So, do you live in a community under the ocean?" He forgot to eat, listening to her.

Her eyes glowed at his encouragement. "Sorry to say, we don't live *under* the ocean. We actually don't build homes on the seamount itself, because that area is a marine preserve. We've built a beautiful white ring, made of the same material as seashells, almost twenty kilometres across. From the air, on a clear day, it looks like a snowflake with a circular turquoise heart set a deep blue sea. It's breathtaking. The marine preserve is the turquoise part in the centre, the snowflake with the lacy arms – at least, that's what it looks like from the sky – are the homes and businesses we build on the Ring. My family, the Romeros, are third-generation Pelagics, descended from the Marcellis."

"Pelagics?"

She saw his confusion, "Pelagics are how we refer to people who live on the open sea. My great-grandfather, Carlo Marcelli, founded the Marcelli colony and designed the floating ring around the seamount. The original colony was made up of four or five families. Over time we've developed into a town, Marcelli Ring.

"We're a prolific bunch. There must be about a hundred families now, all Marcellis – first cousins, second cousins. Actually, I just have cousins everywhere." Maria smiled at the thought. "And of course, thousands of immigrants have come to join us now."

"So, although you're Pelagic, you came ashore to get a degree and find some roots," Ben observed, eating a chip.

"I was a teacher in the seamount school system for a few years. Then I decided to work on this master's degree, hoping it would allow me to do research in seamount ecology. That would be my dream job."

"Seamount ecology?" Another chip was consumed. Ben was enjoying watching her.

"There are tens of thousands of seamounts in the oceans of the world. Many Pelagic settlements are on or around seamounts. Most of the open sea is like a desert, but seamounts are like oases in these sea deserts. There's so much marine life around our seamount, and this makes it a perfect site for farms and ranches. Of marine species, of course."

She took a few bites of her burger. "This tastes great," she said holding it up and smiling.

She warmed to her topic, "Really, there's so little we know about seamounts. The science is young. A better understanding will enable us to use the resources we have responsibly, and not upset the ecology of the whole world really, which is so intertwined with the vast ocean system."

"I can tell you're an enthusiast. That's a great dream." Ben smiled and ate another chip, entranced. "What's it like growing up on a seamount?"

Maria became even more animated, "Oh, it's such a privilege to live on the sea. I feel like the ocean is part of me in my blood, running through my very being. We live suspended between the abyss and deep heaven; I love the beauty and wildness. The ocean has many moods, from profound stillness to storms that feel like they are tearing the very fabric of nature apart. I'm often awed and humbled by the sheer power of waves and wind, sun and darkness, the heights and the depths, the countless creatures that fly and swim. It's what I love, it's my identity." Maria searched for words, "I guess, simply, the sea is my natural home."

The hamburger was suspended in Ben's hand, "That's almost poetic."

Maria laughed. "The sea makes us poets, I guess. In the township, I remember learning to swim before I could walk. I learned the names of creatures and plants of the seamount from my uncles and aunts long before I started school. We're taught to be fiercely protective of our marine sanctuary."

Ben interrupted, "Marine sanctuary? In the centre of the town, right?"

"Yes, no one fishes or farms there. Community consensus allows only minimal human activity and no industrial waste. It's like a nursery for the species which are native to our part of the ocean. In our families and in school, we're taught that each of us is a steward; our behaviour can affect all ocean life. We aspire to live in a symbiotic relationship with the sea. As we protect the sea it then provides us with our livelihood. The plants and animals we farm on Marcelli Rise, for example, are seeded from the populations of the marine sanctuary in the centre of the Ring."

"Marcelli Rise?"

"Sorry, I've kept assuming that you're familiar with this life! Marcelli Township has three parts, the Ring, the Rise, and the Deep. Marcelli Ring is where I live. Then there's Marcelli Rise, where the township's sea farming – or mariculture – takes place. From the air, it looks like a large honeycomb with jewels set in it. Each hexagon is a family farm plot – we call it a seastead – and they earn it by working the farm for five years. The jewels are the lovely family dwellings on the Rise. Then there are sea lanes between the seasteads which make a beautiful blue network accenting the honeycomb.

"Then there's Marcelli Deep – and this is where the light industry is and the services for the township. There's a lot of research going on there as well. From the air, it is a white oval set down-current from Marcelli Ring and Rise over a vast abyssal plain."

"Wow, sounds amazing – and complex. Why have I never heard of it before? When can I visit?"

Maria looked at him for a moment, surprised by his directness, "I'd love to show you. Let me know when you *can* visit. I'll make arrangements." She smiled. "But enough about me. What about you, Ben? If you're collecting muons, something tells me you might have your sights set beyond fixing agri-bots."

The shift in topic startled him. "No, you're right. This is just a… transitional time in my life. I'm doing studies, as well. Muon particles are my focus. I'm in a PhD cohort at the California Institute of Technology."

"Caltech! Impressive." She looked at him again. "Must be a few brains under that sandy hair of yours. And some life experience."

He picked up his burger and bit into it self-consciously. She watched him.

"And yet you wear sadness around you, like a set of old, well-worn clothes."

He looked at her for a few moments. He liked her, and that made him want to be open with her from the beginning. "I'm a recently recovered alcoholic. The jojoba field you saw me working belongs to the community that literally saved my life. I was caught in a self-destructive spiral, running away from loss, pain, grief. The last few years I've been slowly learning how to face my darkness."

Maria was silent but continued to look at Ben with compassion.

Ben answered her unasked question, "You see, my wife and son…" Ben's voice caught, then continued, "were brutally murdered a few years back."

Maria blinked with shock, unsure of how to respond.

He gazed out the window into the night, "They were killed while I was deployed in Africa… a mission during which I was the sole survivor in my military unit. I'm slowly coming to terms with these events. Rebuilding my life."

His words hung heavily between them. Maria could feel the rapport slipping away.

He set his burger down and looked her in the eyes. "I'm sorry, Maria. I shouldn't have accepted your invitation tonight. It was kind, but I'm not really ready for this." He slid out from his seat in the booth and stood.

"Ben," she murmured, looking up into his eyes.

"Sorry." His burger sat on the table with only a single bite from it. He passed quickly through the diner, placing some money at the till.

As he slipped out the door and into the desert, he cast a momentary glance back at Maria. In that instant, her stricken face etched itself into his memory. Reluctantly turning his eyes forward again, he walked into the gathering dusk.

13 April 2063, Grit, Arizona
(the next day)

Maria was walking along a sidewalk of Grit, comparing what was on the paper in her hand against the addresses on the buildings she passed. She came to a door of what looked like a café, but the sign said it was a shelter. She turned the knob and walked through, an old-fashioned bell on a spring above the door announced her presence.

A young woman was seated behind what looked like a reception desk. She looked up from a computer when the bell rang. "Yes?" she asked.

"Yes, hi, I'm looking for a friend. Ben Holden. I think he might be here?"

Maria could tell by the flustered look that crossed the woman's face that she wasn't sure what to do with Maria's request. Maria suspected family members would often come looking for relatives that might be in the shelter. Or someone looking for a fugitive. There would be issues of confidentiality.

"Just a moment." The receptionist pressed a button on her desk and said, "There's a young woman…" she glanced at Maria.

"Maria."

"Maria, looking for Ben Holden."

"I'll be right out." Came from a speaker on the desk.

A moment later a well-built older man, with American Indian features, smooth face and high cheekbones, came out and held his hand out to Maria. "I'm Paul Whitestone, Maria. May I ask why you are looking for Ben?"

Maria took the hand and met Paul's eyes. "I met Ben yesterday out by his jojoba field, and we had dinner together last night." She dropped her eyes, "I seem to have said something to offend him, and I wanted to apologize."

Paul studied her for a moment, then nodded to himself. "I appreciate your candour. Unfortunately, Maria, Ben left this morning for California, related to his research. He'll be back next week; can you wait until then?"

Maria's spirits fell at the news. "No. I have to leave in two days to return home."

"Would you like to leave a note for Ben?"

Maria considered, then shook her head. "No, I think what I need to say must be done face to face." She turned to go.

As she reached for the door, Paul said behind her, "Take heart, Maria, you will see Ben again."

She spun around, but Paul had already gone back through the door. *Nice words. But how can he make such a promise?* She puzzled over the comment as she went through the door.

CHAPTER SEVENTEEN

5 July 2066, Marcelli Ring
(three years later)

Lorenzo Romero opened his eyes. *I can sense them out there in the water, there's something they want.* Pushing chestnut hair from his eyes, the seventeen-year-old rolled out of bed and strode through French doors onto the balcony. He inhaled the soft sea winds. His eyes adjusted to the dim light of the setting moon. Its shimmering path beckoned to him, as it spread across the pre-dawn sea. A shadowy flock of gannets dived nearby, a quarter of a mile out inside the ring, feeding on schools of anchovies.

Looking beyond, he saw the lights of Marcelli Ring itself gleaming in an arc on both sides out towards the still dark horizon. A subtle pride welled in him. *Our town, in the centre of the sea.* His mind's eye pictured the dark bulk of the submarine mountain that provided the foundation for their floating ring, anchored to its slopes. The summit of the mount almost four miles further inside the circle, below the glimmering surface of the sea. Though not an island, because its peak reached into sunlit waters almost touching the surface, the area inside the Ring teemed with sea life which his community relied on for survival and livelihood.

The pelagic community managed this environment with care. The centre of the Ring was dark, a protected marine reserve. This protection resulted in a marine park of constant wonder and provided the seedstock for Marcelli Rise's mariculture activities.

Lorenzo's reverie was broken. *They are insistent, something's urgent.* Leaning over the railing, he searched intently in the dark sea below. *There they are!* Phosphorescence rippled as a pale shape swam back and forth just under the surface. A grey, bottle-nosed head poked up, pointing at him. *Tazia.* Lorenzo's heart warmed at the sight. *There's Lucca as well.*

"Lorenzo, your bottlenose dolphins are below," a soft female voice confirmed.

"Gabriella, please prepare the *Windrider*. Bring it to the inside dock," he ordered, briskly re-entering his room. He reached into a closet to the right of his bed, retrieving an exposure suit, and pulled it on.

Gabriella reported as he finished dressing. "*Windrider* will be ready in five minutes. Be aware, there's a squall to the south-east, about six miles away, moving north by north-west. Its current path will miss the Ring. Conditions inside the Ring is at a sea state one this morning; very calm."

"Thanks, Gabriella. I won't be heading in the direction of the storm. I'll be staying in the Ring, I think." *I wonder what's up with the team? We were planning to start at 3 p.m., after school.* Lorenzo glanced out the window again. *They're very excited about something.*

Opening a trunk at the foot of the bed, he extracted a thin helmet, donned it and adjusted the straps. It contained the communication device he used while working with his dolphin team. He tested the microphone and speakers.

He rummaged through the trunk again, "Has my rebreather been charged?"

"Yes," Gabriella informed him, "it's hanging in your staging cabinet."

Lorenzo opened another cabinet and removed the rebreather, checking the readouts. *Yup, charged. Good working order.* He slipped his arms through the webbing, clicked the harness across his chest, then chose a full-face mask and clipped it onto the helmet. He took a few test breaths. Indicator lights on his forearm readout glowed blue.

"Gabriella, comm check."

"Yes, I can hear you, Lorenzo. Your telemetry's fine as well. *Windrider* is waiting at the inside dock. What shall I tell your parents?"

The young man paused to think. "Tell them I'm taking a morning sail to the north. With Tazia and Lucca. You can track my route. I'll be back in time for lessons," he said, stowing his diving equipment into a backpack.

"I'll inform them."

Anticipation grew in him, he never tired of time with the dolphins. Lorenzo stepped onto the balcony. *Most people in the Ring are still asleep.* Some scattered lights in the buildings revealed just a few early risers preparing for their day.

Lights glowed from the bakery a few houses to the right. *I'll have to grab some fresh pastry when I get back.* He could see his cousin, Angelo through the window, shovelling loaves out of the oven to place on display. Beyond the bakery he could see a portion of the Ring Highway shining softly in the pre-dawn. Shadows of vehicles sped silently past on this primary thoroughfare of the settlement. *People heading to work. And I'm off to mine.* He smiled.

The dolphins, noticing him on the balcony, were now squeaking urgently. He leaned over the edge and dropped the backpack into the half-darkness, hearing it splash twenty feet below. A grey beak grabbed the straps of the pack and pulled it farther out from the balcony. Lorenzo secured his mask to his harness, stepped onto the railing, and in one fluid movement sprang and dived through the fresh dawn air, entering the water with barely a ripple.

Lorenzo's head broke the surface, and he shook the water from his face. Dark hair stuck out at all angles, dripping. A mere hint of green on the eastern horizon heralded the coming dawn. Lorenzo swam with strong strokes towards the lights on his family's dock and pulled himself up onto the walkway. A research boat, belonging to his sister Maria, was on one side. His outrigger floated serenely on the other. He was proud of *Windrider*: a sleek craft, modelled on the outriggers that had been traversing the South Pacific centuries before.

As he jumped into the boat, two grey smiling heads popped out of the water next to him. One carried his backpack in its mouth.

"Thanks, Tazia!" A series of squeaks and squeals from the speakers on his helmet interpreted his words, as Lorenzo scooped up his pack. The dolphin bobbed its head and squealed in response. "Welcome! Quick!" came through his earphones. Lorenzo stowed the pack in the bottom of the boat, then climbed into the stern and took the tiller. The wind was rising from the starboard quarter now.

"Gabriella, release the mooring lines." Ropes whirred on spindles, coiling neatly on the deck.

"Raise the sail." The sheet rose from the boom before him, drawn by the halyard. "Please raise the jib as well, Gabriella." The triangular sail unfurled forward from the roller on the bow stay. In the cockpit, the console sprung to life. The dials adjusted, showing wind speed and direction, water depth and speed of the boat. The boat glided from the dock, a white shadow moving out into the harbour. Lorenzo pulled in the mainsheet and steered towards the centre of the seamount.

"I'm ready. Where to?" he said, turning to the dolphins. His helmet transmitted his words as a series of clicks and squeals to a speaker on the underside of the boat. The two grey shapes took station on either side of the bow.

"Left, follow," came through the helmet speakers.

"What's the problem?" he said quietly. The underwater clicks echoed his words.

"Hurt. Need help. Danger," articulated the speakers. Lorenzo felt the anxiety underlying their words. The image of a struggling calf formed in his mind. *Blood in the water. Something about twine or rope.*

"Gabriella, which med-kit is onboard?"

"A class two kit, Lorenzo."

Class two. That'll include materials for sealing wounds underwater.

"Is there a calf in danger?" Underwater clicks followed.

"Yes," his electronic interpreter squeaked.

The boat now nudged twelve knots, cutting swiftly through the sea.

"Close!" he heard through his speakers.

"Gabriella, furl the jib and take in a reef on the mainsail." The jib pulled back into its roller, and the mainsail shortened one reef. The boat slowed.

"Stop," came through his speakers.

Lorenzo turned into the wind at the dolphin's command. He glanced at the instruments: *forty metres depth here.* "Gabriella, can we drop anchor?" His mind was rapidly calculating what he might need to do.

"It is too deep for the boat's anchor, Lorenzo. However, a Township mooring buoy is sixty metres to starboard."

"OK, Gabriella. I'll jump in here. Please take the boat, secure it to the anchorage, and wait for me."

"Yes, Lorenzo. I detect a dolphin calf. About a year old. Ten metres off the port beam, struggling. Dolphins from the pod are surrounding it."

"I think that's why they brought me here, Gabriella." Lorenzo grabbed the medical kit from inside the cabin, attaching it to his sea suit. He rummaged in the tool compartment, and slipped a knife into the sheath on the thigh of his exposure suit and a multi-purpose tool into a web pocket on his vest.

Lorenzo unfastened his mask from his harness, snapped it onto the communication helmet and took a few test breaths. A glowing blue display appeared again on his wrist. *Ready to go.* The dolphins circled the boat, anxious and impatient.

"Gabriella, turning the helm over to you."

"I have the helm, Lorenzo."

There was a slight tremor in the craft as the mainsail was secured and the electric engines kicked in.

Lorenzo pulled fins from a locker in the cockpit. He slipped them on. In one fluid move, he tucked and rolled backward into the coolness. He uncurled underwater and established a neutral buoyancy position a metre down. *Slow, calm breaths.* Lights on each side of his mask came on. He surveyed the scene below him in the depths.

"Comm check Gabriella."

"I hear you loud and clear, Lorenzo."

The dolphins swirled around him. He spotted Tazia, the leader of the pod. Lorenzo had known her the longest. She'd befriended him two years ago. The relationship blossomed and his supervisor in the Rangers had taken notice. The human-dolphin relations programme had started soon after. Lucca joined them a few months later and the three began training together to develop strategies to use the best of each species for Township defence.

Love my work, Lorenzo thought as Tazia brushed against him.

"This way," came through his headphones, as the grey forms moved off into the depths. Lorenzo followed into the darkness. The water was clear. Motes of plankton floated through the beams. Even kicking energetically, he could barely keep up with the dolphins. *I've never seen them this excited.*

Some forms became visible in the darkness ahead: a struggling calf. Two adult dolphins supported the calf between them and were bringing him up to the surface so that the young dolphin could breathe. The rest of the dolphin pod circled around them.

Lorenzo could feel the calf's panic. He slowed and allowed himself to drift towards the calf.

Tazia was chattering, which seemed to calm the young dolphin. The rapid dolphin speech was too complex for the helmet to interpret.

Scanning the calf's body, Lorenzo spotted the problem. *Monofilament fishing line. Probably drifting in these waters for the past half century.*

Such fishing line had been banned from the Pelagic Territories twenty years ago. The line was tangled around the calf's flippers and tail. *Probably, in his struggle to get free, the filament had tightened and cut into the flesh.* Tendrils of blood drifted from the wound.

"Lorenzo, the Pelagic Array warns me that about six silky sharks are moving towards your position. I believe they detect the blood from the calf." Gabriella cut into his thoughts.

"Thank you. Gabriella, please release a guardian drone from the boat." *Silky sharks. They can be aggressive.*

"Sharks coming." His words were translated by the helmet and some of the dolphins began circling, watching for them.

"We prepare," came through the headset.

"A guardian droid is heading for you," Gabriella said. A barracuda-shaped drone was released from a special tube under the *Windrider*. "I've set it to defend your position."

"Keep calf near surface." He spoke into his microphone while he filled the buoyancy bladders in his suit to hold him near the surface by the calf, adjusting them until he gained neutral buoyancy without effort. The pair of dolphins patiently held the calf at the surface and made room for Lorenzo.

One guardian won't help much if there are six sharks, Lorenzo thought. He studied the tangle of fishing line. *Better bind up the calf before the sharks arrive, stop the flow of blood.*

He inspected the calf's injuries. Taking the multi-purpose tool, he carefully snipped the strands of monofilament in several places with the wire cutters on the tool. The tension eased. Lorenzo carefully teased out bits of line from within the wounds. The calf stilled, trusting his touch and being reassured by the clicks from the pod around them.

Tazia, Lucca and others from the pod were swimming back and forth, trying to locate the sharks. As he focused on the calf, Lorenzo could feel the dolphin pod around him tensing for a battle. Other nearby dolphins, related pods, streamed in and added to the shield of dolphins circling the calf.

Gingerly, he pulled the last of the line from deep within the dolphin's flesh. The calf flinched, making small clicks, but remained calm. Blood streamed more freely from the wound. *Got to stop that blood right away!*

Peeking above the surface towards the horizon, Lorenzo saw dawn spreading as a crimson and orange line on the horizon. He ducked back underwater and moved the medical kit to a convenient place on his harness and opened it. Picking through it, he found what he needed. Taking out and squeezing a small tube of surgical glue, he sealed the edges of the wound, pressing them together. He then wound special tape from the kit around the young dolphin, covering the wounds. *Dolphins heal quickly. This tape will dissolve within a week, he'll be fine.*

He became aware of a spike of anger around him and thrashing behind him. He whirled, all muscles tense. "Sharks are near you, Lorenzo." Gabriella said.

He looked above the surface again, the characteristically small dorsal fin of this species shark was visible, nearing, just outside the pod. *And another. And another.* They circled patiently, looking for an opportunity.

Hurriedly stashing the med-kit, Lorenzo deflated his suit's bladders. He needed mobility. He descended a few metres under the surface. The blinking light of the guardian droid came in view and took station next to him.

Sweeping the area with his lights, Lorenzo saw only dark water, but sensed from the dolphins that the sharks were moving in tightening arcs around them. One shark lunged out of the darkness towards him, entering the cone of light. The barracuda appeared and intercepted it, brushing in front of the shark and delivering a two-hundred-volt jolt onto the predator's nose. The shark twisted in agony and flashed away.

Something tugged on Lorenzo's right fin forcefully. He pulled his knife and turned to strike. A grey bolt shot by him and slammed into the body of the shark. The silky shark hung, twitching in the water, momentarily stunned. Several dolphins circled it, ready to strike again. But then it, too, flicked down into the darkness.

The guardian shocked three more sharks in rapid succession. Other dolphins engaged and rammed sharks around him. A few more minutes and the cluster of sharks gave up and began to swim away. *Good luck at finding easier prey, bozos!*

"Gabriella, I need the boat," Lorenzo directed. He felt the gratitude of the dolphins around him. One dolphin he didn't recognize approached him. *Looks like an older one. Maybe one of the elders of the pod?*

Lorenzo extended his hand. The dolphin rested his beak gently on the palm and held his gaze.

"Yes," the young man said. "My privilege to help you. We are neighbours." The helmet's speakers translated as best it could. *I know you guys understand.*

The old dolphin glided off his hand and disappeared into the sea beyond. Several surrounded the young calf, now swimming slowly on his own. The pod closed behind the elder and followed him into the depths.

As Lorenzo made his way to the surface, *Windrider* was ghosting across the water towards him. Adrenaline was wearing off, he used his last bit of energy to pull himself aboard, settling into the cockpit with his hand on the tiller. The sun peeked over the horizon, revealing the Ring in its glory around him. Windows flashed in the early light, becoming golden stars that traced the western arc of the Township.

*

Back home, Lorenzo stood on the dock next to *Windrider*, hosing down the boat and his equipment with fresh water. His older sister, Maria, approached with one of her interns, pulling carts piled with equipment.

"Mom was looking for you, Renzo." She set the cart handle down, "Where've you been?"

"Out for a morning sail," Lorenzo said briefly.

She narrowed her eyes at him. "You look dog-tired. I see the med-kit on your suit. You don't need that for a sail. You've been out with your dolphins again this morning, haven't you?"

He concentrated on washing the bow of *Windrider*. "Yes, I was out with them."

"Anything you want to tell me?"

Lorenzo glanced at her. "No."

"My brother," Maria rolled her eyes, and turned to her assistant, Fran. "Rugged individualist. Our scientists say he has a special connection with the dolphins," Fran looked at Lorenzo. He ignored her.

Maria and Fran then busied themselves transferring the equipment onto the research vessel, the *William Beebe*. "I suspect you were out for more than a sail with your friends." She glanced at her brother again.

Lorenzo continued to clean his gear. "Going to check the phytoplankton levels today?" he said, not looking up.

"You're changing the subject."

Ignoring the accusation, he finished rinsing and began coiling the hose. "Have a good day, sis. I have to go back for lessons."

She grunted and swung herself up onto the research craft.

Lorenzo walked down the dock.

"I'm interested as to why you didn't tell your sister about your trip," Gabriella whispered in Lorenzo's ear. "Your life was in danger. You fought off sharks with your dolphin pod." There was no accusation in her statement.

"People who haven't experienced the rapport I have with the dolphins don't understand," Lorenzo said quietly. "I get tired of trying to explain. It's like explaining colour to a person born blind."

"Like explaining colour to a blind person. A helpful insight and analogy – I'll add that to my algorithm. What did you experience with that last, older dolphin?"

Lorenzo smiled. "There was a sense of gratitude, but more." He stopped a moment, reflecting. "Probably the closest word I can find was that he spoke a kind of *blessing* on me wishing me good in return for helping them. I can't explain it beyond that."

"I'll record that in your notes on the human-dolphin project."

"Thank you," Lorenzo said as he continued down the pier.

As Lorenzo walked back along the quay, he noticed Tazia again, swimming towards him, trying to catch his attention. Lucca followed close behind. Lorenzo slowed and slipped into the water, pulling on his mask. *Whatever it is, it's important.* He spent a few minutes conversing with the two until he understood their new agitation.

Lorenzo heaved himself back up onto the quay. "Gabriella, alert Ranger Command. The dolphins have discovered several probes snooping around the Ring. The Township's under surveillance. We may be in danger."

"Connecting you with Major Camden now, Lorenzo."

5 July 2066, Pelagic vessel *William Beebe*, Marcelli Ring
(the same day)

The sun was just emerging from the horizon as Fran lifted the last box out of the cart. She struggled to get a grip on the bulky shape; her hands barely reached the handles. *Good thing these bots aren't heavy!*

"Let me help you with that." Maria reached down and grabbed one of the handles to help haul it onboard.

"Thanks," Fran said, "that's the last one."

She climbed up onto the deck of the research vessel and glanced back at the retreating figure of Lorenzo. "Your brother is kinda dreamy."

Maria looked at her, rolling her eyes again. "Don't get your hopes up, Fran. These days, all he cares about are dolphins and the human-dolphin project."

She saw Fran's dejected look and softened, "Just give him a year or so. He'll start noticing you then."

Fran brightened, "Will you introduce me properly?"

"Sure, next opportunity. Right now, though, let's get ready to cast off."

"Of course." Fran climbed the stairs to the bridge, where the instrument panels lit up as she entered. Maria went down to the laboratory to organize the day's work.

"Gabriella, please prepare to cast off lines." Fran said, scanning the instruments.

"Ready," Gabriella said.

"Cast off. Today we're heading outside the Ring, the south-east corner."

There were some chunks and thumps, as the ship crept away from the dock. "Under way," Gabriella confirmed, "Course plotted for Stanton Shelf."

"Perfect, Gabriella. Give me a holo-model of the boat traffic around us." The display popped up to her left. Fran studied it. "Let's go through Ring Channel 3 rather than 2. It looks like they are doing construction on the Channel 2 flyover of the Ring Highway. A lot of congestion there."

"Confirmed, heading east to Channel 3."

Maria came onto the bridge and joined Fran looking at the instruments and readouts. "Good choice of route."

"Thanks, Maria. We'll be there in twenty minutes or so."

Through the window, they observed the Inner Ring activity all around them. Sailboats and water taxis were the main traffic. An ambulance skimmer raced past them heading towards the hospital.

Fran glanced at Maria. "I've been wondering about the name of this ship. Who is William Beebe?"

Maria looked at her intern and sighed. "Don't they teach about scientists any more at school?"

"Sure, they do, but I don't remember that name."

"Better to be a naturalist than a king," Maria said in a gruff voice. Fran looked at her quizzically.

"That was one of Beebe's famous sayings," Maria explained. "He also said, 'The is-ness of things is well worth studying; but it is their why-ness that makes life worth living.' I like that one."

"'The why-ness of things.' I like that phrase. So Beebe was a naturalist?"

"He was a pioneer in the study of ecology over a hundred years ago. He died in 1962. His specialty was studying animals in their natural habitat and context."

They were passing under the Ring Highway flyover for Channel 3. The open sea spread before them.

"I asked the Ring Council to name this research vessel after him since Beebe was the first to study deep sea organisms in their natural environment, in 1934."

"They had the technology for deep sea research back then?" Fran was incredulous.

"Believe it or not, two men went down 922 metres in the sea, encased in a steel ball one-and-a-half-metres in diameter, attached to the end of a cable. They had only two tiny portholes."

"Wow, claustrophobia city!"

"We'll reach the research point and anchorage in seven minutes," Gabriella informed them.

Maria jumped up from her chair, "Let's get ready."

They rode the lift down to the submerged part of the research vessel to reach the laboratory. The large room had floor-to-ceiling windows along both walls, curving to meet in the bow. Computer monitors and lab instruments lined the right side, lab benches the left.

"We're on station, and I've deployed eight beacon buoys to warn other boats that a research operation is in progress. Local traffic will steer clear of the area."

"Thanks, Gabriella," Maria said.

The two women walked into the centre of the room, containing a pool of water in which a submersible floated. The small sub was a sphere, largely transparent, with short wing-like control surfaces on either side. The vessel contained two seats with control sticks and instrument panels. The door of the vessel opened for them.

"Fran, please find a pair of hands for the sub while I prepare the jellyfish droids."

Fran bounced over to a cabinet and pulled out two small fat torpedo-shaped objects with mechanical hands on their ends. She placed them in compartments next to the sub seats. *These are so cool!*

Maria opened the boxes and collected the helmet jellyfish bots needed for this operation. She carried fifteen over to the vessel, slotting them into compartments on the sub floor.

Fran glanced at the devices with curiosity, "Made to look like *Periphylla periphylla*, right?"

"Glad to see that you've been paying attention in class." Maria stowed the last of them.

Fran was already harnessed in her seat, doing a pre-launch check of the submersible's systems. "We're all go here," she said without looking up from the panel.

Maria slid into her chair and clicked the harness in place. "OK. Gabriella, ready to launch." The door sealed shut with a sigh and a click. Mooring cables released the sub to float freely in the pool.

"Take us down, Fran." The younger woman grasped a ball suspended just in front of her right hand, the three-dimensional controller for the sub, and pulled it slowly down. Water rose outside the sphere as the sub sank under the *William Beebe*.

Fran pushed the ball forward a bit and the sub went forward. "Passing fifty metres," Fran said, watching the display.

"Fifty metres," Gabriella echoed.

The sub cruised through an intricate arch of cables, part of the anchoring system for the Ring. As they passed under, Fran gazed at it. "That always reminds me of an upside-down suspension bridge."

Maria glanced up. "Me too. Probably because similar engineering principles are used in both designs."

Fran looked with interest at the robots arranged in their compartments. "These are so cool, I'm so glad we got permission to use these jelly bots."

Marialanced over at her intern. "Pop quiz time!"

Fran rolled her eyes and looked over. "Really?"

"Yep. What are we doing today?"

"We're setting up an experiment to study factors influencing the diel movement around the seamount."

"And what is 'diel movement'?"

"The vertical migration of animals every twenty-four hours from the mesopelagic zone to the surface waters and back down again. Rising after sunset and migrating back down into the depths before dawn." Fran feigned impatience, but she liked showing off her knowledge.

"Mesopelagic zone?"

"Often called the 'twilight zone'; there isn't enough sunlight for photosynthesis. But a surprising abundance of animals flourish down there."

"What's our experiment?"

"Passing one hundred fifty metres," Gabriella intoned.

The waters around them were rapidly darkening to a deep azure. Fran checked the instruments, then continued reciting, "We'll set Sophia's helmet jellyfish drones in strategic clusters within the water column so they can collect information about this migration phenomena, to provide a fuller picture of the migration dynamics around the Ring."

"And *why* are we doing this?"

"This will give us a better understanding of the interactions between predators and prey and the web of life around our seamount. We'll more fully grasp the factors which influence the migration. Plus, this will provide a baseline against which we can evaluate future changes in migration patterns. It's part of our overall goal to monitor the health of the seamount."

"Well done, clever intern."

Fran flushed with pleasure.

"Three hundred and fifty metres." The water was now black outside.

Fran looked over at Maria slyly. "My turn."

"Your turn for what?"

"Questions… such as, 'What makes Maria Romero tick?'"

Maria laughed. "Touché. OK, shoot."

"Yeah, like, do you have a boyfriend?"

"Not presently, cheeky intern. Haven't found the right guy."

"Five hundred metres." The lights of the submersible had come on, and they were now skimming the slope of the seamount as it continued to plunge into the depths.

"Really? No one you're attracted to?" Finger-length tan bristlemouths scattered before their searchlights and vanished into the gloom.

"Bristlemouths are ugly fish," Maria observed.

"You're changing the subject."

"Well, there was one guy I met when I was pursuing a master's degree at Arizona State." Maria stared off into the darkness. "When I met him, I thought he might be the one. I certainly clicked with him."

"Six hundred metres," Gabriella announced. The lights caught a flatnose catshark swimming lazily down a nearby cliff face.

"This sounds interesting. What happened?"

"It was strange. We didn't really have that much time together. We met by chance while I was doing surveys and we had a meal that evening. We were having a great discussion – but I must've asked the wrong question, something too personal." Maria's look was wistful. "He just stopped talking and walked out on our dinner date."

"Seven hundred metres."

"Wow," Fran looked at her teacher with sympathy, "that's a bummer. Did you ever see him again?"

"No. That was three years ago. I guess I should just get over it. It's not like we'll ever cross paths again – my world and his are oceans apart."

"Passing nine hundred metres." The water was inky black beyond the lights. Coldness radiated through their windows.

"William Beebe came down this far in his steel ball."

Fran turned to look at her, "Yeah. While only being linked to the world of air and light by a thin cable. I know I couldn't do that! I wonder what the other guy's name was."

"Gabriella, we're ready to release the first triad of jellyfish."

"Ready on your mark, Maria."

"Release triad one." There was a quiet flush sound and three small devices drifted into the headlights to form a triangle.

"Lights off." Blackness enveloped them. Blue lights undulated across the translucent bodies of the jellyfish devices. "Telemetry check, Gabriella."

"I'm receiving telemetry from the drones, all systems working."

"Good," Maria said. "Now let's head back up slowly, releasing triads every two hundred metres.

"Take us up, Fran." The sub began to retrace its course up along the rocky incline of the seamount. Three more triads were released at their respective depths. Maria and Fran discussed some of the other experiments and studies to be set up over the next few weeks.

At the three hundred and twenty metre mark, Gabriella broke into their conversation. "Maria, I've picked up an anomalous noise in the ocean. I detect a regular pattern amid the random clicks of snapping shrimp. Analyzing it now."

"Can you identify the source of the anomaly?" Maria asked.

Sensing Maria's anxiety, Fran slowed the sub to a standstill in the water column.

"I recommend reconfiguring and sending three of the helmet jellyfish devices to identify the source via triangulation."

"I agree. Proceed." A few moments later three jellyfish appeared in the headlights and spread out along the cliff face.

"Let's follow them, Fran. Keep a distance of a hundred metres." The young woman gently moved the controlling ball and their sub glided forwards, following the jellyfish.

After about ten minutes, they approached a colony of multi-coloured sponges on a small ledge.

Gabriella was rapidly processing the telemetry: "One of the sponges is emitting systematic pulses. I'll highlight it with a laser." A beam came from the submersible which illuminated one of many sponges.

"Launch the hands, Gabriella." Maria donned a special pair of gloves as the two mechanical hands exited the sub. The torpedo bodies the hands were mounted on whirred towards the highlighted sponge while Maria guided their path with her gloves. Carefully, she picked up the artificial sponge with both "hands" and brought it near the sub. The laser beam continued to spotlight the place in the sponge colony, where it had been nestled.

"Scanning," Gabriella said. A moment later the AIA continued, "Confirmed to be a transmission device."

"Send the information to Major Camden."

"Yes, Maria. Connecting now."

Maria continued inspecting the sponge, turning it in the hands, as the Major came online, "Captain Romero? I see you've found something suspicious."

"Yes, Major. We found a transmission device in a sponge on the southeast wall of the seamount. Gabriella, what have you been able to identify about the device?"

"It seems to be receiving and transmitting sound waves, disguised as shrimp clicks, apparently for covert communication between someone on the Ring and something like those probes detected earlier. An analysis shows it is heavily coded, it will take time to break the complex security algorithm."

"Captain Romero, we'll be discussing this with intelligence operatives. I recommend you put the device back where you found it. I'd like to use your research drones, the ones that found the sponge, to continue monitoring the transmissions."

"Of course, Major. We'll change the current configuration of the drones to monitor signals from the sponge."

"Excellent. Thank you, Captain. Be sure to visit headquarters for a debrief on your return."

"Of course, Major. We'll be in this afternoon. Over and out."

Maria carefully put the sponge transmitter back in place and turned off the sub's laser beam.

Fran's heart was racing, "That was unexpected. Do you think it's some sort of threat?"

"We can't be sure, yet, but it doesn't look good. Let's head back to the *Beebe*, Fran, and see what the Major has to say."

"OK. Going up," Fran said. She moved the ball and they ascended towards the light above.

8 July 2066, Marcelli Deep
(the next day)

Lorenzo Romero floated twenty metres below the surface, suspended deep in the vast blueness. He watched the sunbeams sliding slowly past in the waters around him.

A sacred dance, bringing light into the darkness.

In the stillness, he heard only his breath: a quiet whooshing, in and out. No bubbles escaped from his rebreather. It was almost a meditative state, yet his senses were on high alert, watching, with his team.

His suit was barely discernible in the aquamarine light, mimicking the colours around him. To a casual observer, he would be essentially invisible. The active acoustic-cancelling of the suit's fabric allowed him to be largely immune to sonar probing as well, although dolphins could detect him. The same tech that hid him also allowed him to stay in touch with his dolphin team. He and they wore acoustic transmitters that allowed them to communicate with each other, while the sounds produced were camouflaged by the natural din of the sea.

All this tech, yet I feel so vulnerable. Like a lone anchovy expecting a school of sharks to turn up.

The seasteading community of Marcelli Deep rode calmly and serenely on the surface above him. This entrance to the Deep – the south-east approach – was difficult to defend because it opened out into extremely deep water. The abyssal plain was almost four thousand metres directly below him. Many things could hide in that vastness. Which is why, of course, he and the dolphins had been assigned to be on patrol here. *They'll be judging us by how things go today. They need to see that we're capable, that our strategies work.*

Lorenzo was aware of Tazia, Lucca and the extended pod underneath and around him, weaving an intricate net of watchfulness. *They seem calm.* He'd not yet received indication from them that the Green Team was in the area. *Still, something doesn't feel right. And Lucca feels it too.*

He realized his muscles were tense. All senses straining. He willed himself to relax. *Pace yourself, Lorenzo. Still two hours to go.*

He began to swim slowly and methodically, in wide circles. The gentle physical action helped dissipate some of his tension. He regularly looked up at Marcelli Deep, checking landmarks and comparing them with the map inside his helmet, so he wouldn't drift out of their patrol zone. Visibility was so limited underwater. A grey torpedo shape flashed momentarily within his range of vision, then was lost in the depth of blueness. *One of the dolphin recruits Tazia brought in.*

Minutes passed. Lorenzo felt a mental nudge. He heard the dolphins hum and click in his headset. They were about a half-mile away, much deeper. He sensed first their curiosity, then increasing interest, then puzzlement. "What have you found?" he asked quietly into his microphone.

Several other dolphins converged to join the one investigating. An image formed in Lorenzo's mind. *There's something strange in the water, something you all don't understand. Is it a school of fish? Those anchovies aren't acting like normal anchovies. Is there something hiding within the anchovy ball?* Even using their echo-location sense the dolphins couldn't get a fix on the hidden creature.

Tazia triggered her beacon, which sent out a signal of the pod's location, showing up on Lorenzo's helmet map. Lorenzo checked in with command, "Maria, did you receive that ping?"

"Yes, got it, Renzo. What's up?"

"The pod's detected something. They can't get a fix on it. It feels to me like countermeasures. I suspect an infiltrator. Might be Gideon, on *Kestrel*, playing some of his tricks."

"OK. Good. I've alerted nearby guardian bots in the area. They'll observe and deploy on your signal."

Without warning, Lorenzo and the dolphin pod were struck by synchronized concussive pressure blasts. *Feels like someone punched me!* An object whizzed past Lorenzo at tremendous speed towards Marcelli Deep. At the same time, a concussive charge had gone off in the artificial anchovy ball, stunning and disorienting the dolphin pod, scattering them. Lorenzo could hear them cry out in pain.

In that instant, Lorenzo realized his team had lost. He drifted in the water a few moments, regaining his sense of direction. Shock, anger, and despair joined the tingling in his muscles. He felt sick. *We failed!*

He told the dolphins the game was over. They were still disoriented by the shock of the decoy in the anchovy ball. He still felt in a blur himself. *What flashed by? Must've been a cavitating rail gun projectile. They travel at supersonic speeds.*

The dolphin pod sent him a signal that they were unhurt. *I'm so glad you're all fine. Thank you so much. Sorry I let you down.* Lorenzo could feel that they, too, were disappointed as they swam off. The pod's communications faded, their clicks and murmurs blending back into the music of the sea.

8 July 2066, Marcelli Ring Ranger Command
(the same day)

The men and women filed into the room, taking seats around the holo-display for the late afternoon debrief session. Water still dripped from Lorenzo's suit onto the floor as he found his place. He hadn't bothered to remove the rebreather, which hung dishevelled on his chest.

Major Camden observed them all closely, looking for tell-tale signs. She zeroed in on Lorenzo who was wallowing in his defeat.

"Lieutenant Romero!" she snapped. Lorenzo jumped to his feet as if yanked by strings.

"Yes, Major, ma'am!"

"Yesterday you warned us that the Ring's defences were being probed by hostile agents. Your intelligence report, and that of your sister," the Major glanced at Maria, "set the tone for today's exercise. Well done, Lieutenant."

Lorenzo was not moved by the praise. He knew he and his team had been defeated in the war-simulation game. *I've failed the Township, failed my team.*

Major Camden softened, "Why don't you begin? Describe how your part of the mission went today."

Wait! Why me first? She wants to make an example of me. Lorenzo pressed the tumult of emotions down. He took a deep breath and walked resolutely to the front of the room. "Major. Rangers." His eyes met the Major's and then a few in the audience. "I was with my patrol pod in the south-east sector, between the Rise and the Deep. We extended our patrol to a depth of one hundred metres. I was monitoring the dolphin sentinels from the centre of their patrol pattern."

As he spoke, the holo-display in the centre of the debriefing chamber illustrated what he was describing: the security sectors around Marcelli Rise and Deep, Lorenzo's position in the water column, the dolphins weaving a pattern of alertness around him.

"Three hours and twelve minutes into the exercises, Tazia detected something. It appeared to be a school of anchovies. But the school was behaving abnormally." The display zoomed in on Tazia and several dolphins as they cautiously circled a wheeling school of fish.

"The pod suspected something was in the centre. But they couldn't fix on what it was." A yellow undefined blob pulsated in the centre of the school.

"Then the pod and I were simultaneously hit by concussive blasts." The display zoomed out. A projectile trail flashed by the icon of Lorenzo. What the display revealed was a concussive grenade inside the school of anchovies that stunned the dolphins.

"Thank you, Lieutenant. Please be seated."

Lorenzo flopped into his seat, disappointment written across his features.

Major Camden gestured to the young man sitting with a cocky air on the other side of the gathering. "Let's hear from Lieutenant Battuta. Describe your part of the mission, please, Lieutenant."

Gideon stood. "Yes, Major. Our team detected a shadow in the Pelagic Array system, south-east of the Deep. A blind spot. We chose to exploit it." The holo-display spooled back in time and zoomed in on the amphibious vessel, *Kestrel*, at two hundred metres.

"We took cover under a shoal of squid near the thermocline."

The display showed the sub hiding among the squid, hovering where warm surface waters sat on the cold waters of the deep.

"I launched a noise-maker to attract the dolphins towards the anchovy ball. While the dolphins were distracted, we set off a concussive grenade in the middle of the school to stun them all." The holo-display played out Gideon's description of events.

"So, your intention was to distract the patrol, then knock them out," the Major observed.

Gideon smiled, "Yes. It was, and it did! We were able to get shots off targeting the Deep." He sat down, triumph written all over his face. Lorenzo stared at a blank spot on the wall, wishing this moment away.

"Captain Romero, describe your part of the mission, please."

"Yes, Major. If you can just spool back twenty minutes." Maria walked to the centre as the holo-display returned to the requested time and directed the group's gaze to part of the display. "My team and I spent some time beforehand, playing out different scenarios for defence against the Green Team. Choosing from among several good plans, we decided to turn off array sensors in the south-east sector. This simulated a natural, plausible blind spot in the system."

The display zoomed in to that area of sea floor, where lights had winked out in a random pattern. Gideon's face fell. Lorenzo was startled out of his despondency.

"We suspected Lieutenant Battuta was in the area with *Kestrel* in stealth mode. He might be tempted into our ambush."

"Ambush?" Gideon blurted in disbelief. Lorenzo's attention was now definitely sparked.

Maria looked over at him quietly for a moment. "First of all, Lieutenant Battuta is fairly predictable. He would want to show off *Kestrel*'s special abilities. We thought he would notice the blind spot and try to exploit it. Indeed, he did. When he deployed the noisemaker, he exposed his presence. When my brother, uh, when Lieutenant Romero passed on the report about the suspicious anchovy ball, this further confirmed my suspicions. We plotted *Kestrel*'s probable position based on the trajectory of the noisemaker and likely hiding spots in the shadow we had created."

"You knew I was there?" Gideon's face fell.

Maria continued as if he hadn't spoken. "*Kestrel* revealed herself as soon as she fired the warhead towards the Deep. We had solutions within microseconds for both the projectile and *Kestrel*. We took them both out virtually with our rail guns. The assault failed."

The defensive responses were projected in the holo-display.

She glanced at Gideon, with a hint of disdain. Then she gave her brother a quiet smile and returned to her seat.

"Thank you, Captain Romero." The Major's gaze swept the room full of her charges. She was attempting to forge these young people into one strong team. She let the facts of the debrief settle, and for their emotions to clear. Then she left them another moment for reflection before continuing.

"I'd like to remind you that Marcelli Deep was *successfully* defended today. Not because of the work of any individual, but because we worked together as a team. Some defences were defeated," she said, looking towards Lorenzo. "But this is something we must expect. We make multi-faceted defence plans knowing that several of them *will* fail. In any battle there are so many factors to consider, and so much that we don't know about our enemy. This is the famous 'fog of war'. This is also why we test plans, like we did today."

Nodding in Lorenzo's direction, the Major added, "We all know that Lieutenant Romero's dolphin team proved themselves again to be the most effective scouts and sentinels we've ever had."

Lorenzo's heart lifted.

"The dolphins were distracted and defeated by the noisemakers this time. We'll learn from that."

Lorenzo nodded.

"We'll be better prepared next time. If Captain Romero's trap had not worked, we would've fallen back on other defence strategies. There'll always be tactics and counter-tactics. Our best defence is to function as a team. Our strength is our ability to trust and work interdependently, being resourceful as a combat situation unfolds. Well done today. The next exercise will be early tomorrow morning. Be on station no later than 0200 hours."

As the people were filing out of the room, the Major picked out Maria, "Captain Romero, may I have a moment please?"

Maria turned and came back, a quizzical look on her face. "Yes, Major?"

The Major smiled, "I just wanted to congratulate you on passing your reconnaissance training. Not only passing but coming in second in your cohort. You are now qualified for special ops; and this is an area we desperately need more qualified people. We'll talk more about it soon. Well done."

A warmth spread through Maria. "Thank you, Major," she said with a salute.

"Carry on, Captain Romero." Major Camden returned the salute and turned back to the display.

CHAPTER EIGHTEEN

12 July 2066, Pelagic vessel *Kestrel*
(four days later)

Kestrel detached silently from *Oyster* and drifted down-current from the Sea Star, sinking into the depths. The chromatic camouflage on the craft's surface blended with the colours of the surrounding depths, and she faded to become a barely discernible imprint in the sea. Tiny robotic anchovies shimmered in the waters around her. Their electronic activity neutralized sonar and sensory data, and dampened the pressure waves that the craft created moving through the water, making *Kestrel* also invisible to listening and watching electronics. Anyone probing the sea around the craft would detect only empty ocean.

Sea light filtered into *Kestrel*'s cockpit. Ben watched Gideon as he piloted his vessel, working virtual controls for the craft on a glowing holo-interface. Ben squirmed a bit in the seat, his muscles were still sore from the concussion of the depth charge blast. *That was a close call.* His mind kept drifting back to memories of Maria. He shook himself mentally and turned his attention to their situation.

Kestrel stabilized, achieving neutral buoyancy when it reached sixty metres below the surface. The holo-viewer faded as the craft steadied. The sea surrounded them with its vast silence.

"The anchovy bots are just a precaution," Gideon said, turning to Ben. "We don't believe the Chileans are aware of your presence here. But, as my father said, since the Chileans routinely run security around official delegations, watching for threats and potential risks, it's wise to have countermeasures." At the limit of visibility, clouds of real anchovies flickered in the sunlight above them, catching Ben's eye.

"We have a six-knot current carrying us. We'll drift until we're out of range of their security devices, then switch on propulsion. After that we'll return to the surface and steer towards the Marcelli Township. I think it'll be about one hundred and twenty nautical miles from here."

"One hundred and thirty point three nautical miles, Gideon." Nemo said in a stage whisper.

"Right, Neem. Thanks." Gideon rolled his eyes towards Ben. "Smart alec."

'You designed this?" Ben looked around the craft with admiration.

"Yes! Final project for my engineering degree. This beauty has a titanium-carbide reinforced, aluminium composite hull." Gideon touched the side of the craft with pride. "With chromophoric nanocoating. Passive camouflage. We're using that now. There's also an active camouflage mode which can be engaged for reconnaissance or combat situations."

"And what do you do for power?"

"*Kestrel* is powered by the new Alchemist V reactor. I'm testing a new model, from TransmuCorp. It allows me to transition from submersion to air launch in two seconds. Twice as fast as any similar craft."

"A real speedster!" Ben laughed. "I'd love to see how fast it goes."

Gideon grinned. "In a couple of weeks I'll take *Kestrel* into the Western Pacific Exercises – big league war games, for real. That'll be my first chance to test how she flies in actual battle conditions. We'll be pitted against the *Osprey III* that the Rangers now use."

"And what type of weapons does *Kestrel* have?"

"She's designed with three rail guns and three turbo lasers. Two of each in front and one each in the rear. I don't have clearance yet to use the weapons, so they won't be operational until the games. Sophia is also designing some other little tactical surprises for me. Here, I'll show you the specs."

He spoke to his control panel, "Model of *Kestrel*, please, Neem."

A holograph appeared in a pool of light.

Ben looked at the three-dimensional schematic of the craft before him. "May I?" He looked over at Gideon, who nodded. Ben turned the holo-display, zooming in to admire the features. "Extraordinary design. You seem young to be so experienced with this type of craft. How long have you been with the Rangers, Gideon?"

"All Pelagic citizens enlist at the age of seventeen. I've been a Ranger for almost five years now. I started as a cadet, but now I've qualified as a reconnaissance specialist."

"And you specialize in designing aircraft?"

"Well, actually, just designing the kind of plane that I want to fly. First of all I studied many of the Ranger aircraft, and those of terrestrial nations too, before coming up with the plans for this baby. *Kestrel* is the fruit of all that research. I designed it with covert reconnaissance in mind. I hope to show what she can do in those western Pacific exercises. I'll be with the Red Team. I think we should be able to infiltrate the Blue Team lines undetected."

"I hope you succeed," Ben smiled. "It seems a bit unusual, to say the least, that you have your own private warship."

Gideon looked over at Ben, assessing him. "*Kestrel* is cool, of course. But more importantly it's something the Territories desperately need. We've seen the necessity of craft that can respond rapidly to local incidents in the Territory, like with the recent plague of poaching and pirates we've had.

"I've been liaising with the Rangers while designing *Kestrel*. They see her as a potential prototype for local protection and hope to develop some combat protocols based on her capabilities. At this point, the guns don't work, there aren't any armaments on board; but last week I loaded weapons for the first time and did some supervised runs at the test range.

"My dad hopes to test *Kestrel* as a prototype, a plane to defend our Pod and others like it. He's made the request to Ranger Command at Kermadec Seamount. I think they'll approve."

Ben was impressed. "This craft could be a very useful defence for communities like yours."

"We really need some better protection. It's like the Wild West out here. Pirates everywhere you look. A couple weeks ago, poachers stole one of our tuna cohorts. That was five million dollars' worth of fish in one go. If *Kestrel* had been operational, we might've stopped that."

"You do need defence. This is such a different life out here, almost like being on a different planet."

Gideon chuckled, "We *are* on a different planet. A blue one, which just happens to inhabit the same space as the green one."

They cruised the blue expanse of sea for a while in silence. Then Gideon said, "I heard you were in the military too, Ben."

"I did two tours in the Dependency Wars. I was with the Marine Special Forces."

"Really?! Wow. Where were you stationed?" Ben sensed Gideon's admiration.

"Diego Garcia, south of India, east of Africa. But we did most of our forward work based in Kilmia, off the Somali coast. I can't tell you much more about it. Most of the work we did is still classified."

"I understand. So much cloak and dagger these days." The holo-viewer took form before Gideon again. "OK. We're well out of sensor range." His right hand calibrated the virtual controls. The left steadily coaxed the stick back towards him. The robotic anchovies schooled close to the craft, and then filed into a port to be stowed inside once more. Ben could feel a faint vibration awake in the craft as it powered up, moving forward and upward.

"Strap yourself in," Gideon cautioned. "Sometimes the transition is rough." Ben followed his lead, pulling a harness across his chest and clipping it securely.

Ben sensed the vibrations thrumming through his body increase in frequency as they ascended.

"Hold on!" Gideon called out, "I'm gonna purge the ballast tanks." Ben felt his stomach sink as the vessel buoyed upward rapidly.

Ben caught a glimpse of a reflection of *Kestrel* mirrored for an instant on the under-surface of the sea. Then they burst into the air, breaching the surface like a manta ray. With a roar of spray and a small jerk, the air propellers took the momentum of the leap and lifted them smoothly above the rippled ocean. The ocean surface fell away below them.

"Amazing." Ben turned in his seat to examine the twin propellers, fixed on swivel mounts behind them. A single propeller jutted out near the tail. All three propellers now matched the hue of the waters below. "I see you still have the passive camouflage on."

Gideon nodded, intent on piloting the craft, "Precautions still, yes. We could've also done a stealth exit, which is silent. But it was more fun to show you what she could do."

Gideon concentrated again on the interface before him, levelling the craft and increasing the speed. A heavy silence cloaked them. "I've turned on the Active Noise Suppression, based on the principles of Sophia's sphere of silence, so she will run more quietly, and so we can continue to avoid detection. It makes it easier to talk too." Gideon glanced over at him, grinning. Ben now heard only a soft rush of wind over the canopy.

"Would you like to try your hand at the controls?"

"Sure!" A thrill ran through Ben as he leaned forward. Gideon briefly explained the different instruments in the display.

"I think I've got it. These controls remind me of the velocicopters I used to pilot in the Special Forces." Ben relaxed as old skills and reflexes flowed easily into his hands.

"OK, then. You have the stick." Gideon leaned back as the display shifted to Ben's side. Ben's hand tightened on the stick. He experimented with a few rolls, a climb, and descent. "Very smooth." Ben said appreciatively.

"Wow! Nice touch. I've never seen someone adapt to *Kestrel* so fast."

"I cross-trained in piloting in my unit. So, how do I control the camouflage?"

"Those two toggles are for passive. Those three are for active."

Ben flicked the switches, watching out the window as the skin of the craft changed colour and texture.

They flew for twenty minutes. Ben was thoroughly enjoying the chance to fly again after so many years out of the service.

A red indicator flashed in the display. A wavering warning tone surrounded them.

Gideon sat up. "*Kestrel*'s been painted with radar!"

Nemo gave them the details, "Two unknown aircraft, no identity beacons. 126 miles east by north-east. Velocity, 900 miles per hour."

"Where'd they come from? Why are they out here, in the middle of nowhere?" Gideon slid the display back to his side and Ben released the stick to him. Gideon flicked on the active camouflage, while glancing outside.

"Nemo, did they detect us when their radar passed over us?"

"They would have been able to, yes, although it wouldn't have been a strong contact. They might write it off as an anomaly, Gideon. The active camouflage is concealing us at this distance. It won't defeat their active radar when they get closer."

"I was afraid of that. Thanks, Nemo. We could take advantage of those clouds, they'll dampen the radar sweep." Gideon pulled the stick up and to the side, sending *Kestrel* over into the cloud cover.

Ben's adrenalin surged, "If those planes have come over here on a mission, they'll be on high alert. They'll follow up a ping like that. Will *Kestrel* be invisible enough to evade a sustained search with high powered radar?"

"I'm not sure of that, Ben. Hey, Neem, is there a frigate bird drone on board?"

"Yes, Gideon."

"Launch, please." A moment later, a new display appeared. A yellow bird icon left the craft, rising rapidly to 15,000 feet, then levelling out. "Widen the display to include the hostile aircraft."

Kestrel and the bird shrank into smaller icons. At the edge of the display, two red dots appeared, moving rapidly towards them. "Entering close radar range in twelve seconds."

"Gideon, I have an idea." It took Ben just a moment to describe his plan.

Gideon looked at him with awe. "Brilliant! You take the controls."

Ben took back the stick. "Thanks. I saw it about a quarter mile to the north," he said banking northward. Water spattered across the canopy and the clouds darkened around them until it was nearly black outside. *Kestrel* was buffeted as it raced through the storm cloud.

Gideon watched the dots approach on the display.

Ben looked at their position. "This should be about right." *Kestrel* dropped through the cloud ceiling into a heavy downpour above the sea.

"*Kestrel's* camouflage and the rain scattering the radar signal should hide us long enough," Ben said, concentrating on the controls and keeping *Kestrel's* downward movement steady.

Outside, raindrops paused and then fell slowly upwards past the canopy as *Kestrel* plummeted towards the ocean a little faster than the rain was falling. The pursuing jets, avoiding the squall, zoomed above the clouds into a spiral search pattern over the area.

Kestrel slowed and lightly touched the surface of the sea then eased into the silence beneath. Raindrops patterned the waves above them. Ben took a breath. *Not bad, so far.*

"Nemo, deploy countermeasures," Gideon ordered.

"Deployed."

Ben handed control back again. Gideon killed the engines and they drifted silently into the depths. "Take us down to thirty metres, Neem. It's unlikely they will have sonar sensors in the water."

"Yes, Gideon. There is no indication of sonar."

As the sea plane shifted air and ballast to sink deeper, there was a subtle vibration.

He turned. "That was a great idea, Ben. I wouldn't have thought of that."

"It was a close call." Ben's mouth tensed, watching the red dots in the display expand in widening search patterns. "They're persistent."

*

Two aircraft with green Caliphate emblems on their sides banked as they turned down through the lofty cloud canyons. Communications were in Arabic: "Air command, this is Scimitar 3, search sector six. The radar contact we reported appears to have been a false positive. Repeat, false positive; no confirmed contact."

"Acknowledged, Scimitar 3. No contact. Continue on into search sector seven."

"Roger, out."

The planes turned to the south-west and disappeared into a pillar of cloud.

12 July 2066, Seastead vessel *Ossë*
(the same day)

"So, Sheikh, the discussions with the Peruvian delegation went well, the Southern Pacific Territory's request for up to thirteen per cent of the estimated anchovy stock for 2066 was granted. We'll reimburse them in instalments through the year as we monitor what our schools consume.

"Also, our revenues in the Tokyo markets have increased eight per cent in the last quarter with the improved quality of our tuna product, now that we're using the new *iki jime* gate for the slaughtering."

Sul watched the clouds drift outside the windows of the bridge and spoke into his headset, "That's excellent, Hafez. We're prospering under your wise administration. Thank you for the updates."

"My pleasure, Sheikh. Oh, and I'm afraid Cohort 23 lost one of their tuna guides today. That's the second time this month that one of the guides failed. We've recovered the faulty guide and have sent it to Marcelli Deep for analysis; the report will be sent to you and Sophia. I've configured and released a replacement and ordered an additional two new guides to keep for situations like this. Shakeela's recovering from her bout of mono. Jimmy of *Murex* broke an arm this morning rough housing on the main deck but Doctor Maritza was able to treat it without bothering you."

"Nemo, note these in the medical log for the Pod."

"Noted, Captain."

"Well done, Hafez. And thank you." Sul sat in the bridge, keeping an eye on the sea and sky through the windows. "Looks like we might be in for a storm, Hafez. Can we have a weather forecast, Nemo?" Sul glanced at the holo-display of the *Arraa'i* Pod and saw Hafez's *Oyster* was currently about five miles away.

"Captain, barometer falling rapidly due to a low-pressure system moving up from the south. Winds increasing to a sea state six. Waves expected to reach fifteen to eighteen feet in the next half hour. Thunderstorms in the area. Recommend that you submerge within the next fifteen to twenty minutes."

"Yes, Nemo – thank you. Prepare to submerge in fifteen." Sul saw spray and foam streaming off some of the whitecaps outside the windows. The wind whistled as it passed the roof of the bridge.

"Sheikh, I'll contact the other Pod vessels and pass on Nemo's recommendation. We'll submerge *Oyster* in ten."

"Thank you, Hafez. Out for now." Sul glanced at the holograph again, checking the locations of the vessels in the Pod and the schools of tuna. He looked up, "Nemo, make the overhead ceiling transparent."

Where there had been a grey patch in the ceiling above him, Sul now could see through it to the thickening clouds above. The sky was becoming darker, even though it was mid-afternoon.

He heard the lift behind him open, then silence came into the room. He turned. "Sophia!" Sul's daughter approached, her head down. She stopped a few feet from his chair.

"Would you like to sit in my lap?" Her nod was barely noticeable. "Come, *Ameera*, I'll hold you firmly, so you feel safe. Shall we watch the storm together?"

Sophia smiled and climbed into the chair with him. Sul held her closely against him and felt her relax.

"The winds are picking up, I know you like storms, *habibti.*" She nodded, staring out at the steadily growing swells.

It's like watching a silent movie, when her sphere of silence is draped around us. Just the two of us. Sul felt a deep love for his daughter rise within him.

A curtain of dark rain was coming towards them, and then they were in it. Sul could feel the subtle vibrations of the squall on *Ossë*, but no sound. Lightning flashed in the clouds, but there was no thunder. Sophia giggled.

They watched the drama of nature for a while, then Sophia softly said "Mama? A true story, please."

Sul looked down at her, "You want me to tell you a story about your mama?"

She nodded, a small tear slid down her cheek.

"I imagine the waves remind you; it was on a day like today we lost her."

Sophia snuggled closer to her father.

"Sorry to interrupt, Captain. We're ready to submerge."

"Go ahead, Nemo. Take us down to twenty metres. That should be enough."

"Yes, Captain." Outside the windows, the deck began to descend towards the surface of the sea. Spray and waves began slashing against the windows. Then green water swirled around them, rising over the still transparent window above. The sea darkened outside as *Ossë* glided into calm waters below the storm. Sophia sighed again in her father's lap.

Sul looked down at her. "Well, imagine if you will, *Ameera*, a beautiful day in the Southern Equatorial current. A tropical sun in a cloudless sky. Our Pod has joined with the Morning Star community. We're forming a huge Sea Star, to celebrate Resurrection Day together."

Sophia was gazing at the twilit sea, lit by stabs of lightning in the bottle green water.

"There'll be sea games, and I've been chosen to be our Pod's man for the tuna-landing event. You've seen this, *Ameera*. We race to one of the tuna cohorts, capture a fish, and bring it back."

He could feel Sophia nod against his chest.

"Well, I climb down from my parents' vessel to my *Dragonfly* scooter and wait to see who my opponent will be. The Morning Star scooter is idling nearby, waiting for their man to show himself. Your mother steps gracefully onto the deck of her seastead home and dives into the water without leaving a ripple. She pops out of the water, climbs onto her *Dragonfly*, looks over at me, and smiles.

"*Habibti*, I couldn't move. I just stare at her. She is so beautiful."

"Beautiful." Sophia smiled as she mouthed the word, eyes fixed on the flashing sea.

"Like you, *habibti*." Sophia snuggled into his chest.

"The gun goes, *pow!* and she takes off before I can recover. I chase after her. I must get there first! We fly over the waves. I slowly gain on her. She turns to smile at me again, then puts on more speed, pulling ahead of me again."

"*Baba?* Mama wins!"

"Maybe, *habibti*, maybe… But I have to tell the story in order."

Sophia giggled, "She wins."

"Shh, *habibti*, don't give it away! Well, we're approaching the school. We don't want to spook the tuna, or they'll be too hard to catch. As we get near to the school, she slows her scooter, but still gets there a few seconds before me. As I pull up, she is slipping into the water with her stun gun. I pull my gun from the holster and jump in the water near her. I can't help looking at her, wanting to see that beautiful face. I'm so distracted that I miss my first shot. But she shoots well and gets back on her scooter with her fish."

"Mama wins, *Baba*!"

"Yes, *habibti*, you were right. I think you must have heard this before." Sophia quietly laughed and nestled in more deeply.

"Well, she speeds back towards the Star with a fish before I have caught mine. So, I lost the event, but not the opportunity to congratulate her. We had lunch together afterwards, and that was the beginning of our courtship. So maybe I won too, eh?"

Sul felt the regular breathing of Sophia asleep in his arms.

He stared for a while at the turbulent waves above the windows, relishing this quiet moment with his daughter. "I miss her too, *Ameera*. So much," he said quietly to the air.

After a few moments, he stood carefully with Sophia and carried her to the lift, and then below to her room. Placing her in the bed, he stroked her hair and whispered a prayer, then kissed her brow and draped a blanket over her. She smiled in her sleep.

Sul lingered a moment at Sophia's door, gazing at her. *She's the image of her mother*. His feelings were a mixture of anguish and joy.

Nemo whispered, "Captain, Gideon and Ben had some trouble on the way to Marcelli Ring."

"Are they OK?"

"Yes, Captain."

"Brief me as I head to my office, Nemo," Sul said, walking briskly down the corridor.

"They ran into a search patrol of Caliphate jets – but they were able to evade them."

The Caliphate is relentless. Could Ben's wife's data be so important? "Nemo, get me a conference call with Major Camden."

"Yes, Captain."

12 July 2066, three miles north of Marcelli Ring
(the same day)

The sleek hydrofoil sailing yacht sped across the waves in the late afternoon, staying to the transit lanes beyond the customs border for Marcelli Township. A young Arab man was at the helm, glancing below periodically into the yacht's lounge where two other Arab men were donning exposure suits. A third was helping them, then checking their equipment.

The radio clicked to life, "*Desert Dreams*, yacht *Desert Dreams*, this is Marcelli Transit Authority. Please come in, over."

The helmsman picked up the microphone, "This is *Desert Dreams*, reading you loud and clear. Over."

"*Desert Dreams*, I have you requesting a transit berth for the night. Can you confirm?"

The young man pressed the mike button, "Yes, Marcelli, that's correct. Do you have one for us?"

"Affirmative, *Desert Dreams*, you've been assigned berth eighty-seven in the transit docks. I'm sending you a map of the docks with your berth highlighted. Please confirm."

The screen in front of the helmsman flashed to life and he saw the promised map, with the assigned berth blinking. "Yes, I have it, thank you. We're about forty-five minutes out."

"Forty-five minutes, I copy. Be advised that staying at the transit docks means you won't be able to visit Marcelli Township. You must pass through customs and immigration for that. Do you understand?"

"Yes, we understand. We're just transiting for the night."

"Acknowledged, *Desert Dreams*. Thank you."

The helmsman looked below again; the two divers were ready. He glanced over the side of the boat. "We're coming up on a pod of dolphins, get ready to enter the water."

The divers scrambled up onto the deck and sat at the side of the yacht that was dipping down closest to the sea. They each pulled on a mono-fin, then looked to the helmsman. He looked around them. There were no boats within a mile of them and he gave the divers the signal to go. They rolled off the side of the vessel and into the water.

Desert Dreams continued course for the transit docks.

Below, the divers began the three-mile-long swim towards the Marcelli Ring. The shape of the packs on their back, along with the mono-fins, made them look like a pair of dolphins cruising the open waters. They even mimicked the movements of dolphins by regularly skimming the surface for a breath, although their air was supplied by rebreather units.

An hour after sunset, they arrived at one of the more desolate parts of the floating sea wall that protected Marcelli Ring. They swam under the blocks that made up the wall and paused, holding onto the web of anchoring cables. One pulled a screen out of his pack, with a glowing map of the section of Marcelli Ring near them and pointed out a set of buildings. The other nodded.

They waited until 10 p.m. and then continued into the inner side of the sea wall, within Marcelli Township itself, maintaining their dolphin-like behaviour until they reached a dock with several boats moored to it.

Climbing the ladder at the end of the dock, they quietly removed their diving gear and changed into everyday clothes. The taller Arab moved with a fluid, athletic grace and efficiency. His eyes swept the area constantly, looking for threats with a calm, steely gaze. The shorter of the two checked the gear with a quiet intensity, ensuring it would be ready for their departure. He stowed it meticulously in duffle bags and concealed them under the dock, packing a few small items carefully into a satchel to take with them. The two men walked down the street, deserted at this hour, and stopped in front of a door of a darkened house.

The New Caliphate had other operatives in the city, as they did in most cities of the world but not wanting to expose their cover, the men would stay elsewhere. The taller of the two knocked on the door and waited. No response, so he knocked again, a bit louder. A light came on above them on the second floor. They heard steps, a light came on over them, and a speaker next to the door said, "Yes?"

"Good evening, Saeed. We bring greetings from your parents in Bosaso."

There was silence. The two men waited patiently, then the tall one said, "Your parents have been invited to stay at a luxury apartment in the Emir's palace itself. They are being treated very well."

A few seconds went by. "That could change, of course, if you do not open the door, brother," the tall man said quietly.

There was a click and the door swung open, revealing a middle-aged man with a stricken look on his face.

"Thank you, brother," the tall man said as they both entered the house, closing the door behind them.

12 July 2066, training range, Marcelli Ring
(the same day)

Somewhere in the pitch-black waters ahead of him, Lorenzo knew that there was a guardian fish; it was swimming slow enough for him to identify it with the echo-location gear he was testing. A grey body brushed against him, "Listen… with… mind," he heard through his headphones.

Lorenzo's frustration level went up another notch. *What the heck does that mean, "Listen with your mind"?* He knew the dolphins were patiently trying to help him, teaching him something they knew intuitively since infancy.

"Again!" he said. He focused, ignoring everything except for the sounds and vibrations resonating in his skull bones, which were being generated by the echo-locator. He swam forward, swinging his head in a slow arc, searching. *Wait a small change in the pattern.* He swung back to it. *There!*

Tazia came into his field of vision, crossing in front of him, wagging her head. As she neared, the sounds in his head roared. Lorenzo stopped, her body language indicated that something was wrong.

"What?"

"Two… strangers… water… suspicion."

"Where?"

"Outside… Ring… approaching."

"Go… watch."

"Yes." Tazia swam rapidly away into the dark sea.

Lorenzo stopped, suspended in the blackness. "Gabriella, put me in contact with Ranger Command using a security communication protocol."

A moment passed, then Major Camden's voice came through his headset, "Lieutenant Romero, I saw your request and picked it up. What's the security three threat you are reporting?"

"Good evening, Major. Tazia just informed me of two suspicious contacts approaching the Ring, underwater. I wanted to send the information immediately to Command."

"Well done, Lieutenant. Do you know where these contacts were seen?"

Lorenzo talked to Lucca, who was slowly swimming rings around him. "South-east section of the Ring. Apparently, they crossed under the sea wall there. The dolphins lost them, though; they may have turned on active countermeasures in their suits, if they are infiltrators."

"Excellent, we'll investigate. There's been a rise in suspicious activity over the last two days, starting with your dolphins' identification of the probes infiltrating our defences, and your sister's report a few days ago of a covert transmission device. The Ranger exercise has made us more prepared. I'll give you an update soon."

"Thank you, Major. Gabriella, cancel the training exercise. Bring *Windrider* above my location." Lorenzo began to swim to the surface.

12 July 2066, just outside Marcelli Ring
(the same day)

A small puff of mist erupted from the side of a cloud canyon, in the skies, fifteen thousand feet above the shimmering Pacific. *Kestrel* materialized within the haze. It banked, descending towards the vast arc of structures silhouetted against the dazzling surface of the sea.

The instrument panel reappeared. Gideon turned towards the controls. He donned a headset. "Nemo, turn on the military identification beacon."

"Done, Lieutenant Battuta."

"He addresses me by my rank when we shift to military activities," Gideon said, glancing at Ben.

"Marcelli Control, this is *Kestrel*. Pelagic Ranger aircraft, *Kestrel*, Alpha Tango Six Six."

"*Kestrel*, we have you. Take heading two-two-four to enter Marcelli Ring landing pattern."

"Roger, two-two-four. Requesting entrance at the south-east military harbour of Marcelli Ring."

"One moment, *Kestrel*. Switch to channel fifty-six." Gideon tuned to a new channel.

"Marcelli Control. This is a secure channel."

"Is that Lieutenant Raymond Lastra? Gideon Battuta here. I need to report that we evaded two bogeys which, we believe, were hostile. Request permission to land in the military harbour."

"Roger, Gideon. Marcelli Ring is under lockdown, defence protocol three. Lorenzo's dolphins have reported unauthorized undersea probes scouting Marcelli Township, and possibly infiltrators. Your report adds to the concern. Permission granted to land at Seaway One in the military harbour, Gideon. Please report to Marcelli command for a debrief."

"Roger, Ray. Land at Seaway One and report for debrief, thanks." Gideon continued to take headings as he took his position to land at the harbour.

"They're already on alert," he commented to Ben.

Ben shook his head, "Don't they have anything better to do than chase me?"

Gideon turned to him, "Well, from the story you just told me, the Caliphate has gone to great lengths to kidnap you a couple times. Whatever your biodata unlocks, it must be important to them."

He piloted the craft around Marcelli Ring, awaiting his turn to land. He glanced at Ben, "And as my dad said, this is about the Caliphate's bad behaviour, not you. You just happen to be their latest excuse to persecute us and now, apparently, Marcelli Township."

Ben sighed, "Yep, you're right. I keep telling myself that. I hate to be the reason people are in danger though."

He let his heart calm as he watched their approach. "Such a beautiful setting. A city built on a seamount. I met a woman a few years ago who said she grew up here, in the Marcelli Township."

Gideon was focused on turning off the camouflage. He studied the instruments. "Hmm... yes, this is actually the Marcelli Ring. The Ring below us encloses over one hundred square kilometres of ocean area surrounding the seamount. The Township is made up of the Ring, the Rise, and the Deep."

Then he looked up and pointed out the window, "The Ring is basically the town. Homes, schools, hospitals... That's where much of business, trade, community services, and civil government take place."

"OK, that's the Ring."

"Yes, and over the horizon there, to the north-west, about sixty kilometres away – if you could see that far – you'd find Marcelli Rise. The Rise is more rural. Seasteaders there manage ocean farms. They produce food for the Township, as well as to export to China, Japan, New Zealand, Australia, Peru, and Chile."

"Fascinating, I'd like to visit those farms sometime. But what's that on the other side, the south-east?" Ben had spied something on the horizon.

Gideon banked *Kestrel* through the landing pattern, then pointed. "Yeah, you can just make out some structures, about twelve kilometres away. That's the Deep, Marcelli Deep, where most of the Township's industry, mining and industrial services are."

"Yes, I understand. Keeping the industry in deeper waters so that its activities don't harm the reserve or the mariculture. Your dad briefed me."

"Right, you knew that. They don't want to endanger the sensitive seamount and mariculture areas."

"The things that woman told me a few years ago are coming back to me." Ben studied the vista and remembered Maria's description.

As *Kestrel* turned into a new heading, the angle of reflected light changed. Below them, the Ring emerged from shadow and sparkled like a jewel in the sea. Networks of roads, office complexes, parks, and housing extended out into an intricate lacework of humanity. The centre of the development, of the Ring, was an open space. The opalescent blue and turquoise hues displayed the different underwater depths.

"I'm surprised at how much green there is," Ben commented as he watched the city turn majestically under them. "Trees and grass."

"Yes, they might be sea people, but the Ring community still love their trees and lawns," Gideon warmed to the tour guide role. "Most of the founding immigrants became first generation Pelagics. Early in the settlement, there was a movement to 'green' the Ring. They recovered soil from the waste of marine mining operations at the Deep and planted gardens."

Kestrel dipped and slotted into another level of the pattern.

"The central empty space in the centre is where the seamount rises to just four metres below the ocean surface," Gideon continued, enjoying showing off one of the jewels of their Pelagic Territory, "No land actually breaks the surface, so it isn't an island. In fact, there's no naturally occurring land above water here. The Ring creates a floating circle around the submarine peak and is anchored to the slopes of the seamount."

Ben watched the scene unfold below him, fascinated. "So, this empty centre is the marine preserve of the Township?"

Gideon looked at him, surprised, "Yes, how'd you guess? *Baba* again?"

"Yes, but I heard it before. This friend described the nature reserve, and it is consistent with the picture I'm forming of Pelagic culture," Ben smiled.

Gideon laughed, "Early Pelagic settlers certainly understood the importance of protecting indigenous species. So, any part of the entire seamount area closer to the ocean surface than 150 metres was declared to be a marine nature reserve aggressively protected by the Township. The preserve acts as a nursery for natural populations of species native to the Township. The Rise is downstream from the seamount and natural mariculture seedstock drift there with the currents."

"Permission to land," Nemo's voice informed them.

Gideon started the descent. "Heading for the military harbour Seaway ahead of us."

The city spread to the north and west as they descended towards the right-hand sea-lane, one of eight within a large circular breakwater. *Kestrel* adjusted its course to line up with the Seaway, marked by lighted buoys. A set of pontoon skids lowered from *Kestrel* and they landed smoothly. Engines flushed into reverse, as the crafted turned to the right into an access channel between the sea-lanes.

"Take *Kestrel* to berth forty-three near the Marcelli Command centre, Lieutenant Battuta."

"Perfect, Neem!"

They taxied among seaplanes large and small, winding their way through a maze of berths and docks. Then slowing, they neared the inside edge, where the breakwater met the township circle. Gideon piloted *Kestrel* into the empty dock space that had been reserved for them. With a subtle shudder, the engines ceased. A figure was waiting on the dockside, waving them in and coiling a rope. With a practised toss, the rope sailed through the air onto a mooring cleat on *Kestrel*. The man then pulled them in and tied them off to a bollard.

"Moorings have engaged, Gideon," Nemo informed them, "I'll stow *Kestrel* in the secure bunkers."

"Thanks, Neem." Gideon was already popping the canopy open. He leapt from the manta wings onto the quay. "Carlo!" he called out, grabbing the young man in a bear hug.

Ben unfolded himself from *Kestrel*'s seat. He walked more slowly across the wing, onto the dock. "Carlo, meet Professor Holden." Gideon paused for a split second then added, "a guest of the *Arraa'i* Pod. Ben, this is Carlo Marcelli, grandson of the founder of this sea community."

As they greeted one another, *Kestrel* quietly submerged behind them, moving off to be secured underwater.

"Glad to meet you, Professor." The dark eyes under the black hair smiled. Carlo was stocky, but well built; Ben guessed him to be in his mid-thirties, maybe creeping up on forty. "Uncle Suliman informed us that you'd be arriving. We're aware of your recent… situation. Major Camden would like to speak with both of you and debrief you on your journey here."

The three walked over to the low crescent-shaped building just beyond the docks. As they entered, a man in Ranger fatigues, a sidearm strapped to his belt, buzzed them through the security door. "The Major is expecting you."

"This way." Carlo led them down several corridors. They reached a conference room. An officer paced in front of the windows overlooking the air harbour. She turned as they entered. Carlo and Gideon saluted her

"Ah, Lieutenant Battuta. And this must be Ben Holden. I've heard a lot about you this morning, son."

Ben took the offered hand. He looked into a lively and intelligent set of eyes below silver grey hair. She was maybe mid-forties and carried herself with a confidence that made Ben trust her immediately. "Major. Sorry to be a cause of trouble."

"From what I understand, you're not the cause of the trouble. Some aggressive intruders are. We've had indications that marine probes, now identified as Caliphate, have breached our Pelagic Array defences. We're analyzing them, and several other concerning instances which have come to light. And now I hear that you two were pursued by Caliphate fighters this morning?"

"Apparently, Major. Though I can't be sure they were hunting us specifically. They may've been trying to find our Pod, and my father's vessel," Gideon explained.

He then gave a detailed version of their experience with the Caliphate jets on the way to Marcelli Ring that morning.

When Gideon had finished, Major Camden glanced at Ben, "How resourceful of you to use a squall as cover to hide *Kestrel*. Well done."

The door cracked open. A young man put his head in the room. "Major, we're ready for you. The defence scenario is set up. The Security Council has arrived."

"Thank you, Sergeant." Turning to Gideon, she inquired, "Have you eaten yet, Lieutenant?"

"Not yet, Major."

"Go grab some lunch. Then report back here at 1430 hours."

"Yes, Major!" Gideon and Carlo saluted and left the room with Ben.

*

The three of them left the Ring Highway gate of Marcelli Command, walking out onto the main road which encircled the settlement. Small businesses lined the street and housing developments spread out behind them, spaced strategically to allow each home a clear view of the sea.

The sky was a clear blue dome and it was a beautiful day. In the distance, electric cars, most of them driverless, whizzed by on the Ring Highway.

Ben whistled, "Impressive. I saw the green from the air; I didn't expect to find a park filled with trees and grass in the middle of the ocean."

Before them, in the centre of the Ring, a few sailing boats drifted lazily across the nature reserve. Ben glanced back at the seaport. The aircraft in the landing patterns looked like a circling flock of seabirds.

"We call it home," Carlo smiled.

"How many live here?"

"Including the Ring, the Rise and the Deep, about 130,000. In the Ring alone, I think the population's about 90,000."

"So, like a smallish town. How do people get property here?"

"Prospective seasteaders can freely apply to work a plot out on the Rise, for housing in the Ring, or start a business in the Deep. After five years, if they meet qualifications, they can earn a deed of ownership of the farm, house or business. All covered under the 2042 Seastead Act."

They continued along a wooded trail from the harbour, passing through a park with stately firs and flowering shrubs. The path opened to a wide expanse of lawn, bordered by cypress trees next to the Ring Highway. Kids flew model airplanes of a design Ben had not seen before. The planes engaged in miniature dogfights over the green.

Carlo followed Ben's gaze. "The kids are playing with a uniquely Pelagic plane, designed here for defence of the Township. We call them *Sea Wasps*. These models just came out a few months ago. The kids love them; they practise fighter tactics with them. It's one way we grow our own pilots."

"Looks fun," Gideon said. "Would've loved those when I was a boy."

"How old is the Ring? It looks new," Ben said, taking it all in as they crossed the grass towards the Ring Highway.

"The first seasteads were anchored on the seamount back in 2037." Carlo waved his hand out to the east. "My grandfather and a small band of settlers proposed a plan for the Ring in that year. They started construction on one arc of the basic ring the next year. Over the next five years, they completed the full Ring around the seamount. When it was finished, they advertised for outsiders to apply for residence under the Seastead Act. The Rise and Deep were opened in 2043."

"So, what qualifications does an outsider have to meet to gain residence?"

"On the Rise, you have to demonstrate a working farm for five years; same thing for a business in the Deep. To live in the Ring, you must build or buy a house, then demonstrate that you are actively part of and contribute to the Ring community. Most settlers in the Ring order one of the floating modules to build on."

"That gives a new meaning to 'grow your own'!" Ben took in the view with a new interest.

"Sure does." Carlo smiled. "In the Ring there are several companies dedicated to growing the modules using an accretion process. On the Rise, it takes two years to grow the mariculture platforms. After five years, if they've figured out this new way of life, they can apply for permanent residency. For the final step, a local council made up of the applicant's neighbours and peers is convened for a secret ballot on whether the application is accepted or not."

"Quite a process." Ben nodded, then looked down as they walked onto the pavement next to the Ring Highway. "So, the entire Ring has been grown by this accretion process? These blocks look like the same material as the Pod vessels I've been staying on."

"Yep, just the same." Carlo paused to pick up a broken shard, handing it to Ben. "We adapted the accretion technology used to build boats like *Ossë*. My family runs Marcelli SeaShells Complex, one of the first to specialize in this technology to build homes in the Ring."

"Tell me more about accretion technology. I know it was discovered after World War Two and has something to do with seawater and electricity."

"Yes, we like to call it seacrete. It didn't really come into its own until early this century, although it was used for building breakwater barriers in harbours for several decades."

"How does it work?" Ben was intrigued.

"First a frame of graphene is 3D-printed underwater. Then a constant, low voltage electric current is directed through the frame. The seawater reacts to the electrified graphene, causing crystals of calcium carbonate and other minerals to accumulate around the frame. These crystals are called aragonite. The accumulated material, the accretion, is stronger than concrete."

"So, all of this," Ben stamped the pavement with his foot as if to test its solidity, "is basically created out of the minerals in the sea?"

"Yes, several companies do this out at the Deep, each specializing in a different use for the seacrete: modules for the Ring, boats, mariculture platforms; there are many uses. Marcelli SeaShells is one specializing in vessels like the ones in Gideon's community. My sister, Sally, is one of the executives at SeaShells." Carlo glanced slyly at Gideon. "If you are interested, Ben, we can give you a tour of our accretion operations out in Marcelli Deep."

"That sounds like a great idea to me," Gideon chimed in.

"Don't mind him, he is besotted with my sis."

Gideon tried to look nonchalant and changed the subject. "Floating cities are all very well, but, personally, I pity those who are tied to one place on the ocean. The nomadic life is so much more interesting, I always say," Gideon teased, rolling his eyes.

"Not everyone wants to spend their life chasing tuna, *amico*." Carlo laughed. Glancing across the street, he spotted Lorenzo walking on the other side.

"Hey, Renzo!" Carlo yelled. The youth stopped, returning Carlo's wave.

"Carlo!" he called, dodging cars and crossing over. Carlo and the young man hugged.

"You look great," the newcomer said. "How are Ana Lucia and the kids?"

Carlo laughed, "They're well, waiting for your next visit! Izzie wants you to bring your dolphins."

Carlo turned to the others, "This is Lorenzo. My cousin, on my mother's side." Carlo introduced him to Ben. "Where's a good place for an espresso on this side of the Ring, Renzo?"

"I'm on my way to meet my sister at the family bakery. It's near the park. There are nice tables out over the water," the young man pointed down the road.

"Perfect! Can we join you?"

"Sure, that would be great." The four strode purposefully towards the bakery, as Carlo continued the introductions. "Renzo here is a Lieutenant with the Rangers. He's helping us develop an interspecies alliance with dolphins for reconnaissance and patrol."

"Among other things." Lorenzo added, "We're also working with farmers on the Rise to herd fish for harvest. The dolphins get a cut of the fish."

"You work with dolphins?" Ben probed. This sounded vaguely familiar.

Lorenzo looked at Ben, assessing him. "Well, I've developed a special rapport with two dolphins. I've named them Tazia and Lucca. They help me link with dolphin pods in the area. I've just been doing this for a year, barely begun. Dolphins are excellent, of course, for detecting intruders and reconnoitring without raising suspicions." Lorenzo enjoyed introducing his life to others, "But they aren't tools we can use, at our beck and call. With dolphins it's about building relationships."

"Relationships, how so?" Ben asked.

Lorenzo's eyes lit up as he warmed to the topic. "Fortunately, they love working with humans, especially those who build a rapport with them. They've become real friends for me. I look for ways to help them and express my gratitude when they help me."

"Lorenzo is able to empathize well. He relates with those dolphins at a level the rest of us don't quite understand," Carlo offered.

"Fascinating." Ben was struck by the warmth exuding from the teenager.

"Renzo, I hear you had some news for Marcelli Command this morning."

"Yes, Tazia reported some intruders, day before yesterday. They're looking into it. Here we are!" Lorenzo said, as they came to the bakery. "Mm, the smell of brioche, fresh from the oven. They are *squisita* – excuse me, delicious – when warm."

They walked onto the oceanside deck area and chose a seaside table. As Lorenzo waved a waiter over, Ben's attention was caught by ripples in the water. A pod of dolphins cruised just thirty metres off shore. A head poked above water and waggled.

"That's Lucca," Lorenzo said, "inviting me out for a swim. The pod would love me to spend all my time with them."

Lorenzo and Gideon consulted over the menu, ordering lunch for them all.

Ben gazed out at the rim of the Ring, then turned to Carlo, "This looks amazing, considering it's all been grown out of seacrete. How does it stay afloat?"

"It's a modular system," Carlo responded, "made of blocks. Each block is usually the size of a quarter city block and designed for its unique position on the Ring, a bit like a jigsaw puzzle. Each massive block has multiple internal air spaces. Some can be filled with water to adjust height or levelling. This way, each block floats even with the adjacent blocks."

"And how do you keep the whole thing from drifting away with the currents, or from breaking apart in the storms?"

"Everything is attached to anchoring foundations, grown in a ring around the seamount slope, around three hundred metres below us. Blocks are attached to the foundation with carbon nano-thread cable. This forms the anchoring web. Devices on the cable function as shock absorbers. This keeps block movement to a minimum. Plus, we've grown breaker-walls in an outer ring to deflect the larger waves and protect the settlement. The perimeter will continue to expand as the township grows away from the seamount towards the open sea."

"Sounds like an engineering marvel. Thanks for the explanation." Ben scanned along the arc of the ring, admiring the varied buildings and beautiful architecture.

The aroma of the freshly cooked lunch being delivered to their table brought him back to the moment. After a few bites, he said to his new friends, "So, you grow your own food, build seacrete from the sea, have established your own trade, economy, transport, and civil service. Sounds like Marcelli Township and the Pelagic Territory here are fairly self-sufficient."

Carlo mused, chewing his ravioli. "That's right. We're net exporters of goods and services to the terrestrial nations. We've been pretty much free agents up till now, neutral to the politics of the terrestrial nations. There's an increasing awareness that we need to find ways to protect our own interests. The apparent incursion of the Caliphate these last few days is just one example. We've ongoing problems with pirates, poachers, and other outlaws as well. Many in the Territories now feel the time is ripe to establish an independent nation state of Pelagia."

"What would that mean in terms of politics between the seasteads and the…" The conversation was interrupted by an excited chattering rising from the next table.

Ben turned to see what was going on. The children were exclaiming as they watched each other's computer pads. He leaned over to see one of their screens. It was filled with underwater scenes displaying various points in the seamount.

Carlo rolled his eyes, "Those bot-fish are everywhere now. It's your sister's fault, Gid."

"Are those the new lionfish bots?" Gideon perked up, now that his plate was clean. "I haven't seen a working model yet."

"Yes, they were introduced two weeks ago, then in the last few days the Council actually declared a limit on the number of bots that could be active in the marine preserve at any one time!" Turning to Ben, Carlo continued, "Sophia designed these artificial lionfish. They look and act like the real thing. They are equipped with cameras and other sensors. This means children and some adults nodding his head towards Lorenzo, "can explore the reef in non-invasive ways."

"Yes, I have one myself," Lorenzo said proudly. "I've learned so much about the preserve through it, even though I've already explored the preserve for years."

"Anyway," Carlo pressed on, "the kids and Lorenzo guide the lionfish around, using their pads. They observe the drama of the preserve in ways you could never do while snorkelling or diving. The fish accept the robot as part of the ecosystem, so they don't alter their behaviour."

Ben leaned over to look more closely. The boy next to him noticed his interest and handed him the pad, allowing him to experiment with guiding the fish through some caves and then out into a string kelp forest.

"This is amazing, I can see how it can be addictive."

A voice broke in. "If you move it a little to the left, there's usually a moray eel out at this time of day…" the voice trailed off.

Ben glanced up, he knew that voice. He was jolted by the sight of familiar blue eyes. "Maria!"

"Ben?" she stood, stunned.

The others passed questioning glances to one another. "You two know each other?" Carlo asked.

"Wow," Ben puffed his cheeks. "Yes. Our last meeting was a little awkward, actually." He found it hard to look at Maria.

She studied him. "I would have said the same thing, she said quietly.

Ben looked up at her and Maria reached out to shake his hand. At the same moment, they both said, "I'm sorry…"

Everyone laughed at this, and the tension was broken.

"So, who is *more* sorry?" Gideon asked, looking at them slyly.

"Well, I asked a question that was a bit too personal, I think…" Maria offered.

Ben's eyes widened in surprise, "No, not at all. It was me who walked out on you… without an explanation. I'm so sorry."

There was a silence between them as they looked at each other, both trying to gauge the moment.

"Shall we start again? Hi, my name is Maria." She smiled up at Ben.

"Ben." He said shaking her hand now and smiling at the memory, "the guy who collects muons. I'm happy to meet you… again."

"This is interesting," Carlo said watching them closely. "Sit down, tell us more. How did you meet?"

Maria looked at Carlo with a small smile, "In Arizona, when I was finishing my degree. I saved Ben's life. She gracefully sat down at the table with them.

"Saved his life?" Gideon was incredulous. "This sounds like a story worth hearing."

Maria laughed, more comfortable now. She glanced at Ben. "It was only a rattlesnake. He would've noticed it in time, maybe."

Ben also recovered, "Yes, maybe," he said, joining the easy laughter.

He looked over at Lorenzo, abashed, "I think I owe your sister at least a brioche and espresso, if she'll accept."

Lorenzo just nodded his head towards his sister.

"Accepted, kind sir," Maria said lightly. She waved a waiter over to place an order while saying, over her shoulder, "and you're forgiven."

"For rudely abandoning her on our last date," Ben explained.

"You've even been on a date!" Carlo whistled.

"So, tell us the story!" Gideon grinned.

Maria told the story from her side, and Ben chimed in with his version. He also told the small group more of his own background to explain his behaviour.

"Your wife and child were murdered? And you lost all the men in your unit?" Carlo was silent a moment, then said, "I would not have guessed that, you seem so..."

"Normal?" Gideon suggested.

"Yeah," Carlo admitted, "Wow."

"It's been a long road to 'normal'," Ben said quietly. "But that's another story. Maybe for some other time."

"Time! Look at the time!" Carlo said, "Maria and Lorenzo, we have to be back at Marcelli Command in ten minutes!"

"Of course, but only if Ben promises to visit again before you leave. Free for dinner?" Maria looked at him.

Ben looked at Gideon. "We're not expected back at the Pod until tomorrow at the earliest after the Peruvian delegation has left." Gideon replied to the unspoken question.

"Then, of course," Ben smiled back at Maria. "Where, and what time?"

"I had planned for us to stay with Sally out on Marcelli Deep tonight," Gideon interrupted, "but I can leave you here, if you like. Sally won't mind. Carlo, know any place he can stay?"

Carlo smiled, "Well, yes, if you are to be marooned here tonight to have dinner with the lovely Maria, you'd be welcome to stay at my parents' house, the *Tempest*. They love guests and have plenty of room. It's just a few streets down the Arc from here. Would that work for you?"

Ben was touched by this surge of generosity. He took a moment to sort out his thoughts, "Thanks, Carlo. That'd be great if it's not too much trouble."

"No trouble at all. With the family now travelling all over the Territory, the rooms are often half empty. I'll tell Elektra, our AIA to prepare a room for you."

Maria glanced at Ben. "How about the new restaurant, *Diwali*? I hear they have great curries. It's farther down the Arc. Not far from the *Tempest*. Seven p.m.?"

"Seven p.m. it is."

She searched his face, "I won't need to chain you to the table this time, will I?"

Ben smiled, embarrassed. "No, looking forward to it, Maria. My treat... for saving my life."

"Good," Maria confirmed. She squeezed his hand, her eyes smiling.

CHAPTER NINETEEN

13 July 2066, Diwali Restaurant, Marcelli Ring
(that night)

Ben shifted uncomfortably as he stood in line with Maria, his mind drifting over the last few hours. Carlo had rummaged around in the *Tempest* to try to find him nicer clothes for 'the date'. Once they'd all heard the story of how Maria met Ben, and how Ben had walked out on their first date, the group of friends took the couple on as their project. Lorenzo, with his family connections, had made the reservations, Gideon had taken Ben to a local barber, and Carlo had been in charge of obtaining suitable clothes. The shirt was a bit tight, the shoes pinched and the trousers exposed a little too much of the socks. But Carlo had declared that Ben "cleaned up nicely".

As promised, the walk from *Tempest* to *Diwali* was not far, and Maria was waiting in a stunning red dress. Ben's palms were sweating a bit; he wiped them furtively on the trousers.

"Well, Carlo was right, you *do* clean up nice." Maria pecked him on the cheek.

"I feel like the victim of a conspiracy," Ben laughed, relaxing.

"A conspiracy of friendship, I think." She smiled at him, blue eyes sparkling, face glowing under the streetlight. She put her arm through his and led him into the restaurant.

As they walked through the door, Ben was puzzled. There were no tables inside, just a podium at the head of what looked like a pier. "Where are the tables?" Ben whispered to Maria as they stood behind a short queue of customers.

"Watch," she whispered back. They stepped forward in their turn, "Romero, table for two."

The woman behind the podium checked the list, "Yes, and I see you have a reservation for the outer lagoon." She looked up, "My favourite spot. Much more private and further from streetlights; the stars will be brighter."

They followed her to the end of the pier. "Outer lagoon? Are we being exiled?" Ben said in stage whisper. Maria prodded him with her elbow and a smile.

Looking beyond the end of the pier, Ben saw many lights a metre or two under the water and a number of shadowy craft drifting on the surface. Looking closer, he realized each partially submerged craft held diners around a candlelit table.

"Here you are. Gondola seven. Watch your step." A short flight of steps allowed them to enter their gondola containing a tastefully set, candlelit table on wooden decking. The sides of the craft were transparent, curving up and flaring out, resembling a floating fish bowl. The surface of the sea came up two thirds of the clear material, allowing diners an underwater view in 360 degrees.

As they entered their gondola and sat at the table, the stairs retracted behind them.

The hostess above them looked at her pad, "Your gondola will pass through that gate over there to the outer lagoon, where it'll drift in a random pattern, keeping away from the other gondolas. Menus are on the table. When you are ready, press the blue button and clearly state your order. A drone will deliver your meal. If you have any requests or problems, that same button will connect you to the manager. Any questions?" she asked brightly.

"Thank you, I think we can take it from here." Ben said

She consulted her pad, "Oh, sorry, there were special instructions. It looks like this gondola has been reserved for the whole evening, you can stay out until we close at 11 p.m." She read a bit more, "and payment for your meal has been taken care of, so choose anything you'd like from the menu. You have generous friends! OK. Have a great evening, folks."

"Thanks!" Maria waved as their gondola began to move towards the gate.

"The conspiracy deepens," Ben said. Maria laughed, "that last bit sounds like a Carlo touch."

The gondola began drifting. Soon they had entered a smaller lagoon, with fewer gondolas. Stars arched above them, shimmering brightly.

Ben was observing the sea through the walls of their fishbowl. "What's with the underwater lights?" Shadowy shapes darted near them.

"That's why the restaurant is called *Diwali*."

"Ah, the Hindu festival of lights," Ben supplied.

Maria smiled at him, her face beautiful in the candlelight, "Right. We're over the eastern slope of the seamount, which drops steeply to a depth of 2,000 metres. Underwater lights like these attract many small fish, which attract larger predators." They were drifting near one of the lights. "Look, there. Those are squid, hunting their dinner."

As Ben watched, several squid came into view, hovering in place. One suddenly changed from pale brown to vivid red, tensing into the shape of a pointed arrow. In a split second, it struck out with one tentacle, snagging a hapless fish. Then it quickly backed out of the spotlight and made short work of its dinner.

Maria continued, "Squids, like many cephalopods, wear their emotions on their skin; they change colour when they are hunting or mating." She stopped, suddenly flustered. She was glad it was dark and didn't show her own blush.

Ben smiled and moved the subject on, "Fascinating – and what a great design for a restaurant: under the stars, candlelight, ocean view from every angle, moving entertainment."

"And from what I hear, also excellent food." Maria was looking at the menu. "Mmm, I think curried tuna for me."

Ben turned his attention to the menu. "The Rogan Josh looks good, one of my favourites."

After making their selections, Ben pressed the button and placed their orders. It was read back to them and they were told it would be about twenty minutes.

Maria described the drama that was taking place around the submerged lights: the various predators and their habits, but Ben was just watching her. After a few moments, she stopped and looked at him.

"Maria," Ben looked down at the table, straightening his fork. "Thank you for forgiving me for that evening in Grit, at the diner."

She put her hand on his, interrupting, "Stop. We're starting over. All that is forgotten."

Ben looked up at her. She brightened and held out her hand as she'd done that afternoon. "I'm Maria, Maria Romero. Fancy meeting you here."

Ben laughed and took her hand. "Starting over. Thank you. The name's Ben," he chuckled.

"You laugh much easier now," Maria observed. "You don't carry so much sadness."

"Partly, it's the company, of course." Maria smiled at him. "But I've learned so much since I last saw you."

"Tell me," Maria said simply. "I'd love to hear as much as you want to share."

Ben looked into the depth of her eyes, drawn in by their sincerity, and began to trust.

"Well, twelve years ago I was married to a wonderful woman, and I had a great son…"

It seemed only a moment later that the drone delivered their meal, perching on the edge of the gondola so they could collect the warm trays. They ate slowly. Maria mainly listened, asking questions here and there. He told her many stories, some horrible things that had happened to him, but beautiful memories too. When they finished, and the drone took their trays, they continued drifting in the gondola and talking for hours in their small world of candlelight under the canopy of stars.

Soon after 10 p.m., Maria noticed the small button on the table was flashing red. *Oh no, not now,* she thought.

A voice broke their enchantment, "I'm so sorry, but I have an urgent message for Ben Holden. Major Camden requires him at Pelagic Ranger Command immediately." Their gondola changed course and started its journey towards the gate. "A car is waiting at the entrance to take you both to Command."

Ben reached over and pressed the button, "Thank you. We're on our way."

He looked up at Maria. She touched his hand, "It's OK, Ben. Thank you so much for letting me get to know you better." She smiled suddenly as she said, "To be continued…"

"Agreed." Ben put his hand on hers.

13 July 2066, Marcelli Ranger Command
(the same night)

The taxi took Ben and Maria to Marcelli Command where they found Carlo and Gideon waiting. "Wow, Maria, you look great!" Gideon said, then winked at Ben.

"Stop it," Maria said, and stepped out of the street light to hide the colour rising in her face.

"I thought you'd gone on to visit Sally." Ben changed the subject, taking the attention away from Maria.

"The Major called me back. The Ring has gone to security level four," Gideon explained.

"Renzo's coming," Carlo pointed to a figure sprinting through the park across the street.

The sentry waved them through security, where the Sergeant met them, taking them again to the conference room. Major Camden was seated, a holo-display of the Marcelli Ring floating before her above the table.

The Major stood as they entered, returning their salutes. "At ease." She waved them to seats.

"Thank you all for coming." She glanced at Ben and Maria. "Sorry to pull you out of, um, other engagements." She turned to the holo-display, studying it. "Good news and bad news, people. Good news: about two hours ago, Tazia and Lucca detected suspicious activity that looks like infiltration of the Ring by enemy agents. Forewarned is forearmed. However, the bad news is that we've not yet found them and we assume they're in hiding within the Ring itself."

"Excuse me, Major, but that alone wouldn't have pushed us to level four," Carlo observed.

"Yes," the Major agreed, "but there have been several other incidents the last few weeks. As you know, Lieutenant Romero's dolphins detected probes last week. There were four. We located and neutralized these." Four pulsing blue icons appeared on the holo-display. "We're studying the probes now, determining how they got past the Pelagic Array."

Ben studied the holograph before them. The placement of the probes looked strategic. "They were probing your defences, Major. Looking for weaknesses."

"Yes, very good, Professor. A few days after the discovery of the probe, a device was found by Captain Romero..."

"The one in the red dress," Gideon said sotto voce. Maria kicked him under the table.

The Major paused, waiting. "Sorry, Major." Gideon said sheepishly.

"As I was saying, we've been monitoring the device that Captain Romero discovered on the south-east slope of the seamount. We left it in place. It has been continuously active since then, so someone is using it to communicate. We haven't broken the code, though.

"Finally, just tonight, Tazia and Lucca uncovered suspicious activity that looks like covert agents infiltrating the Ring. The dolphins lost track of them when they got out of the water. We are searching, but no luck so far and must assume they are gone into hiding.

"From all of this, we must conclude that there are several agents, probably hostile, active here in the Ring, so we've set security level four. We've no indications of any agents or suspicious behaviour out on the Deep and the Rise, but we can't be sure, of course."

The incidents were projected in the holo-display with dates and labels. Ben got up and walked around the projection, studying placement.

Major Camden addressed Ben, "Professor, as Sul warned us, I suspect these agents are seeking you. Sul forwarded information about you, passed on by a…" she looked down at her pad, "Dr Whitestone. I was told this information has been shared with your permission."

Ben looked up at her, "Yes, of course, Major. You need to know everything necessary about me to understand this threat."

"Yes." Camden said simply. "These files indicate that you were in the Special Forces, and hint that you may have been inserted in hostile areas for reconnaissance. I'm not interested in that – I suspect your missions are still classified – but I'm interested in any insights from your experience."

Ben listened. "Of course, Major. The dolphins detected the infiltrators here," he pointed at the display, "is that correct?"

"Yes," Lorenzo chimed in.

"They would not be able to go far with all their diving gear. If I were leading the team, I would set up operations somewhere in this area."

"That area contains a new development, with recently built homes. Immigrants have just begun moving in there," the Major supplied. "Must be at least a hundred houses to search."

Ben was still studying the map. "Maybe we don't have to search the houses. How is your holo-tech?" Ben asked, glancing at the Major.

"We have some of the latest equipment, Professor. What are you thinking?"

Ben told them his suggestion.

"Excellent, Professor. We can start now," the Major said.

CHAPTER TWENTY

14 July 2066, Marcelli Ring
(the next day)

Saeed stood, watching the two unwelcome houseguests devour the breakfast he'd prepared. They were calm, and under other circumstances Saeed would have thought them professional as they quietly discussed their plans. However, a chill of terror went through him as they waved him to refill their coffee cups.

The taller one looked at Saeed, "Is the car charged?"

"Yes. Everything's ready, as you instructed."

"Good." The tall man rose, walked down the hall into the Saeeds' bedroom. There, his wife and his two daughters were sitting on the floor, tied together, tape across their mouths. They looked up with eyes wide with terror.

The tall man removed a small canister from his pocket, placing it on the floor in front of the bound women.

"What is that?" Saeed's voice quavered.

The guest glanced at him, "An insurance policy." He broke a seal and pressed a button on top of the canister. A blue light began to blink.

He stood and looked at Saeed. "If you follow our instructions, they'll be unharmed."

Saeed looked at the canister, then at the man.

"If you betray us, I'll press this button." From his pocket, he pulled out a small silver oval with a red button in the centre, a guard over the button. "I push this, and nerve gas will be released into the room. Your family will be dead in seconds."

Saeed stared at the canister, then looked at the man. "This is unnecessary. I'll do as you say."

"And we trust you, Saeed, so there'll be no reason to press the button." Their eyes locked tensely.

Saeed looked down and whispered, "Yes."

"It's time to begin," the other man said. They led Saeed out of the room. As he looked back, Saeed saw the wild terror on his wife's face just as the door clicked shut.

*

Later that morning, at a café across the park from Ranger Command centre, the taller man sat at a table with a computer tablet in front of him, reading the news. A mug of coffee sat steaming next to him. *So, informants have seen this Ben Holden. Last report placed him within that military facility.*

"Still no sign," he murmured. This was picked up and transmitted to his accomplice a half mile down the Ring. "I'm almost ready here," he heard through the earpiece.

It would look good on his record if he could find this *jinn*-like man the Emir had been searching for. *I'd be promoted and have a larger team to command. May Allah grant this to me. I need to find the man.*

Patience is a faithful weapon, how well I know that. He took another sip. *Such a beautiful day, a day for Allah to bless my efforts.* He had a clear field of view. Gulls and terns keened as they wove circles over the park which lay between him and the entrance to the Ranger Command centre.

The sun warmed the emerald lawn and stately trees dotted the park. Beds of flowers were scattered in a very pleasing pattern. *Nice touch to cultivate a garden like this in the middle of the sea. We could do that off the coast of Yemen.*

He glanced as an icon on his pad flashed green. His accomplice was preparing a special box in the shipment yard of Marcelli Ring. *Ready to whisk a drugged Holden out of this sea town on a Caliphate cargo plane, right under the noses of these arrogant infidels.*

Saeed was waiting for his signal, parked under shade trees near to the Ranger Command Centre. The tall man could keep watch on Saeed easily. Field glasses lay on the table next to him, he picked them up periodically to pretend to look at wildlife.

How did squirrels get here? he wondered absently.

Always better to work with someone who is like-minded, happy to serve the Caliphate, he mused. Tying up Saeed's wife and two daughters had convinced him to do their bidding, but that was a clumsy way to carry out the task. *I know Saeed will turn us in if he is given a chance.*

The main door of the Ranger Command centre opened and three

young men walked out. The tall man's field glasses swung in to focus on this trio. One was Holden, he'd memorized his face.

The tall Arab pocketed the field glasses, closed his tablet and stood. He left a tip on the table. He didn't walk directly towards the three friends, but chose a tangent course, keeping them in view. A casual observer would see a man on a stroll through the park with no interest in the three.

A police car sped down the Ring Road, lights flashing. The tall man tensed momentarily, then relaxed as it passed on.

The three young men were chattering, oblivious to his presence, not noticing as he slowly curved his path towards them. After a few minutes, two left, to wander off through the park. Holden continued on the Ring Road for a bit, then turned into an alley.

The tall man switched channels on his communicator and spoke quietly, "Saeed, follow us into that small road."

"Yes," came the simple answer.

The tall man looked around briefly, then turned into the alleyway. He walked quickly to close the distance between him and his prey. A car came around the corner, he glanced and saw Saeed sitting stiffly at the wheel.

The young man walking in front of him had slowed, he seemed to be looking at the addresses and glancing at a paper in his hand. The tall man slipped a palm-sized weapon out of his pocket. *The dart will knock him out in milliseconds.* He aimed and pressed the trigger. There was an almost inaudible hiss, as the dart flashed towards his target.

To his surprise, the dart went right through the young man and lodged in a post beyond him. To his horror, he saw Holden dissolve before his eyes. *The young infidel had been just an image, a hologram!*

"Abort, it's a trap!" he said urgently.

He glared over at Saeed in the car and held up the silver oval. A vice-like twist on his wrist made him cry in agony, dropping the trigger. Ben caught it and put it in his pocket. With the help of a Ranger, the tall man was forced to his knees, and his hands bound. The tall man turned his head to see another Ranger holding a gun on Saeed who looked relieved. *The coward!*

Yet another Ranger was speaking over a radio and looking up at the birds above them. Following the Ranger's upward gaze, the tall man's mouth dropped open as the birds fell into a formation and headed towards Ranger Command centre. *They had been the projectors for the hologram!*

*

Saeed was being handcuffed nearby one of the several flashing police cars. Ben walked over. Saeed was distraught, begging the Ranger holding him, "Please! My family are bound at my house. They forced me to work with them."

Ben pulled the oval device from his pocket. Saeed's eyes widened in terror. "Please be careful with that, pressing that button will kill my family. That is how they controlled me. It will release nerve gas in the room where my wife and children are. Oh, please be careful!"

Ben gingerly placed it on his hand, carefully avoiding the plastic guard protecting the button from accidental depression.

"What is the address?" the man handcuffing Saeed asked.

"34 Sunrise Terrace." The Ranger spoke into his headset, then walked over to one of the police cars and pulled out a computer pad and began tapping on it. Ben and Saeed followed, and leaned in to watch.

A map of the Ring appeared on the screen with a flashing icon racing along the Ring Road.

"A SWAT unit?" Ben asked.

The Ranger glanced at him, "Yes, dispatched to the address."

Another Ranger began to lead Saeed away to a car, Saeed struggled to keep the pad in sight. Ben put his hand on the soldier's shoulder, "Let him watch, it is his family. I'll vouch for him."

Saeed looked at Ben gratefully and moved to stand next to him.

The scene had now switched to a body camera on the leader of the SWAT unit. They had arrived at the address and were fanning out to surround the house and block exits. One member of the squad went forward and inspected the door carefully. He stepped back and nodded to someone off camera. Another man came forward and burst the door open.

The SWAT unit swarmed in and began to search the house systematically. At regular intervals, there was a "Clear" as rooms were secured. They worked their way down the hall until they came to a final door. Again, a man checked for traps and wires, then silently nodded at the leader. A camera was slipped under the door, and the scene on the pad shifted to that camera's view.

Saeed's wife and two daughters were tied up, lying on the ground, tape over their mouths, their eyes wide with terror. They stared at the blinking light on the canister in the centre of the room. The camera swept the room, then the scene snapped back to the leader's bodycam.

Ben could feel Saeed tense beside him.

The door was opened and several of the squad came in. Carefully, they lifted each of the women and carried them out of the room. Men in hazmat suits came in and were framed by the door as the leader retreated a bit. The canister was checked, placed in a container, sealed, and taken from the room.

The leader turned and followed the hazmat suits out the front door of the house. The Ranger reached in and turned up the sound on the squad car radio.

"Family released and safe. Repeat, safe." Saeed let out a sigh of relief and sobbed quietly as he was led to another police car.

*

A mile away, the tall man's accomplice walked quickly away from the staging area. *The mission has been aborted!*

Without hesitation, he drew his diving gear out of a bag, changed into his exposure suit and strapped on his rebreather. He collected the rest of his gear, went to the door of the warehouse and looked around warily. *No one there.* Quickly and silently, he ran the short distance to the pier, went over the rail and dropped into the water. Donning mask and the monofin, he dived towards the bottom of the harbour and began swimming through the cover of seaweed towards the channel.

A few moments later, *Windrush* rounded the cargo docks and came to a standstill in the middle of the harbour. Lorenzo slipped into the water, and within seconds Tazia and Lucca were next to him. Lorenzo unclipped an apparatus from his webbing and began attaching it to Lucca, who hovered in the water patiently.

"We've practised this. Do you understand what to do?" Lorenzo met Lucca's gaze.

"Yes." Came through the interpreter and into his headphones. "We… catch."

Lorenzo smiled. "I think you like this." He finished strapping on the device.

The two dolphins swam away and Lorenzo was pleased to see they fell immediately into a classic search pattern routine. The training exercises were working.

*

The co-conspirator had reached the open ocean beyond the harbour entrance, the bottom was dropping quickly away, soon it would be too deep to provide cover. He could not afford the decompression time that a deep dive would require. He needed to get to the extraction point quickly. Since the abort, *Desert Dreams* would be circling back to pick him up at 8 p.m. He still had a three-mile swim.

He stopped for a moment to look around, suspended in the water. The seas were clear, only a couple of dolphins frolicking to the east. He turned back to the task at hand, pacing himself for the endurance swim.

As he moved forward, he was surprised to see one of the dolphins heading straight towards him. A dark object was attached to its right ventral fin. He heard a pop as a line of bubbles came straight towards him. Within seconds, he was entangled in a net. Small floats attached along the perimeter of the net inflated, and he found himself being hauled involuntarily towards the surface.

*

Windrush lay alongside the Ranger patrol boat, and the netted agent was hauled onto the vessel. Lorenzo was in the water trying to remove the net gun from Lucca's fin. The dolphin was leaping around with excitement.

"Calm down!" Lorenzo admonished.

Lucca stilled and allowed Lorenzo to finish unstrapping the net device. Then Lucca bounded off, to leap and dance with Tazia.

Lorenzo climbed back aboard *Windrush* and stowed his gear. One of the Rangers on the patrol boat was watching the dolphins, "What's with them?"

Lorenzo looked at the soldier, then over at the dolphins. "They think it's so funny."

"What's funny?"

Lorenzo rolled his eyes and said, "Catching a man with a net."

*

"Your plan worked perfectly, Ben," Camden said, listening to reports coming in. "They caught the second infiltrator and are bringing him to the interrogation rooms now."

"Only too happy to help, Major," but Ben looked dejected as he sat with Maria and Lorenzo in the conference room.

The Major watched him, then said, "Professor Holden, no one is blaming you; the New Caliphate is causing these problems. You've done nothing wrong."

"Thank you, Major. I appreciate your good will."

Major Camden continued to study the read-outs of the ongoing operation. "It looks like the communication device that Captain Romero found is still in operation. That means we haven't yet found all the agents. I think it'd be safer for you, Ben, and for the Ring community, if you stayed out of sight while we continue the hunt for these people."

Carlo and Gideon entered with grins on their faces, having enjoyed acting as decoys accompanying the holographic Ben to lure the agents out. Carlo overheard the Major's words and jumped in, "Major, Ben is welcome to stay at our family farm for a few days, out on the Rise."

"Good idea, Captain Marcelli. That seems like a safe place to shelter. We've seen no indications of agents in the Rise or the Deep. Still, I'll have Marcelli Rise Security set discrete patrols around your place. How does that sound, Ben?"

"That's fine with me, Major. Thanks, Carlo."

"My pleasure, *amico.*"

"We can fly out in *Kestrel.*" Gideon turned to Camden, "Major, may I draw armaments for *Kestrel,* just in case?"

"Yes, I suppose that would be prudent. I was told that you passed your range qualifications last week with flying colours, Lieutenant Battuta. Well done. I'll grant permission. But keep to defensive rules of engagement at this point, understand?"

"Of course, thank you, Major."

"Captain Romero, you and Lieutenant Romero will join the search for the other agents."

"Yes, ma'am," Maria said, with significantly less enthusiasm than Lorenzo.

Suddenly Ben sat bolt upright. "Major, you just mentioned that two prisoners were being brought to the interrogation rooms?"

"Yes, I did. Is something wrong?"

"Please contact your guards right away and check the prisoners, they must not be left alone!"

Major Camden opened her secure line to query about the prisoners. As she listened, her face fell. "How did you know?" she asked, turning towards Ben.

"Know what?" Maria asked.

The Major's words came slowly. "They've committed suicide, rather than be interrogated."

"The same thing happened to me years ago," Ben said ruefully. "Sorry I didn't think of that earlier. Now we've lost our best sources of information."

14 July 2066, Marcelli Deep
(later that day)

Kestrel skimmed over a rippled sea, its passive camouflage changing to match the hues of the sunlit or shadowed waters beneath it. Ben sat in the co-pilot's seat. Gideon was at the controls. Carlo sat in the rear seat, admiring the craft.

"I like your new design, Gideon!"

"Yes, fresh off the three-dimensional printer nine days ago! Cheng 3D-Print at Marcelli Deep produced it. First of its kind. A prototype."

"I'm amazed you were able to find the time to work on this… what with all the time you are spending with my sister."

Gideon glanced back at Carlo, "There are priorities, and priorities. Your sister is taking top priority."

"Glad to hear it." Then aside to Ben, but so Gideon could hear, "The family was wondering when he was gonna get around to popping the question."

"I heard that! It's done, she has accepted."

"Congratulations! I tried to warn her off, but she wouldn't have any of it…" Carlo smiled.

"Well, it's official. You'll see the ring on her finger soon. You and I are going to be brothers!"

Carlo rolled his eyes. "They let just anyone in the family now."

Gideon punched him from the pilot's seat.

"Careful!" Carlo said to him good naturedly, "Keep your eyes forward. Our lives are in your hands, buddy."

"Well, as a matter of fact, we'll be taking a little detour. I got permission from the Major to visit that sister of yours. She can tell you herself."

"Why am I not surprised?" Carlo laughed.

Gideon glanced back at Carlo. "It was self-defence. I wouldn't hear the end of it if Sally learned we'd passed so close and didn't stop."

Carlo grinned, "Yeah, you don't want to be on her bad side."

A shadow on the horizon had been rapidly approaching and now was resolving into a skyline of buildings.

"We're entering the landing pattern for the Deep now."

Kestrel climbed and joined a line of other aircraft waiting for a turn to land. Ben looked down from this altitude and saw a large oval set in the deep blue of the sea, with lace-like edges like Marcelli Ring, of new buildings growing out from the centre. It looked much more industrial than the suburban Ring, with warehouses, container yards and many cargo ships dotted around the man-made island.

After several turns around the Deep, *Kestrel* began to descend. "We're in final approach, we'll land at the seaway there just on the north end." Gideon pointed.

*

Kestrel taxied through the sea-lane into the crowded air harbour of Marcelli Deep, and headed towards the gates, which swung open for the craft.

"Nemo, stow *Kestrel* in a secure bunker after we leave."

"Yes, Lieutenant Battuta. You have permission to moor *Kestrel* in the military sea hangar on the east end of the harbour."

"Perfect." Gideon was securing *Kestrel*'s weaponry as they approached the pier.

Drifting to a stop at the reserved docking for Marcelli SeaShells Complex, they were met by a pretty young woman.

"Hi, Sis!" Carlo jumped from the craft and hugged her. Her lively dark eyes smiled up at him.

"We've brought a guest: Professor Holden. But he likes to be called Ben," Carlo announced.

She detached herself and came to shake his hand. "Glad to meet you, Ben. Welcome to Marcelli SeaShells," she said, bathing him in the warmth of a natural charm.

"And who," she said, peering around Ben with an arched eyebrow, "is the ne'er-do-well stowaway I see here?"

"Ne'er-do-well!" Gideon stepped off the craft, sweeping her up in his arms, "I'll have you know that I'm your best-beloved and don't you forget it!"

She giggled, "I think hell will freeze over before I forget that."

"Hold out your left hand to Carlo." Sally, still in his arms, did as requested.

"Nice ring," Carlo whistled.

"A diamond mined from our seamount," Gideon beamed.

Gideon set Sally down; she composed herself. "Ben," she said turning to their guest, "what do you do?"

"I'm a scientist, a research scientist. I study particle physics, specifically, how muons behave."

"Which will lead to the next generation of fusion reactors," Gideon said, relieved that the conversation had moved on to a less personal topic.

"Oh, electron replacement to reduce the distance between hydrogen atoms and allow fusion at a lower temperature, some say possibly even room temperature." Sally smiled.

Ben blinked and looked at her as if for the first time. "Why, yes. I'm impressed that you'd know that."

"Not just a pretty face," Carlo quipped. Gideon grinned. Sally kicked Carlo lightly.

"Sally, how about showing Ben how we build our SeaShells," Carlo suggested.

"Certainly, if you are interested, Ben," she turned to him.

"I would love to see how ships like *Ossë* are made. They are beautiful."

Carlo turned to Ben and said, "Sally is learning the family business, working her way up the ladder." Glancing at his sister he continued, "I hear you were just promoted to second production manager."

Sally blushed slightly, "Yes, It is a fascinating job."

A driverless car pulled up silently next to them. The doors opened to welcome them in. "It's a short drive from here, Professor, I mean Ben."

Ben smiled, "Thank you for being so welcoming. I've never been in a Pelagic Township. Tell me a bit about this place, the Deep."

Sally's face lit up, "Certainly. We'll only be going through a small part – but I can explain what we're seeing."

They climbed in the car. The doors sighed shut. "Elektra, my office, please."

"Yes, Sally," a feminine voice with a soft Italian accent responded.

"'Sally, I've heard nice things about you from Gideon's father, Captain Suliman," Ben said, looking at her.

"And from Gideon himself," Gideon said from the next seat.

She glanced from Gideon to Ben, a bit flustered – though she smiled. "And what does Sally do?" Carlo asked with a twinkle.

"Carlo, please." she objected, but she was smiling.

"And where does she do it?" Gideon chimed in.

"OK, guys. Go ahead. Embarrass me a bit more in front of our guest."

Carlo and Gideon said in unison, "Sally sells seashells down at the seashore!" They dissolved into laughter together.

"Now, you've got it out of your system," she only half-scolded, "can we get on with the tour?" She turned to Ben, "A family joke that, apparently, never gets old."

"No, indeed," Carlo said, wiping away a tear.

"Here," Sally changed the subject, "we're passing the corporate headquarters for Williams' Sea Mining operations. Using deep sea excavators, they mine minerals from the slopes of the Louisville Ridge. Most of our manufacturing metals come from Williams and other pelagic miners. A lucrative business."

"But not as lucrative as Sally's seashells," Carlo teased.

She gave him a disparaging look.

"And there's a 3D printing complex, Cheng Sea Prints. They manufacture many products for the Pelagic Territories within the Southern Gyre, primarily aircraft and droids."

"*Kestrel* was printed here," Gideon chimed in, then added, "Sophia has all her inventions produced at this plant and delivered by *Flying Fish* drone service. Very convenient for all of us nomads living within the Gyre."

"And here is Southern Pacific Gyre Research," Sally announced. A gleaming tower stood before them, surrounded by several connecting causeways. "Perhaps you saw the recent documentary about the huge seven-arm octopus. The Gyre Research team captured that amazing deep-sea footage."

"Yes, I saw that a few months ago. It was excellent work," Ben acknowledged.

Sally continued, "They're currently searching for ways to purge microplastics from the marine food web. Despite decades of attempts, a good solution has not yet been found. But there's still hope that we can redeem that ecological mess."

"What a service to the world it would be if they solved the microplastic problem," Ben looked admiringly at the research complex.

"Another idea they are testing provides a way to upcycle plastic garbage retrieved from the ocean into graphene. Graphene is a core component of the accretion technology we rely on."

Just beyond, the car stopped at a gate emblazoned "Marcelli SeaShells". The gates swung open. The car deposited them before a large gleaming dome, the colour of a conch shell. The doors to the complex opened as they neared the entrance.

"Elektra, please prepare showroom three." Sally spoke to the air as they entered.

"Being prepared, Sally," the lilting Italian accent responded.

"Here, let me show you how we make Marcelli SeaShells." She led them to her office which looked out on several large sea pens.

"Those are the construction chambers where we grow the SeaShells. Let's go into the Seashore."

She glared at Carlo and Gideon, daring them to crack a joke. "One of the company showrooms. I'll show you a holo-clip of a SeaShell vessel like *Ossë* being produced."

They stepped into an adjoining room, with a similar view over the tanks. "Elektra," she said, "please turn down the lights." The windows darkened, and the room was immersed in shadow.

"Interface, please." A holographic matrix filled the centre of the room. They gathered round.

"Show *Periwinkle*, from design to completion, six minutes."

"Yes, Sally. Displaying *Periwinkle* construction."

"This is a recent product, currently in production, Ben." She walked around the display.

"Each Marcelli SeaShell is custom-designed by a SeaShell architect. They begin with a core template. Then, after an extensive interview with the family who will live in it, the architect tailors this template to the family's needs and specifications." A line drawing of a large immersed-hull vessel took shape within the matrix. The internal design morphed as Elektra described modifications emerging from the interaction between a hypothetical family and the architect.

Sally easily slipped into her sales persona. "Once a design has been finalized, it is given to the spider bots. They weave the basic framework of the vessel underwater, from 3D-printed graphene, in one of our accretion pens. The vessels are built upside down. You'll see the reason for this in a moment."

Ben watched the holo-image, spellbound as the template was inverted and set in a virtual sea pen. Small spider bots began weaving the graphene framework of *Periwinkle*. The spiders' fragile web quickly formed into the ghostly shape of a vessel – a three-dimensional outline.

"We integrate insulation into the basic graphene matrix. We also integrate bonding interfaces for the artificial sapphire windows, as well as doors and hatches. Then electrical connectors are placed around the graphene matrix at optimum intervals. The electricity flowing into these connectors causes minerals from the seawater to accrete into crystals along the framework. The combination of a graphene frame and dense crystal growth create a light but very tough hull."

As she spoke, the spiders left the holo-display. The animation showed electricity flowing into the web of graphene and the shell of the craft forming.

"Really, we are just copying processes of nature when growing SeaShells. We can manipulate the colour of the shell, as many molluscs do. This causes the final product to look and feel like a seashell, while having stronger physical properties than natural shells."

An orange-white delicate shell steadily grew around the graphene frame. The interior walls took on a multi-hued mother-of-pearl sheen.

"When the basic shell has been completed, we bring in gecko droids to seal, smooth and polish the surfaces."

A swarm of small gecko-like machines entered the shell and dispersed throughout the craft. From their activities, surfaces grew smoother and more reflective.

"When we've done all we need to underwater, we fill the boat with air, bring it to the surface and pick it up with a crane to allow the water to drain. Then it is tipped onto a floating drydock for interior work." The image in the interface followed her description: filled with air, raised, drained, and tipped to the drydock.

"Once in the dry dock, we install all the basic infrastructure for living on and controlling the vessel: wiring for electricity, pipes for fresh water, ventilation, ballast tanks, propulsion tubes, sea vanes, and so on. Next comes installation of the sapphire windows. These are bonded to the hull to retain the structural integrity of the vessel. A basic artificial diamond veneer is often applied to the outside for strength. This texture reduces friction for underwater travel. The hull is conditioned for anti-fouling. One unique feature we're testing as a prototype on the outside surface of *Periwinkle* is a chromo-prism display. This will allow the vessel to camouflage itself in various environments much like cuttlefish and other cephalopods do."

"*Kestrel* uses the same technology," Gideon offered.

As Sally spoke, each of these features was demonstrated on the holo-display. An increasingly complex and beautiful vessel emerged sitting on the staging dock.

"At this point, we install the fusion power plant – in this case an Alchemist IV, like that on *Ossë*. This is linked to engines, desalination, buoyancy and stabilization, safety features, communication, instrumentation, and the family augmented intelligence to manage the vessel.

"Finally, after all this, the living quarters for the family are installed."

As carpet, furniture, appliances, and panelling were added to the ship, the image became an inviting home.

"Most of the vessels we make for nomadic communities in the Southern Pacific Pelagic Territory are single family units. We also grow the modular components for Marcelli Township the Ring, Deep, and Rise."

"And who," Gideon asked, coming near to Sally, "is the *Periwinkle* being built for?"

A blush crept up her face as she lowered her eyes. "You know perfectly well it's for us," she said, entwining her arm with Gideon's. "And I can't wait to move into it after our honeymoon."

14 July 2066, Marcelli Rise
(the same day)

The sun was still high. *Kestrel* skimmed across the stretch of open sea at 150 mph, riding on its own reflected cushion of air above the sparkling swells.

"What a beautiful day!" Gideon enthused, scanning the horizon with an appreciative gaze.

"It is," Ben agreed. Then turning towards Carlo and Gideon he asked, "Tell me more about Marcelli Rise."

Gideon glanced back at his future brother-in-law, "Oh, we can do better than that! We have a presentation with a voice-over by one of the most famous actors in the Township."

An embarrassed look came over Carlo, "No, Gid. Please."

"Nemo, please load 'Seasteader Intro 4 – Marcelli Rise' by Carlo Marcelli."

"Gid…" Carlo repeated.

Gideon faced him and grinned, "This is exactly what these modules were made for, Carlo – to introduce people like Ben to life here in the Township."

"Seasteader Intro 4 loaded, Gideon," Nemo said.

"Play."

A holograph display appeared before them and Carlo's voice filled the cabin. Well-designed graphics, animation, and scenes appeared in the display. Carlo's warm and confident voice was perfectly suited to the commentary.

> As the south equatorial current in the South Pacific Ocean bends southwards, it brushes the eastern coast of New Zealand. Nearing the city of Christchurch, the current crosses the Chatham Rise, a tongue of relatively shallow waters jutting out six hundred miles north-east into the Pacific. At Chatham Rise, the southbound current meets the northbound Southland Current. This produces conditions in the coastal seas that make them teem with marine life.

> Phytoplankton, the minute plants of the sea, bloom in these sparkling waters, feeding on sunlight and nutrient rich seas. Microscopic marine animals called zooplankton fatten themselves on the phytoplankton and each other. Everything from anchovies, sponges, coral, mussels, and clams, to larger manta rays and great baleen whales gorge on the plentiful plankton community. These feeders low on the food chain are, in turn, eaten by a myriad of predators: carnivorous fish, squid and octopus, toothed whales, sharks, and sea birds.

> As this great teeming food web of the sea devours, flourishes, and perishes, it generates an immense amount of mucus, scales, faeces, and even carcasses that fall eternally into the deep – from the delicate gleaming shells of diatoms to colossal blue whales. This "marine snow" rains perpetually from the sunlit waters onto the darkness beneath.

> As the conflux of currents moves beyond Chatham Rise out into the open Pacific, its marine snow falls through kilometres of water to settle on the black abyssal basins. From time out of mind, micro-organisms swarming in those

vast, flat expanses gratefully feed on this gift from the world
of light above.

"'Gift from the world of light.' Nice turn of phrase, Carlo. This is good."
 Carlo waved his hand dismissively, "the Township council pestered me
to do it, they wanted a third-generation Pelagic voice."

Across these deep plains, untouched by the sun, thermo-
haline currents creep at the speed of almost four miles each
week, driven by changes in the temperature and salinity
of the seas. These deep masses of unhurried water now
carry nutrients, a product and gift of the microbes on these
nether expanses. Eventually, these thermo-haline currents
encounter physical barriers like the Louisville Ridge, a
submerged mountain chain, five hundred miles north-east
of the Chatham Rise. The slopes of the undersea mounts
deflect the nutrient-rich waters up towards the surface.

The sunlit open seas of the lower latitudes of the Southern
Pacific Gyre are mostly marine deserts, with scant sea life,
except near geographical features like the Louisville Ridge.
As the abyssal currents rise along the ridge towards the
ocean's surface, only a small amount might enter the sunlit
zone of the sea. In this region, within one hundred metres
below the surface, any accessible nutrients are greedily
absorbed by waiting phytoplankton. The phytoplankton
then reproduce, sustaining the food web and completing this
great cycle of life; a cycle we are an intimate part of.

On Marcelli Rise, the mariculture section of Marcelli
Township, early settlers learned to harness the nutrient
resources of the sea. First, the seasteaders grew extensive
platforms from seacrete. These were randomly uneven in
their topography, in depths ranging from ten to one hundred
metres below the surface. Anchored to the seamount,
these platforms attracted the tiny young of various marine
plants and creatures from the cloud of phytoplankton and
zooplankton, providing them with places to settle.

The settlers used energy from the temperature differences of the surface and deep waters to pump far more nutrient-rich currents higher into the sun zone, and allow these fertile waters to wash across their farms. With this abundant food supply, larvae and spores flourished, becoming forests of kelp, galaxies of sea stars, curling congresses of eels, colonies of clams and scallops, and flashing schools of fish. A diverse web-of-life sprang up within what was once an empty marine desert.

Across the Marcelli Rise farms, seasteaders established systems to make the most of the enriched environment. They discovered techniques to produce the species of fish and crustaceans in highest demand for human consumption, without compromising the wider diversity that makes up the interdependent marine ecosystem.

At the settlers' bidding, autonomous drones circulate among the marine gardens. Some drones crawl among the rocks and along the sand, checking crabs, sea cucumbers, and other bottom-dwelling residents. Others glide through forests of kelp and glittering schools of fish, among pulsating jellyfish and silent sharks. Still others climb among seeded ropes of bivalves. Some of the drones monitor health and size, some monitor the environment, others harvest the plants and animals at a sustainable pace. The robots draw from the abundance to fill the tables of pelagic and terrestrial families alike.

In this dance between humankind and nature, a balance has been found. Systems have been developed that can be sustained and upgraded to serve the community for years, perhaps even centuries. Humans here exert dominion over the marine world as benevolent stewards, mutualists.

Dotted among the undersea platforms, at twenty-hectare intervals, are homes for these sea-farmers. Here, seasteader families become communities who work and live out the

**human drama as they farm these prairies of the seas, which
their pioneering ancestors built out of nothing and nurtured
to fruitfulness.**

The display went blank and faded.

"Embarrassing, Gid. Is this what I have to look forward to when you join our family?"

"Bonding, future brother." Gideon laughed.

"Actually, it was a great intro for new seasteaders, well done," Ben said, looking back at Carlo.

"Thanks." Carlo looked sheepish and pleased at the same time.

"There is the Rise." Gideon pointed out the window. Ben could see a growing dark line on the blue horizon.

Slowly the dark smudge grew and resolved into a network of regularly spaced sea farms. *Kestrel* slowed as they approached the edge of the settlement.

"Here, I'll give you a better view." Gideon glanced at Ben as he adjusted the controls. *Kestrel* rose seventy metres into the air. From this perspective, the arrangement of cages and platforms was apparent: a large network of hexagons separated by clear waterways. Dwellings were set like knots in the net of hexagons, with the clear waterways connecting them and allowing access to the farms. The channels were bustling with a variety of watercraft.

"Beautiful." Ben stood to get a better view.

"Over there, about two o'clock. The second farmstead out. That's my home." Carlo leaned forward to indicate, gesturing towards the front window. Gideon changed course to follow his lead.

A white oval gleamed in the sunshine, with a crescent of green on one end. A jewel set within the honeycomb of farms. As they moved towards it, Carlo explained how the mariculture plots were organized into different seasteads, which in turn were organized into six municipalities.

"Sally and my other cousins were willing to take over the work at our family business, Marcelli SeaShells," Carlo explained to Ben. "This has freed me to do what I've always wanted to do – farm in the sea." Gideon guided the craft towards the white half-domed building. "There's our sector coming up."

"Have you told your wife that we're with you? Ana Lucia is not someone you want to surprise," Gideon interrupted.

Carlo looked at him. "Good point. Elektra, please tell Ana Lucia that we'll arrive in about ten minutes."

"Yes, Carlo, she has been monitoring your progress. Lunch will be ready," came the soft Italian accent.

Kestrel swept down again to the sea surface. They sped towards Marcelli Rise.

"Marcelli Rise Pelagic Command, this is Lieutenant Battuta, Pelagic vessel *Kestrel*, requesting permission to enter your airspace. Please confirm."

"Pelagic vessel *Kestrel*, we read you and have you on our scopes. Permission granted for an armed vessel to enter Marcelli Rise airspace. I have been informed of your mission…" there was a pause, "*Kestrel?* One moment, please. I'm in communication with the Major about a situation here. Stand by."

Ben and Gideon glanced at each other. Carlo spoke their thoughts, "Now what?"

"Thank you for waiting, *Kestrel*. We have a reported act of piracy in progress in the south-west sector near your position. I've asked Major Camden if we could have your assistance. You are the closest asset we have, the only one who can get there in a timely manner."

Gideon looked at Ben and Carlo, they nodded. "Marcelli Rise Command, yes. We are ready to provide any assistance necessary. Please advise."

"Thank you, *Kestrel*. Abalone beds, belonging to the Olsen seastead, have been stripped. We cannot tell from the Pelagic Array how the poachers are doing this. Please investigate. Major Camden has given permission to use appropriate force, if necessary, to stop the piracy."

"High priced abalone for the Japanese market being poached. We have new rules of engagement. Use appropriate force to stop the piracy. Copy."

Gideon turned to Ben, "I bet it's one of those *Tigershark* subs again. We've been plagued with them lately."

Ben was thoughtful, "They need a support vessel, right?"

"Of course." Gideon brightened, "Marcelli Rise Command: can you scan the area around us and tell us if there are any foreign vessels large enough to be a support platform for a *Tigershark* sub?"

"There are three just outside Marcelli Rise territorial boundary." There was another pause. "The closest one is the *Yamamoto* fishing vessel, north-west of you."

"Copy, the *Yamamoto*. We'll investigate, out." Gideon turned off the headset mike. "Almost certainly one of the *Yakuza* organized crime families. Nemo, please give us a fix on this vessel and a course."

"Done, Lieutenant Battuta. Course plotted."

"Elektra, please inform Ana Luciana that we'll be a bit late for lunch," Carlo whispered.

"Done, Carlo." There was a moment's pause, "Ana Luciana replied, 'Hmph'. I don't know what 'Hmph' means."

"It means cold lasagne," Carlo sighed.

"Thank you, I'll add that idiom to my algorithm…"

14 July 2066, Pelagic vessel *Kestrel*
(the same day)

Kestrel held station at twenty metres below the *Yamamoto*, off the starboard beam. Anchovy drone countermeasures were swirling around *Kestrel*, effectively hiding it from detection. Now they retreated into the special compartment for them on *Kestrel*, their job done.

"You were right, Ben. Major Camden had the registry of the *Yamamoto* checked. It's on a watch list for *Yakuza* pirate activity. The Major confirmed that we've collected more than enough evidence to convict the *Yamamoto* of piracy. She said the Japanese now have enough to grant a search warrant for the ship and for their security forces to board the *Yamamoto*. They are on their way."

"Those rail guns are impressive, Gideon." Ben was watching the *Yamamoto* rocking in the swells above them. "You were able to cripple the propellers and stop them dead in the water."

Gideon beamed, "I've been wanting to do something like this for years! I'd love to see the captain's face right now. Even better would be to hear him explain these piracy activities before the Pacific Rim Court." He listened on his headset. "The Japanese troops are on the ship, and they will take it back to Japan for the crew to face justice."

"Roger, thank you, Base," Gideon acknowledged on his radio. He pivoted *Kestrel* in the water and turned to Ben and Carlo, "Now let's go hunt a *Tigershark* sub."

Ben had been thinking, "How deep can a *Tigershark* dive?"

Gideon glanced at him, "I think no more than forty metres, they're made for speed, not depth. *Kestrel* can easily do five times that."

"If my communications were cut, I would be looking for a place to hole up and consider my options," Ben mused out loud.

"Can't go deeper than forty metres. There wouldn't be many places to hide with all the Olsen seastead platforms," Carlo chimed in.

"Where would you hide, Carlo?" Ben asked turning to him.

Carlo considered a few minutes. "There's a thick kelp forest about a half mile in front of us, off to the left. That would be my choice."

As Gideon turned onto the new heading, an alarm suddenly went off.

"Torpedo in the water, Lieutenant Battuta. Bearing 263. Eighteen seconds to impact."

"Or, over in that crevice a quarter mile to the right," Carlo added.

Gideon glared at his friend, "Release countermeasures, Nemo."

"Done, Lieutenant."

Gideon banked steeply, accelerating around the curve. The torpedo was not as agile and passed underneath *Kestrel*. As it turned to try to lock onto them again, Gideon faced to meet it and fired a rail gun burst. The torpedo exploded fifty metres in front of them; their craft shuddered.

"Well done, that was great manoeuvring, Gideon."

Gideon smiled, glancing over at Ben, "Yeah, thanks, but now they've got me mad."

"Nemo, do you have a lock on the sub that fired that?"

"Yes, I've triangulated their position with the Pelagic Array. They are creeping behind that ridge to the right, I believe trying to evade you and get to the open sea."

"Nowhere for them to go, no support ship." Gideon guided *Kestrel* in the direction Nemo indicated, and slowly glided around the ridge both the active camouflage and anchovies keeping the craft invisible to the *Tigershark*.

"There it is." The *Tigershark* was hovering a few metres off the bottom, ten metres below and in front of them; its streamlined shape reminded Ben of a fighter jet from fifty years ago, but underwater.

"They're looking for us," he said, watching the craft slowly turn in place.

"Well, let's show them where we are." Gideon fired a rail gun volley that destroyed the propulsion end of the sub. It could no longer move and was left only with the option to surface. Ballast tanks were blown, and *Kestrel* followed it up.

Chapter Twenty-one

14 July 2066, Marcelli seastead, Marcelli Rise
(the same day)

Half an hour later, *Kestrel* slowed and left the sea lane between mariculture plots, then skimmed the water surface to the Marcelli family's mooring. They unbuckled their harnesses and Gideon jumped out onto the dock to tie the plane onto a cleat.

As Ben stepped out onto the dock, a pair of flippers flew up into the air at the end of the pier, next to a ladder. A small tousled head popped over the edge of the deck and shook water out of her hair. Then the child clambered up the ladder and dropped her mask next to the fins. She beamed at the men next to the plane, then her face broke into joy.

"Papa!" she ran and threw herself into Carlo's arms as he stepped from the plane. Staggering back, he hugged her tightly. "Isabella! *Mia piccola*, my little one! What have you been up to?" he held her out looking at her.

"Papa, this morning I saw a beautiful butterfly fish outside my bedroom window! I ran to get my slurp gun and diving gear. I've been hunting for him for a long time. I want him for my aquarium. But I couldn't find him, Papa." Her face was crestfallen.

Carlo gave her another hug. "Do not worry, *mia piccola*, we'll find him, or a better fish for your aquarium." She brightened at the promise. "Say hello to our guests, Isabella!" She turned to Gideon and Ben, waving enthusiastically.

A short ramp rose from the dock to an open door set in the curved seawall. An older girl, around ten, was standing quietly at the top of the ramp. "Francesca! *Mia principessa*!" Carlo called, "Where is your beautiful mother?!"

The young girl smiled. "She's waiting for you and your friends in the garden. Lunch is ready, Papa. And look, Pietro is arriving from the fields on his *Dragonfly* scooter." She pointed. A small cloud of iridescent spray was approaching rapidly along the water way.

Ushering them all in towards the garden, Francesca rolled her eyes, "I believe Pietro can hear lasagne being placed on the table. Even from out on the oyster cages, Papa."

Carlo laughed, "Yes, *principessa*, he doesn't miss any opportunity to eat!" They walked through the gate in the seawall. To the left was a gleaming white home, and in front lay the green crescent Ben had seen from the air: a thick lawn, open to the cloudless blue sky. In the centre of the lawn was an oval-shaped stone patio. They walked down the steps and onto the grass.

"I heard what you said, Francesca! Your brother is growing, as *you* are." Carlo's wife stepped out of a large glass door on the side of the home, bearing a tray with cups and a salad. She set it down and ran to Carlo to hug him. "Glad you are safe. The Olsens have already sent a thank you. They recovered their abalone and the poachers are in custody."

"Glad to hear that," Carlo kissed her lightly on the cheek. "We're fine, *amore*. Just an adventure, and one that sends a message to poachers."

"I asked Elektra to call Pietro in. He took lunch with him this morning, but we wouldn't hear the end of it if we'd had guests and lasagne without him."

"Introduce me, *marito*," said Ana Lucia, as she nodded towards Gideon and Ben, "I know this rascal who wants to marry your sister. But who is the handsome stranger?"

Ben stepped forward and took her hand. "My name is Ben Holden, Mrs Marcelli. Thank you for letting us surprise you like this."

"And polite too. *Mrs* Marcelli is the mother of my Carlo. I'm called Ana Lucia." Ana Lucia smiled. "We love company, so no apology needed. We're so isolated out here, guests are always welcome."

Ana Lucia straightened and smiled at her guests. "Please come and sit down. You must be hungry."

They followed her down the steps to the table.

As he stood near the table, Ben looked at the huge windows stretched around the curve of the inside wall, on both sides of the stairway they had just come down. The windows looked out on an underwater vista, crowded with waving seaweed and darting marine life. Sunbeams flickered through the landscape in golden shafts.

"What a stunning view," Ben exclaimed.

"Yes, it is," Carlo admired the scene with him. "We call that our garden window. Ana Lucia designed it. She's designed a number of seasteads on the Rise."

Carlo pointed, "Look, I can see some fur seals in the Tasmanian string kelp." Ben spotted the animals weaving fluidly among the kelp forest, hunting lunch; he remembered his recent encounter with fur seals. A lone spiny dogfish cruised just over the sands searching for crustaceans.

Ben's pulled his attention back from the drama of the sea beyond the garden window, "Did you really design this?"

Ana Lucia's clear sparkling laugh rang out. "Carlo always gives me all the credit. At least half of it was his idea." She pointed, "If you look to the left, there, there's a giant cuttlefish lurking in the kelp." Ben stared at the area until he could make out the camouflaged shape.

"And down there," Gideon said, indicating rocks below the cuttlefish, "is a red hand fish. They were endangered thirty years ago. We helped to bring them back off the endangered species list."

Ben noticed Gideon was looking around the farmstead with an engineer's eye. "I see something new, Carlo. Is that a weather shield?"

"Yes, we put that in last month. We can draw a clear cover over the garden during stormy weather and still eat outside. It's open today. The weather is so pleasant. A beautiful day."

A whirring drew their attention. They walked back up the stairs to the door, just as the red *Dragonfly* came alongside the dock, sliding in with a fine spray of water. A tanned, dark-haired teenage boy sprang from the machine and tied it off to mooring rings at the end of the dock. He looked up and waved, then ran to where the men were standing.

"Am I too late?" anxiety was etched in his sunburnt face.

Carlo laughed, "Relax, son. The lasagne sits on the table, untouched. At least, that's where it was a few minutes ago." Pietro flashed a smile.

Ben admired the *Dragonfly* floating at dockside. It was long and sleek, like a wide motorcycle. Two fans were set in the front and one in the stern. The fans were horizontal now, but he saw they could pivot.

"That looks like a fun machine," Ben observed as the teen came over to greet him.

"You must be Professor Holden. Elektra has been telling me about you as I came across from the farm." He held out his hand in greeting.

Ben took it. "That's right. Ben. Good to meet you, Pietro."

Pietro peered around him. The two girls stood in the seawall doorway.

"So, have my sisters left any food for me?"

Francesca scowled at him.

Turning back to Ben, Pietro drew him over to the edge of the deck, by the *Dragonfly*. Enthusiasm shone in the boy's eyes. "This is the newest model. It can do thirty knots when the throttle is full out. Twenty per cent faster than the last version. It's also very manoeuvrable. Papa gave it to me for my birthday three months ago!"

"These are the workhorses for our mariculture activities," Carlo added. "They're versatile, allowing us to handle all the maintenance and work we must do here. Maybe we should take Professor Holden out for a spin after tea?" Carlo suggested. "There are three others under the deck. I can show you some of the farm."

"I'd love that." Ben inspected the machine.

"Count me in, too!" Gideon added.

"Papa, raft twelve had lost one of its anchor lines and was swinging into the other rafts. I tied a temporary fix to the line, but we'll have to go back and resplice it for a permanent repair."

Francesca drifted near to hear the conversation. "May I come, too?"

"Of course, Francesca. You're the best splicer in the family," Carlo said warmly, then turned back to Pietro, "Well done, son. We can look at it when we go out after lunch."

"And lunch is getting cold while you farmers talk about oysters! Let our guests eat!" Ana Lucia chided.

"Yes, Mama." Pietro spun to sprint up the gangway to the garden. The others followed, walking across the grass and sitting around the table.

Ana Lucia poured glasses of iced tea, Francesca served the steaming lasagne, and Isabella passed the large salad bowl.

Pietro snatched a garlic bread from a basket and put it on his plate. "Manners, Pietro. Offer it to the guests first," Ana Lucia said.

"Sorry," Pietro said, passing the basket around.

Ben took a bite of the lasagne that had appeared on his plate. "This is wonderful, Ana Lucia."

"Francesca made this," Ana Lucia glanced at her daughter. Francesca blushed.

"And what a beautiful seastead you have here, Carlo." Ben's gaze took in the graceful lines of the home beyond the lawn.

"In a year and a half, we'll qualify to own this section of Marcelli Rise, according to the Seastead Act. We're farming oysters and scallops on cages in the north-west quarter. In the other three quarters of the seastead, we have artificial reefs. Just this year they've become productive enough to make a profit from the seafood we harvest off them." A touch of pride entered Carlo's voice.

A gentle sea breeze swirled in the bowl around them. A few wispy clouds glided across the expanse of sky above. Seagulls cried to one another overhead, circling with eyes on the lunch.

Conversation was light as they enjoyed the meal. After the main course, Ana Lucia glanced lovingly towards her husband, patted his hand.

Pietro took advantage of a moment's silence. "Papa, there's a dance this weekend, at the Huang Marine Research complex. May I go?"

"Yes, Pietro, if you prepare raft thirty-two for harvesting. I have signalled the *Flying Fish* delivery drone to come by tomorrow to pick up the shellfish."

"Yes, Papa. I'll programme the harvesting bots to strip the lines and package the scallops fresh, just before the drone arrives."

Isabella pulled at her father's sleeve, "Papa, I can help too. Let me go with Pietro!"

He gazed down at her lovingly, "Well, *mia piccola*, we'll have to ask Pietro."

"You'll have to hold on tight, Izzie. Then you can help me inspect and clean the raft after it has been stripped."

"Yes!" the small girl beamed.

Carlo looked at his son, "You'll be a great sea farmer, Pietro. I'll also need you to finish seeding the south-west quadrant with grouper fingerlings from the Huang hatchery by Friday. You do all of this and you can go to the dance."

"Thank you, Papa," Pietro said excitedly, "I can easily finish that."

"I heard Oliana is going to the dance as well," Francesca commented innocently.

Pietro glared at her, then glanced around the table. He suddenly found his food very interesting, as a slow flush rose in his face.

"Francesca! Don't embarrass your brother," said Ana Lucia.

Francesca blinked at her, "I was just making an observation, Mama."

A chime interrupted them. "Carlo, sorry to interrupt," came Elektra's voice from the air, "but I have urgent recording for Gideon from his augmented intelligence agent, Nemo."

There was a moment of silence, then Nemo's voice was heard. The transmission was interrupted by bursts of static, "Gideon... attack... *Ossë*... can't gain access... return to Pod... missing."

"Nemo? Nemo, can you tell me more?"

There was a moment's silence, "I am the most recent backup of Nemo at Pacifica del Sur, Gideon. I was able to preserve these bits of a transmission before communication was broken with Nemo on *Ossë*. It took some time for this backup to be brought online and then recover these bits. I have no new information and cannot reconnect with *Ossë*. I am running diagnostics."

Gideon jumped to his feet. "I must get back to the Pod!"

Carlo and Ben were already on their feet, Ben moved close to Gideon. "Before you rush off, let's see if we can get more information. Take a breath. Carlo and I will help you, no matter what this is." Carlo nodded.

"You're right, Ben. Of course." Gideon composed himself.

Ben spoke to Elektra, "Can you open a secure line to Major Camden?"

"Connecting you now."

In a moment, "Major Camden here, I was just advised that there's a mayday signal from the *Arraa'i* Pod."

"Yes, Major, Gideon's AIA, Nemo, just tried to deliver a message, but the transmission was garbled. What can you tell us?"

"It seems all communication lines are down at the moment with the *Arraa'i* Pod. Lieutenant Battuta, please start back to the Ring with *Kestrel*. I'll keep you informed on the way. I will also see if I can get military support from New Zealand in case this is some kind of attack."

"Nemo did mention an attack, sir, but no details." Gideon was back in control of himself. "Major, permission to bring Captain Marcelli and Ben with me."

"Granted. On your way. See you soon."

Gideon sprinted towards *Kestrel*'s ramp to prepare to leave.

Ben turned to Ana Lucia, "I'm so sorry to rush off like this. Something is wrong on *Ossë*."

"Yes, of course. Go, go." She waved her hand at him as he and Carlo ran off after Gideon.

Ana Lucia and the children followed through the door to the top of the stairs and watched them strap themselves quickly into the submersible aircraft.

"Andare con Dios, go with God," she whispered to herself, as *Kestrel* roared into life on the dock below, rose, and turned towards Marcelli Ring.

14 July 2066, Seastead vessel *Ossë*
(the same day, several hours earlier)

Ossë ghosted through the curling mist on an oily calm sea. Its running lights faded in and out through the tendrils of fog. Up above, the moon sliced like a scythe through ribbons of streaming clouds. Stars sailed serene beyond the ragged strips of mist. The eastern sky was just beginning to lighten.

Far beneath the surface of the sea, a click sounded. It was lost in the undersea chatter of shrimps. A lid popped open, releasing a silent projectile accelerating through black waters. It covered the four hundred metres to *Ossë* in less than twelve seconds, giving little response time for those on board.

Nemo detected the click. "*Ameera*, wake up! We're under attack," Nemo's voice boomed in the darkness, pitched to communicate urgency. Sophia's eyes fluttered open. She slipped quickly from the bed. The deck rocked under her and threw her to the floor; her eyes snapped awake.

"To your *Egg, Ameera*. Now!" Sophia ran from her room into the hallway. She saw silhouetted figures coming down the stairs and into her father's cabin, seconds later they were dragging her father from his room. Sul turned to her and shouted, "Follow Nemo's instructions, Sophia!" The man struck Sul.

"*Baba!*" she cried out.

Nemo's voice was insistent, "Go, *Ameera*, quickly to the *Egg*. It is shielded from the electromagnetic pulse, and I have fed it instructions for your escape. My circuits are destabilizing, I may not be with you much longer."

"Nemo!" She screamed as she fled down the hall. She heard shouts in Arabic behind her. "Yunus, after the girl!" Before she reached the lift, she was thrown to the floor as the deck lurched under her. "Stairs!" Nemo instructed her, "The lift… unsafe."

She jumped for the door and ran wide-eyed down the spiral staircase to the working deck. The door to the stairs closed after her with a loud click as Nemo protected her escape. It was the last thing he was able to do for her.

Ossë tilted towards starboard under Sophia's feet. She scrambled along the corridor that led to the launching bay, her hand bracing along the wall as the floor continued to increase its slope under her. Through the door, her *Egg* was now downhill from her.

Water poured from the brim of the docking portal. The *Egg* floated in the centre of the sloshing pool, still moored. She covered the distance quickly and ran across the ramp onto the craft. The protective shell curled around her even as she set foot onto the *Egg*'s platform. Docking lines released as the clear canopy sealed shut. Ballast tanks flooded. The *Egg* sank swiftly into the dark water, lights extinguished. Robotic anchovies swarmed to surround it, protecting it from hostile sensors. Two large amberjack guardians followed its rapid descent below and behind *Ossë*.

Lights flickered, then went out as she looked up at the ship above her. *Ossë*, her home, became a black hole on the surface of a dark sea. *"Baba!"* she screamed, tiny palms pounding on the glass dome. Her strikes slowed as the minutes ticked away and the *Egg* descended to blackness. Then she was quiet. She sat down. Darkness rushed by, marked only by phosphorescent flashes. The craft moved silently, carrying her to an unknown destination.

She looked around her. "Nemo?" A deathly silence hung in the air. She waited ten minutes for a response. Then she curled herself into a small ball on the floor of the *Egg* as it continued into the oblivion of the dark depths.

*

The dip and splash of oars in the water was muffled by the mist. Fatima leaned over the rim of the rubber dinghy to peer into the darkness, "To the left, I think, Hafez. Pull, *habibi.*"

A soft whisper of rain fell around them, dimpling the sea. Some of the mist cleared. Fatima spied the bulk of *Ossë* emerging from the fog, dark and lifeless. It bobbed awkwardly in the water. "I see it, Hafez." She pointed, "Carefully. We don't know what to expect."

"Oyster, what are you seeing?" whispered an electronic voice of a young woman from a speaker on Hafez's life-jacket.

"Oyster here. There are no lights or signs of activity, Aisha. Is Nemo up and running yet?"

"Negative, *Oyster.* We're recompiling Nemo from backups on Pelagic servers at Pacifica del Sur. It'll take some time."

The dinghy drifted near the derelict craft. Fatima, with surprising strength and agility, pulled herself onto the tilted deck, now less than a metre above them. "Sophia! *Ameera!*" she called as soon as she gained her footing.

"Wait, Fatima!" Hafez called. But his wife had already disappeared into the darkness of *Ossë*.

As she felt her way across the tilted deck and into the bridge area, Fatima could hear another dinghy arriving, and her husband speaking. She paused to listen.

"Mark and Aziz, thank you for coming so quickly. My wife has already gone on board. How is *Murex*?"

"There was no damage to our boat. But our augmented intelligence went down along with Nemo and normal Pod communications. We only have the emergency backup of the radios."

"Have the other vessels reported in?"

"All but two, *Nautilus* and *Pleiades*. But they were the farthest out. We're assuming they are OK, just out of radio range. *Ossë* seems to have been the target of the attack. We'll know more when the network, Nemo and our AIAs are back up and running."

The blackness and silence of the bridge were forbidding, but driven by love, Fatima felt her way to the lift. No power. She found the access hatch to the stairs, leading from the bridge to the interior of *Ossë*. "Sophia!" she called, making her way down the spiral steps. "Sul! Sheikh!"

Bleak, lonely echoes were the only response.

She reached the living quarters level, and heard water sloshing further down the steps in the working levels. "Sophia?" she called, as she staggered along the steeply angled hallway, clutching the handrail. Sophia's door was ajar. She peeked in, fearful. A rumpled bed. She touched the sheets. Still warm. She found Sul's cabin, also empty. Also, warm. She then searched the other rooms. Empty. "Lord of the worlds, keep them safe," she whispered.

*

Hours later, wind gusts cleared the mists surrounding *Ossë*. Low clouds above thickened and began releasing a freezing rain. Hafez sat in the captain's chair on the bridge and slid his hands through his thick curls of black hair. The seat was uncomfortable, the deck was still tilted at an awkward angle. His intelligent eyes flicked back and forth on the panels before him. Most were blank, a few had flickering red lights. "Nothing, Naeema," he said into the speaker on his shoulder, "Is your brother Adam on his way?"

"Yes, Uncle Hafez. Adam and Sam should be there shortly."

In the surrounding shadows, Hafez watched others attaching emergency lights around the bridge and deck. Some were setting up navigation lights outside so *Ossë* wouldn't be a hazard to other Pod vessels. The wind whistled around *Ossë* as she was pushed, helpless, before the rising storm.

"Something seems to have fried the circuits on *Ossë*, Hafez. I wonder if this was a localized electro-magnetic pulse attack, coupled with a virus to disable our network."

"Keep running diagnostics, Naeema. Are all AIAs still down? Is any part of the network back up and running?"

"Yes, several of the Pod vessels had reverted to backups made prior to the attack. We're using those as platforms to rebuild connectivity and do testing. My brother is bringing you replacements for *Ossë*'s damaged modules."

"Thank you, Naeema. Any update on Nemo?"

"Yes, we've reconstructed him from the backups. I'm also sending a linking module for him to communicate with the other reconfigured AIAs in the Pod. They can help him diagnose *Ossë*."

"Good, and the tuna stocks?"

"Hafez, we lost almost half the tuna guides. The schools that were attached to them have gone wild. We're reconfiguring backup guides from the Pod with the pressure patterns of the lost schools. We'll send them out to search and try to recover at least some of our stocks. Any word on Sul and Sophia?"

"No. Sorry, Naeema. We're doing forensic examinations of *Ossë* to look for clues. Apparently, Sophia's *Egg* is missing. That might be a positive thing. She might be safe in the *Egg*. No sign of Sul. There's some indication of a struggle. They may have taken one or both."

"Are we assuming 'they' are the Caliphate?"

"No proof yet, Naeema. It's likely, though, based on the recent activities."

Thunder rolled across the sea outside. The rain increased in intensity. A shiny, rain-slicked figure ran onto the bridge. "Here are the replacement circuits, Hafez." Adam set down one of the two cases he held on the table next to the open instrument panels. The other he set on the floor.

"I'll go below and help get power back online. Sam will be here in a moment to help you."

"Thank you, Adam." Hafez opened the case, removing a small silver cylinder. He set it on the shelf below the windows, now being lashed by rain. He pressed a button in the centre on top. A ring of blue light encircled the cylinder. "This is Nemo, of the seastead vessel *Ossë*. Ready." A pause. "I cannot access *Ossë*'s systems, please advise."

Hafez inserted modules from the case in slots under the panels. "Nemo, Hafez here."

"Captain Hafez of *Oyster*, acknowledged. I can see from telemetry of other vessels in the Pod that *Ossë* is stricken. What has happened?"

"There has been an attack, Nemo. Sul and Sophia are missing."

Turning to the speaker on his shoulder, he said, "Modules are in. Is power ready to come online, Adam?"

"Yes, Hafez. The Alchemist reactor is undamaged in the attack, but it cycled through an emergency shut-down when the systems failed. I have brought it back to normal operations here in the power room."

"Thank you. Switching on system bridge modules and engaging start-up routines." Lights winked on before Hafez and a subtle hum filled the air. Cabin lights flickered then came on brightly around the bridge and out on deck. Another young man climbed onto the deck and walked into the bridge.

"Sam, thanks for coming. Take these other modules in the case and begin replacing the damaged ones in the system stations throughout *Ossë*."

"Yes, Hafez." Sam took the remaining case down the spiral stairs. Hafez continued to place modules in slots under the bridge panels.

"I have basic bridge controls, Captain," said Nemo.

"Excellent. Nemo, tell me, what do you remember before your system failure?"

"A few days ago, we detected an anomalous echo through the Pelagic Array from this general region where *Ossë* now sits. Captain Sul had me maintain a watch of the area. As we approached, I placed *Ossë* on alert status three as a precaution. As we passed over Danseur seamount, a projectile launched from below us. I detected no vessels in the area. It seemed to come from the sea floor. My guess is that we were ambushed by a missile, armed with an electromagnetic pulse warhead, hidden on the sea floor back when the anomaly was detected. Only conjecture, Captain Hafez. I'll do some investigations on this hypothesis when I have access to the logs and sensors."

"Good thing you set alert status three, Nemo. You might have saved Sophia and Sul by your quick response. We'll see." He lowered the panels over the new modules. The screens now displayed diagnostic and start-up routines. "You should have access to all the bridge systems now, Nemo."

"Yes, Captain. I have access." A pause. "Bridge systems normative, coming online." Panel displays shifted to readouts of *Ossë* systems. Most still had red offline symbols. Power and navigation screens flashed green. These then began displaying information on the ship's power and position.

"Captain, optic wiring of *Ossë* is operational, unaffected by the electromagnetic pulse. But all modules aside from power and navigation are out." Nemo informed him.

"Replacements are being installed, Nemo."

"Yes, I see more systems coming online. Damage does suggest a power surge shorted out the systems. Consistent with the electromagnetic pulse hypothesis, Captain."

"Thank you, Nemo. Look and see if there's also indication of a virus that was uploaded before the pulse went off. Keep me informed as modules come online."

"Yes, Captain. My sensors now show that the projectile pierced the hull in storage hold three. The electronic damage radiates from there. The projectile compromised *Ossë*'s Faraday cage which normally protects us from electromagnetic attacks like this. The missile breached the hull before deploying its electromagnetic pulse warhead. The electrical surge destroyed the system modules in *Ossë* that were metal-based. Water has partially flooded storage hold three, but emergency systems sealed the compartment and contained the breach. I'm searching for indications of a virus attack in the *Arraa'i* Pod network."

"Good. Initiate security firewalls for the Pod."

"Done, Captain. I have found and quarantined the virus. It looks to be of New Caliphate origin. I'll have one of the other Pod artificial intelligences analyze the virus."

"Thank you." Hafez watched as more and more systems changed from red to green.

"Captain, I now have control of ninety per cent of *Ossë*'s systems. I have released a repair gecko to seal the breach in storage three. We will be able to pump the water out in five minutes." Hafez could see the glow from below surface windows of *Ossë* as lights came on throughout the vessel.

A few minutes later, Fatima appeared at the top of the spiral stairs. "Sophia, Nemo?" she was concerned.

"Good morning, Fatima," Nemo acknowledged. "No sign of Sophia or Captain Sul on board. I see that emergency protocols for Sophia's *Egg* were engaged. I know that I told her to take the stairs down to the work level. Sophia has possibly evaded the attackers. But I can't be certain from the data here. My systems were going offline at the time and the protocols were running automatically.

"I'm pumping out storage three." *Ossë* began righting itself.

Nemo continued, "Gideon is on his way in *Kestrel*. I have sent him the information you have found, including the triggering of the *Egg* protocols."

The thin figure of Fatima cried softly in the shadows of the bridge, as rising storm winds screamed outside.

14 July 2066, Caliphate vessel *Shaheen*
(the same day)

Suliman Battuta was conscious of lightning flickering on the horizon under a band of dark clouds. Below him lay a calm sea, reflecting the diamond path of the Milky Way. He seemed to be floating above the sea. Gazing down at the stars which were reflected on the ocean's surface, he realized with a shock that he was not part of the reflection. *What is this? Have I died?* Yet everything around him felt peaceful, natural.

"Suliman. Son." He looked up towards the voice.

"*Baba!*" He saw nothing, yet he recognized his father's presence nearby. "Am I dead, *Baba*?"

"This is a threshold. You have a choice, Suliman," the voice continued calmly. He felt embraced by its warmth. Childhood memories, joyful times with his father, flashed through his mind.

"I don't understand, *Baba.*"

Suliman was aware that another Presence was with them now., radiating powerful, intense light and love.

"Lord?" Suliman whispered, bowing in spirit.

"You may stay here with us, or return to face a severe trial," the Presence told him quietly. Suliman felt embraced by love and warmth.

The moment was timeless. It seemed that the universe awaited his answer as stars wheeled in their eternal dance above. He revelled in the freedom, peace, joy. Part of him longed to join this divine Presence and his father.

However, he understood the stakes. A resolve grew in his heart, he knew what he must do. They knew his answer without him saying a thing.

In that instant of choice, he was pulled rapidly into the depths of the sea. A pod of dolphins, then a shoal of squid, flashed past as he descended in the darkness. A black cigar shape on the bottom of the sea, more felt than seen, approached him rapidly. He awoke with a shock to find himself on a cold deck.

*

Too bright. Sul blinked. The lights glaring off the walls of the bare white room assaulted his eyes. He squeezed them shut. He could only manage short gasps. Agonizing pains shot through his body. He lay slumped against the ice cold of the bulkhead. Air whispered from a vent nearby. Faint wafts of engine oil and diesel assailed his nostrils. Thoughts eluded him as he struggled out of twilight consciousness. Someone moaned. He realized the sound came from him.

A door clicked open. Dread gripped Suliman's heart as a man stepped through the hatch. *I recognize that uniform, and that man's face, I've seen him in photographs. Yunus Saleh, one of the 'Faithful' who worked with Abdul Qawwi.* Sul now knew what was coming.

I had a choice, and I chose to return. He steeled himself. Two large men came in just behind Yunus Saleh.

"Suliman Battuta," Yunus scowled at him. "I am captain of this submarine. We've never met. But I know many of your family from Yemen. Some work under my command, serving the Emir of the Somalia Emirates. They seldom speak of you. You are dead to them, *murtadd*, apostate." He spat, the phlegm landing near Sul's head.

Strength flowed into Sul at this point, to his surprise. Raising himself upright into a sitting position, holding onto the railing on the bulkhead, he met Yunus Saleh's arrogant gaze. The two wills struggled, but it was the younger man, Yunus Saleh, who broke his gaze first. "Some deaths are a blessing," Sul said quietly.

Anger flashed across Yunus Saleh's face, but he composed himself. "You are no longer young. We can do this easily and you can meet death quickly."

Sul stared at him, waiting. Yunus Saleh stepped forward and gave him a ringing slap. Pain reverberated through Sul's body, but now he had control over himself. Straightening up, he studied the face of his tormentor. He was surprised to feel pity for this man well up in his heart. "I have seen death. It has no sting for me."

"If you do not cooperate, there'll be a long, excruciating path to death. Pain and torment, old man." Yunus Saleh's harsh voice rose.

"Why have you taken me? What do you want?" Sul asked simply.

"Your grubby community of fish herders has been harbouring an infidel. A Ben Holden. However, we did not find him on your vessel."

Concern flashed through Sul. He replied quietly, "Ben is no longer with us." This was true.

"Where is he?" Yunus Saleh glared. "You should be afraid. Your life is in our hands."

Sul remained silent, staring quietly at his persecutor, aware that his lack of fear was confusing the man. "I'm in the hands of God, Yunus Saleh," Sul said quietly.

Yunus Saleh spun around, walking out the door. "Bring him," he ordered as he left.

The other two men gripped Sul. He cried out and fainted with pain and they carried his limp form from the room.

14 July 2066, Pelagic vessel *Kestrel*
(the same day)

Kestrel banked through cloud canyons above the storm, glinting beneath a clear field of stars. Moonglow engraved the outline of a towering thunderhead and lightning flashed within the monstrous cloud. Thunder rumbled around them. The airship slowed, careful to keep a distance from the perilous wind currents within that column of blackness. Even so, the dwarfed craft shivered and danced, striving to maintain its position in the face of the dark storm.

"Lieutenant Battuta, we are above the first safety point dictated by the emergency protocol in Sophia's *Egg*. The Danseur seamount is directly below your craft."

"Nemo, isn't this where the undersea missile was fired from?" Gideon asked, without looking up. His hands worked deftly to hold *Kestrel* stable in the turbulence. Ben watched the darkening tempest outside the window. Carlo rummaged through storage lockers at the rear of *Kestrel*.

"Yes. However, indications are that it was a pre-set trap, not a current threat. The Pelagic Array doesn't detect any vessels or activities that might endanger this operation."

"Nemo, any signal from the *Egg*?" Ben asked.

"No, Professor. The *Egg* won't release a confirmation signal until it receives the properly coded broadcast. We must move closer to the sea's surface, drop a signal buoy, and send a sonar message. Assuming Sophia is indeed below, then the *Egg* will send a signal in response. My calculations show that the *Egg*'s oxygen supply will only last twenty more minutes."

"Let's hope she's there. We have no option but to descend into the storm." The bank of dark clouds below slowly rose towards them as Gideon massaged the controls. Swirling mists crept over the craft as it dropped into the rainclouds. Charcoal greyness engulfed them.

"Hey, I found the exposure suits," Carlo spoke from behind them.

"Good man," Ben said as he came alongside Carlo to help sort equipment. "Gideon, please let me go down and get her. I'm trained in sea rescue."

"Thanks, Ben. I'd be glad to use your experience in this type of operation."

Ben was already pulling the suit on.

"Carlo, handle the winch," Gideon said tersely. He glanced over his shoulder and added, "Sorry about the tone, I didn't mean that as an insult, Carlo."

"I understand. It's your sister who's in trouble down there."

The craft shuddered. "This is going to be dicey. Put on the other suit, Carlo, just in case I need you to man the lines for Ben. He'll go out through the hatch."

"I've got it." Carlo donned the suit, then swung the winch over the hatch.

Kestrel burst through the cloud layer. The craft lurched as it was seized by the strong winds. They descended until the sea's surface came into view, just twenty metres below. Gideon relied on instruments before him as visibility was minimal. Searchlights beneath the aircraft penetrated only a short distance through the pouring rain. Heavy swells rolled by under the craft. Strain was etched in Gideon's face as he struggled to keep *Kestrel* stable.

"Surface winds are gusting thirty miles per hour, sea state five, rapidly trending towards six," Nemo warned. "I am monitoring swells to keep *Kestrel* clear."

"OK," Gideon muttered. "Nemo, help me stabilize in this wind." *Kestrel* suddenly began to ride more smoothly through the gusts as Nemo assisted Gideon's piloting. "Ready the buoy," Gideon called to the men behind him.

Carlo had attached a mushroom-shaped float to the winch hook. "Done. Nemo, activate the buoy." A brilliant light began flashing from the stem of the float.

"Ben, here's what'll happen," Carlo shouted, over the roar of the wind and rain. "When the buoy hits the sea, it'll broadcast coded messages. If the *Egg* is in the vicinity, we'll get a confirmation signal. The confirmation signal will trigger a raft to inflate around the buoy. After the raft inflates, you rappel down the rope."

"Got it." Strapping rescue and medical kits to his exposure suit, Ben moved to the winch. He attached himself to the cable.

"I found a set of Sophia's gear here, mask, fins and rebreather. Take it with you. You'll need them."

Ben attached the equipment bag to his harness.

"Ready?" Carlo's hand gripped the hatch handle and made eye contact with Ben.

"Yes." The hatch flew open.

Wind swirled through the compartment. The mushroom disappeared into the darkness, emitting strobe-flashes through the rain as it fell. Carlo regulated the fall of the buoy with winch controls. Hitting the surface, the mushroom bobbed for a few moments.

"Beacon is broadcasting the messages now, Gideon," Carlo informed, peering through the hatch.

"And we already have confirmation of the code. The *Egg* is below," Gideon said excitedly. "Help me stay above the raft, Nemo."

The mushroom buoy blossomed into a lighted raft below. The winch clicked and stopped at sixty metres of line.

"We've only about ten metres left on the cable, Gideon," Carlo said looking at the winch spool.

Kestrel's engines began to adjust to the buffeting storm conditions faster than human reflexes could manage. The aircraft fought to stay above the buoy, bobbing up and down, synchronized with the swells below. The wind drove against the raft, straining the cable.

Ben grabbed onto the cable, jumped out of the hatch, slid down the cable through the driving rain, and dropped onto the raft.

CHAPTER TWENTY-TWO

14 July 2066, Sophia's *Egg*
(the same day)

The small *Egg* hung, suspended, in the silent depths. A soft glow etched its outline; a motionless bubble concealed in the vast inky blackness. A few robotic anchovies rolled to and fro below it, jostled by the slight current disturbing the silt under the *Egg*. Their energy was depleted, expended to protect the life of the small form within the bubble of light. Amberjack-shaped guardians still hovered in the shadows nearby. Vigilant, yet impersonal.

"*Ameera*, wake up." The voice came gently to the child. She was curled into a tight ball, asleep on the deck of the *Egg* in the centre of the sapphire dome. Interior lights swelled to a new brightness, pushing back the silent, chill darkness of the sea just beyond the transparent shell.

"Nemo!" Sophia cried, sitting up. "I knew you'd find me!"

"Yes, *Ameera*, I came as soon as I could. You must listen carefully now. Do as I say. Gideon has come to rescue you with Carlo and Ben. They're in *Kestrel* above. But a storm is building on the surface. Do you understand what I'm saying?"

She stood, her pale face peering into the darkness above. Her small hand touched the cold surface of the glass. "Yes, Nemo."

She was drawing in deep breaths. She panted, "Hard to breathe."

"Oxygen is running low in your *Egg*. You must be brave, *Ameera*."

Tears welled in her eyes. "Yes, Nemo."

The *Egg* shuddered as its engines started. It eased out and up from the overhang under which it had been hiding for the last seven hours. It ascended through the darkness. Shadows of fish flickered away before it, some with brief blue flashes. Sophia sat again, shaking slightly.

"Nemo, tell me a true story, please."

"*Ameera*, this story is about you and Ben. You remember him?"

"Yes, Nemo. I like Ben."

"Good. Ben is above you, waiting for you on a raft. The *Egg* is travelling to him. Your *Egg* will get as close as possible to the raft before breaching the surface. When you surface, the sea will be very wild with the storm."

"Nemo, will I lose my *Egg*?" her breathing was more laboured.

"Possibly, *Ameera*, but we'll find you a new one. Relax, breathe slowly. The story doesn't end today."

She looked down at her *Egg*, "I understand."

Nemo continued, "Ben will swim to you. Then comes the hard part, *Ameera*. The *Egg*'s shield will open. Ben will come aboard and help you put on swim gear, so you can go with him into the sea and swim to the raft."

"It'll be cold. I'm scared, Nemo." Her eyes showed fear, her breathing became strained again.

"Yes, *Ameera*, I understand. But you are a fish, are you not?"

She brightened, "Yes, Nemo. I'm a fish. The sea is my friend." Courage rose in her spirit, her small features tightened with resolve.

"Yes, *Ameera*. The sea is your friend. It won't harm you today. Ben will help you swim through the waves to the raft."

"Where is Gideon?"

"He's above, in *Kestrel*. He and Carlo will pull you and Ben aboard *Kestrel*, using a winch. You'll be safe."

"Yes, Nemo."

Another silence. "*Baba?*" she asked, fear creeping into her voice.

"I won't lie to you, *Ameera*. We don't yet know where your father is. Pray and be brave for him."

"Yes, Nemo." The waters were growing lighter around them now. The craft continued upwards until it stopped, suspended six metres below the surface. The storm swells raging above only gently rocked the *Egg* at this depth.

Sophia stared at the mottled surface above. A froth of bubbles swirled there, whipped by the storm. "Be brave," Sophia whispered to herself.

*

Nemo broke into the struggling pilot's concentration, "Gideon, sea state is now seven and moving to eight. There's significant danger if we keep *Kestrel* tethered to the raft. There's about eight minutes of oxygen in the *Egg*. Sophia's breathing is laboured."

"I know, I know!" Gideon muttered to himself as he peered through the rain-lashed window. He could barely glimpse the dimly lit raft below through the searchlights. *Kestrel* was trembling constantly in the gusting winds.

"Ben, Nemo advises us to cut the line to the raft, over."

"Roger, I understand, Gideon. What would be our next move if we did that? Over."

Gideon thought for a moment. "I think I have an idea." He explained it over the radio to Ben.

"Copy, I think that will work," Gideon and Carlo heard Ben's reply over the roar of the storm below.

"Ready for the cable to be cut?"

"Yes, do it now!" Ben yelled. Gideon signalled Carlo to sever the cable with cutters. Released, Ben and the raft were snatched by the next gust of wind and disappeared from the cone of *Kestrel*'s lights.

"Hold on, Ben and Sophia," Gideon murmured. "Nemo, have the *Egg* follow the raft."

"The *Egg*'s keeping pace with the raft as it's being blown downwind, Gideon. Six minutes of oxygen remaining."

"Yes," he said through gritted teeth. "Here we go." *Kestrel* descended into the howling storm winds.

*

Breaking the surface, the *Egg* met the full fury of the storm. Waves and wind lashed against the dome. Lightning flickered in the darkness beyond the glass. Thunder growled, resonating in the air. Sophia put her hands over her ears and screamed.

Waves whipped against and over the shield. Sea foam streamed across it and then was whisked away through the air. Through the spattered glass, Sophia caught glimpses of a raft nearby. A dark figure crouched low in it, holding tight.

"*Ameera*, there's a change of plan." Sophia listened. Her hands were white as she pressed against the bubble shield.

"Is that Ben, Nemo?" Sophia gasped. The raft was upwind from the *Egg*. Both were being tossed before the raging wind and waves.

"Yes, *Ameera*. He'll swim to the *Egg*. I'll open the shield and let him in, then close it again. He'll help you put on your rebreather and gear. Can you do this, *Ameera*?"

"I'll try, Nemo." Flecks of darkness began collecting at the corner of her vision, she felt dizzy.

"Be brave, *Ameera*. Now, lie down on the deck. Ben is almost here."

The child lay prone on the floor of her *Egg* as the shield cracked open. The shriek of the storm and rage of the wind violated her safe environment. The tip of a wave washed into the interior. Cold water and fresh air swirled around Sophia. She screamed.

A blue-gloved hand grasped the edge of the shield. Ben heaved himself inside and removed his mask as the shield slammed shut behind him. Several inches of seawater sloshed across the floor. Sophia crawled over and clung to Ben, drenched and shivering. Ben held her, calming her trembles.

Slowly, Sophia's grip relaxed. With difficulty, she peered into Ben's face. She fixed on his calm eyes, then looked away quickly and sighed.

"Nemo tells me, Sophia, that you're a brave girl."

"I'm trying," she whispered, looking at the dark and stormy sea.

"I also hear that you swim like a fish."

She looked up again, shyly. "Yes."

Ben pulled a small rebreather, mask, and fins from his kit and held them in front of her. "Do you recognize these, Sophia?" She nodded. "I'm going to help you put them on. Then you and I'll go for a swim. We'll be fish together."

She held still, wary, as he put the mask and rebreather on her. He adjusted the equipment, checking that it sealed well. She pulled on the fins. Then she pulled the mask off, "What about my *Egg*?"

Nemo answered, *"Ameera*, we'll lose the *Egg*. But we'll make you a new one. Your life is more important than the *Egg*, yes?"

She paused. "Yes, Nemo," she said, relaxing. Ben helped her refit the mask. Her breathing was quick. *She'll burn air rapidly. I'm not sure how charged the tank is. Hopefully enough for what we must do.* "Are you ready, Sophia?"

She looked at Ben with wide eyes, nodding. "Good. When the shield opens, we'll go into the sea." The girl looked to the edge of the shield expectantly, clutching Ben.

Ben adjusted his mask. The *Egg* opened and Ben pulled Sophia into his arms. He held her tightly as they rolled over the edge and into the sea. Swells swamped the craft.

They were under water, deep enough now to be safe from the fury of the storm. All around was profound silence and stillness. Ben held

Sophia tightly, aware that she was shivering. They floated together, drifting down below the dark surface, their figures outlined in an aura of faint phosphorescence.

A moment later the *Egg* glided past their view. Ten metres away, sinking, tilted at an unnatural angle. The *Egg*'s lights flickered and then went out.

Sophia's sobs were muffled by the rebreather mask. She continued to breathe fast, and struggled to be free from Ben's hug. He released her but kept a firm grip on her hand. He noticed a small cloud of blood from her right leg which had been cut as they rolled out of the *Egg*.

They waited together hand in hand, suspended, watching the shadow of the *Egg* as it faded into the darkness below. Ben could just discern dark forms around the *Egg* as it disappeared. *Whitetip sharks*, he thought grimly.

Sophia glanced at Ben and nodded. They swam together, deeper into the sea.

He watched her closely, noticing that her eyes were wide, frightened. Below them, the cruising shadows were rising, circling them in a slowly contracting ring. Ben watched the sharks warily. *Please, Gideon, hurry.*

Kestrel materialized out of the darkness thirty metres in front of them, its engines slowly urging the craft towards them. Sophia waved to Gideon, now visible in the forward window. He returned the wave, grinning. She pointed at the shadowy sharks and tugged at Ben's hand. He smiled reassurance at her while, at the same time, pulling her more quickly towards *Kestrel* with strong sure kicks. They were closing the distance, but so were the sharks.

Suddenly, Sophia's grip tightened, her other hand tugged at Ben. He looked at her, she pointed to her face mask. *The air supply in her rebreather has given out.* He stopped in the water, using his free hand to search around his gear. There it was, the extra regulator dangling from his right side. He pulled it around and showed it to Sophia. He mimed taking off his mask. She nodded, though her eyes were like saucers. She took one more glance at the sharks. *If I were to reach out, I could touch one.*

Ben whipped off Sophia's mask. She squeezed her eyes shut and screamed underwater. Ben covered her mouth with the regulator, blocking the stream of bubbles. She looked at him and clamped down, breathing very rapidly. *Good girl!* He reassured her with his eyes and his nodding head. As he pulled her closer, he drew a knife from a sheath on his leg.

A shark darted at him, veering away at the last second. Then another. *They're getting bolder.* Ben saw *Kestrel*'s ghostly shape, but it was still maybe fifteen metres away. *If I sprint towards it, the sharks will attack us.* Ben could see Gideon busy talking in his headset, and Carlo opening the underwater hatch, preparing to join them. *He'll bring an anti-shark stick, but there are too many for one stick.*

A shark bumped him in the back. Ben whirled around. Sophia trembled in his arms.

Now Carlo was in the water, approaching with caution. Another shark brushed Ben; he could feel the sandpaper texture of its skin. Sophia clung with a death grip, her glances darting between the sharks and Ben's face.

Two sharks charged in unison. Ben fixed his eye on one of them and was about to strike. Suddenly, a shrill series of squeaks and clicks came from *Kestrel*. The sharks flickered away into the darkness, and the water was clear once again. Carlo had reached them now and helped with leading Sophia the remaining metres to *Kestrel*.

The three of them dived beneath *Kestrel* and swam up towards the mirrored square of light framing the hatch underneath the hull. Carlo pulled himself back into the craft while Ben lifted Sophia up to him. Carlo swathed the shivering girl with a blanket as Ben hoisted himself in and sealed the hatch. Carlo began to examine Sophia's cut.

"Well done!" Gideon exclaimed, turning from the controls. Sophia struggled out of the blanket and away from Carlo, ran to her brother, and clung to him. Startled by this rare display of affection, Gideon returned the hug. After a moment, he leaned back to smile down into her salty face.

"What did you use to scare the sharks away?" Ben asked. Gideon grinned, "I asked Lorenzo to send me the sounds dolphins use when they attack sharks so I could broadcast it over *Kestrel*'s speakers."

"Brilliant." Ben said while removing his gear. Then he sighed, "That was a close shave."

"Too close," Gideon said soberly. Turning to Sophia, he said "Let's get away from this storm, sis. There's still a long journey ahead."

Sophia smiled, her eyes downcast towards the deck.

15 July 2066, Pelagic Ranger base, Kermadec Seamount
(the next day)

Sophia huddled at a table in a dimly lit, bare room. Her tiny hands wrapped around a steaming cup of tea, but she was not drinking.

Instead, her attention was focused on the windows. The night sky was clearing. *Beautiful stars, the storm is over.* A manta-shaped aircraft was silhouetted on the dark landing grid. *My brother's Kestrel. He came and found me.* A lighted sign beyond the landing grid announced: Kermadec Ranger Base.

Sophia turned from the view to stare into the steaming mug.

"Nemo?" she murmured, without raising her eyes.

"Yes, *Ameera*."

"You… weren't there."

"You're right, *Ameera*. You were alone in your *Egg* for almost eight hours," came the soft answer.

"I was afraid, Nemo."

"Yet you found courage. Your fear did not control you, *Ameera*."

"No, it didn't." A tear rolled down the young girl's cheek.

"Well done, *Ameera*. You were patient. You had hope. You believed we would find you."

"Yes." A whisper.

"And we did come. And you were rescued."

"Yes."

"No one forgot you, *Ameera*. A rescue team was organized as soon as possible. Your brother made a heroic effort to save you."

Silence.

"The attack destroyed my circuits on *Ossë*. I had to rebuild my algorithm from backups. I'm sorry I had to leave you on your own for so long."

"Yes. I forgive you."

"Thank you, *Ameera*."

An anxious silence filled Sophia's heart. "Nemo? Find *Baba*?"

"We don't know where your father has gone, Sophia. We're searching for him."

"*Baba* OK, Nemo?"

"We don't know yet, *Ameera*."

She stared into her tea. *Please be OK, Baba. God, take care of my Baba.*

"Nemo, you know God? He helped."

"Did God help you, *Ameera?* I'm merely an algorithm, so such things are beyond me."

"God was with me in the *Egg*," she whispered.

"I believe you, *Ameera*. Many people report a mystical relationship with a supreme being. Your experience is not unique. Is that why you weren't afraid?"

"Yes. God was there. He said, 'Trust. Rest.'"

"Then he helped you trust and wait. It sounds like God was a faithful friend to you, *Ameera*."

"Yes," Sophia said simply. She sipped her tea.

The door opened, interrupting the quiet conversation. "Sally would like to talk with you, Sophia," Nemo said quietly, "Is that OK?"

Sophia looked up. *I like Sally!* "Yes."

Sally Marcelli hurried over to the young girl, who was now staring into her hot drink again, sat quietly next to her and put her hand next to Sophia's. "Sophia," she offered, "*Ossë* is still being repaired. It'll be several days before you can return home. I'd like it if you came to live with me on Marcelli Deep. Would you like that?"

"No." Sophia said emphatically without looking at her.

"No?" Sally was puzzled.

"Help save *Baba*," Sophia insisted, meeting Sally's eyes with a solemn gaze, then quickly turning away.

"Pardon me, Sally," Nemo interrupted. "The Ranger Base is testing prototypes of Sophia's devices. Several of her drone designs may be needed for the search and rescue efforts. Might I recommend that she stay here rather than go to Marcelli Township?"

"Are you sure that's good for her? She's been through quite an ordeal, Nemo."

"Allowing her to participate in the search will most likely help her. She'll be able to process the trauma much more effectively by doing something to help her father. Besides, she knows how to configure and adjust the devices far more quickly than the technicians here. The team could use her skills right now."

Sally considered. "We'd need to get permission. Can you please check with Major Camden, Nemo?"

"I'll do that now," Nemo affirmed.

Sophia was gazing at the table again, but her hand reached over to clutch Sally's arm. "Stay, Sally."

The young woman smiled, "Of course, Sophia, I'll stay. We all want to help rescue your father."

"Major Camden has agreed to the proposal," Nemo announced.

"Well, let's get busy then, Sophia!" Not needing any urging, Sophia rose and gently, but insistently, pulled Sally by the hand out the door and across the tarmac to the command centre.

*

Ben walked over to where Gideon had moved *Kestrel*, near one of the servicing bays at the Kermadec Seamount Ranger Base. In the dawn light, Gideon pulled a utility cart around to the side of the craft and opened the armament racks on *Kestrel*.

Rosy clouds reflected faintly on the sea beyond *Kestrel*. Ben watched for a moment, "Need any help?"

Gideon's eyes were flicking between the open compartment and the load of rail-gun projectiles on the utility cart he'd checked out from the supply shed.

Gideon turned and smiled. "Hi Ben, just checking armament on *Kestrel*. I was going through the stats from that run-in with the *Yamamoto* and the *Tigershark*. It gave me a rough benchmark for *Kestrel*'s abilities in a conflict, so I'm trying to reconfigure it for this next mission. How many rail gun projectiles can I load without affecting the craft's manoeuvrability?"

"May I see your stats?"

"Of course, on that pad there."

Ben studied the graphs and numbers. "Well, Gid. It's likely that a sub is involved, so expect to be fighting underwater. There are many unknowns at this point. Maybe we'll know more after the briefing. However, from your stats, I'd suggest ninety projectiles." Ben joined Gideon at the bay.

"Good, thanks, Ben. That confirmed my thoughts exactly, very helpful." Gideon lifted cartridges from the cart, slotting them carefully into the rail gun racks. "And then there's the problem of power. In a dogfight, the Alchemist reactor won't sustain both rail gun and laser pulses for long."

"You could buffer the Alchemist output with a few more superconducting battery cells," Ben suggested, scrutinizing the power figures.

"Excellent suggestion, Ben. I forgot that you're an expert on power supply. Nemo, are there any superconducting battery modules here at the base that would fit my plane?"

"Just checking, Lieutenant Battuta," Nemo answered. A few seconds ticked by. "Yes. Six in stock which fit *Kestrel* specifications."

"How much additional time will six modules give me while *Kestrel*'s operating at full power, firing rail guns and laser pulses?"

"Six modules should double your engagement time, from ten minutes continuous firing to twenty," the disembodied voice answered.

"Hopefully, that'll be long enough," Gideon said, under his breath. "Ben, will you be joining us on this mission?"

"Yes, I will. Major Camden has graciously allowed me to join your team." Ben watched the first ray of dawn sparkle on the horizon. "This mission is a personal matter, Gid: Your father saved me, gave me sanctuary. The people of the *Arraa'i* Pod have welcomed me, despite the danger I brought. These men we'll be chasing may well be the ones who killed my wife and son. Your fight is my fight."

Gideon put his hand on Ben's shoulder. "Glad to hear that, Ben. We sure can use your assistance." Gideon held Ben's gaze as he continued, "I want you to know that even though I've only known you a short time, you feel like family. I know many in the Pod feel that way." They shook hands and, as Gideon left to find the batteries, Ben stood still a few moments, reflecting on Gideon's words. He also had been drawn towards Sul, Gideon, and the community. Their kindness, hospitality, and friendship touched him deeply. A surprising warmth surged through him, bringing a smile to his face.

He shook himself from the reverie and glanced down the dock. Six metres away, Carlo was gathering equipment from a utility cart: rappelling kits, med kits, provisions, rifles, taser guns, grenades, knives. Ben stepped over to assist him.

*

As Gideon returned to *Kestrel*, he noticed out of the corner of his eye that Maria was approaching. She was carrying a small box and grinning. "Sally told me the great news, Gid! Marriage, is it? A brave step. And about time, I might add. Well done." Her blue eyes twinkled.

"Thanks, Maria. Sally took her time before giving me her answer. The suspense was worse than, well, anything."

She laughed, "Well, buck up. She said 'yes'. You better take care of her, though, or I'll come looking for you!"

"Her love will hold me to that much better than any threat you could make," he retorted, glancing at her with a smile.

She offered the box in her hands, "Sophia said I should give you these, and that you should take them with you."

Gideon looked inside. "Wow, these must be her latest version. They look so lifelike. I wonder why she thinks we need these. I'll take them, though. My sis is often right in almost a spooky way." He put the box in the main cockpit.

He turned towards Maria and ventured, "So… speaking of relationships, how did your time with Ben go? That was some dress."

"A long story." A faint flush rose in her face. "Maybe I'll tell you after the mission."

"Wow, Maria blushing? Haven't seen that before; this *must* be serious!" Gideon responded, with a chuckle.

"I think that's none of your business, Gid," she said, now a bit flustered. "I came over to inform you that Major Camden asked me to be navigator and operations coordinator for *Kestrel* during the mission," she said, returning to the business at hand.

"And, changing the subject. Curiouser and curiouser."

"Stop it! We have a mission to prepare for, and no time to lose."

"Yes, Captain Romero, ma'am." Gideon saluted, continuing to grin. "Carlo and *Ben* will be the other members of our unit on *Kestrel*," he added slyly.

"I'm aware of that," she said, curtly. "Briefing will be in ten minutes at the operations hut." She whirled around and strode away from him.

He watched her go, his grin growing wider.

Gideon spotted four sea-grey velocicopters, manned by New Zealand troops, landing near the mission briefing room. *Good response from our neighbours! We can sure use their help.* News of the attack and the disappearance of Suliman Battuta, a leader well-respected in the whole region, had prompted quick offers of help from terrestrial governments around the South Pacific Pelagic Territory. New Zealand had sent several teams to assist the Pelagic Ranger efforts.

Gideon followed Maria across the tarmac to prepare for the briefing. His mind played out scenarios and strategies of how *Kestrel* might fare in a duel with the sleek velocicopters.

*

Ben saw Lorenzo standing next to the quayside, guiding in the specially built aircraft that was transporting his dolphin team. It splashed down smoothly and taxied to the dock at his directions. As it slowed, doors underneath the craft opened, releasing the dolphins into the sea. Once free, the dolphins dived, then leapt and dived again in the water in a carefully calculated jump, drenching Lorenzo with the resulting splash. Then they swam to the deck, laying their beaks on the edge, looking at him.

"Funny!" The water streamed down Lorenzo's exposure suit.

Ben walked over, sidestepping the splash zone as the dolphins slipped back into the water. *What great animals!*

"Is that your dolphin team?"

"Yes, Tazia and Lucca."

"Hi, Lorenzo," Ben extended his hand in greeting. "We didn't get to talk much yesterday at the restaurant,"

Lorenzo shook his hand and met Ben's gaze. "I know more about you than you think," he said with smile. "My sister told me about you."

"Right, I'm sure she has," Ben acknowledged, a little embarrassed. "I didn't make a good first impression."

"Don't worry. Maria said something similar about herself," Lorenzo glanced towards the dolphins and then back at Ben. "Not many people fluster my sister."

"So, tell me how you work with your team," Ben shifted the topic, "Is it like working with trained dogs, like soldiers do in the K-9 Corps?"

Lorenzo clucked his tongue, in disagreement. "Many people assume that, especially non-Pelagics."

"Well, I'd like to hear what it's really like," Ben assumed a humbler attitude.

Lorenzo smiled again, trusting this man. "Actually, my relationship with my dolphins is more like peer-to-peer. Like how you and I will work together on this team. Tazia and Lucca choose to work voluntarily, as we do in joining the Pelagic Rangers, to defend their friends. They like working with me and have accepted me as part of what is essentially a small dolphin pod."

"Interesting, they *choose* to work with you? What's in it for them?" Ben watched the sleek forms gliding below in the water.

"Well, think about why humans like dolphins, why we try to befriend and communicate with them. We feel like we're kindred species. We recognize signs of intelligence in them. We feel like we're able to recognize, sometimes even identify with, their emotions. In working with them, I see similar motivations from their side. They seem to be as interested in me as I am in them."

"How do you know what they're thinking? Do you have a way to actually talk with them?"

"Well, as I'm sure you know, dolphins have a language made up of squeals and clicks." Lorenzo pulled a set of integrated headphones and hydrophone-speakers from his backpack. "This is essentially an interpreter.

It translates simple English and Italian words into dolphin-speak, and vice versa."

"That's amazing. You can listen in on their conversations?"

"Well, dolphins communicate really efficiently and rapidly, so much dolphin speech goes by too quickly for the interpreter to process. They must slow down to talk to me, like we might do with a small child. In fact, many of the frequencies dolphins use are beyond human hearing. But the interpreter catches those we can't hear."

"Your ability to communicate with each other must come from more than this mechanical interpreter, then."

Lorenzo leaned back, taking the measure of Ben as he had at the café the day before. "You're right. More important than the technology is the time I spend in the water with the dolphin pod, learning to understand their world and their personalities. And they get to know me as well. We've developed a... rapport."

"A rapport, huh?" Ben turned his attention to inspecting the interpreter in his hands. *Fascinating. To be able to eavesdrop on dolphin conversations.* "May I try out the interpreter?"

Lorenzo hesitated a moment, then nodded. "I think that will be OK, but let me check. The dolphins won't be used to you at first. Let me tell them that you're trying it out, so they'll be ready to help you."

He dropped the harness unit with the hydrophone-speaker into the water, attached to a line which he secured to a cleat. He donned a set of headphones, handing another set to Ben. "My friend. Wants to speak to Tazia and Lucca," he said slowly. "Tazia, Lucca, would you like to speak with him?"

The small pod of dolphins leapt into the air, swimming back to the dock.

Chatter and clicks poured forth. Over the headphones came a simple "Yes."

Wow, I can understand a marine mammal! The thought sent a thrill through Ben.

"We must rescue one of our elders," Ben said slowly, moving his face to make eye contact with each dolphin in turn.

"Your elder in trouble?" came the translated chatter.

"Yes. We need your help." He crouched down, looking more intently into their large dark eyes.

"We'll help."

"Thank you."

"Our joy," came through the speakers. They turned and sped off underwater.

"Amazing," Ben said as he pulled off his headset, "to interact even at that depth with another species."

Lorenzo retrieved the hydrophone and stowed the kit away. "It's a privilege to work with them. I count myself blessed." He beamed at Ben, just before being struck in the face again with a stream of water. Ben leapt backwards to avoid the spray, as the dolphins reared up on their tails and leapt with squeaks that sounded like laughter.

"Clowns," Lorenzo exclaimed, as he wiped his face, beaming as he did so.

Some giggles and conversation from behind made them turn. Sally waved, "Hey, Renzo! Hi, Ben."

"Hey, cousin," Lorenzo responded. "I see you have a new friend. A sister-in-law soon, from what I hear."

Sally nodded, "Sophia and I are getting acquainted. She wants to help find her father. Major Camden has given permission for us to stay on Base."

"That's great. I assume it'll involve some of those cool devices you design," Lorenzo said looking at the child. "I have one of your lionfish, I love it." Sophia smiled at the ground.

Tazia and Lucca chattered excitedly as Sally and Sophia neared the edge of the dock.

What's up with the dolphins? Ben wondered, looking over.

Tazia dived and returned with a clump of seaweed, which she tossed towards the newcomers. It landed in front of Sophia, who stepped back, startled.

"It's one of their favourite games, Sophia. They want to play with you. Just throw it back to them," Lorenzo coaxed.

Sophia released Sally's hand to retrieve the tangle of weed. She flung it awkwardly towards the dolphins and Tazia leapt out of the sea, catching it deftly and flinging it again in one fluid move. The seaweed sailed back, landing at Sophia's feet.

"This is a game they play with friends. I've never seen them do this with someone they haven't met before."

The dolphins were splashing, squeaking, and clicking loudly as the game continued. Ben marvelled at this community he found himself in.

Lorenzo pulled out the dolphin communicator, dropping the hydrophone and speaker into the water and tying it off again. "Something curious is going on here. I don't understand," Lorenzo said, "They're engaging in behaviour I don't recognize."

Lorenzo slipped on the headphones, listening to the dolphins. Then he turned to Sophia, as she stared at the ground. "Do you want to try to talk to them, Sophia? They'd like to talk with you."

She nodded without looking up.

He held out the headphones to her. "These phones translate our words into language that Tazia and Lucca can understand. Then their squeals and pops will be translated back to us. It isn't exact, but we can communicate simple things. Do you want to listen?"

"Yes," Sophia said simply, still staring at the ground. She glanced up with a start, "They know my fear."

Sally was puzzled, "Who knows your fear, *Ameera*?"

Lorenzo still held the headphones out towards her, but Sophia walked away from the huddle of people. She knelt at the dock's edge. Two grey heads popped up next to her. They nudged her hands, as she reached out to them.

"You understand me," she said softly. The dolphins calmly stayed at the dock, keeping their heads under her hands.

"Lorenzo, do you know what is going on?" Sally watched the scene perplexed.

A look of wonder was on Lorenzo's face. "Yes, I think I do, but I'm not sure if I can explain it."

The child doesn't need headphones to communicate with the dolphins. Ben just watched in awe.

After a few moments of this quiet contact, Sophia stood and returned to Sally. "Go help *Baba*." She walked past Sally and on towards the Operations Centre.

Sally followed, glancing back at the men with a puzzled expression.

*

The Rangers and the teams arriving with the velocicopters milled around the Base reception hall, meeting one another. Several of the New Zealand soldiers gathered around Gideon, asking him about *Kestrel*'s capabilities, having noticed the strange craft as they landed. Maria hovered near a group of officers discussing tactics, her attention drawn towards Ben, who was in deep discussion with the Maori commander of the team. From another corner, laughter erupted as Carlo finished a joke.

Major Camden entered and motioned to Gideon, Carlo, Maria, and Ben. They gathered around her. "Thank you, Ben, for joining this team. They will benefit from your experience, and from what I've seen so far, your resourcefulness and tactical skill."

Ben nodded, a little embarrassed. "Thank you, Major."

Major Camden turned to the others, "Ben is not officially part of the Pelagic Rangers, but I'm giving him a temporary field commission. Captain Marcelli is the ranking officer and has overall responsibility, but the Professor here has more battle experience than the rest of you in this squad. If it comes to reconnaissance or field work, I suggest you defer to him."

Carlo smiled, "Won't be a problem, Major. We've all seen Ben in action."

"Good." Major Camden looked around the room. *Everyone's here. Let's get this show on the road.* She moved to the front of the room and raised her voice. "Please, take your seats."

The small groups of Pelagic and New Zealand soldiers dispersed and settled into seats with their squads. The chairs encircled a holographic display, now glowing blue, front and centre of the room. All conversation hushed.

"As we speak, Pelagic Ranger craft have identified the most likely route that the submarine is on," she announced.

The route appeared in the display, along with icons representing the *Sea Wasps* and other search craft. The map in the holo-display extended from the site of the attack on *Ossë* to their current position at the Kermadec Ranger base.

"*Sea Wasps* and support aircraft are salting the route with acoustic and pressure sensors."

The drama unfolded in the display: small yellow icons, representing the Pelagic *Sea Wasps*, progressed through a systematic search grid, seeking indications of the sub in the depths. Small pinging blue dots marked marine sonar drones being dropped from the planes and spreading out over the region.

A dot near the undersea ridge began pinging red. The Major felt the change in the room, as faces tensed and stared more intently at the display. A possible contact.

"Captain Lee, I see that one of your drones has detected something," Major Camden said, directing her voice to a virtual participant in the meeting, "Do you have more specific telemetry?"

"Yes, Major. I think we've located the sub. Telemetry gives us ninety-six per cent chance of accuracy."

"Excellent. Well done, Captain. Teams are scrambling as we speak. Release the squid bots."

"Acknowledged, ma'am. Squids have been released into the water. We'll monitor the area until the teams arrive."

"Thank you, Captain Lee, well done." *Good man to have in my command.*

Major Camden looked around the room, "You have your orders. Go to it."

The room burst into activity as the teams sprinted to the doors, spilling out onto the flight deck. Within moments, engines were winding to full power in preparation for flight.

*

Suliman wandered down a garden path, across a verdant lawn. Following the path over a stone arch, he crossed a small stream. On the far side, by the garden wall, a man was loosening dirt at the base of a rose bush. As Sul approached, he saw that the rose bush had wilted. The stems were stunted. The plant's leaves were eaten away. The gardener looked up. "Hello, Sul!" he said, brightly. The man's voice was familiar.

"Can you help me, son?" the gardener asked.

"What can I do, *Ya 'Amm*, Uncle?"

"It's the weed. It has sapped the strength of this beautiful rosebush."

Sul looked around. He saw only neatly trimmed grass, the brick wall, the gravel path. "I don't see any weeds."

"Look on the other side of the wall," the gardener pointed.

Sul stood on his toes to peer over the wall. On the other side spread a large, tangled mass of dark, ugly weeds. The vines snaked away into the distance. Amid the tangle were withered stubs of plants which had already been choked. The weeds' black tendrils came right up to the wall, and pushed between the stones.

"It's on the other side of the wall, Uncle. How can it be hurting your rose?"

"The roots, look at the roots, son." The gardener pointed at the ground at the base of the wall. He handed Sul a trowel.

Sul took the tool and began to loosen the earth, exposing a root as thick as his arm. The root pulsated. It felt like living flesh as he poked it with the trowel. He jerked his tool away, disgusted. Digging a trench from the wall towards the rose, he saw that the root was entangled with the roots of the gardener's plant. As he watched, the weed sucked life from the rose.

"Sul, you must pull the root free from the bush. Save my rose."

Sul knew he must do this, but a creeping horror stole over him. He leaned over, grabbed the root with both hands and pulled. As he did so, more roots whipped out of the ground and snaked up his arms to encircle his neck. They constricted tighter and tighter, pulling him down. He stooped and stumbled, struggling to breathe.

"Thank you, Sul," the gardener said. "Now look at my rose."

Sul saw the stem of the rosebush straighten. The leaves unfurled and turned a lustrous green. Even as he wrestled with the living roots, trying to extricate himself, the rose began to glow, brighter and brighter.

15 July 2066, Caliphate vessel *Shaheen*
(the same day)

Sul woke from the dream, gasping and sweating. He was in a dark room, on a cold metal floor that was wet and oily, and there was a salty tang in the air. The hums and clicks of machinery were his only companions. His pulse calmed as he came to his waking senses.

Memories of the attack, the scene above the surface of the sea, and the conversation with Yunus Saleh flooded into his mind. However, his uppermost thought was, *Where's my little one?* "Sophia?" he whispered.

In the centre of the room, a hatch clicked. The squeaky wheel on top of it began to turn anticlockwise. Sul watched with fascinated dread. As the hatch opened, a head emerged, swivelling to look at him. "Ah, you're awake, *kaafir*. Good. The Emir will talk to you in a few minutes."

"Where am I? Who are you?"

"In good time, Suliman Battuta. In good time." The messenger disappeared back down the ladder. The wheel squeaked again, sealing the hatch. The room was silent.

With effort, Sul pushed himself into a sitting position against the bulkhead. His clothes were soaked, and his arms and legs bound securely. The low ceiling curved tightly over him. *A submarine, probably Caliphate.*

As he sat, collecting his thoughts, a blue sphere emerged in the darkness before him. The sphere hovered and grew larger, revealing an image of a small wiry man in black robes.

"Ah, Abdul Qawwi." Sul's voice came out strong and calm. "It's been a long time, brother. Forgive me if I cannot rise to greet you properly. My arms and legs seem to be bound."

"Emir Abdul Qawwi, to you, Suliman Battuta," Abdul Qawwi retorted. "And don't call me 'brother'. You're not from my family nor my faith." The robed man spat. Sul could feel the venom radiating from him, even though the speaker was merely a holograph. "I spoke with your father's uncle yesterday. He refused to speak of you. But no matter, you're dead to your tribe and to the *Ummah,* the community of the faithful."

Sul's eyes were calm, but his heart went out to his people in Yemen. *Lord, have mercy on my tribe. Forgive them.* "Tell me something new, my brother," he insisted.

Abdul Qawwi gave Sul a cold stare as he repeated, "I am no brother of yours, Suliman Battuta. I hate you, and could kill you now. I would be praised for killing an apostate. You are only here and still alive because I want to find the man, Ben Holden. Where is he?"

"Always in a hurry, Emir Abdul Qawwi." Sul straightened his back against the cold bulkhead. He took his time, then looked at the image again. "Despite my relatives' sentiments, I'm Yemeni still; proud of my culture and identity."

Abdul Qawwi glared at him, "Still muttering blasphemies. A Yemeni without Islam is not a Yemeni."

"Surely you haven't forgotten, brother. Your clan and mine were Yemeni long before Islam came to our land. Being Yemeni is deeper than Islam. Our culture, our identity is more enduring than a passing religious power."

Sul relaxed his features, continuing with a warm tone, "And you, Abdul Qawwi, are you keeping well? How are your father and your mother? How are your wife and your children? How is the clan thriving in our terrestrial homeland? Well, I hope."

Abdul Qawwi almost responded out of habit to the string of traditional greetings, but caught himself. "Enough!" he cut Sul short. "Tell me where you've hidden Ben Holden."

Sul breathed deeply, studying the Emir carefully. "Why do you want this man?"

"That's my business, apostate, not yours!" the Emir barked.

"Forgive me, I'm afraid I can't help you with your business. I don't know where the man is."

The wheel squeaked again. Yunus Saleh climbed into the room. He stationed himself against the wall, watching.

The Emir's voice became colder. "As an indication of Allah's judgment on your foolish choices, He has given your fate into my hands."

Suliman stared squarely at Abdul Qawwi in the holo-display. "You have no power over me unless it has been given to you by the Lord of the worlds. My fate is indeed in my Lord's hands, not yours. He knows how to take care of his own."

"Be quiet, you fool! *I* am in charge of your fate at this moment. *I* can torture you until you reveal the man's location. Make this easy and you can have a quick death. Either way, prepare yourself for hell. However, if you recite the creed with a pure heart, God may yet have mercy on you."

"God has already shown me much mercy, brother. You have an opportunity to receive this mercy also. You already have heard my creed: There is no God besides God, and *Isa al-Masih* is the Word of God, the *Kalimatullah*."

"Blasphemy!" the Emir spat again.

"But listen again, dear brother, Emir. The Qur'an assigns these titles to *Isa bin Maryam,* son of Mary, the Lord's beloved. How can these words then be blasphemy?"

The Emir ripped the sleeve of his robe with passion. "*Kaafir*! You unbeliever! You're twisting the words of the Holy Qur'an, as all unbelievers do. Your family veered from the true path generations ago. You have betrayed our *Ummah*, abandoned submission to Allah, and dishonoured the Almighty."

Sul sighed, "Emir, please forgive me for being candid." He chose his words carefully. "You talk about worship of Allah. Yet the only thing I see you worshipping here is your own ambition."

Yunus Saleh reached over and slapped Sul, "You dog, how dare you! The Emir serves the Caliph, who is Allah's shadow on earth!"

Blood dribbled from Sul's broken lips. He eyed Yunus Saleh and spoke in even tones, "No matter how hard you strike me, you cannot change a lie to become truth, Yunus. I forgive you, though. Remember this later. I realize that you do not really know what you are doing."

Yunus Saleh drew back his arm to strike again. "Stop!" The Emir declared from the holo-viewer.

"Yes, Emir." Yunus Saleh stepped back against the wall.

"No more of this foolish talk. Yunus Saleh, take this *kaafir* away. Do what you need to get the information from him."

Yunus Saleh smiled, "With pleasure, Emir."

The hatch opened again, and a crewman leaned in. "Forgive me, *Qaa'id*, forgive me, Emir," he said, nervously nodding to the image. "There are indications that someone is pursuing us. We estimate they may overtake us within the hour."

The Emir interrupted, "Yunus Saleh, you must bring Suliman to me. Alive, understand?"

"Yes, Emir." Turning to the crewman, Yunus Saleh instructed, "Dawood, begin the ascent. Organize a landing party to meet us at the ladder below the conning tower."

"Yes, *Qaa'id*. We'll be ready in ten minutes. I'll send someone to escort the prisoner." Dawood Naji disappeared down the hatch.

"Do not fail, Yunus Saleh. The glory of the Caliphate may turn on the information Sul holds."

"I won't fail, Emir." Yunus bowed as the image faded. When the room had darkened, he gave Sul a swift, fierce kick.

15 July 2066, Caliphate vessel *Shaheen*
(an hour later)

The school of giant squid began their daily retreat from the growing daylight. As the shoal drifted down into the depths, they continued gorging on the schools of anchovy through which they darted.

Five squid-like mechanisms passed quickly through this swarm. They attracted no notice from the other cephalopods, intent on finishing their breakfast.

The devices continued into the dark deeps. They swam down far beyond the limits of the sunlight's early morning penetration. As the blackness increased, faint lights, flashes of phosphorescence, pulsed across their bodies. By means of these flashes they coordinated their movements with one another and sent information to their controllers, far above.

At a depth of 283 metres, the squid drones darkened their bodies to black. They needed no light to detect the submarine cruising secretively through the underwater valley below.

Below the descending squid, *Shaheen* navigated the undersea cliff formations, hiding among them to baffle enemy sensors in the region. Inside, bent over their consoles, the crew glanced furtively at their commander as he paced the deck of the operations room. The mood in the boat was grim. Yunus Saleh's departure demoralized them, and his next meeting with the Emir would seal their fate, for good or ill.

No alarms announced the arrival of Sophia's squid bots. The sub's sensors were calibrated to ignore bio-contacts like these.

One squid settled on the sub's sonar and sensor array, sending out a brief but intense electromagnetic pulse on contact. The submarine's sensors went blind.

Two squid swam to the front of the vessel and attached themselves, they spread their arms across the torpedo doors, then delivered a brief dazzling flare of light into the inky blackness. The doors were now welded shut, torpedoes neutralized.

The last two squid drifted on either side of the craft. As they moved towards the stern, they were drawn into the propeller's slip stream. They struck the blades and a muffled series of pops sheered the blades from the shaft. The broken blades fell free, drifting towards the bottom of the sea.

Shaheen became dead in the water, sightless and defenceless. As alarm bells sounded, men rushed to battle stations, but their options were limited. After about twenty minutes, they blew the ballast tanks to begin a long, slow ascent to the surface.

*

The morning fog filtered the first rays of sunlight through rainbow refractions and the mist slowly billowed before a delicate breeze, forming a sea upon the sea.

The peaceful scene was destroyed as four velocicopters, *Kestrel*, and the craft carrying Lorenzo and the dolphins sliced through the mist, cruising in formation, low to the water. The pressure wave in front of the aircraft peeled the fog back, like a plough curling soil.

They passed in a moment, with no sound.

A few minutes later, the displaced fog rolled back, obscuring all signs of their passage.

Far above, a formation of five New Zealand jump jets flew, each with three *Wingman-Three* attack drones. Like fighter squadrons of another era, these drones supported the tactics of the pilot in their assigned jet. The jump jets shadowed the velocicopters, *Kestrel*, and the dolphin carrier below, their engines throttled down to stay with the slower craft. The jet's sensors scanned the sea's surface out to the horizons and beyond, offering sentinel cover for the strike team below, alert to threats from sea or air.

*

A column of bubbles marked the ascent of the *Shaheen*. Velocicopters slowly circled the area where the strike force expected the sub to emerge. Soldiers stood guard with rail guns in the open bays of the circling craft. Others held rappel lines, prepared to drop and board the sub as soon as it broke the surface. Inflatable craft maintained a protective perimeter. Several divers were in the water with rebreathers and guns, remaining alert while monitoring readouts in their facemasks; the mist made visibility almost nil.

Fifty-five metres below the surface, *Kestrel* hovered, like its raptor namesake, waiting for its prey. Inside, at the controls, the faces of Gideon, Carlo, Ben and Maria were lit by the glow from the instrument panel. "We have them just coming up to sixty metres," Ben heard Maria say.

Kestrel was using Sophia's countermeasures to remain undetected. But this was only a precaution. As far as they knew, their opponent, *Shaheen*, had lost all ability to detect anything.

Gideon, at the controls, peered into the water column, watched intently for the first signs of the rising submarine. Carlo, in co-pilot position, was quietly coordinating with the other units. Maria monitored weapons and oceanic conditions around them. Ben was suiting up in preparation for action outside *Kestrel* if necessary. He laid out another exposure suit and set of equipment just in case.

"Renzo, give me an update on your situation," Ben requested quietly.

"Tazia and Lucca have recruited a local dolphin pod to help. They are forming a larger perimeter of protection around the area. They'll be in place in about five minutes. I'll keep you posted."

"Thanks, Renzo. We don't want surprises."

"I see the sub, Maria." Carlo pointed. She glanced up from her displays and saw the shadowy outline of the vessel in *Kestrel*'s red searchlights as it ascended from the dark depths to the lighter waters around them.

"Can you make out the status of the missile tubes? There haven't been any indications on the hydrophones that they've opened."

Carlo peered for a few seconds more. "They're closed. I think they can't target or fire missiles without their sensor array. However, I'm not sure what this new class of Caliphate sub is capable of."

"OK, just to make sure, I'll hit three of them with rail gun projectiles, so they can't open." As Maria spoke, her words were accompanied by a subtle vibration as *Kestrel*'s guns fired. They could hear the squeals as the small projectiles scored and disabled the sub's missile doors.

"We'll follow them up," Carlo said. *Kestrel* closed the distance and silently rose alongside the submarine.

"The jump jet pilots say the area and skies around us are currently clear of contacts. Still foggy at the surface though," Maria said quietly.

"Thanks, Maria," Carlo acknowledged

Lorenzo's voice sounded in their headsets, "Ben, the dolphins have set up a perimeter. There are no combatants in the water for at least a kilometre around the sub."

"Good. Thanks, Renzo. The sub will break surface in about three minutes."

*

The conning tower of the sub rose slowly from the surface of the sea, the fog clearing a space for it.

As the deck of the vessel appeared, the special forces in the velocicopters rappelled down onto it. They took positions, their guns aimed at the hatch at the top of the tower. Two soldiers climbed the ladder on the tower and stood near the hatch, ready to blow it if necessary. In the slowly circling velocicopters, men crouched in the open doors with their guns trained on the scene.

"Come out slowly with your hands raised," boomed from a speaker on one of the aircraft. The command was repeated in Arabic.

The hatch slowly opened and men climbed out. The two soldiers on top grabbed them roughly, pulling them out and forcing them down the outside ladder of the tower. The men on the deck quickly cuffed them on hands and legs and laid the twenty-five prisoners flat on the deck in a line.

*

Just beneath the surface, Gideon backed *Kestrel* off as the sub breached, allowing room for the velocicopter troops to handle the sub crew and take them into custody.

Carlo sounded tense, "Something doesn't feel right about all this, Gid. Let's surface in the fog bank and stay hidden." Gideon's hands flew across the controls and moved *Kestrel* as directed.

Hidden by the mists, *Kestrel* surfaced silently. Using its underwater jets, it glided quietly away from the activity, deeper into the surrounding shroud. "Things clear around us, Maria?"

"Nothing on the scopes, except the velocicopters, jump jets with their wingmen, sub, and men in the water. But we have a limited view here on the surface."

"Be advised: eight bogies approaching rapidly from the north-east," the voice of a jump jet pilot crackled in all their headsets.

"Good instincts, Carlo. Sounds like more trouble coming," Ben said.

"Roger, this is Kiwi Leader. These are bandits. I repeat, these are bandits heading towards us. Prepare defence protocol four."

"Acknowledged, Kiwi Leader, protocol four," came the voices from the other pilots.

"Nemo, give us a view of the situation above us," Carlo spoke to the air in the cockpit.

"Pulling telemetry from Kiwi three defence group, Captain Marcelli."

A cube of light appeared before the *Kestrel* crew. Green icons showed the five Kiwi jump jets above, and as they watched, each of the jets launched three smaller aircraft that stayed near them.

Ben leaned in. "Are those the new *Wingman-Three* drones?"

Carlo glanced over at him, "Yes, they significantly increase a fighter's fire power."

On the display, lines now connected jump jets and the drones associated with each.

At one edge, eight red icons entered the pool of light. The bandits. The red shapes spread above and below to take aggressive positions against the defending jets. A blue dot appeared on the sea surface in the centre of the display.

"That's *Kestrel* in the centre," Gideon announced, without looking up. Flashes erupted from the red bandits, targeting the jets and their associated drones.

"They're using lasers. These jump jets and their *Wingmen* are not laser-resistant," Carlo's voice was concerned as they watched. Two of the *Wingman* drones flashed off the screen.

"As they get closer, bandits may also resort to missiles, or rail gun projectiles if they have them – they can cause much more damage"

Even as Carlo spoke, the flashes stopped and were replaced by white dots, firing in a stream towards the defending force. The jump jets and drones spread out and returned fire.

"Two more *Wingmen*, and there goes one of our jump jets." The display held them entranced. "There was no parachute," Gideon said grimly, "Pilot didn't make it."

A deadly ballet of aggressor and defender played out in the holo-display before them. Three of the red icons flashed and begin blinking as they were disabled and dropped towards the sea. Only two parachutes opened as the enemy pilots ejected from the jets.

"Five of the *Wingman-Three* drones are down." Gideon began working the controls of *Kestrel*. "This is not going well," he muttered.

Another of the jump jets flashed and disappeared, and again there was no parachute. Another Caliphate jet was downed, but the mood in the cabin was bleak.

As each New Zealand jet was downed, the tactical linkage of its remaining *Wingman-Three* drones immediately shifted to the control of the nearest jet.

There were now only three jump jets and seven *Wingman* drones against four aggressor planes. "Another of our jets splashed! And two more *Wingmen*. These Caliphate fighters are good." Gideon's hands flew across the monitors, changing *Kestrel's* tactical protocols.

Nemo broke into the drama, "Captain Marcelli, another squadron of eight Caliphate jets has appeared over the horizon. Heading this way."

"Do we have reinforcements coming, Nemo?" Carlo asked.

"Yes, Captain Marcelli, *Sea Wasps* have been launched from a nearby Pelagic Ranger carrier but they are still twelve minutes out. The Caliphate jets will be close enough to engage in seven minutes."

"They will be too late," Gideon mumbled, "This doesn't look good, Carlo. We may need to jump into the fight."

Maria nodded and began working through the weapons system controls. "I have target solutions for *Kestrel* to engage the red bandits above. They won't be expecting us down here."

Gideon and Carlo exchanged glances. Carlo nodded. Gideon then began integrating Maria's combat solutions, as he programmed a protocol for *Kestrel*. "Strap in and tighten your harnesses. This'll get a bit rough. Nemo, are you ready to engage?" Carlo and Ben pulled their straps tight. Maria was already strapped in.

"Yes, Lieutenant. Just refining the protocols to increase efficiency and impact. Standby to execute in five, four, three, two, one, execute."

Kestrel rose and hovered on its propellers, the surface mists boiling around it. The agile craft tilted in the direction of the first fighter and fired three rail gun bursts as it turned rapidly, aiming in three different directions. Then it dropped almost vertically, stern first, slipping into the sea like a stone. The vessel's impeller jets pulled it down quickly into the depths. A line of rail gun projectiles lanced the water where *Kestrel* had been a second before, leaving a trail of bubbles.

"That was close. They have quick reaction targeting. Nemo, integrate that quick reaction time of the enemy rail guns into the solutions and continue this tactical protocol."

"Done, Lieutenant. We took out two red enemy craft with that last salvo. Another jump jet has been damaged but is still fighting."

"Two down and two more to go," Maria said grimly as she worked her monitors. *Kestrel* dived in a smooth arc under the surface and moved rapidly to a new position.

Gideon turned to his crew, "We'll use a breaching offence: we'll jump out of the water, fire, then dive back in and shift course to keep them off balance. Their radars can't track us underwater. Hold on."

Ben grabbed onto a handle near his seat.

Kestrel built up speed as it shot towards the surface at a shallow angle. It burst into the mists above, then spun in the air as it fired off another three bursts of rail gun shots. Slipping quickly back into the sea, it moved in an arc once again, away from the site of engagement.

This time, the responding enemy fire projectile trails in the sea appeared further away.

Kestrel banked as it described a large arc in another direction. "They may have fired wait-and-see missiles, Nemo. Prepare laser cannons."

"Done, Lieutenant."

Kestrel breached again like a giant manta taking to the air. Then it swivelled in the air, firing several rail gun bursts, dipped almost to the surface, banked steeply and rose in the air again to fire two laser blasts. Three explosions sounded a few hundred metres away.

"Just as I thought, the missiles were waiting for us to surface again."

They dropped beneath the sea and curved through the vast blueness two more times, repeating the manoeuvres.

Carlo was quietly vomiting into a bag he'd brought for the purpose as the craft jerked and spun. He grinned sheepishly at Maria and Ben's stares. "I've been on this roller coaster before. I came prepared." Maria was also turning a bit green.

"Status, Nemo?" Gideon asked.

"Between us and the Kiwi three squadron, all eight bandits have now been splashed. The other eight have apparently detected our reinforcements and have turned back. The *Sea Wasps* will be here on station in forty-five seconds. Two of our Kiwi jump jets and six of their *Wingmen* drones have survived, though one of the planes is damaged. It will be escorted back by two *Sea Wasps*," Nemo reported.

"Casualties?" Carlo asked quietly.

"Losses from the Kiwi jump jets: three jets and five *Wingman-Three* drones. One jet damaged but can limp home. Three jump jet pilots were lost, perishing with their aircraft. Three of the aggressor pilots who ejected from their craft have been located and will soon be retrieved. The others were lost when their planes were destroyed."

Kestrel rose to the surface, shifting smoothly from impellers to flight fans. Ascending through the mists now dispersing in the morning sun, they glided a short distance and found the submarine wallowing. Swooping alongside the derelict *Shaheen*, Gideon lowered *Kestrel*'s pontoons and landed on the ocean surface.

"Carlo, requesting permission to go to the sub," Gideon angrily whipped off his harness.

Carlo put a steady hand on Gideon, pushing him back in the seat. "Stay cool."

"These men took my father!" Gideon snapped.

Carlo gave him a steady stare, "We're all concerned about your father; but Gid, I won't let you go near those prisoners with that attitude. Be professional."

Gideon visibly fought to gain control of his emotions.

Carlo turned to Ben, "Ben, can you go with Gideon?"

"Of course." Ben handed Gideon the exposure suit and equipment and Gideon put it on rapidly.

Carlo popped open the canopy door and Ben and Gideon climbed onto *Kestrel*'s airframe. Ben signalled to the soldiers in the dinghy, who ferried the two of them to *Shaheen*. As they bumped up against the sub, they leapt onto the deck and approached the sergeant holding the prisoners.

Ben shook the man's hand. "Sergeant, thanks for your help. Have you located Sul yet?"

The man looked at Ben, reluctant to deliver the news. "We've searched the sub and there's no sign of him." He glanced at Gideon. "I'm sorry, Gideon."

"May I question the prisoners?" Ben asked.

"Yes, of course. I believe this one is in charge. They all are deferring to him."

Ben walked over to the prisoner and pulled the man's head up by his hair to look at his face. He shifted to fluent Arabic, "Where is Suliman Battuta?"

The man gave a bloody smile. Some of his teeth had been broken in the scuffle. He looked over at Gideon, "Ah, he must be the apostate's young piglet." He grimaced as he smiled, "You are too late, *kaafir*. The piglet's father is en route to the Emir."

Gideon rushed over to strike the man, but Ben stopped him. "Don't make me regret bringing you, Gid. We'll work this as a team."

Gideon stopped, nodded, but glared at the man who still smiled mockingly at him.

Lorenzo's voice came over Gideon's headset, "You left your mike open, Ben. I didn't follow the Arabic. What's happening?"

"The prisoner says Suliman has been taken, Renzo."

"That's what I thought. Tazia has communicated that some local dolphins detected the trail of an outboard motor. They've followed the diesel taste in the water for a while. The trail points directly to Raoul Island, about six nautical miles west by south-west. That may be the answer to this puzzle."

Ben passed on the report to Carlo, who responded promptly, "OK, head back. I've been talking to Major Camden. She's asked us to carry out a reconnaissance mission on Raoul. Time is of the essence. They will send us three support units."

"On our way back," Ben acknowledged. The dinghy swung over to fetch them and return them to *Kestrel*.

Once on board, Ben and Gideon strapped themselves in. Maria and Carlo retreated to the back of *Kestrel* to don exposure suits and equipment. Gideon settled himself in front of the controls, "Nemo, plot a course for Raoul Island."

"Done, Lieutenant."

Kestrel swivelled around, heading west by south-west.

"Gideon, I'm coming as well," Lorenzo said in the headset. "I've released the wild dolphins that helped protect the perimeter, and I'm loading Tazia and Lucca in their carrier craft about a mile from your position. We'll meet you at the island. Nemo, please find the best place to release the dolphins."

"I'll send the coordinates to Gabriella, Lieutenant Romero," Nemo replied.

"Make sure you and your dolphins take care, little brother," Maria added, clicking herself back into her harness.

15 July 2066, Kermadec Ranger base
(the same day)

"Major, the Pelagic Array has detected a surface craft, eighty-five nautical miles away, approaching Raoul Island from west by south-west. It's outside the commercial sea lanes. It seems to be a military vessel of some kind," the corporal announced, describing the images in a holographic pool of light before her.

"Send the image to the central holo-interface, Corporal," directed Major Camden, glancing at the speaker's holo-station. *Possible threat to the operation.*

The Major noticed Sophia standing in the far corner with Sally Marcelli, staring at the ground. The girl was clearly uncomfortable in the noisy, crowded Operations Centre. *Sul's daughter. Just survived quite an ordeal in her sub.*

Several of the technicians moved closer to the Major to examine the mysterious contact in the central viewer. "Magnify."

The image expanded until it filled most of the oval of light. Details were now apparent: a sleek craft gliding rapidly above the water on two submerged pontoons. *Obviously designed for speed and manoeuvrability. The flat sides and low profile also look designed for stealth.*

"Identification?" the Major asked over her shoulder.

"None, Major. They are not responding to the international identification protocol. However, the class and shape are consistent with Caliphate patrol cruisers."

"Consider it hostile, then. I expect they're on a mission to collect Suliman Battuta. Propose engagement solutions. The Major was wasting no time engaging the tactical crew. The room filled with the buzz of discussions as tacticians crowded around other holo-viewers to display possible scenarios.

Major Camden noticed the child glance at the holo-display at the mention of her father's name. *She's been taking in every detail.*

The young girl pulled on Sally's sleeve and whispered to her.

"Major Camden," Sally spoke up, "I think you need to hear what Sophia has to say."

Surprised, the Major turned to face Sophia, who was now staring at the ground again. "I'd be very interested in your suggestion, Sophia," she said gently. "Please tell me."

CHAPTER TWENTY-THREE

15 July 2066, Raoul Island
(the same day)

The rubber dinghy scraped the sand of the beach. Waves pushed it further up as four men jumped out and dragged the dinghy to dryer sand. Yunus Saleh and Dawood Naji clambered out, hoisting a heavy, limp body out onto the beach.

"The shore's deserted, just as we hoped," Dawood Naji murmured. Yunus Saleh shook the petrol tank. "Only a few litres left. That's got to get us back out to the ship tonight."

Turning to Dawood Naji, Yunus ordered, "Patrols may be searching for us so make sure you hide the dinghy well. The *Abu Bakr* will near the island in a few hours and we must be ready to go to her."

Dawood Naji dragged the dinghy over towards a narrow canyon, shoving it deep into the surrounding brush until the bow line was barely discernible. He piled a few stones, marking its location. "Secure, *Qaa'id*."

Yunus Saleh nodded absently and turned to the other two. "You two, there's a meteorological and volcanology station beyond those hills to the north. Secure the station and tie up the staff. Contact me on the encrypted channel when it's done."

"Yes, *Qaa'id*." The men shouldered their assault rifles.

"Don't hurt anyone unless you must. This is New Zealand territory. We don't want to sour relationships more than necessary," he added just before they ran up the trail, into the hills. Dawood Naji watched as they left. *Looks like a tough climb over those hills,* he thought.

"Dawood, let's take this *kaafir* to the cave near the south end of the bay. We'll wait there for the *Abu Bakr*." Yunus Saleh retrieved an oar from the dinghy. They trussed up Sul's hands and feet, ran one of the oars between arms and legs, and carried him hanging from the paddle. The man moaned, then slipped back into unconsciousness as they lifted him.

"Some of our *jihadis* visited this island a few years back," Yunus Saleh explained, as they picked their way carefully through the brush, "to secretly establish safe quarters in one of the volcanic caves; one of a network of such places around the world. They left behind a cache of supplies. We can wait there, shielded from any drones or scanners."

"Yes, *Qaa'id*." Dawood Naji found himself carrying the bulk of Sul's weight as they negotiated the twists and turns on the trail.

*

Fifteen minutes later, Dawood Naji pushed aside a shrub on the canyon wall. "*Qaa'id*, I see the entrance to the cave here." As they laid Sul on the ground. Dawood Naji noticed Sul stir slightly.

"Go look for a wooden door, about five metres inside. I'll stay with him."

Dawood Naji felt his way into the darkness. His skin crawled as he brushed against the walls, which were damp and slick from a stream on the slope above. Something crawled on his arm, and he brushed it off swiftly. A few minutes in, he called out from the blackness. "Found the door, *Qaa'id*." A moment later, a flare of light illuminated the cave, as he lit a hurricane lantern, setting it near the entrance.

They both carried Sul past the door into the cavern beyond and eased him onto the damp stone floor. Dawood Naji set the lantern on a table near the western wall of the cavern. A rough wooden cupboard and a trunk stood against the far, dark wall.

"Basic, but adequate." Yunus Saleh looked around, then pointed, "In that cabinet, Dawood, there should be supplies."

Dawood Naji grabbed a large rock. Smashing the lock repeatedly, he knocked it out of the rotting wood. The cabinet swung open, revealing stacks of MRE rations and water bottles. There were also small arms, grenades, and ammunition. Dawood Naji was relieved. *Enough food to sustain us, and we can defend this place if we're discovered.*

He explored the cabinet thoroughly, taking stock of what was there.

Suddenly the floor quivered under them for a few seconds. "*Qaa'id*, what was that?" Dawood Naji asked, freezing in place.

Yunus Saleh was calm, walking around and inspecting for damage in the cave. "A small quake, Dawood. Apparently we're on an active volcano; that is why there's a research station here."

"Yes, *Qaa'id*," Dawood Naji said, his voice subdued, not at all reassured.

They lifted Sul onto mats covered with a blanket from the trunk. Yunus

Saleh checked his pulse. "He's weak. We had better not let this infidel die." He sprinkled water from a bottle over Sul's face. Sul sputtered and opened his eyes.

"Drink," Dawood Naji insisted, lifting Sul's head and offering his water bottle. Sul took a mouthful, sighed, then lay back, watching them through half-shut eyes.

"He's too weak to run," Yunus Saleh commented, cutting loose Sul's wrist and ankle restraints. The cave was cold and damp, so Dawood Naji pulled out a blanket for each of them, throwing one over Sul who lay still, on his side.

"He'll stay alive until they fetch us tonight, *inshallah*." Yunus Saleh turned away from the prisoner, clicking his tongue in disgust.

Dawood Naji took some meals from the shelves, handing one to Yunus Saleh. They ripped the packs open and ate hungrily. Dawood Naji opened one and put it beside Sul on the floor. With a soft moan, Sul reached for morsels from it, bringing them to his mouth with trembling hands.

"*Qaa'id*, I saw a radio in the cabinet. Should we call the *Abu Bakr*?"

"No, we can't risk the signals being intercepted," Yunus Saleh muttered, opening another meal. "Let's wait for the prearranged rendezvous location and time."

They continued eating in silence.

"Water, please," Sul asked from the shadows.

Dawood Naji looked at Yunus Saleh who nodded. Dawood took a bottle and set it down next to Sul.

"Thank you, Dawood Naji." Dawood paused, looking at the older man. An apostate, but still polite.

"Dawood, take the first watch. Wake me in three hours."

"Yes, *Qaa'id*," Dawood Naji agreed, stifling a yawn himself.

15 July 2066, 105 miles due west of Raoul Island
(the same day)

The lone velocicopter flew rapidly, low to the water. It sliced across the glittering path of light cast by the morning sun. No light reflected off its matte skin and it appeared only as a shadow passing over the sea. The men inside bustled about in the cabin, preparing for the drop.

The pilot spoke into his helmet microphone, "The ship's over the horizon still. We shouldn't go any closer, or we'll enter detection range."

"This is close enough," the co-pilot said. "Seed the area. We're on top of the projected path of the ship."

"Yes, sir, dropping now."

The aircraft slowed. It began a sinuous route along the predicted path of the oncoming ship. The side doors of the velocicopter opened. The men inside began tossing out small translucent objects. These tumbled into the ocean below, sinking quickly. Several Shearwater Observer Drones were also tossed out the open doors and, after the last of the drones had been launched, the copter pivoted. It set a straight course back to base, hugging the surface of the sea.

"Seeding and launch complete, sir."

*

Captain Fa'iz of the Caliphate patrol ship *Abu Bakr* absently noted four seabirds wheeling around his ship. *Sooty shearwaters, the beggars! Hoping for scraps we throw overboard.*

"Captain, sir, there's a holo-communication for you from the Emir," a seaman announced, peering around the hatch into the bridge.

"Very well, project it here on the bridge." He smoothed his tunic. *This mission is an unexpected and unwelcome diversion from regular patrol – and has kept me up all night.* He rubbed his weary face but, resolving to appear fresh, he smoothed his jacket and straightened his back.

In the room's holo-display area, the robed Emir materialized, with startling realism. *These holo-projectors are becoming too sophisticated.* In these moments, he longed for the days when communication was only written. "Emir," he said, bowing slightly, his hand on his chest.

"Captain," the Emir acknowledged, "I see you're due to arrive at Raoul Island in two hours."

"Yes, Excellency. We should have visual contact with the island before noon."

"The party you are scheduled to pick up, some crew from the submarine *Shaheen*, will be waiting on the south coast."

"Yes, Emir, we have the position. Your staff sent us maps," the officer said. *Just stay calm, the Emir is not actually in the room, just in the image.*

"Captain Yunus Saleh has a prisoner. It is imperative that you deliver that prisoner safely back here to the Somali Emirate. Yunus Saleh's men have subdued the staff at the research station on Raoul Island, so you should have no problems."

"Yes, Emir," he began. Then, with some reluctance, "I just read a report of recent seismic activity in that area, Excellency."

The Emir considered. "Let us hope that won't be a problem. Get in and out quick. Once you have the prisoner you will rendezvous with the Caliphate support ship, *Medina*. It's on its way to your position. It has jump jets onboard, which will then transport the prisoner to me."

Who is this man? Why such an effort to retrieve this particular prisoner? "Excellency, are there any special orders concerning the prisoner?"

"He's an infidel and apostate but he has important information. His name is Suliman Battuta – you may have heard of him."

"Ah yes, I know one of his cousins."

"Your orders are to keep him alive."

"We will, Emir, and we will send him safely to you. We serve the Caliph." Captain Hassan touched his chest and bowed again.

The image of the Emir faded from the room. Out of the corner of his eye, the captain spied one of the shearwater birds perch for a moment outside the open hatch on the railing of the bridge wing. Then it lifted its wings, caught the wind and drifted off. *Strange, I've never seen one land on a boat like that before.*

A sailor approached him with a clipboard and the captain thought no more of the bird. He signed the clipboard, and began to give orders to prepare for taking the shore party aboard.

*

Just below the sparkling surface of the dark sea, a small cluster of moon jellyfish pulsated – but the crew on board the Caliphate ship *Abu Bakr* were oblivious to their presence.

The jellyfish devices beat their way through the water towards the oncoming ship. As they touched the vessel, they did not bounce off but, instead, adhered to its metal surface. The ship continued to surge forward and, in a few moments, more than a hundred jellies were clinging to its sides.

*

Two hundred miles away, Major Camden listened in on the conversation between Captain Hassan and the Emir by means of a transmission from the shearwater drone perched on the Caliphate ship's railing. Major Camden kept her eyes fixed on the ship in the holo-viewer before her. "From what I hear, the vessel has hostile intent. Do you concur, Lieutenant?"

A legal officer, a young man with a bit of a harried look, standing next to her said, "Yes, Major. They're talking about a kidnapping which is currently in progress. Under international law, they can therefore be classified as hostiles."

"Ready?" The Major turned to a ranger peering into another nearby holo-interface.

"Yes, Major."

"Ignition, Corporal."

"Ignition." The corporal pressed a virtual button with her finger, whispering to herself. "Fire in the hole."

Two hundred miles away, the hundreds of moon jellyfish affixed to the ship exploded in unison. Within ten minutes, the Caliphate ship was foundering. Lifeboats had been flung over the sides and the crew were scrambling to safety.

The wheeling shearwater drones flying above the ship jammed surrounding airwaves. The ship was deaf and mute in the water, unable to receive or broadcast messages.

"Well done, team. We've neutralized the threat. Now it's up to the rescue team to finish the job." The Major congratulated those around her. As her gaze swept the room, she noticed a faint smile on Sophia's face.

15 July 2066, Raoul Island
(the same day)

Kestrel drifted like a silent apparition in the dim light into a clearing of the forest. Only the ferns and shrubs four metres below betrayed its passage as they were stirred by her fans. The camouflaged craft was a shadow within the shadows of the trees.

After a few moments, *Kestrel's* landing gear unfolded, and the craft settled gently into a field of ferns.

The canopy lifted and four dark figures clambered to the ground, virtually invisible due to their exposure suits. Maria, Gideon, and Carlo gathered around Ben who had been designated as lead for this reconnaissance mission, as per Major Camden's suggestion.

Ben was relaying a report from Nemo, "Lorenzo says he's located more dolphin pods willing to help. The pods have formed a watchful perimeter around Raoul Island and gull drones are scanning the meteorological station on the north coast. The telemetry from the drones should be on your displays."

An area on the lower part of Ben's mask showed a map of Raoul Island. *There we are.* An icon indicated his team here on the peak of Expedition Hill. A meteorological and volcanology research station sat on the north coast, north and down the slope from their position.

Nemo continued, "As you requested, Professor, the velocicopter Blue team is now on standby north-west, on Meyer Island. Green team is on standby to the east, at Hutchinson Bluff. Red team is ready south-west, on the ridge above the Milne Isles. All await your team's tactical report. Twelve jump jets are on patrol in a fifteen-mile radius around the islands. The jets will be regularly relieved on station, in rotation, by replacements from the Pelagic Ship *Triton*, twelve miles to the south-east."

"Thank you, Nemo, acknowledged." Icons for the blue, green, and red teams blinked in the locations just described by Nemo.

"Blue, Green, and Red teams, communication check." Ben spoke into his helmet mike.

"Reading you, loud and clear," each team leader's voice sounded in turn.

Ben looked at his comrades. The viewing shield of his mask cancelled the camouflage of the others' suits, so he could see them clearly. "The gull drones are in the air. Are you seeing their data?"

Gideon interrupted, "Ben, I just remembered this box that Sophia insisted I bring with us. How could she possibly have known we would be searching Raoul Island? She is always full of surprises like that."

Gideon retrieved the package Maria had given him from *Kestrel* and handed it to Ben, who opened the lid. Sixteen life-like rats were packed in the box. Ben pulled one out and inspected it, "These are very realistic."

"That's my sis," Gideon said proudly.

"How do they work?"

"We activate and release them and they each have sensors calibrated to look for indications of people. They will cover a much wider area of the island than we can, much faster than us. They are linked to the gull droids which will monitor them."

"Excellent," Ben said, placing the one in his hand on the ground.

Gideon pulled the rest out and put them near the first.

"Nemo, work out the most efficient search pattern for these reconnaissance droids."

"Done, Professor, I'm displaying it on your map."

Ben studied it. "That looks great, ready to deploy them?"

"Ready, Professor."

"Reconnaissance droids, go," Gideon mouthed the words without a sound. The helmet's communication device translated his muscle movements into speech, now heard in the earpieces of Ben, Carlo, and Maria.

The rat bots scattered and scampered away, blending into the underbrush.

"I suggest we hide *Kestrel* in Denham Bay down there, Gideon," Ben said.

"Good idea." Gideon put the empty box in the airship and the canopy closed. "Nemo, hide *Kestrel* in Denham Bay. Twenty metres down."

"Yes, Lieutenant." *Kestrel* rose on a whisper, gliding down the hill, out over the water and sank deep into the bay.

Ben studied the map on his helmet's screen. "Are you all getting this readout from the drone on your maps?"

"Yes, looking at it now," Carlo said. Gideon and Maria nodded.

Maria studied the ghostly images on her display, "I'm zooming in on the research station. Thermal imaging shows that staff are being held in the south-west room. Probably bound, they aren't moving. I count six people."

Ben also zoomed in, examining the station and surroundings. "I see only one person moving in the building."

"The others might be in the jungle," Maria suggested.

"I think you're right, Maria. That'll make them much harder to find. Nemo, can you adjust the pattern for the rat droids in that area to do a perimeter search around the station?"

"Yes, Professor. Done." Ben watched the shift in search pattern. "Red and Green teams, deploy," he mouthed. "Blue team, launch inflatable dinghies."

"Acknowledged," came each team leader's response.

"Renzo, are the waters clear?"

A second of silence passed, and Lorenzo replied, "The dolphins have found no humans in the water around the island. Something is spooking them, though."

"Any idea what it is?" Ben asked.

"No. I sense their anxiety. I don't think even they know why."

The ground beneath their feet trembled.

"Nemo?" Ben asked.

"Professor, there seems to be some seismic activity on and around the island."

"I think that's what is disturbing the dolphins," Lorenzo observed over the headsets.

"Nemo, can you tell us more?"

"No, Professor, I do not have enough information to evaluate what this seismic activity means. The best source of data, from the research station to the north, is offline."

"OK, well, no choice. Let's stick with the plan and try to find Sul. Keep us posted, Renzo. Thanks, all of you. Over."

Switching to the local team channel, Ben continued giving out assignments: "Carlo and Gideon, go towards the station – Green team will meet you there. Blue team will patrol the western coast and Red team has the southern bay. Maria and I will take east of the ridge; we should be able to rendezvous with Red team on the beach if our search has no results."

"Got it," Carlo acknowledged.

The four crossed the ridge together. The wind gusts grew stronger and a squall passed across the sparkling sea far below them. The four melted into the night in two pairs, one pair moving swiftly south along the ridge, and the other two going north towards the meteorological station.

*

An hour later, Maria and Ben trudged along the crest trail, moving towards the south-west corner of the island. Denham Bay lay to their right, and Milne Bay to the left. The ferns surged around them, whipped by the rapidly shifting air currents of the ridge. Breezes from both bays met here and gusts of wind sheared through the myrtle and palms above them. A sudden rain shower passed over and pelted them. They moved off the trail and into the cover of the shrubs and trees to wait for it to pass.

"The reconnaissance rat, in the valley to the left, just went offline," Ben reported.

"Maybe he was a snack for one of these feral cats we've seen slinking around," Maria teased, perching on a convenient rock to massage her calf. "Those rats looked very realistic, and tasty."

"Maybe," Ben's mind was elsewhere as he focused on his magnified display. *Looks like the droid was half-way down the valley when we lost it.* "Before it went offline, the rat sent some thermal images. They might've been cats, but this contact looked larger. On the map, it looks like there might be a cave down in the valley. We'll have to check it out."

"I'm definitely a *marine* mammal, not a mountain-climbing one," Maria sighed. "Well, at least the cave is downhill from here. And Red Team can give us a ride from the beach."

Ben was studying the dark valley and its opening onto the sea.

"OK, I'm done whining. Ready to go," she flashed Ben a wry smile. He laughed.

The headphones clicked, "Ben, we've neutralized the bad guys here at the meteorological station. There were only two; one inside guarding the hostages and one in the jungle as Maria figured. I would guess more are hiding out on the island. Gideon and I are just releasing the staff now."

"Acknowledged, Carlo. Any sign of Gideon's father?"

"Negative, and these guys aren't talking. Blue team are on their way from the Meyer Islands to evacuate the meteorological staff and the prisoners to the *Triton*."

"Acknowledged. One of the reconnaissance rats got an interesting reading before going offline. We're investigating."

"OK," Carlo acknowledged.

Gideon cut in on a secure channel to Ben, "You might be interested to know, Ben, that Nemo has been looking at the data from the station here. The island's been seismically unstable the last few weeks. Small quakes and such. Apparently, we're walking around on a volcanic caldera – there's a huge chamber below us with a pool of magma in it. Take care."

"Roger. Just what we need. Thanks, Gid." Then, turning to Maria, he said, "I saw a trail leading down into the valley a while ago, let's backtrack and see if there's a quicker way to climb down."

Maria was peering down the steep slope next to them. "I'm all for finding an easier way."

They turned and started back down the trail they had just come up. A hundred metres down the path the ground trembled.

"Oh, I forgot to mention it, Maria, but Gid said we happen to be on an active volcano."

Maria rolled her eyes, "Better and better." There was a stronger tremor. She looked at Ben; they stopped. She knelt and put her hand on the ground. Birds in the nearby trees screeched and took to the sky and soon the sky was filled with many flocks rising from the trees. Maria looked at Ben, "This doesn't look good."

In the next instant, the earth heaved, sending Ben and Maria sprawling in the dirt.

"What was that?" Ben lifted his head. "Gid, did you feel that at the station?"

Nemo cut in. "The Pelagic Array reports an earthquake near the island. Six point six on the Richter scale. There's volcanic venting in Denham Bay. Sea temperatures are rising in the centre of the bay."

The earth jolted again.

"Nemo, do you have a profile?" Ben asked as he steadied himself.

"Yes, Professor. This kind of quake precedes ongoing volcanic activity in eighty-six per cent of recorded cases."

"Ben, if it is venting in the bay, then *Kestrel* is in danger."

"Roger, Gideon, go ahead and bring your ship up near you."

"Thanks, Ben. Nemo, bring *Kestrel* to our position here on the northern coast."

"In progress, Lieutenant Battuta."

"Ben, are you and Maria OK there?"

Ben looked at the map display, "Yes, Red team is at Wilson Point…"

"Sorry to interrupt, this is Blue team. Ash clouds are also now venting from Blue Lake crater. The plume is crossing the ridge to the south, cutting off Red team. Volcanic ash is bad news for our engines. They won't be able to fly through it, Professor."

"OK, Red team circle to the east around the plume and rendezvous with Blue team. Assist in evacuation of the staff."

"Acknowledged, Professor."

"Gid, I'm losing the dolphin pods. They were spooked by the volcanic activity," Lorenzo chimed in.

"Renzo, get back to your plane and evacuate Tazia and Lucca," Ben ordered.

"Yes, will do. They'll be happy to leave the area – the other dolphins are long gone."

"Green team, can you get across Denham Bay and pick us up?"

"An ash plume is rising from the bay so we may have the same problem as Red team. I'll send a team in the rubber dinghy around the volcanic activity in the middle of the bay."

"Roger that, Green team. We'll get down to the beach and sit tight, waiting for you to pick us up in the dinghy."

Ben glanced over at Maria and they started back towards the trail into the canyon that led to the beach. Ben reported as they travelled. "We found a way into the canyon. I'll keep you posted on our progress. We're making for the beach a few hundred metres east of D'Arcy Point. Gideon, the last position of the rat droid was down that canyon. If we can, we'll try to check it out on our way to the beach."

"Acknowledged, Ben. I see it on the map."

"Did you catch all that, Maria?" Ben asked, glancing at her.

"Yes, never a dull moment with you, Ben," she smiled, and braced herself against a tree. The earth trembled again.

"Let's go back to where the two spurs meet. I saw a stream. It looked like the path went along the stream, down the valley to the shore."

They trotted briskly back along the ridge trail. After a few hundred metres, a massive explosion from the east threw Ben against the base of a tree. Maria lost her balance and tumbled down the steep hillside, swallowed up by the ferns and shrubs.

"Maria!" Ben shouted into his mike.

Silence.

His stomach tightened. He ripped off his mask, "Maria!" All he heard was a deep rumbling in the bay behind him.

Mask back on, he turned towards the bay. White smoke billowed from the centre. "Green leader, do you read?"

Silence again. *This can't be happening again!* Ben willed himself calm.

"Professor, I've lost contact with the Green team aircraft and dinghy," Nemo's calm voice sounded in his headset. "I fear they were caught in the eruption. I also detect poisonous gases, hydrogen sulphide and carbon dioxide pouring from the volcanic vents. The fumes are spreading around the island. There's significant threat of asphyxiation."

"Red and Blue teams have rescued the staff. They are all travelling north, upwind of the venting," Carlo reported. Gideon's voice cut in, "And *Kestrel* is now approaching."

Ben's priorities quickly shifted from the mission to survival in the escalating volcanic crisis. "Carlo, please take responsibility for the station staff and prisoners. Maria has fallen down the hillside. I'm not getting a response. I'm going down to look for her."

"Acknowledged, Ben. Red and Blue teams are off with station staff and prisoners."

"Thanks, Carlo. You and Gideon try to come around the island and approach underwater from the south in *Kestrel*, that will reduce *Kestrel's* exposure to the ash cloud. I'll find Maria and we'll meet you at that beach."

"Roger that, Ben, we'll be there. *Triton* just detected a radio burst from near your position. Possibly in the valley below."

"Caution, Professor," Ben heard Nemo say. "Volcanic plumes are on either side of you. The spread of the vapours into your area will become life threatening within twenty-five minutes."

Ben was already working his way down, carefully picking his way and following the trail left by Maria's tumble through the foliage.

15 July 2066, Raoul Island
(earlier the same day)

Yunus Saleh lay on a mat at the far end of the cave, draped with a blanket. He was asleep within seconds.

Dawood Naji found a rickety chair near the wall, one of its front legs broken. It was near Suliman and so he propped the chair against the wall and sat next to the prisoner. Shadows from the hurricane lamp danced on the dusty walls and ceiling as the minutes ticked by slowly. Yunus Saleh's snores drifted from the rear.

"Dawood Naji." Hearing his name, Dawood was startled out of a half-sleep. "Where are you from, son?"

Confusion seized him, he knew he shouldn't talk to this apostate – but Sul had kind eyes and had shown him respect. He whispered, "I shouldn't talk to you."

"Then don't. I'm just interested in you."

Moments of silence passed.

"I'm from Bosaso, Sheikh." There was something about Sul that made Dawood Naji add the title.

"No need to call me 'Sheikh'. I'm just a child of Allah, like you Dawood Naji. Where are you from in Bosaso? I've visited there."

"I come from a slum area outside the city, Sheikh. My parents were killed during the Dependency Wars and the Emir brought my sister and me into his household to train. I owe everything to the Caliph and *Qaa'id* Yunus Saleh."

"Yes, I remember that orphan programme. There were almost two hundred of you, right?"

"Yes, Sheikh."

They sat together in the flickering hurricane lamplight for a while, quiet.

"Sheikh, why do you not rejoin the true faith of Islam? You have lost so much, so many people hate you. Why do you choose to remain an apostate?"

"Do you find peace in your faith, Dawood Naji?"

Dawood hesitated, then said, "Yes, of course. Especially doing *Salaat* prayers in the mosque. I feel that God is close during my prayers."

"Yes, I feel the same in my prayers." Sul studied him. "But Dawood Naji, this life you lead, are you happy with it? You must have thoughts of your own."

"Sheikh…" The younger man hesitated again, but there was something about this man Suliman Battuta that drew Dawood Naji to trust him. Dawood's voice was quiet. "It is true. I have done terrible things. Things I'll be ashamed to give an account for on the Day of Judgment."

Sul did not respond, but waited, sensing the young man had more to say.

Dawood Naji continued, "A little over a week ago, I had a dream. I was sitting in my father's fishing boat on the sea. It was dark, no stars or moon. I was afraid out there on my own, in that vast darkness. But as I waited in the boat, I saw a light on the horizon. It moved towards me until it reached the boat. The light was a man, standing on the water." Dawood hesitated.

"The man came to your boat?" Sul's gentle voice encouraged him to continue.

"Yes, he approached me where I sat. I was trembling but he held his hand out. I wanted to reach over, but I was terrified. 'Don't be afraid, Dawood Naji,' he said. And my fear left. I wanted so much to be with him. He radiated so much goodness and love – I had never experienced that before."

"What did you do, Dawood Naji?"

"I took his hand, Sheikh. I stepped out. He held onto my hand. I stood with him on top of the water! I even looked down and saw fish flashing beneath me. He said, 'Dawood Naji, follow me.' His voice, it had authority… and power. I wanted to bow down, kneel at his feet."

"You were drawn to this man, what happened next?"

"I asked him, 'Who are you, *Sayyid*?' He let my hand slide from his grasp and began walking away, still on top of the water. He turned back to look at me. My eyes were riveted to his. He said it again, 'Dawood Naji, follow me!' I took a step, but I started sinking under. The water was deep and I was terribly afraid. So I turned and grasped the side of the boat, pulling myself over and back into it, and I watched the shining man walk away to the horizon."

"He walked away?"

"He did, but he called me a third time, 'Dawood Naji, come with me!'"

Then I woke up. It was such a vivid dream. Sheikh, do you know what it means? I don't know who he is. I wanted to follow him, but something in me held me back. I felt... unworthy I think."

Sul sighed. "Dawood Naji, I know many people who have had dreams like this, dreams with this shining man. My grandfather Jadan had such a dream, which started him on a profound journey. A pilgrimage, really, closer into the heart of Allah."

"But your grandfather was the one in your family that became an apostate, Sheikh. I know the story." There was fear in Dawood's voice. "Did this shining man cause your grandfather to leave the faith?"

Sul looked at the young man with compassion. "I would be glad to tell you the story, Dawood Naji, but I must warn you, it will unsettle you, it will demand all you have. Truth can set you free only if you choose to embrace it."

A resolve arose in Dawood Naji. "Sheikh, remembering my dream has set my heart on fire. I do want to know more – so please tell me."

"Dawood Naji, the poet Rumi said, 'Respond to every call that excites your spirit.'"

"Yes, Sheikh. I love the poetry from that Persian mystic. Rumi was hungry for the love of God, as I am."

"Rumi also said, 'Not only do the thirsty seek the water, but the water seeks the thirsty.' Are you thirsty, Dawood Naji?"

Dawood Naji's eyes lit up as he swallowed. "Yes, I'm thirsty to know God more."

"A man named Yahya said, 'God is love,' Dawood Naji."

"I'm thirsty to know if he is really a God of love... How I long for that to be true," Dawood Naji said wistfully.

Suliman Battuta and Dawood Naji whispered together for several hours. When they had finished speaking, Sul slept softly, and Dawood continued to think. As he thought, he drowsed. The next thing he knew, he was startled awake by a soft scurrying sound. He glanced over at Yunus Saleh. *The captain's still snoring.*

The scurrying seemed closer. He peered into the corner shadows. *There it is, a small rat.* The beady eyes focused on him. Dawood Naji's hand slowly extended towards the broken chair leg lying nearby. *I hate rats.*

With a rapid flick of the wrist, he threw the block of wood. *Wah! A direct hit!* However, instead of a squeal and a spurt of blood, the creature surprised him with a *ftzz* and a spray of sparks.

333

Alarmed, he shook Yunus Saleh awake. "*Qaa'id, Qaa'id!* They've found us!"

*

"*Qaa'id*, there's been a response to our radio message," Dawood Naji said, looking up from the radio set with a puzzled expression. "Instead of the *Abu Bakr*, a submarine will be waiting for us. Same rendezvous position, a mile south of Nash Point."

Yunus Saleh's face was disturbed. "Something must have happened to the *Abu Bakr* – but the Emir always has a back-up plan so we'll proceed as planned, Dawood Naji. Go to the beach, prepare the inflatable boat, then come back and help me transport the prisoner."

"Yes, *Qaa'id*."

Sul was in a deep sleep on the mat on the floor of the cave. Dawood Naji shook him and said quietly, "Sheikh, we must go."

As Sul began to rise there was a great explosion. The cave shook, rocks and debris fell as the ceiling and walls began to crack. The cabinet toppled to the ground, its rotten frame crumbling.

"Hurry! Collect some supplies so we can leave the cave, Dawood!"

Dawood Naji scrambled to collect provisions from the broken cabinet, throwing them in a bag. He noticed a gun and taser pistol lying among the jumbled contents. He gave the gun to Yunus Saleh and kept the taser for himself.

The earth trembled again. Dawood made his way quickly towards the cave door, eyes wide. Glancing behind, he saw Yunus Saleh pull Sul roughly to his feet. "Walk, *kaafir*, if your life means anything to you. The island is erupting around us."

Sul stood unsteadily, leaning on Yunus Saleh. Together, they made their way out of the cave. The earth continued to tremble, and rocks tumbled across their path into the ferns on all sides. The three of them picked their way down to the stream, then onward through the small valley opening out onto the sea.

Nearby they heard shouting. "Maria!" Yunus Saleh stopped, placing a warning hand over Sul's mouth.

"Ben!" Sul said involuntarily. The hand tightened on his mouth. Yunus Saleh placed his gun against Sul's temple. He whispered in Sul's ear, "Silence, *kaafir*, or I'll shoot your friend."

*

Ben climbed carefully down the rock face, feeling for toe holds. He scanned below for any sign of Maria as another rumble made him cling tight to the cliff face. Then he jumped the last metre to the valley floor.

"Maria!" he called. He emerged from the undergrowth onto the trail next to the stream. He walked carefully along the path, peering into the bushes and bracken, fearful of finding an unconscious body, or worse. He called out several more times, "Maria! Maria!"

He went back up the trail, systematically searching the area below where she'd fallen. The earth trembled beneath him again and he stopped, steadying himself.

"Stop there!" Ben froze and turned around slowly. A man in a traditional Arab robe and *keffiyeh* had Sul in an arm lock, his gun was trained on Ben.

"Who are you?" the stranger demanded.

Sul shook his head almost imperceptibly. "Answer the question, or your friend dies." The man tightened the armlock on Sul, making him call out in pain. He shifted the gun to Sul's head.

Ben was cautious, and spoke with calm. "You don't need the gun. My name is Ben."

The captor's eyes widened. "Ben Holden?" As Sul struggled, the man clenched him more tightly.

Ben's eyes narrowed and his skin prickled. Inner alarms were going off. "So you know me." A surprising peace settled in him. "Look, put the gun down and let this man go. I'll go with you."

The man relaxed his grip on Sul. "Allah has favoured me. He's delivered you into my hand." He waved the gun at Ben, "Move towards the beach."

Ben hesitated.

The man shook Sul. "This man dies unless you do as I say."

Ben didn't want to see Sul harmed more and did as the man requested, walking the fifty metres to the sand. The captor forced Sul to walk ahead of him, arm still around the neck.

Ben glanced back as he walked. "This island is covered by patrols, you won't get far on foot."

"That doesn't matter. Stop there on the sand."

Ben stopped as commanded. Waves were lapping the beach a few metres in front. He heard the man come up behind him with Sul. *Only a little bit nearer,* Ben thought.

"The island's erupting around us, toxic gases are spewing out..." Ben did not finish the sentence as the ground jerked under them again. Ben crouched and whirled around. Sul and his captor had fallen to the ground. Ben sprang towards the gun. Just as he was about to snatch it and roll, his body stiffened in mid-air. *Tasers!* He landed with a thud and darkness closed around him.

*

Dawood Naji stood near the line of bushes at the head of the beach, the taser in his hand. Yunus Saleh looked up and smiled. "Well done, Dawood Naji. Your quick action will be rewarded."

Sul crawled over to check Ben. Yunus Saleh jumped up quickly and struck Sul on the head with the gun, knocking him out.

Dawood Naji was shocked, "*Qaa'id*, what will the Emir say?"

"We don't need this apostate, Dawood. This other man is Ben Holden. He's the one the Emir really wants."

"The boat's ready. Are we taking both of them, *Qaa'id*?" Dawood Naji was uncertain.

"Leave the traitor to die on the beach," Yunus Saleh snapped, "This is the one we want."

"Yes, *Qaa'id*," Dawood Naji said, glancing with regret at Sul's unconscious form. "*Qaa'id*, there's something else..."

"Not now, Dawood! We must get away. The submarine will already be offshore. Help me carry him."

Together they carried Ben, stowing him in the waiting dinghy. Dawood Naji looked back towards the brush in the canyon and spoke quietly to Yunus Saleh. Yunus looked surprised. "Show me!" he barked.

"Yes, *Qaa'id*. There in the brush," said Dawood, as they hurried over together.

*

Kestrel moved cautiously through the shallow waters, avoiding undersea rocks and shoals near shore. Just outside the breakers, the craft rose to just under the surface.

"Nemo, how's the air outside?" Gideon asked, as he piloted the craft.

"In about seven minutes, the toxic fumes will be life-threatening, Lieutenant," he heard in his headset.

"Carlo, be ready. The valley that Ben described is in front of us. I don't know what we'll find on the beach."

"Be advised, Lieutenant, that electrically charged ash from the volcano is interfering with radio frequencies. There have been no communications with the Professor for fifteen minutes now. I'm currently connecting with you through the undersea Pelagic Array. However, I'll lose contact once you're above water."

"Got it, Neem. What about the ash? Will it affect *Kestrel*'s engines?"

"Concentrations are at a safe level now; in about ten minutes there'll be enough debris in the air to stall the engines."

"We'll be out of there by then," Gideon murmured, scanning the instruments.

Carlo was checking his gear. "We're ready. Your rebreather is next to your seat there, Gid. Put it on before you pop the canopy. I have two extras strapped to my harness for Ben and Maria."

"Good. Blowing the tanks." *Kestrel* rose to the surface, then hovered a metre above the small waves rolling towards shore. Gideon opened *Kestrel*'s cover, Carlo stood and scanned the beach.

"I see something that looks like a body. To the left, there," he pointed.

"Just one?" Gideon asked, looking up.

The craft rose, its fans beating rosette patterns into the sea surface. Gliding to the beach below the bluffs, the pontoon skids made a soft crunch as they set down on the pebbles. The fans continued whirling.

"Gideon, stay with the craft in case we need to make a quick escape. This could be an ambush." Gideon nodded as he adjusted his rebreather and mask. "I'll check who's out there." With this, Carlo jumped from the cockpit onto the shingle. He sprinted to the figure and turned it over, then waved excitedly to Gideon.

Gideon piloted *Kestrel* into the air. Cautiously, he flew the craft up six metres and moved to the head of the valley. He studied his instruments and sensors – there was no indication of movement or thermal signatures. He would have to take a risk, although there were no indications of ambush. *Kestrel* landed a just a metre from Carlo, who had put a rebreather and a mask on the fallen person.

Kestrel settled to the ground and Gideon vaulted out of the cockpit, running towards Carlo, his heart pounding with recognition. "*Baba!*" he shouted.

CHAPTER TWENTY-FOUR

16 July 2066, Caliphate submarine *Uthman*
(the same day)

The dark conning tower rose from the deep under a starry sky and the sea around grew turbulent as ballast tanks were emptied. Dawood Naji, seated in the boat as they neared the submarine, saw distant fire reflected on the wet surface of the tower. He turned to look back towards Raoul Island, where flames flickered from the sea. A fountain of incandescent lava shot into the air. Columns of smoke rose above and spread into a black canopy blotting out the stars.

At the tiller, Yunus Saleh glanced at the figures slumped in the bottom of the dinghy. "Dawood, check the bonds."

Dawood Naji squatted down to inspect the cable ties on their captives for at least the eighth time. "Yes, *Qaa'id*, they're are tight. The gags are secure. The drugs'll keep both of them out for another two hours at least."

Yunus Saleh tapped the handle of the small outboard while looking at Ben. "He won't escape us again."

"No, *Qaa'id*." Dawood Naji watched him from the darkness.

The dinghy bumped against the deck of the surfaced sub, *Uthman*. A tower hatch opened. Several men scrambled up and over the ladder onto the deck. Dawood Naji threw the bow line to them and the small rubber boat was secured to the vessel's deck.

"Bring two stretchers," Yunus Saleh snapped.

A man spoke gruffly into his headset. Moments later the stretchers were conveyed to the men on the deck and they rolled the limp body of Ben onto one, strapping him down, and the second body onto the other stretcher. Using a small crane fitted into the top of the tower, the men winched the stretchers up alongside the tower and lowered them into the hatch. Yunus Saleh followed Ben's body, climbing up the ladder into the sub.

Dawood Naji and the crew quickly stowed the dinghy and scrambled up the conning tower. The air from the volcano was foul, even at this distance. *Let's leave this cursed place!* Dawood Naji glanced once more towards the island. There were many things he regretted in his life but leaving that good man on the beach to die had just moved to number one. Just then a stream of rocks and molten lava blasted high into the air and he sealed the hatch quickly.

*

Yunus Saleh waited in the dark room as the glowing orb grew before him. *I'm developing a distinct hatred for holo-displays.*

The image of the Emir emerging in the orb startled him as always. Yunus Saleh touched his chest and bowed.

"Emir. That was superb planning, Excellency. We have met the sub you sent as a back-up to the *Abu Bakr*. The captain of the *Uthman* has informed me that the ship we had been expecting had been sunk. What happened?"

Abdul Qawwi's face clouded and Yunus Saleh regretted asking.

"We don't know. An investigation's in progress. This sub had been protecting the ship and its sensors showed the sea was empty around them. We do not know where the explosives that sank the ship came from. Another trick of the infidels. No matter. This submarine will take you to an aircraft carrier near New Zealand, at which point your prisoner will be transferred to my palace by jet."

"Excellent plan, Emir." Yunus Saleh was going to say more, but the Emir interrupted him, "Give me your report, Captain!"

"Emir, sir. We had word that a Pelagic Ranger unit was coming to intercept *Shaheen*. We were not far from Raoul Island so we surfaced. I took a party in the rubber raft to shelter the apostate in our safe house on the island, sending my crew to secure the meteorological station. We discovered that a Pelagic Ranger unit had somehow tracked us onto the island."

"You managed to evade them?"

"We did evade them for the most part. As God willed, a volcanic eruption happened soon after I lost communication with those two crewmen at the station. We had to evacuate quickly, so we left them behind. Then, *alhamdulillah*, as we were coming out onto the beach, Emir, God delivered into my hands the infidel you are looking for."

"You mean Ben Holden?" Abdul Qawwi was incredulous.

"Yes, Emir." A glow of satisfaction flooded through Yunus Saleh.

"Finally. Well done, Yunus Saleh. What about the apostate, Suliman? Did you kill him?"

Yunus Saleh squirmed, looking down. "We left him behind, Emir, judging that you'd want us to bring this other man. The volcanic gasses were overpowering us and we left him there to die in the fumes."

"Idiot! You should've made sure he was finished." Abdul Qawwi glared at him.

Glad I'm eight thousand miles away, Yunus Saleh thought.

"Yes, Emir. But I've got some more good news." Yunus Saleh looked up, smiling. He'd kept the best card for last.

17 July 2066, Palace of the Emir, Bosaso
(the next day)

Ben stood on an urban street at twilight. Crowds milled around him, anxious. "It's coming," someone screamed from down the street. A group clustered at the corner of a building, peering around into the next street and Ben watched as a ripple of panic went through the crowd. People began yelling and running from the corner.

Ben walked against the crowd, jostled by the mob now sprinting past him. He pressed against the flow of people, pushing through them, drawn towards the danger.

"Watch out!" someone warned, stumbling against him. "Wrong way, kid!" another called as he passed. "What're you doing?!" a woman screamed, looking at him with horror.

Ben continued towards the source of the panic. The masses thinned as they all rushed towards safety. Ben turned the corner.

The street was eerily empty. At the far end, a grotesque, gorilla-like creature thundered towards him, the ground trembling with its every step. It tossed cars in its path to the sides effortlessly and its arms spanned the avenue, crushing the sides of buildings on either side as it advanced.

Someone was next to him. It felt like Paul Whitestone, but he knew it wasn't. Without turning, he asked the Presence, "What is this?"

"Walk closer. You'll see," came the answer. Against all his self-protective instincts, Ben obeyed.

He continued towards the monster that towered above him, blotting out the stars. When he was about five metres from it, the terrifying shape shimmered and changed. Ben took a few more steps and it shrank until it was no more than a gibbering monkey, a metre tall. The monkey grimaced at him, sniggering as it did so.

Ben looked around, amazed. The road, buildings, and cars were not damaged, there was no sign of the destructive spree he had just witnessed with his own eyes. The monster and its devastation had all been an illusion.

"Be gone," the Presence next to him said softly and with authority. The monkey screamed as it scampered into the shadows of an alley.

"What was that?" Ben asked, watching the tiny creature flee.

"The Father of Lies," came the answer.

The scene around him changed and Ben now stood at the edge of a sea. He turned his head, wanting to see who his companion was – but saw only a brilliant light. Brighter than the sun, although his eyes didn't hurt. As he watched, the light grew smaller and smaller, receding away from him and into the sky. It ascended into its place as the brightest star, above a horizon split with the first streak of dawn.

*

Ben slowly opened his eyes. At least, he tried to; one eye was swollen shut. Through the other, he found himself looking at the morning star through an open balcony door.

A chilling breeze blew in from the sea beyond the veranda. Shifting, he found himself bound to a hard chair, his arms and legs were tied.

Then he felt the pain. *My ribs, back, and head.* He groaned softly. His mind struggled to remember. *How did I get here?* A memory surfaced, *The struggle on the beach… Sul!*

He stayed very still – there was a conversation going on in the room in Arabic. He closed his eye again and listened.

"Emir, everything is set now. The drilling companies have moved their equipment into position and only await the data from the memory device to know precisely where to inject super lubricating fluid to release stress points in the faults."

"Good Yunus Saleh, as soon as this data device is unlocked, we'll stream it to our operatives. *Alhumdillah!* After so many years, we're now close."

"Yes, Sheikh."

Ben's chair was moved and he groaned.

"He's awake, Emir," someone in the shadows observed.

Ben lifted his head to look around the room.

A gecko stalked a fly on the ceiling above the window. A man in black robes with gold trim was standing in a dark corner. The figure waited a moment, studying Ben, then walked into the light. "Ah, Professor Holden. Professor Ben Holden. I'm glad to see you awake – I've been looking forward to our meeting for many years."

Ben's eye narrowed as it took in this man. "Who're you?" His voice caught; his words came out slurred. *Did they drug me?*

"I am Abdul Qawwi, Emir of the Somali Emirate. Yunus Saleh, bring the man some water."

Yunus Saleh. Ben recognized the man from the beach. *He had a gun to Sul's head.*

Yunus slipped out and returned with water, holding the cup to Ben's lips. Ben stared at the man as he took sips, he was very thirsty.

Abdul Qawwi, Yunus Saleh. Where have I heard these names before? Ben struggled, fighting to think clearly. In a flash, he recalled the face of that prisoner calmly committing suicide in the police cell in Grit, Arizona. *That man mentioned Abdul and Yunus before saying, "I go to paradise."*

"I would have liked to have met under different circumstances, of course," the Emir continued. "However, the Pelagics have interfered with our plan. All praise to Allah, who has finally brought you into my power. I have been looking for you for a long time."

Ben consciously took note of the men in the room, memorizing their faces, watching their stance, seeing how they were armed. *An elite squad, probably the Emir's bodyguard.* As his gaze swept the room, he noticed a familiar object lying on the table across the room. Lisa's data device. Anger welled up in him. Ben fought for calm, to detach himself from the internal rage at this man. Then a voice in his head, Lisa's voice, said *"Forgive them Ben."*

It was like a switch went off. Peace spread through him along with a calm, clear mind. He studied the man in front of him and said matter-of-factly, "Yes, I know who you are. You murdered my wife and son. And that data device belongs to my wife." His eyes turned steely.

"Very good, Professor. You catch on quickly."

"And I know about your plan to unleash a cascade of earthquakes on the North American continent." This was still mainly guesswork, but Ben was gratified to see the startled look on the man's face, quickly followed by a new wariness.

Ben glanced at the device which glowed a steady blue. "And you need my help to access that data."

Abdul Qawwi composed himself, "Yes, Professor. The device has confirmed your biometrics, but now you must say the password, to provide your voice print." He smiled before continuing. "Apparently, the sensors on the device can detect stress. If there's no sign of duress, the files will open. A thorough encryption package, I must admit. So, if you please, please speak calmly."

"And why would I want to help you?"

"Yes, that *is* the topic we must address. It seems we must convince you to help. Of course, torture is out of the question, it would only add stress to your voice." A smile spread over the Emir's face. "However, I think we've found something persuasive. Yunus Saleh?"

Yunus Saleh left swiftly through a door on the other side of the room, then returned. He pushed a wheelchair bearing another figure. As they passed the window, the first rays of dawn caught the blue eyes of the woman in the chair. She looked up and gasped, "Ben!"

Ben tensed; the device which was still scanning him shifted to a blinking red.

"Ah, as I thought. I see she means something to you, Professor." Abdul Qawwi sounded almost gleeful.

A spasm of panic had rippled through Ben, then disciplined calmness returned like the stilling of a pond. The pod shifted back to a steady blue.

Ben considered Abdul Qawwi with a firm gaze. "Yes, I do have feelings for her."

Maria gasped, eyes wide. Ben's eyes flicked to her and then back to Abdul Qawwi. "But that doesn't matter. Your plan could kill thousands, maybe millions." His eyes lingered over Maria as he added sadly, "I couldn't live with that."

Maria smiled at him, whispering, "Yes, that's the right choice, Ben."

Yunus Saleh slapped her. "Quiet!"

Maria moaned and Ben struggled in his bonds. The data device flashed red. Abdul Qawwi looked back and forth between them, then held Ben's eyes, musing. "I wonder how strong your resolve really is, Professor. We'll have to test it. Dawood Naji!"

A thin, bearded man entered, hoisting a bag onto a table near the French doors. The man glanced over and Ben was surprised by the sadness in his eyes. Abdul Qawwi walked over, "Thank you, Dawood Naji." Opening the bag, he pulled out an ancient looking metal instrument.

"A thumb screw. This one dates back to the days of the Ottoman Empire," Abdul Qawwi said casually. "Used to crush a person's fingers. It takes quite a while. I've heard that the pain is excruciating. When finished with one finger, we go on to the next. Then we start on the toes…"

Lisa's data device flashed red again. Ben willed himself relaxed.

Blood drained from Maria's face. She looked over at Ben and shook her head slightly. "Still not worth it, Ben," she whispered. Yunus Saleh struck her again. She straightened her head and glared at him.

A gecko chirped on the ceiling above them.

"Hold her hand, Yunus Saleh." Yunus reached down, gripping Maria's right hand, and forced her smallest finger out. Abdul Qawwi calmly attached the torture instrument to it and began turning the screw, all the while watching Ben.

Maria calmly held Ben's gaze and smiled. As the pressure increased, the smile froze and turned to a grimace. She closed her eyes, tension written across her brow in beads of sweat. A slow moan, then an involuntary scream escaped her lips.

The data device flickered blue then red, blue then red. Frantically, Ben's thoughts whisked through scenarios, searching for a plan. *Nothing.*

The device turned blue again, though tendrils of despair began to brush against the edges of Ben's soul. He glanced out the window, the star was still above the horizon. Somehow seeing the steady light held his inner darkness at bay and allowed an irrational hope to grow.

The gecko chirped again, stalking a fly, seemingly oblivious to the drama going on in the room below. Ben noticed a second gecko had joined the hunt.

*

Twelve crouched figures, guns held low, crept out of the water. They became shadows within shadows among the rocks at the base of the overhanging cliff. A dark craft with rotors whirling noiselessly glided after them and rested on the sand at the water's edge.

Six of the soldiers climbed onto the outside of *Kestrel* and squatted down, keeping their centre of gravity low. The aircraft rose against the darkness of the cliff and began depositing them at regular intervals on the southern face. As they came to their appointed spot, each leapt off, and clung to the rock, their camouflage suits rendering them invisible. They placed chock anchors in crevices around them and attached lines to secure their position. Then each slowly worked his way upwards, until they came to their assigned position to wait just under the cliff edge.

Meanwhile, *Kestrel* ferried the other six around the point, to the northern cliff face and deposited them in the same way. Just above the clinging combatants, over the cliff edge, was a plateau: the palace and grounds of Emir Qawwi of the Somali Emirates. Guards paced the palace gardens and kept vigil over the surrounding sea. Several sea gulls keened noisily in the skies above them.

Beyond the cliffs where the headland sloped down to the beach, a wooden dock ran out into the Gulf of Aden. The Emir's yacht was tied up alongside and a guard stood smoking at the end of the pier, the cigarette glowing at slow, regular intervals.

A squeal in the water caught the guard's attention. A grey bottle-nosed head appeared and nodded at him. He turned to look at it more closely and, without warning, another dolphin shot from the water. Jumping over the dock, it knocked the man into the sea. Once he was in the water, waiting hands pulled him down. Another figure climbed the ladder at the edge of the dock and took the guard's place. He picked up the dropped cigarette pack and lighter, then casually lit another cigarette. Water dripped from his trouser legs.

"Carlo, we have eyes at the end of the dock." Lorenzo held position twenty metres beyond the end. "Dolphins report the waters are clear of divers. We'll disable the patrol boats off the coast."

"Roger that, Renzo." Carlo watched the display in front of him intently as Gideon piloted the craft. "Green team, I'm sending you live positions of the guards in the gardens taken by the gull drone and thermal images of inside the palace."

"Roger, *Kestrel*, we see them on our displays." The unit leader mouthed silently, swinging from a rope on the rock face.

"Blue team, do you have the data?"

"Roger, *Kestrel*, copy. They're on our screens as well." A man peered over a boulder, with a line of crouched men behind him in the ravine to the east of the palace grounds. He signalled to his team to spread out and begin working their way up the slope leading to the palace entrance that faced inland. Their movements were unseen by the cameras mounted at regular intervals along the walls.

Carlo straightened in his seat in *Kestrel*, "OK, all teams. The mission is go. I repeat, the mission is go."

Simultaneously, twelve grenades were lobbed up onto the plateau of the palace grounds. They bounced and rolled on the lawn. Each had blinking red lights which attracted the attention of the guards. Each red light blossomed into a brilliant white flash, followed by an explosion which blinded and stunned the guards. *Kestrel* rose above the cliff edge and its rail guns silently took down fifteen of the Emir's men. Its lasers then quickly targeted the cameras around the compound. The Emir's security shield had been penetrated.

The commandos quickly climbed the few metres onto the grounds and spread out through the gardens. One of the guards who had evaded the *Kestrel* attack by hiding behind a tree now shouted towards the house. It was the last sound he made.

*

Sweat glistened on Ben's brow. Maria's scream echoed in his mind, the end of her little finger was now a bloody mess. She had fainted.

"Yunus Saleh, wake her." Yunus Saleh put smelling salts under Maria's nose and she woke, wild-eyed and struggling to thrash out. Abdul Qawwi calmly moved the instrument up to the next section of finger.

The data device glowed red.

"This can stop any time, Professor. Just calm yourself and say the password," he said, glancing at Ben.

The woman Ben now realized he loved was being tortured. *I might lose her. Like I lost Lisa. To the same man!* It would be so easy to stop this but he could not do that – even at the risk of Maria's life. His felt his soul being shredded within him.

His mind flashed to Paul, to Paul's certainty that there was order behind the universe. *Where is that order? Or is Paul's belief a lie?*

Then he remembered the image from his dream of the raging monster being reduced to a gibbering monkey. An unarticulated prayer flew from his heart as he noticed the star still gleaming in the night sky outside. What he saw outside the doors made him suddenly squeeze his eyes shut and turn his head away.

A blinding white light crossed in front of the star as it hurtled towards them, flooding the room.

"Dawood Naji! What is that light?!" Abdul Qawwi snapped, blinking.

One of the guards stumbled towards the balcony, cried out, and collapsed before he could step outside, blood streaming from his head.

Seeing the guard yelp and fall, Dawood Naji flattened himself against the wall, inching towards the window with caution.

"Get down, Emir!" Yunus Saleh shouted, standing next to Maria, "Guards! Cover the Emir! We're under attack."

Ben's instinctive move to close his eyes saved his eyesight. He knew what the light indicated: enhanced magnesium grenades, designed to blind as well as stun.

Now he opened his eyes and surveyed the room. The guards were crouched in a circle as they sheltered the Emir. Two guards, temporarily blinded, were in the lead, feeling their way towards the exit. Abdul Qawwi was on his hands and knees, cowering within his human shield. A bullet deflected off a guard's shoulder and struck the wall to Ben's left.

Once out of range of the window, the guards lifted the Emir bodily and sprinted through the door. Abdul Qawwi glanced across the room as he left, sending Ben a furious glare. "Take the girl to a safe place," he called to Yunus Saleh.

Yunus Saleh backed away from the danger of the open window, pulling Maria in the wheelchair with him. Yunus could not follow the Emir and his guards because crossing in front of the window would expose him to the gunfire. He continued backing and went out another door. As they left, Ben noticed something fall from the ceiling onto Maria's lap.

Dawood Naji had pulled out his gun but was making no bold moves. *Probably wise, there are snipers in the trees by now*, Ben thought as he watched. Another guard remained behind with them and Ben spoke to them in Arabic, "My brothers, you are surrounded by snipers. Surrender and save yourself. There's no shame in admitting defeat."

Dawood Naji looked at him, uncertain. He glanced at the other guard and his features hardened, "We cannot, *kaafir*," he grunted.

Something landed on Ben's shoulder. He turned his head to see the small gecko that had been on the ceiling a moment before. The gecko fixed its eyes on him, then spoke with Carlo's voice, "We're here, Ben."

The tiny robot scuttled down his arm. He felt a flash of intense heat on his wrists as it melted his bonds. The creature then ran down his leg and melted the restraints there.

Ben surveyed the room, considering his options.

Yunus Saleh reappeared at the door, glanced at Ben, then at Dawood Naji and the guard. "Watch them, Dawood Naji. I'll be back with reinforcements." Yunus slammed the door as he left again.

Dawood Naji crouched next to the balcony opening, gun at the ready, peering at the garden. The gecko was now on the floor, next to Dawood Naji. Plaster suddenly exploded near Dawood's temple – he dodged it and grunted at the guard, "Move the prisoner further away from the window, we mustn't let them take him from us."

The guard lay on the floor, reached over, and grabbed the leg of Ben's chair, and Ben allowed himself to be pulled closer to the guard and Dawood Naji. The gecko skittered closer to the balcony.

"Dawood," the guard muttered, "they'll be storming the room any minute. What do we do?" In a flash, Ben whirled out of the chair, grabbed the gun from the guard, and slammed the unsuspecting guard into the wall with a powerful kick.

Ben and Dawood Naji crouched, guns pointed at each other. "Dawood Naji, if you shoot me, that data will be useless." Ben nodded at the table where the data device lay. "The Emir won't be happy about that."

"No." Dawood Naji's voice wavered as he glanced at the pod, then the guard. The man lay senseless.

"Carlo," Ben said out loud, "Maria's been taken by the Emir and his men."

"Who is Carlo?" Dawood Naji looked around. Ben took advantage of the distraction, closed the distance and wrested the gun from Dawood Naji in one quick twist.

"On the ground!" Ben commanded.

Dawood Naji lay down. Ben looked around but there was nothing to tie him with in the empty room. "Sorry, Dawood Naji," he whispered, and knocked him on the head with the gun.

"Copy, Ben," the gecko said. "We're monitoring the movements of Emir and his guards in the building using thermal scans. It seems that they're headed for a safe room in the centre of the Palace. We'll leave them be for the moment. A team of three are coming to get you and Maria. Nice work, by the way."

A grappling hook clanked on the balcony and three black figures scrambled into the room. Ben directed two to watch the doors. The remaining one came alongside Ben and assessed Ben's wounds.

"No time for that," Ben said. The man nodded and backed off.

"Carlo, where've they gone?" Ben took the gecko off the wall, fixing it to his shoulder.

"To the right, out the door. Down the hall twenty metres, then turn left.

We're on the clock, Ben. Caliphate reinforcements are on their way. We won't be able to hold this plateau long. You only have a few minutes, then we've got to get out of here."

"Roger that." Ben waved the three men through the door with him. They sprinted down the hall. One moved in front, peeked around the corner and gave the "all clear" sign and they swept into the next hallway.

"Ben, the guards have taken the Emir down the stairs. Their thermal images have disappeared, I think they have him in the safe room in the sub-basement."

"Maria?"

There was a pause, "She's still in the wheelchair by the elevator. I dropped a gecko into her lap as she left, and it has melted her bonds but I can't communicate with her. There are five men with her. They're fifteen metres to the right around the next corner."

"Copy, going silent."

"Roger, good luck," Carlo said.

The four crept quietly in a line to the next corner. They heard the elevator chime. This hall opened out onto a rooftop garden, with colonnades along three sides – in the centre, a fountain splashed, incongruously peaceful in the midst of the violence. Ben peeked around the corner and saw the elevator to the right.

"Go!" Ben directed. "Don't let them get in the elevator."

The lead commando unclipped two devices from his belt and rolled them along the pavement towards the elevator. The first exploded in a brilliant light and a stunning explosion and the second gave off a local electromagnetic pulse that fried the circuitry of the elevator, leaving the doors half open and stopping the communications of the guards. The guards with Maria shot blindly into the hall.

"Stop!" Yunus Saleh shouted. "Hold these *kaafirs* off while I get her into the stairwell."

During the seconds of confusion, the commandos with Ben sprinted to bushes and rocks in the garden for cover, maintaining fire on the men near the elevator. Two of the Caliphate guards fell under the hail of bullets, and two managed to squeeze inside the elevator, using the half open doors as shields.

The guards sustained cover fire from the elevator, while Yunus Saleh rolled Maria onto the stairwell landing. One of the men inside the elevator began to crank the doors closed by force. When they were shut, two commandos sprinted forward and checked the vitals of the fallen guards, they looked at Ben and shook their heads.

Ben signalled the third commando to follow him to the stairway entrance. Ben took one side of the door, and motioned the commando to take the other side. He counted to three with his fingers, the commando opened the door and Ben rushed through with his gun ready. He was greeted with the sight of Maria calmly standing next to her wheelchair.

"What took you so long?" she smiled.

Ben whirled and looked around. *Nothing.* He looked back at Maria.

"All sorted," she pointed down the stairs – Yunus Saleh lay sprawled at the next landing.

"He was talking to his friends down the stairwell. I quietly rolled up behind him and gave him a good shove and the stairs did the rest. I think he's still alive."

The gecko on her shoulder said, "Ben, Maria, we've got to get out of here. All the commandos are evacuating except for those with you. Caliphate helos are on their way, they will be here in ten minutes."

"I love these geckos, Carlo!" Maria said, winking at Ben, though he saw her eyes were strained, and she cradled her damage hand. A drop of blood fell to the floor at her feet.

"Maria, you need to move!" the gecko scolded.

They went back out the elevator and joined the three commandos. The medic looked at Maria's broken finger, skilfully and swiftly applying a dressing and splint. "That should hold you until we get to better medical facilities," he whispered, efficiently repacking his kit.

"Thank you," Maria mouthed as they gathered in a defensive formation to return to the balcony.

As they began to move back the way they had come, shots erupted from the far side of the garden and Ben, Maria, and the commandos took shelter behind some rocks. They were still ten metres from the safety of the hallway they had come out of.

"The Emir's men have just entered the garden and pinned us down, Carlo," Ben said to his gecko.

"We're on it," the gecko chirped.

Within seconds, they saw *Kestrel* sweep up and open fire on the troops at the far end. A number fell before they could take cover.

It was enough of a distraction, the three commandos became a shield, moving towards the corridor with Ben and Maria crouching behind them.

But just as they reached the entrance, one of their commandos was shot and fell a few metres from the hallway entrance. Ben, Maria, and the other two made it into the hallway. The wounded commando began crawling towards them.

"Cover me," Ben said and crept out under the hail of covering fire. He grabbed the commando by his collar and dragged him back into the hallway. The corpsman picked the wounded man up into a fireman's carry and started running down the corridor with Maria. Ben and the other commando backed quickly behind them, covering the retreat.

They turned the next corner and sprinted to the room where Ben and Maria had been held captive. They entered cautiously, but Dawood Naji and the guard were apparently still unconscious.

"Hurry," the gecko said. Running to the balcony, one commando vaulted over the railing and down the rope. Ben helped the corpsman hand down the wounded commando. The corpsman followed down the rope and Ben watched them carry the injured man to a velocicopter that touched down on the lawn and took off just as quickly. Carlo was below, waving them to come down.

Ben turned to help Maria but, just as she reached the rope, something grabbed him from behind and pulled him back. Ben twisted and rolled, finding himself facing the guard, who now pulled a knife. They circled each other, the guard lunged, Ben took his momentum and threw him, but the guard gripped Ben's shirt and they rolled on the floor, fighting.

The guard ended up on top of Ben and began forcing the knife towards his chest. Ben gripped his hand and twisted. Suddenly, there was a crash and the guard went limp.

Ben looked up into Maria's eyes. She was holding the remains of a chair. Ben smiled with relief. "I had him!"

Maria pushed the man off and smiled back, "Let the record show that I saved your life yet again. The cost of the next dinner keeps going up."

Ben laughed, "Worth every penny."

The gecko chirped, "Down the rope. *Now.*"

Ben ran to the table, grabbed the red winking data device and shoved it into his pocket. "What's that?" Maria looked at him curiously.

"No time. I'll explain later."

Sprinting to the balcony, Maria swung over and grabbed the waiting rope. She slid expertly to the ground. Ben looked on in admiration. She looked up at him, "Come on!"

Ben followed quickly and, once on the ground, Carlo came over to them. "Ben. Maria. Glad you're safe. Caliphate reinforcements are four minutes out. Gotta leave. Now."

Mist rolled across the headland. Ben took in the scattered bodies and signs of struggle. Shadowy velocicopters were taking to the air in the fog nearby. Navigation lights were all off. Figures were climbing aboard the last one in disciplined groups in the dark. The aircraft lifted off into the streaming haze.

Kestrel landed nearby. The canopy popped open to reveal Gideon at the controls. He waved them on.

Sounds came from the balcony above them. They turned to see another figure clambering down the rope. Carlo trained his gun on the man, tracking his progress to the ground. It was Dawood Naji. As he turned to walk towards them, he held his hands in the air. Blood streamed down the side of his head.

"Don't shoot," he quavered. "Please take me with you."

Gideon had run over to his waiting comrades. "He was one of our captors," Maria explained.

"Wait!" Dawood Naji shouted, dropping to his knees and staring at the ground, trembling. "I seek sanctuary with Sheikh Suliman."

Gideon walked over and grabbed the man. "What do you know about my father!"

Dawood Naji looked up, "You are the apostate's son?"

Gideon struck him.

"Please," Dawood Naji whimpered. "Your father helped me. I was with him in the cave. Ask him. I want to come with you. I want to join the Sheikh's clan."

Gideon looked at Ben and Carlo, then at *Kestrel*, "This is our ride. The last one. The bad guys are two minutes away." Gideon looked back at Dawood Naji.

He spoke into his microphone, "Kermadec Base. This is Lieutenant Battuta, please put my father, Captain Battuta, on."

Seconds ticked. They moved to *Kestrel*, and Ben, Maria, and Carlo got inside and strapped in.

"Gideon, son, this is your father." His voice was weak.

"*Baba*, do you know a Dawood Naji? He said he was in a cave with you."

There was a moment's silence. "Yes, son. What does he want?"

"He wants to come with us."

"Then let him come, son."

"*Baba*, he is one of the men who captured Ben and Maria."

"Bind him then, son. But bring him. If he has asked for sanctuary, we must be merciful, as our Father is merciful."

Carlo jumped back down and pulled Dawood Naji's hands roughly behind him, securing them with zip ties.

Gideon grimly kept his gun trained on Dawood Naji. "Get in the aircraft then. Carlo, watch him."

"Like a hawk." Ben helped to pull Dawood Naji into *Kestrel* and Carlo followed him aboard, his gun pointing at Dawood Naji's back. Gideon pulled himself up onto the craft and the canopy quickly closed behind him. He rolled into his seat and breathed a sigh of relief.

"We just have time to get out over the water, active camouflage will protect us for a while."

Kestrel lifted off quickly, spun towards the open ocean and sped away through the thickening cloud. Mist swirled in its wake.

17 July 2066, 45 miles south-west of Socotra Island
(the same day)

Kestrel raced along, seven metres off the rolling swells of the sea. They were just west of the island of Socotra. *Kestrel's* skin mimicked the bright surface beneath them, making them invisible from above.

"Caliphate fighters are still pursuing you, Captain Marcelli, they're searching for you. I detect a new Caliphate fighter group swinging around from the eastern point of Socotra. They will cut off your escape into international waters beyond the sea border of the Caliphate. The velocicopters are just crossing into international sea-lanes, but still in range of the fighters. Pelagic *Sea Wasps* will join them in ten minutes, as escorts to the nearby Mascarene Plateau Township's airbase."

"Thanks, Nemo." Carlo watched the pattern of the jets on his display.

Ben now sat in the rear jump seat, an eye on the bound Dawood Naji.

Maria glanced at Ben. In his hand Ben had pulled the still blinking data device he'd taken from Abdul Qawwi's palace. "What *is* that thing?"

Ben was silent for a few moments. Finally, he said, "Because of the data on this device, my wife and son were murdered, I was kidnapped, and this whole mess took place."

"Wow," Maria said simply, "what type of data is it?"

"Something the Caliphate is desperate to get their hands on," Ben said, his voice tinged with sadness. "Nemo, please give me a secure link to the US Geological Survey headquarters. I want to relay the final algorithm of Dr Lisa Holden."

"Yes, Professor, I'm opening a channel."

Ben spoke with calmness to the data device, "Open most recent algorithm and data construction of Dr Lisa Holden."

"Biometrics of Ben Holden confirmed. Decrypting algorithm and data. Please confirm password."

"Sand dollars," Ben said.

"Password confirmed."

"Transmit to US Geological Survey data banks on a secure channel."

"Voice print of Ben Holden confirmed. Checking channel. Channel secure. Transmitting... Completed."

Nemo's voice resumed, "Director Banks at the Geological Survey confirms secure receipt of transmission, Professor. He sends you thanks for this valuable material and will alert Professor Hakim. He has a number of questions for you."

"Thank you, Nemo. Please inform him I'll contact him soon to fill in the details he needs."

"Done, Professor."

"Erase memory," Ben spoke to the device again, a deep weariness in his voice.

Maria watched him intently, "I'm so sorry Ben," she said as she reached out with her good hand to touch his hand.

Ben looked up and put his hand on top of hers.

"Current estimation based on the search pattern of the fighters: they will reach us within six minutes," Nemo reported.

Ben abruptly broke his reverie. "Carlo or Gideon, do you know anyone nearby?"

"Yes, I've got a friend in another pod called Dilshan Al Kuri," Gideon said, "He married a girl on Socotra and I think he still lives there. What're you thinking?"

Ben explained his idea.

"Excellent," Carlo said.

Gideon scrolled through a list of names on his display. "Nemo, connect me with Dilshan Al Kuri on a secure line please."

"In progress."

Gideon spoke Arabic quietly into his microphone while Carlo scanned a holographic map of the area south of Socotra. "Nemo, take us to where the continental shelf drops off, near the village of Mahfirhin on the south coast."

"There's a bay south-west of Mahfirhin which will conceal *Kestrel* well, Captain."

"Perfect, guide us in."

Turning to the others, Carlo said, "We can hide under these cliffs here." He pointed at a point where the underwater canyon connected with a cave at the base of the sheer rock face in the holo-display.

*

The young navigator turned to the pilot, "*Qaa'id*, I detected a brief blip, three miles south south-east of Mahfirhin – but now it's gone."

"It could be them." Toggling his mike, the Caliphate pilot announced, "Investigating possible contact just south of Mahfirhin on Socotra Island."

"Roger, Companion One leader," they heard in their headsets.

"Bearing two-four-six, *Qaa'id*."

The pilot of the search and rescue aircraft swung to the new bearing.

"Release a set of sono-drones when we're over the area," the pilot called to the navigator.

"In twenty seconds, *Qaa'id*."

The sleek craft swung over the spot where the contact had briefly appeared. Six small torpedo shapes were dropped into the choppy seas.

"Fish are in the water, *Qaa'id*."

"Very good." The two men listened intently to the pinging on their headsets, their eyes concentrating on the displays.

After a few moments, the pinging increased. The icons of the sono-drones on their display converged on an area where the continental shelf dropped into a undersea canyon.

As they watched, a piece of the cliff seemed to detach and *Kestrel* emerged from its hiding place to plunge deeper into the marine canyon.

"Companion Two and Three Teams, I think we've found them," the pilot spoke into his microphone.

"We're moving towards you. Paint a target on the craft."

The navigator released drones to follow the craft that was wending through the deep canyon.

The pilot watched the drama below intently. "Fire at it, Hassan."

"Yes, *Qaa'id*." A bright light shot out of one of the drones, exploding near the drifting shape.

The shape began to ascend quickly towards the surface.

"Quick! They're attempting to reach the surface and make a run for it."

"This is Companion Two leader. Our jets are closer to the target. We'll fire from here."

The small search and rescue aircraft trembled as the Caliphate jet roared past. *Kestrel* leapt from the surface of the sea about a mile and a half ahead of them, banked to the left, then re-entered the sea.

"They're trying to hide in the water," the jet pilot's voice sounded in their headsets. The jet turned and circled the area. "They can't escape, the sono-drones are tracking them."

Kestrel burst from the sea again – this time, half a mile to their left. The jet corrected and moved towards its target but *Kestrel* banked sharply right and disappeared in the sea again.

"We've got them next time they surface," the jet pilot's voice was confident in their headsets. "Missiles armed."

Kestrel appeared in a spray of sea water a few miles further ahead and the pursuing jet launched a barrage of missiles. *Kestrel* jerked down and slipped into the water. The missiles overshot, exploding, impotent, just beyond the wake left by the amphibious craft.

"No!" they heard on their headphones.

A moment later, *Kestrel* appeared again to the right. The jet fired another volley of missiles as *Kestrel* rose above the sea. In less than three seconds, there was a deafening explosion. *Kestrel* was blown to pieces.

"*Yaha!*" the fighter pilot cheered. "Another infidel has fallen by the sword of the Caliphate! Let's head home."

The jet and the search planes veered north-west, swooping over the island of Socotra and back towards the coast of Somalia.

18 July 2066, Socotra Island
(the same day)

A vivid starry expanse arched above four shadowy figures as they emerged from the waves and walked onto the shore – two of them were carrying a fifth body. They pressed past the surf, onto the shore, then paused to remove masks and fins and evaluate their surroundings.

The beach was deserted. A steady wind swept from the sea and whitecaps formed beyond the waves. There was no sign of any vessels on the sea or in the air.

Carlo set Dawood Naji on a rock, a gun trained on him while he removed Dawood's mask and cut the bonds on his legs. "Walk," Carlo ordered.

"There," Gideon pointed, "by those rocks." The four other silhouettes followed him to the base of the cliffs and piled their gear on a flat stone.

"So sorry about *Kestrel*, Gid." Carlo glanced at his friend, then back at Dawood Naji.

Gideon sighed sadly, "Yes, I loved that craft. But the sacrifice was worth it. Our velocicopters wouldn't have got safely into international airspace without the diversion."

He brightened, "I have ideas for the next one, anyways... how to improve some of her best features..."

"Shh..." Ben cautioned, as headlights swept across the road above the beach.

Hands instinctively went to the weapons on their hips and Carlo put his hand over Dawood Naji's mouth. Dawood sat quiet, watching.

The car stopped and a door opened, then clicked shut. "We come out of nothingness..." a voice recited quietly above them.

"Scattering stars like dust," Gideon responded. *"Alhamdulillah!* Dilshan!" Gideon climbed up the small cliff onto the road and the two friends embraced.

"Just like you to use a quote from Rumi as a countersign," Carlo commented, looking at Gideon. Dilshan smiled as the others climbed up to join them.

"My father's influence," Gideon admitted.

Then he introduced his comrades, "My future brother-in-law, Carlo."

"Mabrook, congratulations!" Dilshan embraced him.

"The lovely Maria."

"Indeed," Dilshan bowed his head towards her.

"And Ben – it was his idea to contact you." Dilshan shook Ben's hand. "Glad I could help you, Ben. I owe my life to this guy," he tilted his head towards Gideon. "He saved me from certain death."

"There were only two barracuda, Dilshan." Gideon laughed, "and we were only small boys."

"They seemed big at the time, Gid. Here," Dilshan turned to the car, opening the back. "I brought dry clothes for you all. Baggy things, so they should fit. Put your gear in this duffle bag."

"Perfect. Thanks, Dilshan." Gideon handed out the clothing.

Carlo had brought Dawood Naji up the trail and Dawood watched the excitement, wary.

"Cut the bonds on his hands, Gideon. Give the man some dry clothing." Carlo nodded at Dawood Naji. Gideon reluctantly obeyed.

Maria took her pile of clothes and disappeared back down into the shadows of the cliff. A few minutes later she reappeared, dressed in a local outfit. She stuffed her exposure suit and other gear into the waiting duffle. The men had done likewise.

Carlo bound Dawood Naji's hands again and Dawood didn't resist.

Dilshan watched them, interested. "Who is the bound one?"

"A servant of the Emir of Somalia."

Dilshan clicked his tongue, expressing disapproval, "Then he's dangerous."

Dawood Naji looked at Gideon, voice full of contrition. "I'm with you now – I won't betray you. I'm finished with the Caliphate."

Dilshan was sceptical, "Really. How can we trust you?"

Dawood Naji looked at the ground, "You're right, there's no reason. The Emir has used me to cause you much harm."

Gideon shifted uncomfortably and stepped over. "Dilshan, my father was kidnapped by the Caliphate forces some time ago. He met Dawood Naji there and got to know him. My father vouches for him, which is why we let him leave with us, and why we brought him this far. It's your decision, though, Dilshan. You're putting your life on the line by helping us."

Dilshan considered. The silence was heavy. "Gideon, I've known your father almost as long as you have."

Gideon smiled, "Yes."

"'If you wish mercy, show mercy to the weak'," Dilshan recited.

"Rumi again," Gideon said wryly.

"Your father's always been a good judge of character. It *is* a risk, but I think that since we trust your father, we can trust Dawood Naji."

Dawood Naji looked up with wonder and Carlo leaned over towards him, "We'll trust you – but remember, I have a gun and I'll be watching you."

"Yes, I understand," Dawood Naji whispered.

They piled into the old Land Rover and Gideon chuckled as he slammed the rusty door shut, "I think my *great-grandfather* owned one of these."

"You should be so lucky to have one yourself," Dilshan retorted. "Easy to fix. Dependable."

The engine came to life, Dilshan put the car in gear and turned around towards the interior of the island. The mountainous spine loomed dark before them.

"Make yourselves comfortable, it'll be a long drive over those hills, across the island to the capital, Hadibu. I've made arrangements for you at the western port." No other cars were evident as they wended through the canyon and over the ridges on the rough, dirt road.

Maria lay her head on Ben's shoulder and was soon asleep. Ben watched out the window as the strange, dark landscape went by. The presence of Maria, her closeness, brought a deep peace over him.

A spontaneous prayer of gratitude welled up in Ben's heart as he remembered Lisa, Sammy, and his life with them. He sighed. *That chapter is now over.*

The act of handing the geological data into government hands seemed to have closed a door in his life. *New horizons are opening.*

Gideon and Dilshan chatted softly in the front seat, Carlo was in the far back, leaning against the side, keeping watch on Dawood Naji. The gun gripped in his hand pointed steadily at their guest. Dawood Naji dropped into a deep sleep.

*

In the early hours of the morning, the Land Rover pulled to a rest on a street next to the port. Dilshan led the group through a rip in the fence surrounding the container yard and they crept along the rows of containers, keeping to the shadows.

"A boat will be waiting for you at the docks. My friend, the owner, is a local pilot for ships coming into the harbour."

"What did you tell him about us?" Ben asked.

"I didn't need to explain. He's in this work for the money so he doesn't ask questions. He's not a friend of the Caliphate and he helps anyone who wants to leave without being noticed. This kind of thing is more common than you might believe."

Ben nodded.

They reached the end of the stacked containers. A clear, well-lit sandy area stretched between them and the dock, where a pilot boat sat ready to ferry the harbour's pilots to container ships anchored offshore. No sign of life. Then they heard a cough.

A guard was leaning against a lamp post twenty metres to the right of them, smoking a cigarette.

"Hameed won't start the boat, or even show he is there, while the guard is around."

"Gideon, give me your taser," Maria whispered, moving to the edge of the containers.

Gideon drew it from his holster and handed it to Maria, puzzled. She tucked it into her belt at the small of her back and let her loose top drop over it, hiding it from view.

Maria stepped out into the light, walking towards the guard, swaying, unsteady and stumbling.

"Soldier, do you have another one of those?" she asked, her voice slightly slurred.

From the shadows, the men watched her act, fascinated. Ben placed his hand on his pistol.

The guard straightened up at her approach, looking her over – he smiled as he pulled out a pack of cigarettes.

Maria fumbled a bit, then took a cigarette. The guard struck a match, but it went out in the wind.

Maria glanced around, and then caught the guard's eye, "Let's go behind those containers. There'll be less wind there."

His smile broadened as she turned towards the stack of containers. The guard followed her like he was on a leash and they disappeared in the shadows of the boxes. A second later, there was a flash of light, a soft *fzzt*, and Maria stepped back out of the shadows, smiling. She waved them towards the wharf.

At the end of the dock, lights came on aboard the pilot boat. The boat captain had also been watching. Dilshan led the men towards the moored boat and Maria caught up with them halfway down the dock. She reported, "I took his wallet, so it'll look like a robbery."

Dilshan whistled softly, "Wow, that was impressive. Well done."

He turned to the gathered group, "Hameed will take you out to the sea lanes. A Pelagic Territory cargo ship is due to pass by in the next hour and Hameed has arranged for you to go aboard that one. You remember Farouk, from university?"

Gideon nodded.

"The captain of the cargo ship is Farouk's father. Captain Zanafi. Zanafi knows your father well, Gideon."

"Thanks, Dilshan." Gideon embraced his friend again.

"It is a joy to see you again, my friend. And I expect an invitation to the wedding!"

"Of course!" Gideon stepped onto the boat. The others followed, each shaking Dilshan's hand in turn and thanking him. The boat pulled away into the dark night.

Chapter Twenty-Five

20 July 2066, Palace of the Caliph, Mecca, Saudi Arabia
(two days later)

Abdul Qawwi knelt on a balcony on one of the highest minarets of the Caliph's palace. There was no railing before him as he looked out over an early morning in Mecca. Brown dust clouds rolled in slow motion towards him from the horizon; as they advanced, they blotted out sections of the city below. Manacles bound Abdul Qawwi's hands and feet together; a chain ran from the manacles and were attached to a ring just behind him on the floor, constricting his movement.

Sturdy Bedouins stood guard, one on each side. Alert. Motionless. Each clenched a naked, curved executioner's sword. A black-and-white checked *kufiya* shrouded each face, allowing only gaps for their dark glittering eyes.

The wind increased in force with the approaching sandstorm. Abdul Qawwi squinted to protect his eyes; terror kept him from shutting them completely. He licked his lips, and the fine grit ground between his teeth. He wanted to hide his fear from these men but his trembling body betrayed him. The roiling cloud swept in, engulfing them and even at this height the airborne streams of sand stung and tore his skin raw.

The guards watched, impassive, as the force of the sandstorm increased. Abdul Qawwi coughed, choking on the dust. He held his head down, trying to protect his airways.

Hearing firm steps approaching from behind, Abdul Qawwi tensed. He felt a presence move in front, facing him, temporarily shielding him from the blast of sand and dust and he blinked, lifting his head, to meet the eyes of the Caliph. A shock of dread made him drop his head again.

"Look at me," Abdul Qawwi involuntarily raised his eyes again, spellbound. The world fell away and he saw only the eyes of the Caliph.

"I've entrusted you with three missions, Abdul Qawwi. And you've failed me – three times." Abdul Qawwi's limbs trembled even more.

"You have humiliated the Caliphate each time you have failed to carry out the plan." The eyes held his gaze, cold, merciless.

"My faithful fighters, my *mujahidin*, discovered you cowering in the safe room of your palace while the infidels gained control of your prisoners! Your head should be off already, cast onto the stones below."

Abdul Qawwi glanced at the guards, then at the Caliph, and wondered why he had not yet been beheaded.

The Caliph sidestepped to allow the storm to blast Abdul Qawwi again. A wave of sand whipped against his face, stinging the patches which were already red and raw. He detached himself from the agony by turning his mind inward, preparing his soul for death. Under his breath, he began to say *Al Fatiha*, the first Surah in the Qur'an: "*In the name of God, Most Gracious, Most Merciful, Praise be to God, Lord of the universe…*"

The Caliph watched him for a moment, then stepped in front again to block the sand. "However, despite these recent failures, I have noted that in the past you served the Caliphate with distinction. Part of our successes in Europe come from your efforts. You spurred many into action. Because of these past acts of faithfulness, I will give you one more chance."

Hope stirred in Abdul Qawwi's heart and the shadow of death receded just a little.

"We must teach the ocean-dwelling infidels a lesson." The Caliph turned to look beyond the swirling eddies of sand. "Especially Suliman Battuta and the seamount community who protects him and other apostates."

Then the Caliph held Abdul Qawwi's gaze. Abdul Qawwi strained to catch the next words over the howling of the wind, "You will lead a retaliatory strike against Marcelli Township. Do not fail me."

Abdul Qawwi immediately bowed further down in his chains and knocked his head against the tiled floor. "Yes, Commander of the Faithful. Your mercy is too great. I won't fail."

The Caliph studied him, "May it be. This is your last chance."

He nodded to the guards, then strode through the doorway without looking back.

The guards sheathed their swords. They released Abdul Qawwi's chains and he collapsed. Grabbing him under the arms, they dragged him to the coolness and protection inside the minaret. Then, binding his hands again roughly, they marched him, stumbling, down the spiral stairs. As they descended, blood seeping from Abdul Qawwi's raw skin left a trail of red on the marble steps.

24 July 2066, Marcelli Rise
(four days later)

With the light of the morning sun dancing on the waters around him, Pietro watched the progress of the robots below, displayed on his *Dragonfly's* monitor. *Almost half done.* The harvesters were stripping scallops off raft number twenty-three. *Might get 500 kilos of scallops from that raft. One of our most productive sectors. And the prices are high this month, Dad says.*

He looked around. *I love being out here on the open sea. In a little over a year, Dad says we'll have completed the seastead contract and the farm will be ours to keep.*

Seven-year-old Isabella was snorkelling on the far side of the scallop raft, hunting for new fish to inhabit her bedroom aquarium. She lifted her head, tossing back dark wet curls, and waved. Pietro waved back and shouted, "Izzie, I'm gonna check raft twenty-one, just over there. I'll be back in a few minutes."

Her little head bobbed up and down, dark curls throwing off flashing water drops, and she returned to the hunt. Pietro checked that a guardian drone was monitoring her, then spun his *Dragonfly* towards raft twenty-one.

Still ten minutes before the harvester finishes. Enough time to check my special project. He deftly steadied the hovering *Dragonfly* and guided it to the nearby raft which had strings of green mussels hanging below it. One line, however, held oysters he'd custom-seeded at the Huang Marine Research complex a few months ago.

He set the *Dragonfly* down next to the raft and opened its utility compartment in front of the seat. Pulling out several items, he clambered onto the raft, the boards creaking under his weight as he searched for the oyster line. *There it is – the red nylon rope.*

He pulled the line up, smiling as the oysters clicked shut one by one, in response to coming out of the water. Laying the shells carefully on the dock, Pietro took the spectre-scope from his belt and passed it over them. The screen on the device displayed the inside of the oyster shells. He paused over one shell, watching the animal inside pulsate. He measured the growing pearl inside, and continued along the line.

As part of his study of marine genetics at Huang Mariculture school, he was testing out a new strain of oysters, exploring how hereditary lines could be manipulated. *This strain is delicious and produces beautiful pearls.* He'd developed the hybrid with Professor Zhao last semester. His family had exclusive rights to the new strain and already there was a growing market for it within mainland China.

There! Among the last oyster images, he spotted one spherical object within the shells which seemed large enough. Most of the pearls were still too small to harvest, but the third oyster from the end seemed to have a good one. *I ought to let it wait another week. Maybe just a peek.*

Pulling a knife from its sheath on his exposure suit, he slit the oyster open. He scooped out the meat, popping it into his mouth. *Mmm, tasty.* He gently teased the pearl loose from the back of the shell, holding it up to the light. It sparkled, sea blue.

Judging from the size of this one, the others will be ready in time for mom's birthday. She'll love them.

An image flashed in his mind of a string of these same pearls around Oliana's neck. He was falling into a reverie, enjoying the daydream when a roar of engines jolted him back to reality. He looked around, alarmed. *Two jets above the neighbouring Visiniago farm!*

Dark objects were dropping from the jets. *What is that!?* A flash of explosions among the mariculture cages on the nearby farm sent him springing onto the *Dragonfly*. The pearl fell from his palm, rolled across the catwalk and dropped into the sea unnoticed.

"Izzie!" Pietro yelled above the growing whine of the *Dragonfly*. His sister's head popped up from the water, alarm in her eyes.

Pietro banked his machine around the raft, leaned down and scooped her out of the sea. The *Dragonfly* almost capsized, but Pietro regained control as he pulled Isabella onto the seat behind him. She clung to him in terror.

Pietro continued the momentum of the turn to circle the scallop raft then pushed the *Dragonfly* to full speed, back towards their farmstead. Several more jets roared overhead. A geyser of water erupted as bombs struck the rafts behind them.

"Elektra, alert Pelagic Defence. We're under attack!"

"Major Camden has been informed," his AI responded promptly. "There are multiple explosions along Marcelli Rise. Sea Wasps are scrambling to engage the attackers."

"Please, tell my mother that Izzie and I are safe. We're heading back to the seastead."

"Message sent, Pietro. She was concerned."

Pietro leaned into the wind, willing the Dragonfly to go faster. *Home is still two miles away.* He steered in the centre of the access channel between the cages and he could see that the attacking planes were targeting the mariculture plots. *But why?*

To his right, he noticed a shape tumble into the oyster cages. Instinctively, he turned towards where the inevitable explosion would come from and the sea erupted in front of him, a steep wave advancing rapidly. The *Dragonfly*, already travelling at high speed, continued to glide up the swell, becoming airborne at the crest. The shock wave hit them, but the *Dragonfly* provided a shield, protecting them from the water and debris coming directly at them.

Pietro could hear his sister screaming. "Hold on, Izzie," he yelled, as they landed, miraculously upright, on the other side of the swell. Oysters, ropes, and raft fragments rained down around them. Izzie was crying quietly, holding onto him with a death grip.

He let *Dragonfly* idle while he turned to hug and calm his sister. The water and debris finally stopped hissing, other explosions still sounded, but further and further away from them. Pietro shielded his eyes with his hand to track the flight path of the attacking planes through the haze. Then the explosions ceased altogether.

Izzie raised her tear-stained face.

"Brave girl," Pietro said. "Ready to go home?" She nodded her head vigorously.

Pietro turned back and revved the *Dragonfly*'s engine. *Seems to be fine. What a great machine!* He slowly picked his way through the debris, returning to clear water. As he increased the throttle, he heard a different sound in the sky above them.

He looked up and saw Pelagic *Sea Wasps* in the air, giving chase to the now fleeing attackers. Even as he watched, an enemy plane was hit by a laser blast from a *Sea Wasp*. There was an explosion on the enemy jet, sending the escaping aircraft into a spin. A few seconds later, a parachute appeared above the doomed aircraft.

Pietro let the *Dragonfly* settle and stop on the water, then he and Izzie stood up on it and cheered.

24 July 2066, Twenty-five miles north-west of Marcelli Ring

(the same day)

The squadron of seven sleek, flying-wing style Caliphate bombers skimmed the tops of the clouds at sixteen thousand feet. A group of three led the formation – about five minutes ahead of the second wave of four bombers. A Caliphate fighter escort of three squadrons had joined them an hour ago from the Caliphate air carrier *Zeynab*. There was a bright sun in a blue sky above them, but below the clouds were dark. Flickers of lightning flashed in their depths.

Abdul Qawwi stood between, and just behind, the pilot and co-pilot. His knuckles were white as he gripped the backs of their seats. The turbulence was significant, but he kept his footing, rolling with the jerks and shudders of the aircraft.

The pilot glanced uneasily at him, "We're over a storm front, Emir. Wouldn't you be more comfortable strapped in the chair there?" He nodded towards the communications officer's seat.

"I'm fine here, Captain. This is an important mission."

"As you wish, Emir."

"What's the status?"

Reluctant respect made the pilot turn again to face Abdul Qawwi. "The first three bombers," he pointed at the holo-display, "are timed to drop the first wave of torpedoes as the storm front nears the Township." He glanced at instruments, "Six minutes from now."

"Good, what is the tactical advantage of two waves?"

"Eminence, the torpedoes of the first wave will gather telemetry on the infidel community's response profile and feed this into the guidance system of the second wave. This'll allow the next drop to be far more destructive. We'll keep our fighter escort beyond their radar horizon to increase the chances of our bombers remaining undetected."

"Excellent!"

"Thank you, Emir." There was relief in the pilot's face as he turned back to his instruments.

Yunus Saleh sat nearby, strapped into what was normally the navigator's seat. Abdul Qawwi noticed the fear lurking at the edges of his eyes; the man did not look comfortable. He looked away. *Nausea can be contagious.*

"The fighter escort will be standing by at this current waypoint."

"Roger, see you soon," the pilot acknowledged.

Minutes ticked by.

The navigator poked his head in, "The timing is perfect. The first wave of bombers is coming up on the leading edge of the storm front, just six miles from Marcelli Township. They will be dropping munitions in about ninety seconds. The squadron confirmed that they will synchronize their bombing sequence, then relay telemetry to us, *Qaa'id*."

"Acknowledged," Abdul Qawwi and the pilot said at the same time. The navigator looked from one to the other, then ducked back to his temporary station. Abdul Qawwi knew that his presence made lower ranking officers uncomfortable. *I'm sure he'd be more comfortable at some distance from me.*

"Are you sure the Township cannot detect us, Captain?"

"Detection is highly unlikely, Emir. The storm below us will confuse their radar and monitoring systems. We'll drop the torpedoes just behind the leading edge of the storm, then we'll turn. The storm will give us cover as we make our way back to join our escort. Our fighter squadrons are out of detection range and they'll join us after the bombing run." The pilot moved with a calm professionalism, checking and rechecking his instruments, "The *kaafirs* will only have minutes to respond once the torpedoes have been dropped."

The pilot listened to his headphones, then looked at Abdul Qawwi. "The communication officer reports that the bombing of the sea farms has begun already."

"Too early," Abdul Qawwi growled.

"Yes, Emir. But still, this sea village below won't have much warning before the first wave of bombers strike." The pilot and co-pilot now concentrated on their instruments, steadying the plane. Tension built in the cabin as the silence stretched.

They heard the lead pilot of the first wave speak into his headset, "Release on the bombardier's mark. Three, two, one, mark!"

Three bombardiers acknowledged almost at once, "Payloads released."

On the holo-display, they saw the pilot of the lead bombers put his aircraft into a graceful U-turn and head back towards the fighter rendezvous point. The other bombers followed his lead perfectly.

"Torpedoes are in the water, Emir. We are receiving telemetry from the torpedoes," the co-pilot said, with a nervous glance at Abdul Qawwi. The Emir ignored him, a look of triumph filling his face.

24 July 2066, Marcelli Ring
(the same day)

Ben was nervous. *This is worse than the day I faced the Emir.*

Carlo looked over at him as they drove along the Marcelli Ring Road. "Relax, buddy – she likes you."

Ben's effort to smile came out like a grimace. Carlo rolled his eyes, slowed, and pulled up outside the Davy Jones restaurant. He turned to his friend, "Maria loves this place. She likes your company. You just need to show up, be yourself... and here we are!" he said reaching across and opening the door.

Ben pulled himself together and looked over at his friend. His face was a little less pale. "Thanks, Carlo. I know it's only a lunch, but..."

"But you like her too. Yeah, we know."

Ben grimaced, "That obvious?"

"Yep, *amico*, my friend. She knows too."

"Oh," was all Ben could say.

Carlo gave Ben a little push out of the car. "Go on. I'm off to meet Gideon. He just received his latest model of *Kestrel* today, fresh from Cheng 3D printers. He wants to show me all its new tricks. I think he wasn't that bothered with the destruction of his first model! It gave him an excuse to test some more ideas."

"Less than a week? That was a super-quick turnaround – Gid must be a highly valued client! Tell him I'll expect a ride soon." Ben stepped out, then looked back at Carlo. "Thanks."

Carlo smiled, called out, "Relax, Ben," then drove away.

*

Ben stood alone in front of the restaurant, allowing the tang of the salt breeze to wash over him. The sea sparkled before him like a carpet of diamonds. Above the horizon, a dark line advanced. *Hmm, a storm front.* He closed his eyes for a moment and revelled in the sun's warm embrace.

People were coming and going on the pavement around him, busy in their own worlds. He took a deep breath and the knots in his stomach relaxed a bit. He could almost hear Paul's words, "and for this you will need emotional courage. Allow love in."

A moment later, a driverless taxi pulled up. The door opened and Maria stepped out. Her dark hair was swept back and she wore a shimmering dark blue dress that hugged her curves.

Ben looked at her, stunned. A moment passed. "Wow," he said finally.

Maria smiled. "I'll take that as a compliment. For a minute, I was afraid you'd lost your voice and that I'd have to resort to sign language."

Ben laughed and the tension melted. Maria took his arm.

"How'd you know this was my favourite restaurant?"

"Your cousin dropped a hint."

"I'll have to pay him for that." They laughed together.

"What's so special about this place?"

"Well, besides the food being exquisite, if we are given a table in one of the undersea domes, there'll be a super view of the marine reserve. I heard there's an aggregation of zebra sharks in the park this month and I'd love to see that. By the way, the seared abalone is my favourite."

Ben drew her towards the entrance, "I'd love to hear more stories of what it was like to grow up here. I'm a stranger in a strange land and I'd like to understand your life better." Ben smiled down on her. *This felt so natural, to let love in.* She squeezed his arm.

As they neared the entrance, the wailing of a siren rose as red lights began to flash up and down the street. Ben and Maria both froze mid-step.

"What is it?" Ben looked around and tensed.

"Of course!" Maria said, stomping a foot and glaring at the lights. She glanced at Ben and softened, "Civil defence alert. Another date we have to postpone, I'm afraid. I'm beginning to wonder if there's a conspiracy against us."

"Something's happening so I'll have to go to my station." She smiled sadly up at him.

Ben watched all the people scurrying to their assigned places, and offered, "Is there any way I can be of help?"

Maria considered for a moment before responding, "Gideon mentioned you handled *Kestrel* very well. Are you familiar with other aircraft?"

"Yes. I'm qualified in velocicopters and jump jets."

"Major Camden knows you now; she gave you a field commission. I bet she'll let you pilot a craft. We're short of pilots here on the Ring."

"What type of crafts do you need pilots for?"

"*Sea Wasps.*" An official-looking driverless car pulled up next to them.

"Captain Romero, I'll take you to your station," a disembodied voice said as the door opened.

"Romero, authorization number 65PT390. Request permission from Major Camden for Ben Holden to be given temporary Pelagic Pilot status."

"Your authorization confirmed," the car acknowledged. "One moment."

The streets around them were emptying quickly.

"Permission granted. Major Camden has given Ben Holden temporary Pelagic Pilot status for this emergency. She thanks Ben and wishes you both luck and Godspeed."

"Let's go!" Maria jumped in the car and Ben followed her in. The door clicked shut and the car sped away.

24 July 2066, Marcelli SeaShells Complex, Marcelli Deep
(the same day)

Sally Marcelli watched with satisfaction. The sun glinted off an opalescent structure emerging from the water in the Production Tank. Her eye was on the air release rate meter. The *Periwinkle* must rise at a measured rate, to avoid over-straining the unfinished hull. The webbing of the crane now took on the weight of the vessel and the crane lifted the craft and swivelled, allowing water to drain from the vessel for a few minutes, before continuing around to bring it over the track. *I'll finish processing it in the Gecko Shed after lunch.*

Her mind drifted to Ben and Maria's recent ordeal. The Pelagic authorities were keeping it quiet because of the sensitivity of the operation. But the Caliphate was also keeping it out of the press. *Maybe their defeat at the hand of the Pelagic forces is too shameful?*

The water had finished draining, so Sally slowly manoeuvred the *Periwinkle* and left it hanging above the tracks leading to the Gecko Shed. She began shutting down the console.

Meanwhile, I have a wedding to plan! As she gazed at the *Periwinkle* swinging below, her heart swelled with the promise of life to come. *Only a few more months!*

She glanced pensively at the sea stretching to all sides. A dark storm front was advancing on the Deep from the north, riding on its shadowy curtains of rain. The ocean swells were being whipped up before it. *I don't like the look of that storm.* "Elektra, tell me about that storm please."

"The storm is due to hit Marcelli Deep in seven minutes. Conditions around the Deep are approaching sea state five. SeaShell complex has been secured for stormy weather," she responded.

"Thank you, Elektra." Sally said as the tablet in her hand pinged with more messages for her. *Yet another order for SeaShell modular components for the Ring. The Township is having a bit of a population boom.* Her mind raced through the list of new orders. Housing on Marcelli Ring was in high demand. There had been talk of building a suburb on the uninhabited seamount eighteen miles south-south-west of the Ring. *We'll need to build more growing tanks to produce the modular sections in a timely way. I'll convene a planning meeting to talk about it on Friday.*

The wail of civil defence sirens interrupted her thoughts and red warning lights flashed around the complex. "Elektra, clear the tanks and complex of all personnel. Have them assemble in the shelters."

"Yes, Sally." Moments went by, then, "Civil defence staff are at station. All civilians are proceeding in an orderly way to the shelters."

She looked below at *Periwinkle* swinging over the breakwater.

Her gaze swept across the docks, then outer gates and on towards the horizon, "What's the emergency, Elektra?"

"Four minutes ago, unknown aircraft dropped charges in the mariculture cages on the east side of Marcelli Rise. The situation is being monitored. Your command post is being activated."

The lift would take too long so Sally ran up the stairs to her office, two at a time. She sprinted through her office into the attached reinforced command bunker for Marcelli Deep.

Display screens, stretching from wall to wall, activated to her biometrics as she stepped into the command bunker. The windows offered clear views of the sea wall on three sides.

"Captain Rosalia Marcelli, Marcelli Deep Command. Identity confirmed. Defence station 5 of the Township: western industrial park. All systems nominal and ready."

Sally caught her breath and responded, "Thank you, Elektra. Display my Marcelli Deep defence sectors." She paced around the room, examining each screen. "Could this be a retaliation by the Caliphate?" she muttered, pulling her chair up to the display.

Elektra's calm voice responded, "The planes are unmarked; however, their actions are consistent with Caliphate tactics and protocols. Marcelli Deep defences are on screen four. Civilians have been evacuated to shelters, monitored on screen two. Damage control parties have been mustered, status showing on screen three. Lorenzo is forming a dolphin perimeter to the north, between the Deep and the Ring. Marcelli Deep *Sea Wasp* flights one, three, four and five are ready to launch. Two and six have just come online. Station 5 defensive forces are at the ready: aircraft and pilots in place, fixed rail guns and lasers are coming online. No threats have been detected in a three-mile radius around the Deep. A storm front is moving in from the north-west."

Sally surveyed the screens as she listened, noting each system as it blinked according to readiness: red, yellow, then green on the holo-display. Various members of civil defence were signing in that they arrived at their stations.

"Major Camden," Sally announced as she pressed her signal for readiness. "Ready for action at Marcelli Deep Command." Her heart surged with satisfaction as all sectors under her control flashed green. *A good team.*

"Reading you loud and clear, Captain Marcelli," came the Major's voice. "This is your first experience in real combat. Stay calm, trust your instincts. You will do well. Keep us apprized of your actions and observations."

"Thank you for your confidence, Major. I'll keep you posted." Sally's brows now tensed as she initiated defence protocols.

"All *Sea Wasp* flights ready for launch," Elektra informed her.

Sally moved to the screen displaying a hangar with a fleet of graceful delta-shaped aircraft, each with a sleek bump for the cockpit, ready for action. Pride stirred in her. *Those planes were designed and built here at the Deep, even their fuel has been processed from algae grown at the Rise.* "Elektra, launch *Sea Wasp* flights five and six immediately. Put three and four on high alert, pilots in planes. Have one and two on standby."

"Done, Captain Marcelli."

She watched as the ten aircraft, five in each flight, launched from hangars around the Deep. The delta wings began slotting into defensive patterns over the industrial complex.

"*Sea Wasps* from Huang Marine Research complex at the Rise have engaged the unknown aircraft. Two of them have been shot down. One parachute was seen."

"Thank you, Elektra." All her senses concentrated on the screens and windows.

"Lieutenant Romero reports that the dolphins have spotted torpedoes heading for the Ring and Deep."

"Torpedoes? Where've they come from? Ready the rail guns. Fire at will."

"Source of torpedoes unknown. Rail guns ready. Locking on targets." There was a pause. Elektra then continued, "Rail guns now firing. Major Camden believes the bombers used the advancing squall to shield their approach from our sensors."

"Launch all *Sea Wasps*. Flights one, two three and four. Now! Find those bombers!"

More planes flew into the air, racing off towards the dark storm.

"Your rail gun capacity will be insufficient to take out all torpedo targets. Eighteen seconds until torpedoes reach the Deep. Flights from Marcelli Deep are joining those from the Ring to hunt for the bombers."

Sally studied the battle map before her. *Swarms of torpedoes are approaching the Deep.* She looked up and saw the faint traces of bubble trails spreading out from the Deep as the rail guns fired on their targets. Explosions began dotting the sea before her, and torpedo icons began to wink out on her display.

"What percentage can we take out with our guns, Elektra?"

"Eighty-six per cent of those aimed at the Deep will be defeated. The Ring defences will take out ninety-three per cent of those targeted at the Ring."

Sally's thoughts were moving almost faster than she could speak. "Concentrate fire on those that will strike critical Deep industries. Allow the tanks at our SeaShell complex to be exposed. They are expendable."

She could see the battle now raging outside her windows. *Reduced production will be a small price to pay if we can save lives and save the systems critical for the Township.* Still she felt a pang of grief as she watched the outermost tanks explode into fragments.

Periwinkle jolted in its webbing. One of the torpedoes sped through the opening of a damaged tank, striking the foundation of the crane holding Sally's dream home. As it crumpled, *Periwinkle* fell onto the breakwater and smashed.

Part of her heart broke with it but she swallowed the emotions quickly. *Time for that later.* Explosion after explosion filled her windows as torpedoes aimed at nearby Deep industries were destroyed. The damage was significant, but much less than it would have been if they had not had those few seconds of warning.

"Damage control teams are arriving at the site of torpedo strikes. Expect assessments in five minutes."

Billows of smoke and debris wafted across the windows. "Thank you, Elektra."

What a setback to the Township! Her gaze swept over the damage. But we'll pick ourselves up again, as pioneers have always done throughout the ages.

She stared at the wreckage of *Periwinkle* being dispersed by the waves.

CHAPTER TWENTY-SIX

24 July 2066, Marcelli Ring (the same day)

Ben and Maria sped along the boulevard in the driverless vehicle. Lights flashed and sirens wailed to give them priority, but the streets were already empty. Outside the tinted windows, the midday scene was surreal: shop lights glared in vacant buildings, doors of some houses had been left wide open, bicycles and footballs lay in the gutters near the park. The only people visible wore civil defence armbands.

The car passed an alleyway between apartments built facing out to the open sea. Ben saw a small boy crying in the middle of the road and a woman ran out to him, picking him up and sprinting back into the building.

"It is likely that these are Caliphate forces attacking us," Gabriella said from the air.

Maria was watching Ben, "Everyone is safe now, in the shelters or their defence station." Then, as if reading his mind, she added, "Ben, this isn't our fault. Not *your* fault. Caliphate forces are attacking because they chose to be aggressors, to try to bully us."

Ben squeezed her hand, "You're right. Still it's terrible to feel like I'm the reason for the attack."

"No one here blames this on you. We know our enemy well." She returned his squeeze.

He smiled at her then and relaxed, "Thanks for your vote of confidence, Maria."

His mind quickly shifted to focus on the next steps. "Maria, thank you for letting me be a part of this fight."

A voice interrupted Maria before she could respond, "Professor, I see that you're fully qualified to pilot a jump jet."

Ben was startled, "Nemo?"

"Yes, Professor. I have been assigned to brief you. The *Sea Wasp* is faster and easier to manoeuvre than the jump jet. I have configured the control panel to be like that of a jump jet, so it'll be familiar to you."

"Excellent, thank you Nemo."

"Based on your experience, I think you'll have no problems. I'll be with you as co-pilot and navigator as well, Professor."

"Our flight suits will be waiting for us in the hangar, underneath the Ring. It's coming up on the right in a moment," Maria's voice was brusque.

Major Camden's voice now came over the car's speaker, "Captain Romero, you and Ben are part of the fifth Flight. Captain Carlo Marcelli will be lead pilot. Your mission is to overtake the bombers that dropped torpedoes on the Ring and the Deep. You have permission to engage your hydrogen turbo to overtake them after you gain altitude above the Ring."

"Normally, we aren't allowed to kick in the hydrogen engine assist so close to the Ring," Maria explained.

The car skidded under them as explosions rocked the Ring near them.

"Some of the torpedoes have broken through the rail gun defence," came Major Camden's voice again. "I must coordinate damage control and first responders. I'll sign off now. Good luck."

"Thank you, Major," Maria said, as emergency vehicles zoomed past them, towards the smoke clouds further down the Ring Road.

Their car increased speed and squealed around the next corner, rushing through a gate which lifted at their approach. Beyond the gate, a ramp curved down and under the Ring. In a moment, they skidded to a stop behind five planes which resembled something out of science fiction movies from a previous century. The delta wings were shaped for speed and minimal radar reflection. In the centre of each wing was a canopy, now open, which was the only break on the smooth curve of the wings. Stabilizer tail fins were at the tip and centre of each wing.

Around the planes, flight crews scrambled to fuel and arm them, and trucks and ammunition carts moved under the bright lights of the hangar. The noise was almost deafening.

"Wow," Ben said, climbing from the car. "If this weren't so serious, it'd be fun."

Maria looked at him, her eyes dancing, "Yes, they're exciting to fly."

A ground crew member brought them flight suits and then ran to continue preparing the planes for take-off. Maria glanced at the suit and then at her dress. "Turn around," she said.

Ben did as he was told, while putting on his own suit.

"Done," he heard Maria say. He turned back and she kissed him on his cheek.

"What was that for?" he asked, confused, but not unhappy.

"For actually turning around, and not looking."

Ben laughed and sized up her bright orange outfit. "We match," he said, plucking at his suit, "Though I have to say the blue dress was more flattering."

"You, on the other hand are rather fetching in vivid orange." They laughed as they moved briskly towards the planes.

"That's yours, number four. I'm five, on the end," Maria called out as they ran to their aircraft, climbed up ladders into the seats, and pulled on their harnesses. Crew helped them settle in and slip on helmets.

Ben activated his headset and looked over at Maria, "Any last tips, Captain Romero?"

She smiled over at him and spoke into her helmet mike, "The launch will take only seconds. Be ready for a couple Gs coming off the rails, it's quite a rush. We will use the hydrogen turbo immediately after gaining altitude and forming up. We'll need that boost to overtake the bombers and stay with our Flight. Once we're clear of the Ring, we'll rendezvous with the other Flights in our squadron."

"Ben!" Carlo's voice came over Ben's headset, "Great to have you in my Flight!"

"Thanks, Captain. A privilege to fly with you."

"Hey, Ben!" Gideon's voice now came over the radio. "I'm part of Carlo's Flight too. These planes aren't as fun as *Kestrel*, but they'll do."

"Gideon, please. In a *Sea Wasp*, I could easily defeat *Kestrel* in a dogfight," Maria cut in.

"Oh, you're *on*, Maria. You'll eat your words. Especially when you see my new, improved *Kestrel*. These jets might be faster, but *Kestrel 2* has the advantage of underwater offence and defence tactics."

Maria smiled over at Ben as she spoke into her headset. "Overconfidence. Always your weakness, Gid."

Carlo's voice cut in, "OK, time to be serious now. No more chatter. Fifteen seconds to launch."

The canopy closed over Ben. "Any questions about the instruments, Professor?"

Ben scanned the display before him and tested the yoke. "No, Nemo. It looks pretty straightforward."

One of the switches flashed yellow on Ben's display. "Press this switch to power the hydrogen turbo engines once you are at altitude."

"Got it, Nemo. Thanks."

Carlo's voice sounded in their headsets, "Our Flight will circle the Ring clockwise as we gain height after launch. Then form up with our squadron and go after those Caliphate bombers."

"Acknowledge readiness for launch. You are all green on my panel."

A "Ready" sign flashed on Ben's panel. "Acknowledged," Ben said in turn after the other pilots.

"OK," interrupted Carlo. "Let's turn it over to Ranger Command for a precision launch."

Nemo counted down, "Launch in three, two, one. Rails hot."

The sudden acceleration of the plane as it zipped along its rails pressed Ben flat against his seat. The flight suit protected him from blacking out under the G-force.

The five planes of the Pelagic Flight burst out from the hangar openings. They turned as one, above the Ring, in front of the still advancing storm.

The curtains of rain rose just beyond the dark clouds and neared the settlement.

"Light up hydrogen boosters on my mark. Four, three, two, one, mark!" Ben toggled the hydrogen thrust switch. He was pressed back sharply into his seat again as the small plane jumped forwards.

As the acceleration eased, Ben looked down for a moment. More than a dozen columns of smoke and debris rose from the settlement. *The torpedo hits.* The violence of the explosions had broken the Ring in several places and there would be significant loss of life. Fire crews swarmed around the rubble already from boats and trucks, fighting to contain the damage. Ben turned to his controls with a look of grim resolve.

The five Pelagic planes swept around the Ring again and climbed rapidly above the storm front which now eclipsed the stricken town below.

Above the clouds, the sky was clear. Sun glinted off the cockpits of planes to Ben's left and other planes joined them to make up their squadron of fifteen aircraft.

"Reports from the gull drone should be on your displays," Carlo said over their comms link.

"Got it, Captain," Ben said over the comms channel.

"Radar estimates the hostile bomber group at course 284, twenty-six miles to the west," Carlo's voice filled Ben's headset. "Two other squadrons are forming up with us. We have lead position."

A holographic image appeared before Ben. He watched as the three groups of aircraft formed into an arrowhead with Carlo's Flight in the front.

"Stay sharp. Likely the bombers have come with fighter escorts. Waiting for final confirmation of bomber group positions." Ben scanned the instruments and display reflexively as he listened to Carlo.

The holo-display zoomed out. There were two formations of bombers, three moving away from them and four more approaching the Township.

"There's a second wave of bombers approaching Marcelli Township. I repeat, a second wave," Carlo announced over the headset.

"Acknowledged, Captain Romero. You have permission to engage hostiles," Major Camden replied.

24 July 2066, Caliphate bomber group
(the same day)

Abdul Qawwi had unclipped his harness, impatient. He strode behind the flight deck, where the navigator bent over a display. The crewman glanced up, stiffening when he saw the Emir.

"Emir," his voice faltered, and then took refuge in a professional confidence. "The first wave of bombing took them by surprise. Three planes have gone to rendezvous with the escort fighter group from the Caliphate aircraft carrier *Zeynab*. Just ninety seconds until we drop our ordnance."

"Good," the Emir was satisfied. He turned back towards the flight deck. *This is going well.*

"Er… excuse me, Emir," the navigator looked up. Abdul Qawwi whipped his head around and fixed his eyes on him. "We're picking up some confusing and inconsistent readings."

He stared at his display, then looked again at the Emir. "There seem to be several hostile fighter squadrons in pursuit. They are rapidly gaining on us."

Disbelief flashed across Abdul Qawwi's face, then he snapped, "Where have they come from?"

"*Qaa'id*, it looks like they have come from the sea settlement we just bombed."

"How many?!" Abdul Qawwi barked.

A tremor appeared in the navigator's hand as he adjusted his display. "It's h-hard to say, Emir," he stammered. "This cloaking technology... I'm not f-familiar with it. I see thirty hostiles, perhaps fifty?"

Abdul Qawwi ran into the cockpit, and yelled at the pilot, "Turn the plane around."

"But Emir, we haven't released our torpedoes yet."

"Never mind," Abdul Qawwi snapped. "Let the other three bombers finish the run."

Abdul Qawwi stared out the windscreen. "We're exposed now. Bring the fighters forward, three to protect us, the others to attack the hostiles."

"Yes, Emir." The co-pilot began giving instructions to the other bombers and fighter squadron.

A large holo-display appeared in the open deck. Three bombers continued the bombing run, and Abdul Qawwi's bomber had turned to catch up with the first wave bombers. Most of the fighter escort had broken off from their defensive formation around the forward bombers and turned back towards the new threat, ready to engage as directed.

Abdul Qawwi stared at the random glints of lights indicating possible hostile aircraft still pursuing his plane. The flickers of the Pelagic *Wasp*s disappeared completely as the Caliphate fighters turned. "Emir, they seem to have turned on active cloaking of some kind."

How can they hide like that? Abdul Qawwi's stomach tensed – he did not want to contemplate what another failure might mean.

"Do we have countermeasures to this cloaking?"

The navigator's brow glistened. "We're reconfiguring our sensors, Emir. There is a possibility we can defeat this technology of theirs."

The two fighter plane forces were now entangled in desperate dogfights. The Caliphate pilots were forced to engage visually, an almost impossible task at these speeds.

Some of the glints began to reappear, sporadically, then more consistently. "We can see them now, Emir."

"Well done," Abdul Qawwi spoke though his smile. Enemy glints appeared on the screen, and some began to plunge towards the sea. His smile froze as, with growing horror, he watched now one, two, three of his second wave bombers disappear from the screen.

"Only two of the bombers released their payloads. All three have been destroyed by the incoming fighters." Fear was in the face of the navigator as he relayed this information.

We were right to turn back. The Caliph will understand. Abdul Qawwi's attention was fixated on the holo-display, on which Caliphate fighters continued to flash off, out of existence.

"Emir, we've already taken down at least nine of their planes. However," the mission control leader averted his eyes, "there's a third squadron still pursuing us."

Abdul Qawwi spun and ran up to the flight deck. "Take us below the cloud cover," he shouted. "Tell the three remaining fighters to create a protective formation around this bomber."

The pilot's voice was tense, "But Emir, there's a severe gale below us. If we take the fighters with us, it will leave the other bombers exposed, defenceless."

Abdul Qawwi stared the man down. "Descend, now. Give my orders to the fighters."

Without a word, the pilot turned to his yoke and pushed it forward. The co-pilot ordered the fighters to form around them to shield their aircraft.

The bomber slid beneath the boiling clouds, three dark jets following.

"Emir, we've lost one of our three escorts to enemy fire."

The deck trembled and jittered beneath Abdul Qawwi's feet as he half walked, half fell back into his seat and clicked his harness across his chest.

The plane shuddered violently as it plunged through the darkness.

Breaking through the cloud ceiling, the rain and wind screamed across the air frame of the bomber. The pilot struggled to pull the yoke back and stabilize the craft.

"*Bismillāh ir-rahmān ir-rahīm,*" Abdul Qawwi whispered to himself. "In the name of God, the most gracious, the most merciful. Spare me, Allah, for your work. If you deliver me from this, I'll commit all my waking hours to the spread of Islam."

This vow did not remove the dread from his heart.

24 July 2066, Pelagic *Sea Wasp* squadrons
(the same day)

The three Pelagic squadrons were closing quickly on the hostiles. As the forty-five *Sea Wasps* drew closer to the enemy bombers, the pilots could see smaller dots appearing in a cloud behind the large planes in their holo-displays. *Those must be the Caliphate fighter escorts.* As Ben watched, the

Caliphate fighters turned to face the oncoming threat of the Pelagic planes. Ben counted seven bombers and thirty-six escort planes.

"OK, we have bandits," Carlo announced as he surveyed the massing of enemy jets. "Turn off hydrogen thrusters and prepare for battle. *Wasp* Squadrons Bravo and Charlie: engage the Caliphate fighters. We'll go after the three bombers still approaching the Township."

"Copy, Alpha *Wasp*," the Bravo and Charlie captains said in their headsets.

These two squadrons moved to the front of the Pelagic formation and reconfigured their positions, meeting the oncoming Caliphate fighters. Carlo's squadron dropped back to engage the bombers.

"One of the second-wave Caliphate bombers has turned around."

"Thanks, I see that, Ben. OK, Squadron Alpha Flight 3, take the bomber on the left; Flight 2, take the one in the centre; we'll take the one on the right."

"Roger, Alpha 1."

"Our target bomber is releasing torpedoes. I repeat, releasing torpedoes," Flight 3 leader said urgently.

"Yes, ours as well," Carlo acknowledged. "Let's take them all out."

The bombers, focused on their targets and still too far out from the protection of the approaching Caliphate fighter escort, were relatively defenceless. The three Flights of Squadron Alpha engaged and all three enemy bombers were quickly dispatched by rail gun fire and missiles. The third bomber had not dropped its cargo and exploded spectacularly.

"Well done," Carlo acknowledged. "Let Bravo and Charlie continue engaging with the Caliphate fighters, we'll chase after the four bombers. The bomber that turned around still has a payload. Take evasive action to avoid the enemy fighters and pursue our targets."

"Copy, Alpha 1," the other two Flight leaders acknowledged.

Carlo's squadron of three Flights slid into a cloud bank. While the other two *Wasp* squadrons were fully engaged, Carlo and his group ascended to hop over the fierce dog-fight, then sped after the bombers.

Ben stole a glance at the display below him, fascinated. He wanted to watch the dogfights but was forced to maintain concentration to stay in formation with his Flight in Carlo's squadron. He focused on the view on his front screen. *Things are happening too fast.*

"Nemo, please describe the dogfight behind us!"

"Yes, Professor. The thirty-six Caliphate fighters have turned to engage

Squadrons Bravo and Charlie but they are unable to detect the planes due to the Pelagic cloaking technology."

"A neat trick." Ben concentrated on staying on station. *Maria's a little too close off my right wing.* He adjusted to make space.

"Squadrons Bravo and Charlie have lost two fighters to the enemy. Three of the Caliphate craft have been hit and disabled.

"We have lost a third aircraft. A fourth hostile aircraft has been dispatched. Correction: fifth, sixth, seventh hostile aircraft dispatched... A fourth Pelagic fighter is down…"

"Squadron Alpha, disperse and engage the retreating bombers," Carlo's voice said in the earphones. "Flights 2 and 3, target bombers now."

"Roger, Captain," crackled in Ben's headset.

"Our target is bomber 4, extreme right," Carlo said over their Flight channel.

"Professor, the targeted bomber is highlighted on your display. Three more Caliphate fighters and one Pelagic have been disabled in the dogfight."

"Thanks, Nemo, you can stop the narration now. I have to concentrate." Ben watched his instruments.

"Yes, Professor. Narration stopped."

Defensive fire was now coming from the bombers, trying to pick off the pursuing Pelagic fighters. "Rail guns ready?"

"Ready, Professor."

"Fire."

The metal projectiles zipped at supersonic speed from the Pelagic fighters, tearing through the wings and engines of Caliphate bomber 4.

"They're releasing smart flak!" Carlo said in his ear.

Clouds of black particles bloomed behind the bombers. Out of the corner of his eye, he saw a *Sea Wasp* explode as it hit one of these clouds. Then another.

"Breaking right!" Ben shouted.

Maria peeled off to his right as Ben dived and swerved to avoid the mass of particles before him. The outer edge of his left wing was shredded as it passed through the cloud.

Maria's voice called out, "You OK, Ben?"

Ben inspected the damage, then tried the controls. "Seems OK. My plane's pulling a bit to the left. Nothing critical."

"Let's come up and under bomber 2." Ben saw Carlo rise on his left.

"Bomber 1 is down. Three casualties to the flak." The voice of the leader of Flight 2 sounded grim.

"Bomber 3 is down. Two Pelagic planes also lost to the flak," the leader of Flight 3 added.

"Sorry, Flights." A pause, then Carlo said, "We lost good pilots today. But that was good work, Flights 2 and 3. Combine to form a new Flight 2. Let's make their sacrifice count. Come with us to take down the final bomber," Carlo commanded.

"Roger, Alpha 1," the leader of Flight 2 confirmed.

"Carlo, three remaining Caliphate fighters have formed up to defend the remaining bomber," Ben announced, "while another four enemy fighters have turned to engage us."

"I see them, Ben. We'll engage the bomber and escort," Carlo agreed. He informed the other Flight of the plan, "Flight 2, can you engage these fighters?"

"Yes, we've got them, Captain. Go ahead after the lead bomber."

"Thanks. We're diving into the storm." Carlo's team changed course to pursue the bomber, now plunging below the cloud layer.

"It's rough below the clouds. Be ready for turbulence!" Carlo warned his Flight.

"Captain, I've got fighter 3 next to the bomber," Maria said.

A second later the plane exploded just within the top layer of storm clouds.

"Nice shot, Maria!" Carlo responded.

Ben wrestled with the yoke as his plane plunged into the streaming clouds of the storm. The plane juddered underneath him.

"Spread out a bit in this turbulence," Carlo cautioned.

It was almost black outside Ben's cockpit. "Nemo, I need status reports for the bomber and two fighter escorts ahead of us."

"Storm conditions are affecting radar, but I calculate Caliphate fighters and bombers are just five miles ahead of you, Professor."

"Professor, Squadrons Bravo and Charlie have broken the Caliphate fighter defence shield and are now pursuing the last remaining fighters trying to flee."

"Thanks, for the update, Nemo." The wind howling around his plane, Ben fought to keep it on a straight course in the rising gale. Hail rattled along his fuselage and Ben pushed the yoke forward to get below the turbulence in the cloud. He broke through to a rain-lashed view below dark clouds.

"Professor, the bomber we're pursuing has also broken through the storm ceiling at 1,000 feet. They're at twelve o'clock, four miles away. The two Caliphate escort fighters have pulled away from the bomber, preparing to attack our Flight."

A moment passed. "Lieutenant Battuta has splashed the fighter on the right."

"Well done, Gid!" Carlo said in his phones.

"Captain Romero is pursuing the fighter on the left," Nemo continued. "The bomber has descended. One hundred feet above the sea surface. Moving right and left to evade us."

"And they're succeeding," Ben murmured in response to Nemo. The conditions required intense focus. "That's a dangerous game, flying that low. A sudden wind shear could send them into the drink."

Rain lashed across his canopy in a steady roar. Lightning flickered in the clouds above. A roll of thunder resonated through his aircraft.

"Nemo, can you use Sophia's trick to make things quieter?"

"Of course, Professor." The sound immediately diminished and Ben could concentrate more easily.

"Range?"

"Three miles to the bomber. The remaining fighter is attempting to flank us. Captain Romero has turned to engage it and the Caliphate fighter has locked onto Captain Romero's aircraft."

"I thought we were cloaked, Nemo."

"The enemy sensors are apparently tracking water displaced by our fighters as we move through the rain, Professor."

Ben focused on the bomber inching into his sights again.

"Captain Romero's jet has been hit, Professor, she's lost control." Ben wanted to turn around, but it took all he had to focus on the target and avoid catastrophe. Another bloom of smart flak came from the bomber. Ben dived under it, a mere thirty feet about the wave crests. *Not good.* He slid to the right, made a half-barrel roll around the cloud of flak, followed by a snap roll to level above the bomber again.

Tense seconds passed. "Maria?" Panic sounded in Ben's voice as he spoke into the mic.

"Captain Romero's ejection seat has been triggered. A parachute is descending to the surface, Professor."

Ben's chest tightened and his breaths were shallow and rapid.

"Lieutenant Lastra in fighter 2 has destroyed the last enemy fighter," Nemo continued.

"Maria, be OK," Ben whispered.

"Lieutenant Lastra has circled back to check on Captain Romero. He's dropped flares and a smoke pot in the vicinity. The bomber is firing at you and Lieutenant Battuta, Professor."

Ben snapped his focus back to the fight. "Run evasive course, Nemo."

The plane began jerking from side to side randomly. "Evasive protocol engaged."

An image of a parachute landing in stormy seas haunted him. Ben concentrated with a new vehemence as the bomber drifted into the crosshairs. "Fire!"

The holo-display showed him virtual tracer trails of his shots. Ben watched as engine three on the aircraft was struck and exploded. However, the bomber continued flying, though descending and slowing.

"Any hydrogen in my burners, Nemo?"

"A few seconds, Professor."

"Light it off. I want to get closer."

Ben barely noticed the acceleration as his jet closed on the bomber. "Take out engine four, Nemo."

The plane steadied. The engine crept into his sights. "Fire."

A second later, the fourth engine erupted in flames. The bomber slowed abruptly and curved towards the streaming swells below.

Ben and Gideon both pulled up, just avoiding collision with the crippled bomber. They circled tightly around the failing plane as it crashed into the sea.

Carlo cut in across the comms, "Ben, weather ahead looks rough. Possible tornado cells forming around us. Bad news for our small planes. Nice shooting, Ben. The other squadrons have downed all enemy aircraft, though we lost at least fourteen planes. Reports still coming in. Time to go home."

Ben and Gideon pulled their two planes up through the dark cloud ceiling. A burst of hail rattled on the fuselage, then they burst into sunlight and a clear sky.

In his peripheral vision, Ben spotted Carlo and Raymond's jets popping above the clouds off to the right. Gideon was on his left and they turned to join up.

"Maria?" Ben asked. He was flying next to Carlo now. He turned to look at his friend through the canopy.

"We marked the position of her chute, Ben. No radio contact yet.

Search-and-rescue crews are racing to the scene as we speak." There was a pause.

They made eye contact through the canopies. "Sorry, Ben. We don't know yet whether she made it. Her radio beacon is on but haven't received a voice response. That was a rough ejection – she may be unconscious."

Ben pushed his yoke forward and turned it slightly, his *Wasp* slid out of formation and turned around.

"Ben!" Carlo shouted. "We must head back! There's barely enough fuel to return to the Ring. You don't have any margin."

"Sorry, Carlo," Ben switched off the communication with Carlo. "Nemo, give me a fix on the smoke pot and flares where Maria went down."

"Yes, Professor. On your display."

Ben adjusted his course. "Nemo, what kind of survival gear is in this plane?"

"A small, two-man raft with a survival kit."

"Enough. Lock onto the radio beacon dropped near Maria."

"Done, Professor." Ben abruptly began his descent through the clouds again and then beneath the ceiling into the storm. Visibility was poor as he brought the plane closer to the sea surface. In a few seconds, he spotted the smoke pot floating on the rolling swells ahead. He banked into a circle with the smoke pot in the centre, climbing for altitude while scanning the water below.

"Nemo, are you picking up Maria's personal distress beacon?"

"Scanning frequencies, Professor. There's a faint signal just to the northeast. If it is Captain Romero, then her beacon has been damaged and is only broadcasting at minimum power."

Ben turned to the north-west and came low over the swells. He saw a dark shape bobbing on the sea not far from the smoke pot, a faint light flickering from it. "Professor, I have confirmed that is Captain Romero ahead of us. At this range I am picking up some of her telemetry from her exposure suit. She appears to be unconscious, and she has a weak pulse – she may be bleeding."

Ben pulled his *Sea Wasp* up and kept it in a tight circle over Maria's position. He then toggled Gideon on his comms, "I have a favour to ask, Gid."

Ben gave his request, got the answer he wanted. His hand went to the ejection lever and he pulled.

CHAPTER TWENTY-SEVEN

24 July 2066, Pelagic *Sea Wasp* Flight
(the same day)

Carlo's Flight of three *Sea Wasps* dropped from the late afternoon sky, now clearing from the storm. They circled Marcelli Ring, awaiting their turn to land.

Carlo reluctantly opened his channel to Pelagic Command. "Captain Marcelli reporting fourteen aircraft lost, seven pilots unaccounted for," *including Maria and Ben*, "six *Sea Wasps* limping home with escorts. The Caliphate fighters were brutal, Major. We had significant losses, despite the cloaking. But, thank God, we were successful. Only two Caliphate fighters escaped, and all seven bombers were splashed."

"Acknowledged, Alpha *Wasp*. Well done. Thank you, Captain."

Carlo turned the channel off. "Elektra, any updates on Ben Holden and his *Wasp*?"

Elektra's soft voice came over his headset, "Captain, no current updates to report." After a brief pause, "There's no contact with Professor Holden, or Captain Romero. Both are currently presumed missing in action until we gain contact."

"Please relay that to the rest of the Flight, Elektra," Carlo sighed, glancing at the fuel gauge. *I'm running on fumes.*

"Done, Captain."

He looked down and counted eighteen smoking wounds in the graceful lines of the Ring. *Torpedo damage was even worse than I thought. Good thing those last two bombers didn't drop their payloads – that would've broken the infrastructure.*

"Elektra, give me current damage and casualty reports from the Township."

"Current news reports from Township Security put the casualties at 1,238, with another 2,340 wounded or hospitalized. A total of 359 residents are still missing and unaccounted for. Eleven of the eighteen fires are now contained. Efforts are being made to restore utilities around the Ring."

Carlo watched the drama below: vehicles clustered like swarms of ants near the damaged sites, streams of water jetted from fire boats working to extinguish the last fires, red-suited rescuers combed the rubble for survivors, yellow-vested medics quickly moved the wounded towards hospital tents, damage control teams shored up the Ring blocks shattered by the torpedoes and placed buoys to keep sinking sections afloat.

Ambulances and police vehicles raced with flashing lights around the dusk-lit Ring Road that was still intact. *They look like toys from up here.* Carlo's heart was weighed down – many family and friends lived in the areas that had been torpedoed. He suppressed the emotions welling up. *There will be time to mourn later.*

He glanced at the approach pattern unfolding over the military landing area. *One more Flight, then our turn.*

"Captain Marcelli, you have permission to land your Flight on the south-east sector, Seaway 9."

Finally! "Thank you, Ring Command," Carlo acknowledged, then toggled his Flight channel. "Gideon, lead us in. Ray, follow Gideon. I'll bring up the rear."

"Acknowledged." The Flight began their descent.

"Captain Marcelli, Major Camden has sent a gig to bring you for a debrief immediately after landing."

Carlo sighed. *Not looking forward to this debrief.* He could already hear the Major, *"Tell me exactly why you let Ben Holden ditch that expensive Sea Wasp!?"* He began marshalling the facts in his mind, replaying the events and rationales for decisions he made.

"Elektra, please tell Ana Luciana that I'm fine and have returned to base."

"Done, Captain."

The skies over the Ring were free of air traffic now, except for a few ongoing patrols. Theirs was the last Flight except for the ones escorting damaged planes. Carlo concentrated on Ray's plane, directly ahead, maintaining the correct distance. He toggled a switch and felt the answering vibration of landing pontoons as they lowered.

Ray's *Wasp* landed ahead and twenty seconds later Carlo's *Wasp* pontoons touched down as well. Carlo's aircraft settled its weight onto the floats and impellers in the pontoons helped him brake so he could quickly move out of the landing lane. A tug came alongside and hooked onto his plane to take it to its berth.

Carlo popped the canopy; ground crew clambered up the ladder from the tug, saluted him, and helped him out of the fighter. "Sir, please board the gig next to the tug. They'll take you directly to debriefing."

"Thank you, Sergeant." Carlo returned the salute and stepped quickly onto the gig.

As the gig cut gracefully through the small swells in the harbour, Carlo's eyes assessed the damage on the *Wasps* he passed. Battle scars were evident: scorch marks, holes, shredded composite.

Carlo leapt onto the dock and took the stairs at a pace. Entering the Command building, he was welcomed by those from the squadrons who had arrived earlier. They all shook hands and exchanged hugs or pats on the back, grateful to see one another alive and well. Some looked towards the entrance, with the faint hope that others might walk through. Conversations were subdued, grief and relief mixed in equal measure. There was so much to talk about, but they knew it would come out during the debrief.

A lieutenant approached them, "Major Camden is ready to debrief your mission. Please follow me." She led them into a conference room, dimly lit, where they took seats in a semi-circle around an empty area. A holo-image formed in front of them, and Major Camden appeared, in her office at Ranger Command.

"Thank you, Rangers. You've performed admirably and I hope you can have a good rest after we debrief. I apologize that I cannot join you in person but I'm debriefing the various Ranger groups involved in today's events. Holographic footage has been compiled from the various Augmented Intelligence Agents to give us a picture of your mission. As you know we're still awaiting damaged planes which are still returning, as well as news on Professor Ben Holden and Captain Maria Romero."

CHAPTER TWENTY-EIGHT

24 July 2066, Caliphate bomber wreckage
(the same day)

Abdul Qawwi woke, dazed. His feet were cold and, glancing down, he saw they were soaking in seawater. He looked forward, at the pilot who slumped unnaturally against his yoke. On the other side, the co-pilot moaned, struggling to release his harness.

This is a disaster! Abdul Qawwi snapped open the latch on his own harness and rose unsteadily out of the seat. His ribs ached, but he pushed the pain away in his mind.

He went over to the co-pilot and checked the man, but even as he checked the pulse, it faded under his fingertips and stopped. *He has passed on to paradise.* Abdul Qawwi felt vibrations beneath him, he turned and walked the few feet to Yunus Saleh who was seated across from him in the cockpit. Yunus Saleh stirred and looked up at Abdul Qawwi. "Emir," he said thickly.

"Can you get up?" Abdul Qawwi released Yunus Saleh's harness buckle. Yunus slumped lower in his seat with a gasp.

"The plane is sinking, brother. We only have moments." Abdul Qawwi grabbed his shoulder.

Yunus Saleh staggered to his feet, "Yes, Emir. I think so." Abdul Qawwi gripped his arm, helping him up, back into the main body of the jet. *It's a miracle this plane is afloat. It won't be for long, in this storm.*

The plane shifted with a jolt under them. Angry swells were now crashing against the windows and lightning flickered in the dark clouds above. They moved quickly past the navigator, also sprawled unconscious over his station, a pool of blood forming under his head.

Abdul Qawwi spotted the exit door and he left Yunus Saleh to support himself in the aisle while he walked over to pull the emergency lever. The hatch popped with a loud hiss and freezing seawater gushed through the opening. With relief, Abdul Qawwi watched the attached life raft inflate. Behind him, Yunus Saleh had recovered somewhat and was opening lockers, looking for survival kits and exposure suits.

Another of the bomber's crew climbed up the tilting deck towards them. Abdul Qawwi grabbed him and pulled him up. It was the plane's security chief. Abdul Qawwi stopped him, deftly drew the pistol from the man's holster and pointed it at him.

The man looked at him calmly, "Brother, we are in the same emergency together. There's no need for a gun, we must help one another."

Abdul Qawwi jammed the weapon into his belt. "Help us with this raft."

Soon the raft was detached from the door. "It's ready, Emir," the security chief said looking over his shoulder, "We must leave quickly. The plane is going down and if we don't leave now, we'll be sucked into its vortex as it sinks."

Yunus Saleh hurried to join them, tossing the kits and suits into the raft. Yunus and the security officer jumped out the door into the numbing sea, holding onto the raft ropes and thrashed their way onto the raft.

Just as Abdul Qawwi was preparing to join them, he felt the bomber give a great lurch. He could feel the plane rapidly sinking under him and he clung to the edge of the door as the cabin floor swung to become a vertical cliff-face of metal. The plane gave a shudder, the rain and clouds outside the door became sea, and Abdul Qawwi watched the surface recede above him.

He pulled himself out the door and into the open ocean above him, kicking furiously to reach the surface of the frigid water. Panic squeezed his heart, the pain spurring him to swim with even more frantic strokes upwards, towards the light, fighting the suction of the wreck. Bit by bit, the pull of suction weakened, allowing him to gain headway.

A moment later, he broke surface, gasping for air, drawing in great gulps. The raft with his comrades was caught in the whirlpool eddies over where the bomber had gone down and was spinning around slowly. Yunus Saleh and the officer paddled vigorously to gain control and keep near the site in the face of the storm winds. The vortex faded as they cautiously approached Abdul Qawwi. The security chief tossed a rope, the end landing a few feet away from the Emir who kicked and, with one last effort, grabbed the line. Yunus Saleh and the chief heaved him aboard.

The gale pushed the raft downwind from the crash site and lightning flashes revealed massive swells on all sides of the tiny craft. Rain continued to fall in a deluge, lashed by the wind. Abdul Qawwi lay gasping in the bottom of the raft, then twisted himself to grab the safety ropes to avoid being thrown overboard as a swell carried them up a wall of water.

Yunus Saleh and the chief retrieved the paddles again and straddled the sides of the raft. They paddled furiously, trying to maintain control and avoid being capsized.

Fuel from the sunken plane was now spreading across the ocean surface, towards a part of the wing that was still afloat and burning furiously. The men fought frantically to distance the raft from the threat of the fire when a concussive explosion came from behind. Yunus Saleh fell into the raft, the security chief fell into the water, Abdul Qawwi was flung halfway out of the raft but dragged himself up and lay on the pontoon and Yunus hauled the crewman back into the boat. Abdul Qawwi watched as the last wing of the aircraft slipped below another advancing monstrous wave. Fire flickered at the wave's crest.

The wave moved under them, flinging the raft up once again. The three men fell into the bottom, clinging to the ropes and the raft dropped into the trough between waves, a tiny yellow cork driven before the wind between mountains of water. Patches of flame began to spread around them, but the raft was moving away into clear water.

Alhamdulillah, may God be praised, I may yet survive, Abdul Qawwi prayed amid the frenzied turbulence. *Allah, please accept my vow. Ya Allah, now hear me again, help me escape from the wrath of the Caliphate.*

He eyed his two companions in the raft through the haze of the storm. Yunus Saleh is trustworthy but *how can I get rid of the other man? We should have left him in the water.*

As he was calculating, Abdul Qawwi heard a roar. He looked up and saw a plane descending towards the sea and, as he watched, the pilot ejected and floated down on a parachute. *Good, another Pelagic plane downed.*

The plane hit the water and exploded about a quarter mile away.

As the pilot splashed in the water, Abdul Qawwi noticed a streaming column of smoke near him and, as the next massive wave lifted the raft up, the scene became clearer: a small raft had inflated as it hit the water, and there were *two* people in the water, about twenty metres apart.

*

Ben splashed with his parachute into the side of a wave and rose with it. He quickly released himself from the harness and let the chute drift down current. There was the raft to his left, that Nemo had released from the plane. With a few strokes, he grabbed the rope and pulled himself into the raft. He found the survival kit attached under the rim, opened it, and took stock: exposure suit, rations, water, beacon, flares, and a knife. The beacon was already active, relaying coordinates of the raft via the Pelagic Array to the Command Centre. He quickly changed into the exposure suit.

Then he scanned the area around the raft, as it rose and fell with the waves. The streaming wind and spray reduced visibility. *There!* He spotted the smoke pot, maybe fifteen metres away. He used it as a reference point and started searching in ever-widening circles, with each lift of a swell, looking for her orange flight suit.

In his peripheral sight, he spotted something slip over top of the wave. A flash of orange. He waited for it to come into view again and was startled to see another raft beyond the orange figure, barely visible. *Someone else is out here.* As he crouched down and peered over the edge of his raft, his hand reached back and strapped the knife with its sheath onto his calf.

He studied the distant raft. *Larger than mine.* Waiting for a clear view when they were below him in the valley between waves, he counted three people and just beyond the raft he spotted floating wreckage. *Survivors from that bomber. Caliphate men. Too close for comfort, but not an imminent threat.*

He continued scanning the sea for Maria. He thought he caught another glimpse of orange at the top of a roller between him and the other raft, but it disappeared over the crest. He watched the spot, waiting for it to reappear, his gaze flicking between the wave and the raft.

Yes, it's her. The body bobbed, face up, about twenty metres away. Without delay, Ben looped the raft's mooring rope, slipped his right arm and head through it, and dived into the water. He swam, head above water, towards Maria, towing his raft behind. His course was bringing him closer to the other raft, but there was no other way.

He reached her within minutes and, with his raft shielding him from the Caliphate raft, he checked her quickly. *Pulse is good, but weak. Swelling on her face, possible concussion. One leg might be broken.* Climbing into the raft, he carefully pulled her in next to him. She moaned, her eyes flickered open and connected with his. "Ben?" she mumbled before she fainted.

He laid her carefully in the bottom of the raft, then kneeling, he wedged himself next to her so she wouldn't roll about too much on the swells.

Stripping off her life vest, he created a makeshift splint for her leg, then looked back at the other raft.

He was shocked to see them paddling towards him. *This is not good.* Ben glanced at his watch. *Maybe fifteen minutes.*

He dived back into the water and began towing the raft away from their pursuers.

*

Yunus Saleh had balanced the binoculars on the side of the raft, trying to get a fix on the other raft.

"What do you see?!" Abdul Qawwi snapped.

"Emir, it's hard to tell, with the spray and the waves. OK. The pilot released his parachute. He's in the raft. Now he's back in the water, towing the raft. I think he's searching for someone. Maybe another pilot?" Yunus Saleh swung the binoculars, "Yes, I see an orange flight suit in the water."

He turned again to look at the swimmer, then looked up from the field glasses and back at Abdul Qawwi. "Emir, you won't believe this, but I think Ben Holden is towing the raft."

Abdul Qawwi snatched the binoculars from Yunus Saleh. He slowly stood and balanced, trying to get a stable view, as the raft rose and fell with the waves. The man was now swimming towards the other pilot. Now he was next to the pilot, apparently checking him. In another moment, he was pulling the injured pilot into the raft.

He concentrated on the image in the glasses. Something was familiar. Could it be? *Allah has delivered them into my hands again!*

"Start paddling!" Abdul Qawwi shouted.

The security chief looked at him, "Brother, it would be better to save our strength. We don't know how long we'll be out here."

Abdul Qawwi drew the gun and pointed it. The security chief held up his hands, "OK, we'll paddle." Both he and Yunus Saleh reached for paddles, straddled the side of the raft and paddled towards Ben. Abdul Qawwi kept the gun pointed at the chief. The man glared at him but kept paddling.

As they neared, Abdul Qawwi was staring intently at the other raft. The security chief chose his moment, swung his paddle in an arc, and knocked the gun out of Abdul Qawwi's hand, into the raft. He then lunged for the gun, but Yunus Saleh was on top of him in a second. Abdul Qawwi reached down and grabbed the gun, slamming it against the security chief's head. The man slumped in the bottom of the raft.

Yunus Saleh looked up, "What should we do, Emir?"

"Throw him over." Abdul Qawwi took his hands, Yunus Saleh reluctantly took his legs, and together they pushed him into the swirling sea.

They watched for a moment as the man's body drifted down current from the raft. As it crested the next swell, fins emerged from the wave and circled the body. The scene disappeared over the wave but, a minute later, their raft rose on the next wave crest and they saw white foam as the sharks thrashed. The figure of the chief was jerked back and forth and, in another second, it was pulled under, leaving only a red stain on the surface.

"Get back to the paddles," Abdul Qawwi said. Yunus Saleh crawled meekly to pick up his paddle, eyes and mouth frozen in horror.

*

Something bumped against Ben's leg. As he reached for his knife, a bump came from the other side. As quickly as he could, he hoisted himself back into the raft.

That was close. I won't be any use if I become a shark's lunch. Pulling the rope in, he peered over the edge as more shadows gathered in the waters around the raft.

Glancing back at the enemy raft, less than twelve metres away, he saw there were now only two men. He looked around quickly and spotted the flare gun in the survival kit. He picked it up, draping his white pilot suit over it.

Ben's raft was climbing a wave, the hostiles were below him. He stood, waving the hand draped in the pilot suit, and called out, "We need help!"

Concealing the flare gun beneath the suit, he aimed at the forward flotation chamber on the Caliphate raft and fired. The flare paralleled the slope of the wave, striking the other raft with a brilliant flash, burning a hole through the rubber. The pierced chamber deflated immediately, but other chambers still held air and kept the raft afloat. The men didn't seem to notice the damage.

Now ten metres away, one of the men aimed a gun at Ben, "Stand still!"

Ben was incredulous, It's Abdul Qawwi, the Emir.

Anger welled up but, with an act of will, he pressed it back down, forcing his emotions to calm. Ben glanced at his watch as he raised his hands, "Don't shoot."

Maria moaned again. She was coming around.

"Ben Holden. Kneel! Make your peace with Allah." Abdul Qawwi waved the gun. He looked at Maria, then smiled at Ben, "We'll take her with us. I'll make her one of my wives."

Ben slowly knelt, balancing, taking stock of his options. *Too far to jump. I have no gun. Too many sharks.*

"If you kill me, Emir, you'll lose access to my wife's data."

"We no longer have the device. You do!"

Ben held his gaze, "You're clever – I know you made a back-up."

Abdul Qawwi was silent.

The two rafts swirled in the calm of a valley between the massive waves.

Ben's eyes flicked at his watch. "I will make a deal with you, Emir. Take me. Leave Maria. Rescuers are on their way. You're out of time."

Abdul Qawwi's mind remembered the cold, ruthless stare of the Caliph that day on the balcony. *I failed again. Even if I obtain the data, the Caliph won't spare me.* His mind was racing. He considered, then made a decision.

The rafts ascended the next swell. Abdul Qawwi shouted above the rising wind, "I'll give you a few seconds to recite the *shahaada* before you die, Ben Holden. Allah might then have mercy on you." Allowing only a slight pause, Abdul Qawwi's finger squeezed and fired the gun.

At that moment, Ben's raft had slipped over the crest of the swell and the bullet skipped off the water. The wind whistled over the swell, driving spray and foam. Abdul Qawwi cursed, waiting for his raft to crest the wave. Yunus Saleh stared at the Emir.

In a few seconds, they too slid over the crest. Now Ben and Maria were below them and Abdul Qawwi knelt in the raft, steadied his arm on the side, and took aim again. His finger began to squeeze the trigger.

Only ten metres away, Ben stared at Abdul Qawwi and his gun. "It's now or never, Nemo," he whispered.

As if on cue, to the left of the Emir's raft, the water boiled. *Kestrel 2* broke the surface, bursting into the air.

"Shoot the raft, Nemo!" Ben shouted.

The rail guns whispered, filling the Emir's raft with holes. As he toppled, Abdul Qawwi shot his gun. The raft flooded and collapsed around its occupants and the bullet sliced across Ben's shoulder and on into the water.

A stretcher descended from *Kestrel 2* while it hovered above the raft. Blood streamed down Ben's arm as he readied Maria to be lifted up. He gingerly lifted her into the wire stretcher and strapped her in and then stood, feet straddling the stretcher, with a firm hold on the cable. Nemo began hoisting them in.

Their raft drifted away below them, towards the struggling men who were grasping onto their paddles and fragments of raft. "One moment, Nemo." The winch stopped mid-air. He and Maria swung in the wind.

Abdul Qawwi looked up and their eyes locked. A grimace of hate contorted the Emir's face. "You will burn in hell, infidel."

Ben looked down at this man who had literally made his life hell. He was surprised by pity welling up inside. The faces of Paul, Sul, and their communities flashed through his mind, calming his heart. "Somehow, I think not," he called.

Abdul Qawwi screamed obscenities.

"All right, bring us up, Nemo." *Kestrel 2* rose in the air above the waves, pulling in the cable. Buffeting winds swung the stretcher. As they reached the hatch, Ben clambered in and pulled Maria in after him.

"Professor, the weather system in this area is becoming increasingly unstable."

"Let's get out of here, Nemo." Ben sealed the latch, and while he secured the stretcher, *Kestrel 2* rose above the storm.

*

Abdul Qawwi, clinging to the last air pocket in the raft, watched *Kestrel 2* vanish into the clouds. His cursing dwindled into impotent silence. Yunus Saleh gulped and struggled next to him. Abdul Qawwi struck Yunus Saleh's head, "Stop panicking, brother." Yunus became calm.

Abdul Qawwi continued quietly, "We can survive this. Stay calm, brother. Hold onto the air pockets. The raft around us will protect us from the sharks. I see the other raft just over that wave. The wind is blowing it towards us.

Yunus Saleh looked at him, "Yes, Emir." His voice was less than confident.

The other raft was close now. "Can you grab the rope, Yunus?"

Shapes swirled in the water around them. Trembling, Yunus Saleh reached. A fin ran under his arm and he flinched back.

"Try again," Abdul Qawwi commanded. Yunus Saleh made a quick grab and gripped the rope.

Yunus pulled the raft closer as they crested another summit, spray and wind whirling around them. Abdul Qawwi tied the paddles onto the end of the rope and tossed them into the raft now bouncing below them. They each grappled with the sides of the raft and tumbled in.

Yunus Saleh retrieved the paddles while Abdul Qawwi pawed through the survival kit. "Allah has spared us again, Yunus. If we're careful, we can last a week out here." *The wind is blowing us east, towards commercial sea lanes. That's good. Should Allah spare us, we can join with the Indonesian groups and rebuild.*

Looking up from his musing, Abdul Qawwi noticed Yunus Saleh across from him, eyes wide with fear. From behind him came a primal roar, like a train rushing towards them and he looked over his shoulder in time to see a dark grey column rising from the sea into the clouds, less than a hundred metres away. It approached rapidly, sucking up the sea as it came.

Abdul Qawwi reached for a paddle, but it was too late. At that moment, the raft and the men were sucked into the water spout. Up they whirled, far overhead, disappearing into the dark clouds.

24 July 2066, Ranger Command, Marcelli Township
(the same day)

Carlo and the other exhausted pilots filed into the debriefing room. The grief for the friends they had lost was tangible. There was a holo-image of the Major in one corner and, in the centre of the room, a holo-display with frozen icons of the seven Caliphate bombers coming in two waves, their thirty-six escort fighters forming a protective cloud around them, and the forty-five incoming Pelagic *Wasps* preparing to engage…

Carlo held his breath, waiting for the action to begin.. Nothing happened. He looked again towards the image of the Major in the corner of the room. She seemed to be talking with someone just off camera. The Major turned her attention back to the gathered viewers. "I've just received word from air traffic control. They have *Kestrel 2* on radar now," Camden announced. "Captain Romero is in a stable condition and *Kestrel 2* will be landing at the north-west hospital within the next fifteen minutes."

Spontaneous cheers and applause broke out around the room. Carlo stood up and said, "Major, may I have permission to go meet *Kestrel 2*."

Major Camden fixed Carlo with a stare for a moment, then relented. "OK. Go meet your comrades." She now turned to the gathered virtual community, "This debrief will continue at 1900 hours. Go." The holo-image faded.

*

The sun was just setting as the bus whisked the squadron members to the north-west hospital on the empty Ring Road. They sprinted to the receiving deck, where nurses and doctors were already waiting with a stretcher, all watching a dot on the horizon which was growing rapidly as the craft raced towards them.

In a matter of minutes, *Kestrel 2* slid onto the emergency seaway and taxied to the hospital deck. The canopy popped open and Ben climbed out. Medics lifted the mesh stretcher onto the dock and waiting nurses unstrapped the figure on the stretcher, transferring her deftly to another stretcher. A nurse blocked Ben as he attempted to stay by Maria's side, "Let us do our job now, sir."

His eyes followed Maria's face as they rolled her into the hospital. *Pale. Almost lifeless. Her pulse was so weak during the journey here.* Fear felt like knots in his chest.

Gideon put a hand on his shoulder, "She's in the best hands, Ben. My father will look after her himself."

Suliman, robed for surgery, gave a nod to Ben and Gideon from the entrance, before hurrying inside after the stretcher.

24 July 2066, Ranger Command, Marcelli Township
(the same day)

After an hour and a half of waiting at the hospital, Ben and the pilots from the squadrons were summoned back to Command Centre for the debrief. It didn't last long and afterwards, most of them returned to the hospital and sat outside the operating theatre doors. Lorenzo, extended family, and many friends were gathered there. Maria was known by many in the Ring.

The small crowd waited in silence, watching updates on the aftermath of the attack which were displayed on the wall screen at regular intervals. Power was being restored to affected areas of the Ring and damage to the Deep and Rise was being assessed. International news feeds were picking up the story of the attack and the Pacific Rim Council was demanding an investigation. Nearby terrestrial nations were outraged at the attack on their peaceful neighbours in Marcelli Township.

Ben stared out the window, neither hearing nor seeing the drama unfolding before him. Time had stopped as he waited to hear about what was happening in the operating theatre. *It's been three and a half hours since Sul took her in.*

Finally, the double doors to the theatre swung open. Suliman came out, pulling off latex gloves as he approached. He smiled and relief swept through Ben like a flood.

Suliman addressed the crowd, "I can report a broken femur, two cracked ribs, and some internal injuries, for Captain Romero. She's had a rough landing but she is now stable. We'll keep her under sedation for at least twenty-four hours to let her body heal. In a day or two, she can have visitors."

Everyone began talking at once. Suliman caught Ben's eye, beckoning him into a corridor. Ben followed him.

"Ben, Paul left a message for me. He's leading the investigation into this attack for the Pacific Rim Council and he'd like to interview you. A room has been prepared for a holo-link. Down the hall, just to the left when you're ready."

"Of course," Ben responded. Suliman was studying him. Ben blurted out, "Will Maria be OK?"

"Yes. I expect a full recovery. Be at peace, son." Suliman's face softened as he continued, "I see she means something to you. That's good – and from what I've observed, I think the feeling is mutual."

Suliman put his hands on Ben's shoulders and spoke out a blessing of peace over him. "Now, go talk to Paul. He's waiting."

Ben hurried off down the corridor. He did feel more at peace.

*

Entering the indicated room, Ben spied his friend Paul. He was sitting on a hay bale, bent over a leather saddle that he was oiling. Above Paul's right shoulder, the shaggy head of his favourite horse – a roan named Buck – stared placidly at Ben. The scene was stunningly vivid; he could almost smell the fresh hay. Memories flooded back of the many times he had entered his friend's barn, seeking advice.

"This must be a new standard for holo-tech." Ben took a seat in his darkened end of the room, while admiring the view.

Paul looked up, "Ben, good to see you, son. Yes, a friend is letting me beta test his holo-suite technology."

"I'd love to just ride up into the hills with you right now, Paul. Do you still have Vienta, the pinto? She was my favourite. Very spirited."

"Yes, she's in the stall next to Buck here." Paul put down his cloth. He looked straight at Ben before continuing, "A ride along the ridge would be good for you, I'm sure. We're having beautiful weather now. In fact,

Buck and I just returned from a trip to the Indian reservation. We visited Red Hawk. He has a new grandson and he wanted me to lead a service of dedication. So, how is Maria doing?" Ben felt Paul's gaze probe him as he continued. "She'll pull through, Ben. Suliman gave me a quick briefing a few moments ago. You really like her, don't you?"

"You know too?" A sheepish smile appeared on Ben's face. "People keep telling me it's obvious."

"Yep. It's OK, son. It's even a good thing. It's time for you to move on, start a new life."

Ben thought for a moment, "I almost lost her, Paul. In that battle. My whole life changed this week and even though I felt like I was being pulverized in a meat grinder, it has been cathartic."

He reflected a moment, "I feel like a snake that's shed its skin, the skin of my former losses and grief."

"Good to shake off that old skin," Paul smiled.

"Yeah. What comes back to me now is that dream I told you about so many years ago. The one with Lisa and Sammy saying goodbye. That felt like the beginning of my journey towards healing."

Ben hesitated, still moved by the emotions stirred up by that dream, but he took a deep breath and went on, "I sent Lisa's data and algorithm off into safe hands. When I did that, it felt like I'd reached a door, a way out of that long, dark corridor, out into light."

He paused a moment, reflecting. "The Caliphate has no more reason to hunt me. Now I can step into whatever lies on the other side of this door."

"That's good to hear. You've tamed grief, anger, and bitterness. Well done, Ben. Welcome to a new season of life."

"A new season? Yes, summer, maybe."

Paul set the saddle down and changed the subject. "Actually, Ben, I asked for this meeting for an important reason. As Sul probably told you, I've been tasked to investigate the attack on the Township for the Pacific Rim Council. I need to take a deposition from you about the events leading up to today's conflict, including your previous interactions with the Caliphate forces. I'll be recording this as testimony for possible actions being taken in the international court. Are you ready to do this?"

"Of course, Paul." Ben shifted uncomfortably in his seat.

"Take your time, son. Start with what you remember of your latest kidnapping. Recording is on."

Slowly at first, then more quickly as the memories flooded back, Ben recounted everything that had happened to him over the last three weeks. Only three weeks?! He began with the conference in Singapore.

Paul listened intently, asking a few clarifying questions.

An hour and a half had passed and Ben finished recounting the downing of the bomber, the return to Marcelli Ring, and the doctor's report on Maria. He sighed with exhaustion.

"Stop recording," Paul said to a machine off camera, then sat, thoughtful. "Good, Ben. Thank you. There's a lot there. The Council will have to consider the evidence. I believe this will result in sanctions against the Caliphate. This can possibly spur an agreement on containment by other nations who have felt the sting of Caliphate terror attacks. We'll have to wait and see. I know the Caliphate won't be allowed to act with such impunity again within the Pacific Rim."

Paul stood up and stretched. "Tell me about your special friend, Maria."

Ben reflected for a moment about his history with Maria. "Well, actually, Paul, I first met her there, outside Grit. She was doing a survey for the national park and she saved me from a rattler," Ben smiled at the memory. He went on to describe her personality and their adventures together.

"Sounds like quite a gal. I'll be praying for Maria's recovery." And Ben knew he would.

"Yes," Ben said simply.

"Thank you, Ben for this testimony. It'll be very helpful. I must go now as I've got other interviews to conduct. Good talking with you again. We miss you around here."

"I miss you all, of course – although I'm beginning to feel at home here in the Southern Pacific Gyre."

"That wouldn't have anything to do with that pair of lovely blue eyes, would it?" Paul's grey eyes twinkled.

"I can neither confirm nor deny," Ben laughed. "Give my love to the Robinsons, Paul. And the rest of the crew there. You all literally saved my life." He felt an urge to step into the holo-image to embrace his mentor.

"Of course. Will do." Paul had returned to oiling the saddle on his lap. The image began to fade.

"Oh, and Ben," Paul said without looking up, "You might start thinking of baby names, three boy names and one for a lovely girl."

The image was gone.

25 July 2066, Marcelli Ring
(the next day)

Sul peeked through the window. There was Dawood Naji, slumped on a steel cot in the spartan cell. He signalled the guard to open the door.

"Open cell forty-one," the guard said.

"Biometrics confirmed for prison officer Jalisco," a disembodied voice said.

The door opened. Dawood Naji sat up and jumped to his feet as Sul entered with the guard. "Sheikh!"

He put his hand to his chest, a gesture of respect, then took Sul's hand in both of his.

"Dawood Naji, please sit. The authorities want to question you, but I've asked to talk to you first."

"Thank you, Sheikh." Dawood Naji backed to the cot and sat down. Sul sat on the steel stool bolted to the floor and studied the young man.

Dawood Naji lowered his head, unable to look Sul in the eyes.

"Sheikh," Dawood Naji began softly, "we did a terrible thing, leaving you on that beach to die. It was by the Almighty's favour that your son found you in time."

"Yes," Sul said, "and I forgive you, Dawood Naji."

Dawood Naji looked up tentatively, surprised. His eyes welled with tears, "Thank you, Sheikh." He looked at the floor again, "That lightens my soul a bit." His voice fell to a whisper, "But I've done many terrible, evil things."

"Yes, Dawood Naji. You have. You deserve to be punished for those things. You could be in a cell like this for the rest of your life."

"Yes." He now looked into Sul's eyes. "I see no hope. After that dream I told you, I had hope. And the stories you told me gave me more hope. I looked in the *Injil*, where the stories of the prophet *Isa* are found. I read so many beautiful stories of *Isa*, whom the infidels call Jesus. Thank you for introducing me to this book. As I must go to prison for my crimes, I can at least continue to learn about *Isa*."

"Is this the life you dreamed of leading, Dawood Naji?"

Dawood Naji reflected, "No, Sheikh. The Emir took me into his household when I was young. I was an orphan. The life I lived is the only life I've known. I believed I had no choice about what course my life would take. Since I was a boy, my only choice was to obey the Emir. I never questioned that, or the truth of Islam. Even when it meant committing terrible deeds."

"And now?" Sul watched him.

"Oh, if I did have a choice about my life, I would have chosen to live with you and the *Arraa'i* Pod. To live the freedom of the seas, to be a part of your clan, and work alongside you."

"Under different circumstances, Dawood Naji, we would have taken you." Dawood Naji sat silent.

"Dawood Naji, I must ask you something, and you must think carefully before you answer."

"Yes?"

"Are you willing to tell the authorities about your life with Abdul Qawwi and Yunus Saleh, the things you did in the name of the Caliph?"

"Sheikh, you know if I did that, it would make me a traitor. They would hunt me down and my life would be forfeit."

"Yes, likely."

Dawood Naji considered, "And yet, my life is already finished. I'll pace back and forth in a cell like this for the rest of my days."

Sul waited and then asked, "What would be the right thing to do, Dawood Naji? The just thing in the eyes of God?"

Dawood Naji considered for a few moments, "If my testimony would bring justice, if it would save more from needless suffering and death, then I would gladly risk being assassinated as a traitor for that."

"Good answer, Dawood Naji. I'll arrange for the investigators to come question you. Be honest and tell them everything, even if you participated in the evil deeds."

"Yes, Sheikh, I will. It is the right thing to do before God."

Sul rested his hands on Dawood Naji's head, speaking out some words of blessing in Arabic. Dawood Naji broke into tears. Sul got up and signalled to the guard to open the door. He glanced back as he left, at the man sobbing on the bed.

A severe looking lawyer was waiting for Sul in the corridor. "I heard all that, Dr Suliman. You didn't tell him about the possible amnesty or reduction of his sentence if he testifies."

Sul looked at her, "No, I didn't. I wanted Dawood Naji to choose to do this for the right reasons."

"That was a very unconventional approach."

"Maybe, but I believe Dawood Naji now understands himself better – and understands the choices he faces."

Sul started walking down the corridor, then stopped and turned again to the lawyer. "If he gives you his testimony, will you offer to resettle him under witness protection?"

"It depends what he can tell us, of course, and whether it is verified by other sources. But from what it sounds like, he knows a lot about the inner workings of Emir Abdul Qawwi and the Caliphate and if all that is true, then I think, yes, he will be eligible."

"If that is the case, then we'd be happy to take Dawood Naji, and his sister, into our community and work with them."

"I can't promise, but I believe the court would look with favour on that request." She scribbled some electronic notes on her pad.

"Thank you," Sul said and walked on down the corridor to check on his patient Maria.

25 July 2066, Marcelli Ring
(the same day)

Ben emerged from his doze. His body ached, slumped in the uncomfortable hospital chair. He looked around the room, then at the clock. *Renzo must've left hours ago, looking for food.*

A moan came from the bed next to him and the darkly-lashed eyes fluttered open. Maria caught sight of Ben and smiled, "Sleeping on the job again, Ben?"

Ben jolted into alertness, "Maria!"

"Who were you expecting?" She shifted in the bed and groaned, "Has someone been hitting me with a baseball bat while I was sleeping?"

"I think you ejected a little too low." Ben kissed her forehead.

Maria looked at him, surprised, "Wow, a show of affection. Who are you and what have you done with my Ben?"

Her eyes softened at his embarrassment. "Been there long?" she indicated the seat.

"Just a day."

"Thank you," she said simply. "I'm glad."

Her voice grew serious, "So, fill me in on what happened. Last I recall, the canopy shattered above me and launched me into the blue."

An unfamiliar happiness flooded Ben's heart. Encouraged, he told Maria what had happened since her *Wasp* was hit by the bomber's guns. When he got to the part about his talk with Paul, he noticed she had fallen asleep. A faint smile painted on her lips.

Chapter Twenty-Nine

26 August 2066, Marcelli Ring
(five weeks later)

Ben had about an hour to spare, so he strolled along the Ring Road. Repairs were in full swing at the sites damaged by torpedoes but it would take months before the Ring approached some semblance of normality again, probably years more for the Ring community to come to terms with their grief and loss.

He came to a park, marred by a jagged hole. Debris had been cleared away, and the grass was even beginning to grow back but it hadn't been cordoned off for repair like the other damages in the Ring. This area seemed to have been overlooked.

Ben noticed a young man on a bench glancing at the ragged ruins, then drawing on a computer pad. Ben approached and stood a bit behind him. He could see the artist was sketching a series of designs.

The blonde young man broke from his concentration and turned. His eyes were rimmed with red and sadness was etched on his brow.

"Your drawings are beautiful," Ben said. "Are those for this spot?"

"Yeah," the young man sighed. "I'm submitting designs for a memorial here, in the torpedo crater, to commemorate those lost in the attack and I'm trying to capture hope."

"What a great idea. I'm Ben." Ben held out his hand.

The young man took it with a firm shake and a wan smile as he responded, "My name's Jered."

"Mind if I join you?"

"Not at all, I'd appreciate some company."

Gulls screeched above the waves crashing just beyond the seawall. The sun glittered on the water and the late afternoon seemed bright, full of hope.

"It's been a rough few weeks; a memorial is a good idea to help people focus their grief and find solace."

"Yeah."

Ben studied the quiet man next to him, noticing how he kept staring at the damage at the end of the park. His body language spoke of despair.

"I'm guessing this place means something to you," Ben said softly.

"Yes, my wife Evelyn and our two-year-old son…" Jered hesitated, the words choking him, then he gained control of himself and continued, "Charlie. We lived together in an apartment out there beyond the park." He glanced at the rubble stretching between the green before them and the sea. It's no longer there." Jered paused, lifting his head to stare at the open sea beyond the park. Each move of his body was slow, as though he was bearing a great weight.

"Charlie loved to play here," he turned his gaze back to the park and continued quietly. "I can almost see him kicking his orange ball across the grass…" His stylus froze above the pad, his mind caught in memories.

"It feels like someone ripped the bright core of life out of you, leaving an empty dry husk, with no reason to go on."

Jered turned and stared at him. "How did you know? Those are my exact feelings!"

Ben held his gaze. He told Jered simply, honestly, his own story of loss, grief, and anger. How he had tried to hide from these overwhelming emotions by drinking. How he wandered onto a path of increasing isolation and self-destruction. Then how he slowly recovered hope and control over his life again with the help of a supportive community.

Jered listened without interruption, sighed thoughtfully, then said, "Man, you've been where I now find myself."

"Yes, I thought so," Ben said. "Please tell me what happened to your family."

The young man laid the stylus softly on his pad, setting both on the bench. He looked at Ben. "You really want to know?"

"Yes, I do."

The artist gazed out towards the horizon, remembering. "I'm an architect. I was at my office on the Ring when I heard the sirens. I rushed to join my defence crew and we were assigned to protect a section of the Ring. I knew that we'd be given news about our own families and homes as soon as it was known."

Jered stopped for a moment, letting the memories unfold. Ben let the silence hang in the air.

After a few moments, Jered continued, "Six hours in, my crew chief came to me. I could tell something was wrong by the look on his face. A wave of panic rose in me; it felt unreal."

"I've been there," Ben said quietly.

"Reluctantly, my crew chief broke it to me that Evelyn and Charlie were still among the missing. He released me from my duties and I rushed home." Another silence.

"There was only a smoking ruin, here." He pointed to empty sea.

Jered's voice went dead, "By the end of the day, the list of the missing was compiled, Evelyn and Charlie along with 231 others. That news ripped out my heart and left me empty.

"I wallowed in that grief for weeks – until my crew chief approached me with an idea. He had asked the Ring authorities to allow me to work on a memorial design, hoping it would help my grief, I suppose. I took it on, just last week, but the ache was still there, burning a hole in my soul."

Ben and Jered sat silent for a while, brothers bonded by a common sadness. Then Ben touched Jered's shoulder, looking into the eyes of the young man. "At my lowest point, a friend told me that my wife and son were standing before God. I didn't believe him. Then I saw Lisa and Sammy, in what must have been a vision, as I recovered from a drinking binge. They were happy, at peace. It somehow convinced my heart it was true and that vision stayed with me, it allowed me to forgive those who murdered my family. Once I forgave them, the evil acts they had done stopped controlling my life. I chose life again, and healing began."

Jered still sat in silence, looking at his hands.

"If anything," Ben continued, looking out at the sea, "I'm a man growing into faith. I have this steadily increasing hope that God indeed works things towards his good, even things which began as evil. I can only be a witness to the fact that he is doing this in my life – and I pray that you'll recognize his presence as he walks with you through this valley shadowed by death."

"Thanks," Jered said looking at Ben again, his eyes showing he meant it. "Your story gives me a little hope."

"I hope it will," Ben said, then, with a deep breath, changed the subject. "You look like you work out, Jered. Are you a runner?"

"Yeah," Jered said, "but I haven't run since… since the attack."

"I've been looking for a running buddy. Would you be interested?"

"Sure."

"OK. Meet me here tomorrow morning at 6:30. It's about five miles to Inner Harbour South, and we can grab breakfast after the run. Will that work for you?"

"Yeah, thanks!" A small hint of life had come back into Jered's voice.

Ben glanced at his watch. "OK, I gotta split," Ben shook Jered's hand again as he got up, "I'm due for a meeting."

Jered raised his hand to wave as Ben walked off, then picked up his pad and stylus. He paused for a moment and watched as Ben walked along the Ring Road, then turned to his pad and began to sketch again.

26 August 2066, Marcelli Ring
(the same day)

Ben's eyes were transfixed by a school of anchovies, glinting in choreographed movements above and around the crystal dome over the tables in the café. Through the water, the sun gleamed, high in a blue sky. *Must be almost noon.*

Ben was shocked to realize that, at this moment, he was deeply at peace with himself. *What a novel sensation. Maybe this is the start of a new normal for me.*

A grouper drifted slowly up towards the shimmering school and, with a sudden movement, gulped down several anchovies. Then several tuna burst through the ball of fish, sending them into a frenzy of erratic movement.

I wonder if those tuna belong to Sul's Pod. Sul had mentioned that the nomadic Pod community would be stationed north-east of the Ring for a few weeks, to engage in repairs and replenishment.

In fact, Suliman and Major Camden had asked to meet him at this café for lunch. *I wish they'd told me in advance what this meeting is about.*

The anchovies reformed into a ball after the predatory disruption and Ben reflected on how quickly the school regained its sense of order. *What a relief to see life in the Township returning to normal too.* On the walk to the café, Ben had noticed lots of repairs and building in progress. He'd also begun meeting, at Major Camden's invitation, with several committees planning on how to upgrade the Township defences.

Now the anchovies moved away, as a school of squid swarmed into view. *Already three weeks since Maria got out of hospital.* He mused, remembering wheeling her outside to be greeted by the cheers of her gathered friends, a driverless car whisking them to her parents' home where she could complete her recovery.

At the invitation of Carlo and Sally, Ben had been staying at the Marcelli family home, a few doors down from where Maria was recuperating. *Convenient.* He smiled to himself.

The door to the underwater café opened as Sul and Major Camden strode in. Ben stood to greet them. *What a privilege it is to work with these leaders.*

"Thanks for agreeing to meet us here, Ben." They settled into the chairs and concentrated on the menu.

"I recommend the abalone, fresh from the Rise, one of my favourites." Major Camden pointed to the selection.

"Apparently, that's Maria's favourite as well," Ben said. "Abalone it is, then. I'm fond of abalone myself. When I was a boy, my dad and I would dive for them off the coast of southern California. My job was to pound them out with a wooden mallet, then mom would fry them with a bit of butter and garlic. Delicious."

A waitress came to take their order. After she left, Sul got right to the point, "You're probably wondering why we asked you to meet with us."

"It has nothing to do with the loss of an expensive *Sea Wasp*," Camden quipped.

Ben smiled sheepishly.

The Major reassured him, "Ditching the plane was a wise choice, Pilot Holden. Your action certainly saved Captain Romero."

"We have a proposal for you, Ben," Sul began. "After discussion among the Ring Council, there's been a unanimous decision to invite you to become a citizen of Marcelli Township."

"Wow. Thank you." Ben was taken aback, "A citizen? What an honour. Do you mean I can submit an application under the Seastead Act? I was thinking along the same lines."

Sul and the Major looked at each other. "No, Ben. We intend to grant you citizenship outright, including providing you with a homestead plot of your choice," Camden clarified.

"You've proven yourself to be a valuable member of the community, several times over," Sul smiled.

Ben was surprised at the emotions welling up in him. After years of feeling rootless and adrift. *They want me to become part of their community and this epic endeavour to pioneer the seas? Can this be true?*

Major Camden continued, "Your fusion research may lead to the next generation of reactors. The Ring Council would like to give you a grant to do that research here. By building our own reactors, the Pelagic Territory could rise to a new level of self-sufficiency."

Sul touched Ben's arm, "Paul Whitestone has forwarded a proposal to the President of Caltech. You could continue as a professor there, while conducting your research here in the Ring. We suggested that he should establish a Caltech campus here, for both terrestrial and pelagic students. He seems interested in hearing more about the idea."

Ben looked at the two, sensing their eagerness to hear his response. Smiling, he said, "I think this is a no-brainer. Of course I'd love to live and work here in the Ring."

"Ben, you have demonstrated courage and resourcefulness and kept a cool head throughout all the challenges of these last few months. I would like to offer you a place in the Pelagic Rangers as a captain. It would be a privilege to welcome you into the Ranger Corps."

"Wow, I'm speechless. An honour, Major. Thank you."

The food arrived. They spent the next hour and a half discussing the forthcoming changes in Ben's life. Ben hadn't felt this happy in years. *There's just one thing missing.*

27 August 2066, Marcelli Ring
(the next day)

After an invigorating morning run and breakfast with Jered, Ben had an appointment with Gideon. They met at Southwest Park, off the Ring Road. Sitting next to his friend on the bench, Ben glanced at the sky. *Only 9 in the morning and it already feels like it'll be a scorcher of a day.*

Grass ran down from their bench to the man-made beach about thirty metres away. Some children were already playing in the water, laughing and screaming as they splashed at each other.

Gideon pointed, "It's down by those rocks there at the end of the beach. Sophia's made it top priority over the last few days. Cheng 3D printed it last night. How *did* you get Sophia to give you priority over her other projects? She's really taken a shine to you."

"I don't know why, but I'm glad she has. Thanks for putting everything in place, Gid." Ben put his hand on Gideon's shoulder and pushed him, "Now, get outta here! She'll be coming any minute."

Gideon grinned as he jumped up. He jogged away, down a nearby street, quickly moving out of sight. A moment later, he peeked back around the corner and Ben, noticing him, waved him away.

Ben sat back on the bench, closed his eyes, and gloried in the warmth of the morning sun.

"Asleep at his post… again."

Ben's eyes jerked open. "Maria!" he jumped up. "Ready for our walk?"

Maria looked at him for a moment, "What are you up to, Ben Holden?"

"Me?" he said innocently, checking down the street that Gideon really had gone.

"You sure are squirrelly this morning." One of her eyebrows was arched.

Ben stepped towards her, took her arm, pulling her with him as they walked past the grass and along the sand near the water's edge. "I feel so alive on this beautiful day. And now I've got a beautiful woman on my arm." He smiled at her. "Life is good. I went out to the Deep yesterday and looked at my new lab. All the latest equipment! I can't wait to begin the work."

They jumped to avoid a stray splash from children playing in the waves. "And, I hear you've been given a plot on one of the new sections of the Ring," Maria said, matching the rhythm and pace of his steps.

"Yes, I'll be talking with the architect in two days, my friend Jered. Do you want to help design the new place?"

"Of course, I'm sure a feminine touch will help it feel more like a home."

Ben glanced at Maria, "Now, would I be right in thinking that me splashing that bomber kind of makes up for you saving my life twice? The time with the rattlesnake and that palace attack?"

She looked at him, "I think it'd count only if you'd destroyed the bomber *before* it shot me."

"So, I seem to still be in your debt."

"Without a doubt. Might take you years to pay that debt off."

They neared the rocks that Gideon had indicated.

Maria stopped and pointed to a place near the stones. "I see a spider crab there. I'm surprised to see it close to shore like this. Usually they remain in deeper water."

"Really? I guess you'd know. You are, after all, the resident expert on spider crabs." Maria, surprised by his tone of voice, glanced at him, frowning. Then she turned her attention to the crab in the shallows, which began to crawl towards her. Her eyes widened as it stood up on its spindly hind legs and danced around, spinning and pirouetting.

"Are you seeing this?" she glanced, unbelieving, at Ben.

"Is that abnormal?" Ben bent forward, with feigned interest.

Maria looked back at the crab. It paused its dance, and the shell popped open. Out flared a little flag, waving slowly, with the words, "Will you marry me?"

Maria frowned, "Now, why would I marry a crab?"

Ben poked her. "Me. Marry me."

Maria acted surprised, "Oh, you!" She looked into his eyes, smiling and, without hesitation, said, "Yes, of course."

Ben nodded to the crab. Maria looked – the crab stood with one claw extended, offering a ring to Maria.

"Sophia's idea." Maria took the ring from the crab and Ben took it from her hand and slid it onto her finger.

A sly look crossed Maria's face, "We're going to have so much fun!"

Ben picked her up and swung her around, singing out, "You don't know the half of it."

3 April 2067, Pacific Rim Council Auditorium
(eight months later)

Six months after Ben and Maria's wedding, the Pacific Rim Council was convening. In the great hall of the Pacific Rim Council, Ben and Maria sat next to Paul Whitestone, among the members of the *Arraa'i* Pod.

Ben turned to Paul, whispering, "Maria is four months pregnant."

"Well done, you two," Paul congratulated.

"I've suggested that we name him Paul. Maria thinks it is a bit early to assume it's a boy, though."

Paul laughed, "I'm honoured. I'll happily be the godfather, of course."

"Wouldn't have it any other way."

Sophia slowly wended her way towards their seats, eyes on the ground. She paused in front of Maria and placed her small hands on Maria's stomach. "He will have blue eyes," she said, looking up for a second at Maria, "like yours."

Sophia continued down the row and sat next to Fatima.

"What have you been telling her, filling her head with?" Maria whispered to Ben.

"Nothing," he shrugged his shoulders, "all her idea. I haven't talked to her about the baby at all."

Representatives of the terrestrial nations surrounding the Pacific Rim filled the auditorium around them and the crowds were stirring in their seats. A hush fell on the room as Suliman Battuta stepped up to the podium at the centre of the auditorium and everyone stood.

"Representatives of the Pacific Rim nations, I'm honoured to address you today," Sul began. The crowd applauded. "Please be seated." They sat and focused their attention on him.

"Yesterday's vote was historic. You granted the Pelagic Territories the authority to chart their own destiny. In doing this you've been midwives at the birth of the first oceanic nation: Pelagia South Pacific."

Cheers rose around the hall, especially from the pelagic settlers.

"This vote creates the possibility of a new endeavour – for families and communities to create permanent societies on the open sea. Humankind has stepped beyond the boundary of the good Earth which has nurtured us all since time immemorial, and stepped out onto the open sea. We embrace our oceanic identity. This is the next frontier in the world we all share.

"This agreement opens the way for pelagic nations to develop, flourish, and defend their maritime cultures, industries, enterprises, and civil authorities. These new nations will join with their terrestrial neighbours in the common polity of nations.

"For all of us who live on the sea, we recognize this agreement as a trust. You trust that we'll be good stewards of the sea on which we live. A healthy marine environment is important for the pelagic nations whose livelihoods and lives intimately depend on it. And we understand that a healthy marine environment is just as critical for you, our terrestrial friends. The health of the world's seas impacts your health and livelihood. In fact, the seas impact all life on the ocean, the land or in the skies of our blue planet."

Murmurs of assent swelled among the seated crowd.

"So, we pelagic settlers regard the protection of the oceans as our *sacred* trust. Just as the continents' forests, mountains, and plains are the sacred trust of the terrestrial nations. We pledge ourselves to make good on that trust through treaties, collaborations, and initiatives. We pledge to work with you as part of the Pacific Rim community, as well as with other nations both terrestrial and pelagic as a united effort in the next decades.

"While your vote has been shaped in part by the recent aggression of destructive forces, the desire for clearer identity and nationhood has been growing in our hearts over the past several generations. My father was one of the first pelagic pioneers and I remember as a child how often he told me of his dreams for a nation of Pelagia. This dream grew in my heart also, and I discussed it many times with the next generation who joined us. Now our dreams are being fulfilled in time for our offspring. Thank you for becoming part of this powerful dream, empowering settlers to be wise stewards of the open sea. As terrestrial nations believe in our dream, pelagic families gain the freedom to create new ways of living in peace and good will with one another."

"My fellow pelagic citizens, you have honoured me by electing me to be your first president. As President of Pelagia South Pacific, I will serve our interests willingly. We will work together and be good neighbours. We will shoulder our responsibilities in the family of nations. Thank you."

With one motion, everyone in the chamber rose to applaud.

Ben looked down at Maria, "Can't think of a better way to spend a life," he said, patting her stomach, "or raise a family." She snuggled closer to him.